The Imperceptible Adjustment

James & Cynthia Runyon

WestBow Press books may be ordered through booksellers or by contacting:

WestBow Press
A Division of Thomas Nelson & Zondervan
1663 Liberty Drive
Bloomington, IN 47403
www.westbowpress.com
1 (866) 928-1240

ISBN: 978-1-5127-3218-4 (sc)
ISBN: 978-1-5127-3219-1 (hc)
ISBN: 978-1-5127-3217-7 (e)

Library of Congress Control Number: 2016903078

Print information available on the last page.

WestBow Press rev. date: 3/3/2016

PROLOGUE

JANUARY 1, 1802, EVENING

Forcing his way into the mudroom, Peter turned and wrestled with the heavy oaken door to prevent the icy wind from exposing the toasty entryway to the elements. He stood there a moment dusting the snow from his coat and boots while putting a tray on the counter. "Whoa Boy! Sho is cold out."

Betty bustled over to help close the door. Peter smiled. Mama was an opposing force the blizzard couldn't match. When the wind had finally given up its fight and quit wailing through the tiny crack under the entry, she turned her motherly displeasure on the still shivering young man. "What you doin'? It's freezin' out there. You goin' to catch yo' deth o' cold being out dis late." She bent to her knees, drying the melting snow from her spotless wooden floors.

"Well, I gots to bring the Mastuh some muffins. You know what he says. They is a…"

"I know, I know," the older black woman muttered as she brought herself up from the floor. Her hands sucked to her hips like magnets. "He says they is a great luxury to him," throwing her arms in the air to add some exaggeration.

Peter smiled, "Mama, don't make fun. If he wants muffins, he's gonna git muffins." Kissing his mother on the cheek, he turned toward the window within the door. "Ya needs to git Wormley out on that terrace and move that snow. I tells you that the whole place is just goin' to fall in with all of that snow." Placing the covered tray on a table, he let Betty take his coat and hang it on a stand. Arms crossed, he spoke with a hint of amusement in his young voice. "Seein's how the gardenin' appears to be on hold 'till spring. He oughta just start shovelin' in the mornin'."

"Honey, don't you think I knows it. I'll git him on it tomorrow," she smiled back. The steaming muffins were arranged on a delicate piece of china before she carried them into the Tea Room. "I believe he was hopin' for a longer reprieve from harvest and autumn gardenin' before he started the snow shovelin'. Poor man is just gettin' mo' and mo' tired every day it seems."

"Hey, Mama." He crept up behind her. "I made extras. You wants some?" She turned kind eyes toward him. He'd been allowed to keep the extra muffins since he'd begun baking them, but Peter kept up the charade of secrecy as if his muffins were the greatest of treasures.

"What you got there?" said Joe walking in from the Dining Room. "It sho smells good."

"Now Mistuh Fossett, why is you here at this time of night? Don't no one sleep no more?" Betty grumbled. She'd lost much of her matronly control of the slaves years ago as each one had grown into adulthood.

The thin black man hung his coat and satchel on a rack and pulled a chair up to the table. Peter followed suit.

"You two better git up from that table," Betty whispered forcefully. "This is the Mastuh's 'Most Honorable Suite.' He will hang you two from the nearest tree if he sees you there." She gestured, "You can sit there on the window seat."

The young men looked around the Doric-styled room to the busts of Benjamin Franklin, John Paul Jones, Lafayette, and George Washington. The marble eyes of the replicas each showed different character; some kind, some haughty. At the moment nearly all appeared to be raising eyebrows and looking down their noses with disapproval.

Knowing the primary house servant was right, the two fellows looked at each other and slipped quickly over to the window seat.

Betty smiled and brought in a pot of hot tea wrapped in a floral cozy. "Mistuh Fossett, you never answered me," she said pouring the steaming drink into waiting tea cups.

Peter chimed in, "Yeah Joe, you ain't going out tonight, ah ya'?"

Joe took a bite from a muffin and answered, "The Mastuh has some letters going out. I got to get them to Charlottesville." He spoke around the muffin with a light of honor in his eyes, proud to be chosen for such an important task.

"Child, it's freezing out," the mother figure sat next to him and took a sip of her tea. "Can't they wait 'till tomorrow?"

"Nope," he said taking another bite, "there's a stage leaving in the morning from Charlottesville, and he wants those letters on it."

The older woman stood and headed for the door, "I better get Jupiter to readying a horse."

Joe rose to catch her, "No Miss Hemings, I already got Jupiter on it." He pulled her back to her seat. "Let's just sit here and fill up on muffins," he said with a smile.

"You best not eat no more muffins," Peter turned in fierce protest to guard his offering. "The ovens are cold, and it'll take an hour to get 'em back hot." Joe looked at Betty and the two laughed. "I show knows how to get him, don't I?" Joe grinned. "Come back Peter, I won't take any mo' o' your precious muffins."

"You's right, you won't," Peter said getting in on the joke.

The cook took out one more muffin, "Here, you gots a long ride."

Joe smiled and moved to place it inside his overcoat pocket. "Miss Hemings, you always been a slave?" he asked sitting back in his seat.

The woman looked at him amused. "I was born into it." She poured more tea and looked out the front glass windows. The full moon was reflecting off of the snow illuminating the thick Virginia countryside. "But I have been here with the President almost 28 years now."

Peter continued the story, "Before that, Mama was with his father-in-law, ain't that right?"

"That's right," she said walking over and putting another log in the fireplace. "I came here when he and Miss Martha married." Betty looked at a silhouette sitting on the mantle, "She's been dead a long time, but I still miss her. I sure knows the Mastuh does."

"Do you think he'll find another wife?" Joe asked.

"I'd say no. He loved that woman too much." Betty turned to the window seat once again. "He grieved evah so long when she died. I don't think he wants to go through that again."

"What are we discussing this evening?" The good-natured voice of the President floated into the room from the main hall.

Everyone immediately stood to welcome the owner of the house.

"We just talkin' befoe bed," said Betty with a smile. "Would you like some tea? Peter made you some o' your favorite muffins."

Peter smiled awaiting approval.

"Yes, Elizabeth, that would be pleasant," Jefferson bent his almost six foot three inch frame forward as he pulled a chair back from the table. "Joe, are you prepared for travel?" He sat and pulled a sealed letter from his jacket and studied it for a thoughtful moment before handing it, along with several others, to the slave.

Joe took the official parchment. "Yes Mista Jeffason, I's ready. I'll git these to Charlottesville real fast." Donning his woolen jacket, he buttoned the placket and placed the letters into his satchel. "You can trust me," he smiled turning from the room to put on his gloves and a thick scarf. Before he could step into the next room the President's voice stopped him. "I know that you will, Joe." He turned back, embarrassed for a moment that he'd not waited to be sent on his way.

The tall man filled his own cup with tea and his plate with three muffins. "I would normally never ask you to leave at such an hour. However, this is official business that requires quick attention."

"I undastand, Mista Jeffason," the slave nodded and began backing toward the door.

"Elizabeth, please have sustenance prepared for the young man upon his arrival."

"Yes, Mista Jeffason. I'll see to it."

The man smiled and took a bite. "Thank you Peter, these are a great luxury to me."

"Yes, sah. Thank you for the compliment," he said backing away with a Cheshire cat grin embedded in his dark features.

The President's eyes drifted to the mantle and the silhouette of the young slender woman above it.

"Come, boys, we's got work to do," Betty said pushing everyone from the room and leaving the now pensive man in silence.

Once out of the President's presence, Betty gave Joe a big hug and pulled his collar closer to his throat. "Be safe now. Anythin' ya' need?"

"No Miss Betty. I gots to go," he said hugging the older woman and heading toward the back door of the house.

Joe crossed through the Entrance Hall and worked his way to the Piazza before stopping to check that his coat and satchel were secure. When he felt certain that he was bundled as tightly as possible and that his bag would hold its contents, he took a deep breath and headed out into the cold along the upper terrace.

At the first set of stairs, he crossed to the lower level and found the stables. Jupiter was good to his word and had the horse ready for its winter trek.

"She been fed and watered, Jupiter?" he questioned attaching his bag to the saddle.

"She'll run for hours," the man boasted while sitting next to the fireplace. "When you plan on bein' back?"

"I hopes by mornin'." He climbed onto the back of the brown and black steed. "Wish me luck," the black man said with a grin.

"Ya' don't need luck," Jupiter yelled as Joe sped away. "That animal's doin' all the work!" Jupiter closed the stall door and trudged to his quarters in hopes of getting some rest before the sun snuck back over the horizon.

The well-trained animal kept a good pace. The pair passed through fields and jumped streams. They trotted on the roads and took short cuts through the woods. On many occasions, Joe laid forward on the horse placing his head next to the horse's neck, hoping to gain some warmth against the frigid night air. The full moon allowed the duo to have minimal light, but did not alleviate the deep cold of the early winter journey.

After hours of solid riding, Joe decided to give the dedicated horse a well-earned break. The man dismounted, looped the reins over a branch and grabbed the feed bag. After setting the horse up with some midnight sustenance he pulled a blanket from the saddle and rested against the tree to enjoy his muffin.

It was much warmer being out of the freezing wind. Sliding his back closer to the wide tree, the heaviness of sleep weighted his eyelids. The long day and strenuous ride made fighting slumber difficult.

Only minutes later, the slave's eyes flew open with the realization that he was no longer alone. An apparition in black was going through the satchel containing the letters from his Master. He stood to face the dark figure and shouted even as fear crowded into his voice. "That's my Mastuh's. Be gone!" He rose from his position and started toward it. The eerie shape merely turned and stared. The thing's eyes glowed green from its misshapen face. Attached to its waist were belts containing devices the man had never seen.

"Demon!" he screamed and backed away in terror. "You're a demon! Jesus, help me! Lawd, protect me from this demon o' the night," immobilizing terror prevented his escape as the shadow started toward him grabbing one of the things hanging from its belt. Aiming it at the delirious man, the figure pulled the trigger, sending 10,000 volts through the petrified slave. The young man began to writhe on the ground, crying for mercy from his God.

Returning to the horse the shadow began looking through the satchel once again. Finding a letter he held it to a dim light source produced from another pocket, and pulling an identically labeled one from his vest, the night demon switched them, taking the President's letter with him and leaving the new one in its place.

Once he had tied the leather bag tight and returned it to its original position, he walked back toward the sobbing slave and bent over him. Ghastly green eyes peered down for a moment before speaking, "If you are wise, you will never mention this to anyone, and will continue on to Charlottesville as if nothing ever happened." He turned abruptly and started to walk away, speaking one last time he removed his night vision goggles, "If you don't heed my warning, I will be back." The shadow walked deliberately into the woods until he disappeared.

After a few moments more, Joe recovered his breathing and full movement enough to stand. He untied the horse, lifted himself astride and ran the animal as fast toward Charlottesville as its legs would carry them.

Approximately one mile down the road, a huge surge of light appeared, terrifying the pair further. The illumination disappearing as quickly as it had come. A short time after the light filled the sky; an imperceptible sonic boom emanated throughout the countryside.

The fear of the incident surged both the horse and rider on toward the city. Joe never mentioned to anyone what had happened on that lonely winter night in January. And only in his dreams did the haunting apparition return.

1 — TUESDAY EVENING, OCTOBER 17

Hudson steered the stolen Mercedes S-Class through the rolling hills of the Allegheny Mountains. With the sun setting in the west, the last rays of daylight were igniting the maples and poplars like a blaze of red and yellow fire along the hillside.

Normally, a drive like this brought a chance for the ex-Secret Service agent to ponder the greatness of God, his beautiful wife, and two rambunctious children. Not this time. Instead, every curve gave a turn to his stomach. Every glorious tree reminded him of a world wasn't right. And of the job that now fell to him.

Gently purring beneath them, the finely-tuned automobile made quick work of the quiet rural roads, reducing the drive by half.

"Hudson, are you sure this is going to work?" Todd poked his head into the space between the front seats.

Sara turned in the passenger seat to hear the response.

"It has to. He's the only one who'll know where to find it," he replied maneuvering the Mercedes over a single lane bridge.

"You mean we came all the way out here as fugitives, and it might not even work? There's a chance our lives won't be restored?" The fair-skinned woman flushed with panic, setting off her bright blue eyes. Tears pooled as she continued, "I want to get back to my life. I don't even know why I'm involved in this."

Deeply aware that she could not know everything, Hudson fought back his own emotion as he touched the beautiful woman on her arm. "Sara, believe me, I want you to return to your life as badly as you do. I'm doing all that I can to set the world right."

The woman pulled her arm away and looked out the window. From the back seat, Todd watched his partner and friend go through a grief he could not imagine. *Lord, make this right,* he prayed as the luxury vehicle made its last turn and entered the long circle drive of their destination.

"Wow. Look at that," Hudson mumbled as they slowed their progress to take in the size of the complex.

Everyone sat forward in their seats.

"I've only heard of the Greenbrier." Sara's eyes widened. "We aren't dressed for this place."

"There have to be shops in there where we can buy what we need. Hudson, do we have any money," Todd asked.

"I have enough. We can't use any identification or it will put us on the grid. Hopefully, cash will solve that problem."

The Greenbrier began in 1778, and was known for over a century as White Sulphur Springs. People traveled from miles around to "take the waters" and restore their health. Although renowned for its luxurious spas and world-class golf courses now, throughout the Civil War, the resort had been occupied by both sides and was eventually bought and expanded by a railway. Today, however, Hudson was here because of its affiliation with the United States Government. The agent brought the vehicle to a stop just short of the large canopy on the circle drive.

Turning and speaking to the woman, he lifted her hand to gently claim her attention. "Sara, I need your help." She looked inquisitively at him. "I need you to act like my wife."

The passenger in the back looked at Hudson.

The woman pulled away, "Why is that?"

"You have to trust me. If the resort has been alerted, they will be looking for two men and a woman, not a married couple."

"What about him?" she questioned pointing to Todd.

The professor pulled himself up between the seats and looked over at Hudson with the same question, "Yeah, what about me?"

"Todd, I need you to hide here in the car. We'll go and check in then I'll come back out and park the car. We'll go in the back door after that."

"Okay, you go and have all of the fun," Todd smiled knowingly at Hudson.

Hudson furrowed his brows at his partner and turned back to the woman, "Sara, everything will be proper between us, but I need you to help me. Hopefully, tomorrow we can have our lives back."

"Okay, but keep your distance, big guy," she said pointing her finger at him then smiled. "I'm a pretty good actress. We'll get in," she said with certainty.

"You are a very good actress," the agent answered.

She looked at Hudson oddly.

"I mean, I know that you'll be very believable. Now for a story…"

Before he could finish she had pulled a blanket from the back and shoved it under her denim shirt. After she had smoothed out the lines well enough and formed a nice belly, she pointed toward the door and started speaking with rapid breaths. "Let's go."

Hudson left the vehicle and quickly ran over to open the passenger door while Todd lay in the floor board.

"Oh, honey, help me," she yelled jutting her hand out of the car. "I'm having early labor."

"But, honey," he played along as a doorman looked their way. "We have two more weeks before you're due."

"I know, but I'm having terrible contractions. I need to lie down."

"Help me," Hudson yelled to the doorman as he assisted in pulling her small frame from the car. Sara placed her arm on his shoulder and faked a pregnant waddle.

Running over, the doorman grabbed the pained woman from the other side.

"Oh, honey, I need to lie down," she cried as tears fell from her eyes.

"Run in and check in sir, I will help her into the lobby."

"Thank you, you're a hero," he smiled as he ran in through the large doors.

Taking a deep breath, the agent halted his progress a bit as he took in the vast size and beauty of the early federalist design. Large chandeliers were positioned with medallions around them every twenty feet along the ceiling and each anterior room was colored differently. The main dining room glowed in tangerine and white decor. Next to it a sitting room sparkled with crystal blue and white. Every room had large molding and heavy chair railing. Hearing his feet scraping on the carpet runner surrounded by marble, he was reminded of his mission and continued forward.

Hudson ran straight to the long registration desk where a young man in a suit and tie was standing and typing into a computer.

"I need a room," he said breathlessly.

"Yes sir, let me pull your reservation." He continued typing into the computer.

"I don't have a reservation. This was a spur of the moment trip. I wanted to get my wife away, so that she could rest before the baby comes..."

"Aaahhh," yelled a woman as she struggled through the large main doors. The doorman was struggling with all his strength to help her in.

The young man's eyes doubled in size.

"She says she's having early labor. I think if she can lie down she'll be alright, but we need a room right now. Take her right to the elevator," Hudson yelled to the doorman.

"Uh, sir, yes sir, let me have your identification. I will get you a room."

"I left it in the car."

The woman screamed again and fell against a large marble column in the lobby.

"Here's some cash," the agent said throwing out five $100 dollar bills. "Get me a room and I'll come back when she calms down to give you all of the information."

"Sir, I can't, I mean, I need your identification."

"Aaahhh!" Sara wailed all over the hapless doorman.

"I need a room. Here is more cash," he said pulling more bills from his wallet.

"Sir, just give me a license or credit card…"

"Help me," the pregnant woman screamed as the doorman hobbled around trying to keep his balance under the climbing woman's weight.

People in the lobby began murmuring under their breath.

Seeing the situation was not helping the ambiance of the Greenbrier, the doorman yelled, "John, just get her a room! We'll work it out later," he grumbled trying to get the writhing human to the elevator.

"Honey, I need to lie down! I feel like I'm going to drop this baby right here."

More murmuring occurred from the guests.

"Yes, darling, this kind man is helping us," Hudson said looking at the concierge with pleading eyes.

"Okay, sir," he said typing furiously, "you can have room 4102. He handed over the magnetic card. "The night crew will be coming on in a few minutes. Once you settle her in, just come back down and give them all of your information."

He looked at the poor man's name tag. "Thank you, John, you're a life saver."

"Honey, do we have a room?" she cried.

"Yes, darling, John's kindly helped us," Hudson said while patting the young man on the arm.

"Oh, thank you!" she panted as the nervous doorman pushed the button on the elevator. "Let's call our son John when he's born. Would you like that?"

Hudson ran over and relieved the crumpled doorman from his charge. He placed his arm around the woman. "Yes, I think that would be a perfect name for our son," he said smiling at the man who checked them in.

Grinning back with satisfaction, John watched the couple disappear as the elevator doors closed.

Looking over every inch of the elevator, the agent found no cameras and dropped the façade. "You are great!" he smiled as he hugged her.

"I try," Sara spoke as she realized she had to crane her neck to look up at him from this close. "Now what?" Backing away, she pulled the blanket from her shirt.

"We get into the room and bring up Todd."

The two quickly found their room and could not believe its opulence. The walls were covered in vibrant wall paper replete with roses and bows. The windows were decorated in heavy white cotton, edged in green piping. The bed held large pillows embroidered with the resort name and a thick down comforter. Everything matched perfectly from the checkerboard covered chairs to the design laden carpet.

"Wow, we should have taken our honeymoon here," he said looking around.

"What do you mean?" Sara asked not sure of the comment.

"I mean, I need to take my honeymoon here when I get married. Let me go and get Todd." Hudson quickly left the woman alone in the space.

The agent took the elevators back down but exited the building through the Crystal Terrace and made the trek back around the building to his waiting Mercedes. He entered the vehicle and started driving it toward the main parking area.

"Hey man, you still here?" he said looking forward.

"Sure am, I was getting a nice nap. Did you get a room?" he asked starting to rise in his seat.

"Yeah, Sara got us in. It just reminds me of how much I love her."

"Hudson, it's going to work out," he hoped he sounded convincing.

The next few minutes were quiet as the vehicle found a parking spot. After backing it into a place where the license plate was pressed against a bush, the men got out with their equipment and headed for the building.

"Todd, you go through the outside entrance first," Hudson said giving the professor a magnetic card. The agent ran over to the grass and picked up an acorn. "Here, put this in the lock hole, and I will come through in a few minutes and meet you in 4102."

Todd made it to the room first and let himself in.

Stifled weeping drifted from the furthest bed, and he found Sara on her side, crying into a pillow. "Are you alright? Is there anything I can do?"

"No, I'm just scared." She sat up as Todd headed to the bathroom to find a Kleenex. "This last 24 hours has been a whirlwind," she said. "I was abducted, put in some type of prison, for a reason no one explained.

Then, I was rescued by two men I don't know and asked to pretend to be someone's wife. I don't know if my friends and family are alright, and evidently there is a lot more to come." She stopped and gratefully accepted the Kleenex he offered. "It has been a day."

Todd looked the young woman in the eyes, "You must trust Hudson. We have been through the thick of it before and made it out every time." He paused, "Sara, understand that Hudson will give his life to protect yours. That's a promise."

Sara dropped her head. "Why am I involved in this? Why me?" Stopping and thinking she looked up, "What do you do? Do you work for the government or something like that?"

The man chuckled and stood up, "Nope, I'm a seminary professor."

She fell back onto her pillow, "A seminary professor. I've been rescued by a seminary professor? We're all going to die. And I'm going to die first."

Hudson entered the room to find Sara babbling to herself. "What's going on?"

The professor spoke up, "I just told her that she was rescued by a seminary professor." Looking over and pointing at her, "Needless to say, she doubts our future possibilities."

Furrowing his eyebrows, Hudson tried to assure, "Sara, it's going to be alright," he spoke as he took some architectural drawings from his backpack. "This guy is pretty handy."

Poking Todd on the chest, Hudson whispered, "Don't make her more nervous than she already is. I don't want her upset." He faked a smile.

"Hey, she asked me what I do. I'm a minister, I can't lie," he said shrugging his shoulders.

"Uh-huh," Hudson mumbled while laying the drawings on the bed.

Everyone looked on while Hudson got down on his knees and began tracing his finger across lines on the page. Each sheet represented a level within the building and the agent had to look at one page on top of another to trace connected lines and areas of intersection.

"Todd, over on the nightstand is a book of services, bring that over," he said pointing.

Hudson continued tracing lines, "The Greenbrier is a world renowned five diamond resort; however what most people don't know is that in 1959, the U.S. government rented the entire facility for almost three years to build a bomb shelter under it." Todd and Sara looked at each other. "They built this shelter large enough to house the entire Legislative branch for an extended period of time.

Todd, open that book up. There has to be a floor plan or site map."

"Got it."

"Bring it over here." Hudson kept one finger on a spot on the drawing and started scanning the floor plan diagram for a match. "There it is."

Sara sat in a wingback chair. "What did you find?"

Standing up, Hudson straightened his back and then sat in another wingback across from her. "We know that he's in the shelter below us. It's pretty obvious that he's going to be well guarded, but only at the main entrances. We need to get to him through another way."

"What is the other way?" Todd spoke up.

"The bomb shelter became public knowledge in the late 90's. Changes were made around the grounds to bring the resort back to its original glory. In that time, certain doors and passageways were covered." Hudson stood and walked back over to the drawings. "I found a ventilation shaft that should get us down to the bunker. We'll have to do some welding, but we can get down there."

"Where is the access point?" Todd asked.

"The Cameo Ballroom," he said pointing to the name on the floor plan.

Picking up the television remote, Todd keyed in the channel describing the events going on at the hotel. "Hudson, it says that there is a formal dance taking place in that room in a little over an hour."

All eyes went to the agent, "Well, it looks like we need to get ready for the ball. Todd, you need to find a server's outfit, and I will get us some clothes," he said pointing to Sara. "I suggest you take a shower and start primping. You need to look beautiful."

"But I don't have anything. No makeup or even a brush," she complained throwing her arms in the air.

"I'll get you what you need," Hudson said heading for the door.

"But you don't know what color of makeup I use or what size I wear."

The agent smiled, "I'll figure it out."

2 — TUESDAY EVENING

Both men left the room and entered the elevator. When it arrived at the lower level, they headed in different directions.

Hudson found a formal shop on one of the lesser floors of the facility. Greenbrier Avenue, as it is referred to, is lined with high-end shops to meet any desire. Walking in the men's shop about half way down the hall, he found the formal section and pulled his size of tuxedo from the rack. His eyebrows lifted at the price, knowing that it would normally take him a month to pay for the garment. Resolving the amount was worth it for the mission at hand, he went to check out. Usually a suit of this caliber would be exquisitely sized, but after telling the cashier he was happy with the fit, he quickly paid and walked to the nearby women's boutique.

Looking through the ball gowns, Hudson smiled and picked a slender and strapless black dress. He looked forward to seeing Sara in it. Next, he found a purse, brush, and some makeup he knew would work for her and headed for the register.

"Hello sir, how is your wife?" John asked picking up a candy bar from a shelf. "What, uh, why do you need all of that?" He pointed to the formal clothing Hudson was carrying.

"I..., we, uh, well, she was so depressed. You know how pregnant women can be. She was so depressed that I wanted to cheer her up," he tried to explain with a smile.

"How does that cheer her up?" the young man asked pointing to the gown.

"Well, I wanted to perk her up," the agent said quickly, "She's been complaining about feeling so big that I thought this gown might be something she can look forward to after the uh, the baby is born."

"Well," the poor man blinked in confusion and doubt.

"Like hanging your swimsuit up to motivate you to lose weight for the summer. It's that kind of thing. Right?"

The woman behind the register looked as confused as John did.

"Here, John, move up in front of me. You've earned it for all of your help."

The man paid for his candy bar and looked back in puzzlement before he left. Hudson paid with a roll of cash quickly and made his way back to the room.

~

Todd began searching through closets around Draper's Café and found a white garment designed to be a uniform for a chef. Because of its straight shape and tall fit, it looked like it might work. He grabbed it nonchalantly and headed back upstairs.

~

It had been close to twenty minutes by the time Hudson arrived to hear the shower running and knocked on the door. "I have some things for you to wear," he said hanging them on the doorknob.

An arm slipped around the door, the bags were quickly snatched, and the door once again slammed shut. Hudson placed his things on the floor and lay down on the bed to rest his eyes for a few moments before he had to go again.

"Oh, God, I need your strength and guidance. Please protect us in this mission…."

The door released and Todd came in with a room service cart. "I found a chef's uniform and grabbed this cart sitting against a wall down the hall. I hope it works."

The agent craned his neck up and looked over at the professor's acquisitions. "It should be fine." His head dropped back down as Todd plopped into one of the wingback chairs.

"You hangin' in there?" Todd asked.

"The world's in a mess, Sara doesn't know me, and we're supposed to set it all straight. I'm lost and feel beaten."

"Hey buddy, we've been to the edge of the world and back, and God got us through it. He *will* get us through it again."

The bathroom door opened and Sara walked out. Her lean hourglass figure shaped the dress perfectly and even with wet hair and no makeup, she was a stunningly beautiful woman.

Hudson sat up. "Wow, you look…striking."

"Thank you," she said with a blush. "The dress fits perfectly. The makeup is the same color I wear and you even bought the same type of hairspray I use. How could you be so accurate?" she said as she walked over to the vanity in the room.

"I guessed," he stammered, picking up his bags and walking toward the bathroom. "Give me a few minutes, and I'll be ready."

Sara sat at the makeup desk and started on her eyes. "How long have you known Hudson?"

The professor pulled his head through the chef's shirt. "Not long, less than a year."

"How did you two meet? Were you in the military together or something like that?" she lowered an eyelid to apply liner.

"No," he mumbled pulling on the chef's trousers over his own. "He was working for the government, and they needed my expertise."

"What would that be?" she asked inquisitively.

"I have a Ph.D. in Hebrew and Ancient Israeli studies," he answered with a smile.

"What would the government be doing that they needed your type of help?" she asked powdering her nose.

"It's kind of long and drawn out, but needless to say; we had to *protect* an important Jewish figure several times."

Continuing the line of questioning, "What do you know about Hudson's background? Is he married?" she said rather shyly.

Todd sat on the bed and donned the large round hat. "Uh, hmmm, how do I answer that? I, uh, I… I would say no."

"Is he divorced or going through a divorce? Is he a widower?" she questioned out of frustration.

"No, he isn't divorced or going through one and he hasn't uh,…, he isn't a widower," Todd said banging on the bathroom door trying to get away from the barrage of questions.

"Then why the odd answer?" she queried turning in her seat staring at the obviously nervous man.

"I, uh, think, well, I think it depends on your perspective." He banged on the door until it opened. "I need a break," he whispered.

Hudson looked oddly at him and entered the room wearing a tuxedo. Sara had finished her makeup and stood to meet him.

"You look very handsome," the woman spoke as she moved to straighten his tie. "In another world and another time, this would be a fun evening."

"I couldn't have said it better myself," the agent replied, looking at her piercing blue eyes. The woman dropped her head and turned to busy herself on other things.

The agent picked up the architectural drawings and looked over the passage ways once again as Todd reentered the room.

"So what's the plan?" the professor asked.

"Sara and I will take a few minutes to feel out the room," he said pointing to the fair-skinned woman. "Let's say about 15 minutes after we enter, you'll come in with that cart as if you're changing out some food on the buffet tables. Have the gear underneath covered with the white cloth, and then we'll get to business."

Looking his friend in the eyes his voice lowered with intention, "Todd, you know that this will have to work like clockwork. The more time that maniac has, the more the world might be changed. I need you there."

"You don't have to worry about me."

"Let's pray, and then we'll go." Everyone agreed. While the three formed a small circle holding hands, Hudson continued, "Lord, we thank you for getting us this far. We praise you for your sovereignty and protection. Lord, we need you to guide our steps and allow us to accomplish this mission. Be with us in the next few minutes as we try to right the things that have been made wrong. We love you and thank you. Amen.

"Let's go."

Leaving the room, Todd pushed his cart and took one elevator while Hudson and Sara took the other. The couple looked stunning standing together. The agent's strong features and tall muscular frame made a pleasant backdrop for Sara's petite hourglass shape. The pair looked as though they were walking a red carpet for a movie premier, not preparing to break into the underground of one of the most luxurious hotels in the world. The elevator door opened as they proceeded down the hallway to the ballroom.

Taking her arm in his, Hudson whispered, "Keeping up appearances." The two walked a little farther, "By the way, you look gorgeous." His words caused her to blush as they entered the ballroom.

The Cameo Ballroom was a large space covered with bright white walls and massive golden chandeliers. The carpet was a deep red with a gold paisley design holding hundreds of guests dressed formally and dancing to an orchestra playing a Gershwin tune.

Placing her delicate hand in his, he looked her in the eyes, "Care to dance?"

She replied with a smile, "I would love to."

Todd made it to the first floor and was pushing his cart toward the ballroom, when he was stopped. "What are you doing?"

"Excuse me?" he replied.

The heavyset woman carrying a clipboard was very upset. "You aren't supposed to be walking the halls when we have guests around."

"Yes ma'am, I'm sorry ma'am. I was going to check on the refreshments in the ballroom when I got lost. It won't happen again."

"You are right, it won't happen again. I have had enough of breaking protocol. I am going to walk you back to the kitchen myself and tell the manager what I think."

"No, ma'am I haven't got time. I'm supposed to bring out the meatballs so they can bring in another tray. It's vital I get to this," he said continuing his forward trek.

"There is plenty of time. You come with me," she said pointing the opposite direction.

"Ma'am, I can't. We had a complaint by one of the more important guests – if you know who I mean," he said putting his hand alongside his mouth. "He was very upset that we were out of meatballs."

The woman looked terrified. "He was upset?" she asked incredulously.

"Yes, I would do something for him. Possibly send a flower or fruit bouquet to his room. His influence is important, and we don't want to lose him as a happy guest." Todd stopped his movement. "I'm just a lowly waiter, but if I were you, I'd make this thing right."

"I'll do that right now, but we will talk about this breach of protocol later," she said pointing her finger at him as she ran down the hallway.

"Thank you," Todd whispered looking to the ceiling. He continued forward to the ballroom.

—

The couples floating around the floor looked like a kaleidoscope of color and movement. Each pair took their spot to perfect the beauty of the choreography. Hudson and Sara were no different. As the singer completed the song "'SWonderful" and began "I've Grown Accustomed to Her Face," the seasoned agent was overcome with emotion.

They stopped their movement. "What is it?" she asked wiping a tear from his eye.

"I'm sorry. It has to be a combination of things; the pressure of the last few days, the time ahead and the beauty of the night."

She hugged him close and started the movement again. "Just think about now," she whispered.

Several minutes later, Todd wheeled his cart along the side wall of the room, passing the beverage and food tables, and headed directly toward a storage closet at the back of the area. As Hudson and Sara caught his movement, they slowly followed. Once hidden in the dark nook, Todd pulled up the sheet on his cart revealing a general tool set and two small gas cylinders connected to an acetylene torch.

The agent tried the door and found it locked. Picking up a long flat-head screw driver, he jimmied the locking bolt so that the door would open. Quickly wheeling in the cart, they closed the door behind them. Hudson turned on the light.

"Where is it?"

"The vent opening should be behind this wall." Hudson started tapping on the sheetrock. The sounds went from that of high pitched to much lower. "I found it."

The violins swelled over the Bossa Nova beat of *Begin the Beguine*. "So how was the dance?"

"Hand me a hammer. It was great," the agent said with a smile.

Thrusting the claw of the hammer into the sheetrock, he started pulling the wall covering down in large sections.

"I'll tell you this, next time I'm going to be the one dancing," Todd said looking over at Sara. "I'll bet she's a good dancer." He poked Hudson in the side.

Sara blushed and folded her arms.

"There was a woman out there who gave me some problems. I almost didn't make it. She wanted to take me to some manager."

"There's no way that you'll be doing the dancing. I look too good in this tux," Hudson said jokingly. "We're through. Hand me the torch," he said breathless.

The work soon revealed a large circular metallic grate. Bending down on his knees the agent turned on the tanks of gas. "If the drawings are right, this will be a straight drop down to the underground shelter."

Sparking the igniter, the flame came to life. "Todd, take off your shirt and place it under the door. We're about to produce a lot of light."

The top layer of shirt and pants came off quickly and were stuffed under the door. Slipping on the protective eyewear, Hudson tuned in the flame until it was white hot.

"Everyone, turn around. Todd, stand in front of Sara, so she won't get any sparks." The agent began melting the connecting spots on the grate.

The large covering was held on by a few welded connections. After several minutes of tedious work, the grate was ready to drop. "Todd, get over here and find a way to catch this thing so we don't stop the party outside with a lot of noise."

The professor found a box of tablecloths and after wrapping them around his hands, he grabbed the hot thick metal. "Ready."

Another minute of the torch and the grate came free. Looking down the long drop, Hudson thrust his arm behind him, "Give me the flashlight and the rope."

Sara bent over and found the necessary equipment and placed it in his hands. Recognizing the dainty hand, Hudson pulled his head from the hole and looked at the lady whose hair was now falling from its earlier style. "Thank you," he said sincerely, shining the beam down the angled descent.

"Todd, tie this to that table over there, and then sit on it, so I don't fall," he said pointing to a piece of heavy furniture being stored.

He threw the other end of the rope down the hole and backed himself into the opening. "Don't go anywhere. I'll be back as quickly as I can."

"Be careful, Hudson," Sara said with concern.

"I will, honey," the agent said with a crooked smile as he began down the opening.

She looked at him awkwardly.

The air shaft for the lower levels was very smooth and because of its 30 degree angle, the agent made the descent easily and painlessly. Had it been a straight drop, he would have needed extra gear, especially for the ascent back up. But the daily time in the gym paid off, and made this a cake walk.

Upon reaching the last few feet of the drop, the vent went horizontal, and Hudson backed his way through the canal until he found an air grate into the room. This cover was not like the one on top, but rather like those found in houses. A small kick and the grille fell to the floor twelve feet below.

The agent backed out of the opening until he was holding on with his hands. The four foot drop was quick and forced him into a position staring directly at the man he had come to find.

"Hello, Hudson." The man was wearing silk pajamas and holding a cup of tea.

"Hello, Dr. Keith. There isn't any time. The sphere has been compromised, and the world is at stake. I need you to come with me now!"

3 — LATE SUNDAY EVENING, TWO DAYS EARLIER

Dr. Todd Myers looked at his watch and sighed, wiping his hand over his face. Nearly an hour had passed since he had set aside the lesson plan for the Church History class for which he was substituting, and picked up the Bible. He knew the lesson well enough – had discussed the very topic with the history professor last week – but this scripture was branded into his mind at the moment, for a reason only God knew. And He didn't seem to be revealing it anytime soon.

Jeremiah 29:11. For I know the plans I have for you; plans for good and not for evil, plans to give you a hope and a future.

Crossing ankle over knee, he leaned back in his massaging desk chair. The press of a button started the thing buzzing while he stared at the ceiling. Ah, he loved his chair. *Jeremiah 19:11 For I know the plans I have for you; plans for good and not for evil, plans to give you a future and a hope.* The verse came crashing back into his thoughts with an overwhelming sense of importance as if some deeper meaning that had eluded him consciously had triggered an awareness in his spirit.

He dropped his foot back to the floor, turned off his chair and faced the Bible once again. Pressing his elbows onto the desk he read the entire passage for the third time. For the life of him he couldn't put his finger on the source of this strange mix of foreboding and peace. *Lord, I know I don't often understand Your purpose before it happens, but something in me senses that I need to be very alert right now. Help me to stay vigilant and not miss what You are trying to show me, or be too distracted with circumstances to apply Your Truth to my situation.* A new thought hit him this time. *Lord, protect Hudson wherever he is. Keep him on his guard and give him peace. Your peace that goes beyond our limited comprehension.*

For thirty minutes he prayed, burdened beyond his normal concern for his family and Hudson's, for his church, his country, even the world. Head aching and elbows now numb, he finally lifted his head from his hands and blinked at his watch. It was 7:45 pm. His wife would be worried. *Or angry that I made her burn dinner,* he smiled to himself. She still wasn't accustomed to their new electric oven.

Gathering his papers, he shoved them into his brief case absent-mindedly. Right now he could use a cup of coffee and the company of his wife at the kitchen table. Her spiritual senses had been finely tuned into the Lord in a way that few could ever understand. He wanted to pray with her tonight, and then hold her for a very long time - feeling the baby move in her pregnant belly. Moments like this were rare and usually preceded God's work in some area of their lives. He stopped a moment and looked at his desk.

Papers lay strewn about, uncharacteristic of his usually tidy nature, but this evening a clean desk seemed unimportant. Dr. Sampson had asked him to sub for his History class at 8:00 am, and in studying the lesson he'd left books and copies of articles everywhere. With one last glance at the mess he threw on his jacket and picked up his briefcase.

He knew the topic well enough: the beginning of "separation of church and state" from Thomas Jefferson's letter to the Anabaptists, in 1804. His secretary had made copies of the letter for the students Friday afternoon, and he had three or four history books about it on his desk; with the copies he needed between the pages like a bookmark. He threw the books, the articles and the student's copies into his briefcase and headed for the dark seminary hallway. Right now his wife was waiting for him, and he needed her spiritual wisdom. Locking the door behind him, he headed home.

MONDAY MORNING, OCTOBER 16

"Good morning, class." The thick briefcase landed with a thud as it slammed onto the table posing as a desk at the front of the room. "Is everyone awake? Eight o'clock Monday morning comes earlier every week, doesn't it?" He shrugged out of his navy blazer and slung it around the desk chair revealing a crisp blue shirt pulled slightly taut around his well-developed arms and chest, and tucked neatly at his trim waist.

He had recently begun spending hours a week keeping his body more healthy. Truth be told, he'd had a wake-up call earlier in the year when an arm injury had forced him into rehab. After that, he figured the true purpose of a gym was to keep your body prepared for anything. His wife said she didn't mind the side effects either.

"Dr. Myers?" spoke a young man sitting front and center. Thin build and thinner hair made him look older than his twenty-three years. At the moment he just looked confused. "I don't have you until Hebrew at ten." Stopping only a split second he added, "Although I *am* ready with my translation." He rose to hand in his work. "I spent quite a bit of time working on…."

"Later, Jim. We can talk about your translation in class at ten. I'm only filling in for Dr. Sampson." Disappointment registered momentarily before the man sat and arranged his already neat desk. Jim was an excellent student majoring in Biblical translation, but his social skills were seriously deficient. *Good thing he'll be working with computers and not people,* Todd thought not for the first time. The other fourteen men and three women took their seats and readied themselves for a good dose of Church History.

Todd sat on the front table and loosened his tie. "Good news or bad news. Which do you want first?"

The professor put his hand up as a cacophony of both options rose from the students. The room echoed with calls for both choices. Smiling, he took over, "The bad news is that Dr. Sampson is sick. As a Hebrew and Ancient Israeli Studies professor, I don't usually fill in to teach Church History. Believe me, I try to avoid Baptist History like some of you try to avoid turning in your Hebrew homework."

"Not me, sir, I would never . . ." Jim interrupted, his eyes wide as boiled eggs.

"I know, Jim." The professor smoothed the young man's ruffled feathers with a kind look. "However! Nathan and I were conversing about the reasons behind the fracturing of the Anabaptists just a week ago, so he called me yesterday afternoon asking if I would prep you for your test on Wednesday." The room grumbled at the reminder.

"What's the good news?" Jim asked from the front row.

"It should be obvious," standing from the table and rifling through his papers, "you have me." He smiled for effect before adding, "Since I'm just a sub, I'm not going to give you a quiz like Dr. Sampson does." Good-natured applause broke out across the room.

"For those of you who don't know me, I'm Dr. Todd Myers. I've been on staff at Southern Seminary for a handful of years now. I've written several text books, am a Flight Instructor on the weekends, and have a black belt in Taekwondo. I enjoy scuba diving and rock climbing, sunsets, longs walks on the beach and Elizabethan poetry." The class chuckled good-naturedly.

"Now that you know who I am and why I'm here, let's get down to business." He pulled the copies from his briefcase and quickly passed them out before reaching for his own stack of prepared notes. Grasping the articles he'd copied the day before he turned to sit on the table.

A hand went up, "Yes, Jim," the professor said almost expecting the question.

"Do you want me to take roll? I usually do that for Dr. Sampson. I think he gives us extra credit for perfect attendance." He whispered the last part behind his hand as if he was avoiding the ears of the other class members.

"I don't think he's too concerned about it today, Jim, but. . ."

"I'll just take the names and give it to him tomorrow." He began quickly writing down names.

"Great idea, Jim," he exhaled softly and smiled kindly as he waited for the student to finish. The rest of the class nodded understandingly. Jim's Bible translation skills from original text in Hebrew and Greek to other languages and dialects were beginning to surpass even the brightest students. His extreme attention to detail, although maddening, made him capable of great potential in the field as a translator, bringing the Word of God to remote tribes and cultures.

Jim set his pen down and looked to his professor. Writing utensils poised around the room, ready to take notes as Dr. Myers started his lecture.

"Today we're discussing how the Baptists, in particular the Connecticut Baptist Association, helped to form the relationship between the church and the government." A few hands stilled as faces lifted around the room. Todd sat on the desk and continued, feet dangling beneath the table.

"The problem starts in 1796, with George Washington. You see, our illustrious first President proclaimed a National Day of Thanksgiving to commemorate a small and seemingly unimportant achievement; the ratification of Jay's Treaty which addressed some of the differences America had with Great Britain. One wouldn't think the simple act could cause such a problem, but the precedent had been set.

Then came the Treaty of Amiens. This piece of paper states that there was peace in Europe and that America was essentially delivered from danger. This is a big deal in comparison to Jay's Treaty." He stood from the table and began to pace, noticing again some faces lift to his as he paused. He had not seen students this attentive in a while.

"The Boston Columbian Sentinel, a New England Federalist paper stated that, 'It is highly probable that...the President will issue a Proclamation recommending a General Thanksgiving.' Now, the paper and its readers knew Jefferson would never issue that Thanksgiving proclamation. For to him and the Republican faithful in the middle and southern states, presidential thanksgivings and fasts were anathema, and an extreme example of the Federalists' political exploitation of religion.

The Federalists knew Jefferson wouldn't declare the day and wanted to show him as having contempt for Christianity. They thought he was an atheist," Myers said folding his arms and pacing. "If you lived back then, you might have thought that yourself. He did give 'citizenship' to Thomas Paine, offering the nation's hospitality in moving him from France to the United States. If you remember, Paine wrote *The Age of Reason* better titled 'the atheist's bible.' The Washington Federalist charged that his actions were, 'an open and daring insult offered to Christian religion.'

Our third President had suffered in silence the relentless and deeply offensive Federalist charges that he was an atheist and against the church," he said stopping in front of Sam's desk. "That brings us back to the Baptists." The professor sat on the table.

"The Danbury Baptists were a religious minority in Connecticut. They wrote a simple letter to Jefferson. After some congratulatory comments about his new presidency, they got down to business complaining that, in their state, the religious liberties they enjoyed were not seen as immutable rights, but as privileges granted by the legislature. They felt as though they were favors or rewards given.

Now remember, I told you that Washington had taken a beating over the thanksgiving issue. Well, Jefferson decided to take the gloves off and fight back, and he used his response in this letter to make it happen." Now all heads were up and staring at him in rapt attention.

"The President's final letter is fairly benign even though it has a line in it that we will discuss in a few minutes. What's important are the circled areas and inked out lines. It is in these areas that he says thanksgivings and fasts are 'religious exercises.' He was going to 'refrain from prescribing even those occasional performances of devotion.'" The professor stopped a moment to look at his notes. He shuffled the papers around a few times looking for today's lesson. *I must have started lecturing without the right page in front of me.* Returning to his briefcase he found everything he owned on this era of history, but nothing referred to the separation clause. *I must have been in too big of a hurry to get out of here last night.* "Sorry, about the delay. I seemed to have misplaced my notes. Good thing for you all I have them practically memorized." A few chuckles twittered across the room.

"Jefferson went on to say that these were 'practiced indeed by the Executive of another nation as the legal head of its church. He was saying that George III of England had practiced religious rule as a monarch of the state, and Americans had left England to get away from religious control. Our President attacked the act of making religious dictations of any kind to the British, thereby condemning them in American eyes.

In the unedited draft, he opposed proclaiming fasts and thanksgiving, not because he was irreligious, but because he refused to continue a British practice that was an offense to republicanism. To emphasize his resolve in this matter, he inserted a phrase with a defiant ring: 'wall of separation between church and state.' Of course, this simply emphasized the 'Establishment Clause' in the First Amendment, but his words took on a life of their own." Now all of the students were focused on him completely. Jaws were dropped all over the room, and heads inclined like parrots listening for their next important phrase.

"Now, it is difficult to determine Jefferson's true religious beliefs, and we don't necessarily know how much he really believed in the separation idea in the first place. For on January 3rd of 1802, just two days after the letter was written, the President appeared at church services held by John Leland in the House of Representatives. He attended these services twice more during his administration.

It seems Jefferson's public support for religion was more than a cynical political gesture. Many have argued that in the 1790's Jefferson developed a more favorable view of Christianity that led him to endorse the position of his fellow Founders that religion was necessary for the welfare of a republican government, that it was, as Washington proclaimed," the professor looked at his notes, "in his Farewell Address, indispensable for the happiness and prosperity of the people. By Jefferson attending church services in the House, he was offering symbolic support for religious faith and for its beneficent role in republican government."

The professor continued to pace the floor, reciting, without his notes, the topic he knew so well. "Our third President never compromised his views that the government couldn't deal in the religious sphere by legally establishing one creed as official truth and then supporting it with financial and coercive powers. However, by 1802, he seems to have come around to what the New England Baptist leaders such as Isaac Backus and Caleb Blood believed that, provided the state kept within its well-appointed limits, it could provide friendly aids to the churches including putting at their disposal public property that even a separationist like John Leland was comfortable using."

He looked at the class a moment. "Jefferson was a very complex man. On one hand he said that there should be a wall between the church and the state, yet on the other, he allowed religious services to be held in the House chambers. He is a very interesting figure, and yet his religious views are clouded forever by the single sentence, 'make no law respecting an establishment of religion, or prohibiting the free exercise thereof, thus building a wall of separation between Church & State.'

When the Danbury letter was originally written, it was published in a Massachusetts newspaper, and then disappeared for close to half a century until it was put back into circulation in an edition of Jefferson's writings. However, it wasn't the writings that truly brought it back to societal consciousness; it was several Supreme Court decisions.

The first decision was Reynolds versus the United States which was an authoritative declaration of the scope and effect of the first amendment. The second was McCollum verses the Board of Education which essentially forbade religious instruction in public schools. The courts had used Jefferson's 'wall' metaphor as a sword to sever religion from public life.

Before we move on to something else, are there any questions?"

A hand rose from the back. "Dr. Myers, where can we find out more about this?"

Several within the room nodded and other hands went up.

"Your book does a fairly good job on this, you need to read the lesson," he said pointing to another hand.

"Sir, I've read the lesson. Unless I read the wrong pages; that wasn't today's lesson," the student started skimming through his book. "It was interesting information, something I hadn't heard before, but not today's lesson."

The professor walked back to his papers. "Of course it was." Pointing to the class and looking at his notes, "Someone look at your syllabus and tell me what pages you were to have read last night."

Hands went up holding papers all over the room.

"Just read it out to me," he said looking at his notes.

A woman of Middle-Eastern descent in her twenties started to speak first. With a slight accent she read, "Pages 224-256, Dr. Myers."

"Exactly. It looks like you read the wrong pages," he said to the confused man. With a slight smirk, he added, "It is a good thing we didn't have a quiz today."

Beginning to start another subject, "Sir, I read those pages also, and it doesn't say anything about a letter that Jefferson wrote," another student muttered.

Picking up his personal copy of the text book, "This is the book that you are reading from, isn't it?" Dr. Myers asked out of frustration.

A unanimous yes resounded from the class.

"What edition do you have? Mine says the sixth. Is that what you have?"

Another unanimous yes.

"Well then turn to 224. It's on Jefferson." Opening his book, he found a small description of the early colonial government and its relationship with the church. Jefferson wasn't part of the reading. The professor went over to Sam's desk and read from his text.

Looking to the same pages, he found the identical information that his book revealed; no Jefferson.

"Am I being...?" he said with a flustered laugh. He mumbled to himself, "I studied from this book last night. I read the information starting on page 224." Turning to the front, "It has my name on it."

Picking up his notes, he reread his summaries on what he was to teach. His notes were fine, yet the book was different.

The professor looked at the index of the text and found nothing about the Danbury Baptists, the Connecticut Baptist Association, or Jefferson with relation to them. "What is going on here? I read it out of this book last night.

Well, it's on the pages I prepared for you. Look at those."

They all looked up.

"It's there isn't it? I prepared the information for you myself."

There were a few mumbles and heads shaking back and forth.

The Professor picked up one of the handed sheets and read it over. The information was not there.

"You have heard about this letter, haven't you?" Dr. Myers said out of frustration and confusion.

The students were shaking their heads no. "No sir," one said. "Me either," another answered looking at her fellow classmates. No one had ever heard of the "Church and State" letter by Jefferson.

Todd Myers sat in a chair behind the table in the front of the class and thumbed through the textbook. It mentioned information that was benign in content but new to the seasoned professor.

Tossing the book on the table in front of him, he stared blankly at the back wall. *What is going on*, he thought? *It is not there. The information is not there. It's as if it never happened.*

"Dr. Myers," a middle aged woman said raising her hand in the row to his left. "Dr. Myers."

Breaking from his stare, he looked over at her as she waved at him, "Yes…yes, what is it?"

"Are you alright? I think this Jefferson information is fascinating. Can you tell us more?"

Feeling like he was in the Twilight Zone, the professor rose and started to load his materials back into his briefcase. "No, Sally, I can't. Not right now."

He put his coat back on. "Guys, I'm going to need to do some research. Take the rest of the hour off or prepare for your next class, but I need to go." The students sat puzzled, exchanging raised eyebrows, as they watched him practically sprint out the door.

Todd turned toward his office hoping some quick computer research would render the information he had learned years earlier and studied the night before. A troubling connection between last night's prayer session with Aaliyah and today's turn of events was beginning to form in his mind. God's message of reassurance in a time of relative calm could only mean one thing. The storm was on its way.

4 — MONDAY MORNING, OCTOBER 16

Hudson Blackwell always enjoyed Monday mornings. There was something fresh and freeing about the idea of starting a new week: new possibilities and opportunities. The last several years of working on the project had been challenging and rewarding and except for rare circumstances, he worked nine to five; something very important for a man with a beautiful wife and two children.

He programmed in a new frequency on the radio. While turning onto the George Washington Memorial Parkway toward Alexandria, Hudson found a station playing classic rock and started drumming on his steering wheel.

The 36-year-old hadn't always wanted the family life. Having been a high school wrestler, six foot two with a muscular 210 pound frame, he'd worked his way through college as a security guard for top sporting events.

He came out of college with a Master's in Electrical Engineering and a new wife. But, he enjoyed the role of protector, and being recommended after every job he worked gave him the idea that he might be good at it. Not long after that realization, came a call from the Secret Service. He was the perfect candidate, tall, great eyesight, a Master's degree and the right psychological profile. He could remain cool and perform well under any circumstance.

When the joys of his life, Michael and Amy, were born, Hudson knew protecting the President at all hours and traveling the world away from his family had to end.

Hearing a cell phone ringing, the agent fumbled in his pocket to answer the call. "Hello."

"Hudson, you forgot your lunch," came the words on the other end.

He glanced at the empty passenger seat where a brown bag should be, "Honey, you're right. Can you bring it to me?"

"No, Babe, I'm a chaperone on Michael's field trip. I'll be gone all day. Just pick something up when you can."

"Okay, Love. By the way, what did you make for me?"

"Some of the enchiladas we had last night and a protein bar."

"Man, those were good. I'll look forward to them tomorrow. I love you, Sweetheart."

"Love you too. Bye." The phone went silent.

Hudson took an exit from the Parkway and drove into a quiet area north of Alexandria. Up on the right through the trees, he could begin to see his destination.

Cox Manufacturing was an ordinary-looking building. The typical cinderblock structure had a single glass entrance opening to a small desk guarding the door to the plant. A parking lot in the front and a delivery dock in the back completed the setup along with some shrubbery and a modest sign bearing the company name.

No one really knew what Cox Manufacturing produced. No one had ever cared to find out. The few sparse businesses around it were only concerned on the building's effect on their property taxes. So far, Cox Manufacturing had proved quiet and tidy, earning its keep on the block.

Not seeing many vehicles, Hudson looked at his watch. It was seven-thirty and still early, so many of the scientists had not arrived yet. But this building never sat empty. A prompt greeting would welcome him inside.

After parking his car, he strode up to the back door and popped open the very normal-looking dead bolt lock. Pressing his thumb against the surface, Hudson waited for the print analyzer to recognize him. Upon acceptance, the analyzer sent a small current of electricity into his thumb pad, designed to calculate the resistance within the person's body. And, unless Hudson had gone through a large body mass change within the previous 24 hours, the second stage of security would allow him through.

After the slightly irritating electrical surge, came a retinal scan. In the center of the back door, about eye level was a large peephole. One must submit to staring wide-eyed through the peephole into a red laser. When the blood vessels matched the database, the door opened to an inside chamber where a guard stood ready to examine the visitor and ask for the password of the day. The word changed daily, and today's word was troposphere. *I bet tomorrow's word will be stratosphere*, he thought knowing the week's passcodes often had a connective theme. *Government work at its best.*

Hudson tensed as Joe, the guard – actually a very large, well-trained Army Special Forces Sergeant – okayed him from the inner chamber. The facility had been compromised before, resulting in the death of several agents. Now, Hudson prepared for the worst every time he entered. Seeing that everything was normal today, he relaxed a bit.

His eyes were naturally drawn to the center large open area, about fifty feet below. Employees and the occasional guest entered at the street level and were immediately ushered to the metal railing that kept them from falling into the large pit below. The agent pushed the button next to the support and called the open-air elevator up to the top level.

"Hudson, is that you?" came a voice from below.

"Yeah, Brad, it's me," the agent calling over the chasm.

"Well, get down here. We have a lot to get done."

The elevator reached the top, and Hudson stepped inside. "It's not even eight thirty. I'm here early," he mused aloud.

"This is a busy day! We need you to wake from your peaceful slumber, and get to work," the voice laughed up at him.

Hudson smiled as he rode down in the open elevator. "I'm coming. Just hold your horses."

The agent had been in the white painted space hundreds of times and had used the equipment more often than he liked. A heavy breath caused his chest to lift then fall in a weighty sigh.

It still overwhelmed him. Computers designed to drive the large apparatus in the center of the room concealed every inch of the fifty foot high walls surrounding it. Two bulky generators rested in opposite corners providing immediate and heavy-duty backup when the apparatus was running. If there were a power failure, the computers would continue to ensure accuracy crucial to the functionality of the mission. The entire space was covered in a clear, rubber-type substance that minimized static electricity.

In the middle of the room was the main piece of equipment. The top-secret purpose of this craft had already resulted in the murder of its creator and designer Dr. Keith, among others.

"Hurry up, sir, we have guests," Brad yelled.

"Coming," the agent mumbled as he crossed the room.

Hudson exited the elevator and walked by the piece of equipment for which the building was designed. The sphere, as it was called, looked like a giant pearl cut in half with the top portion suspended telescopically from the lower half. When placed together, the machine was about seven feet in diameter. The base consisted of four tubes that shot straight up into the mother-of-pearl exterior of the lower half, supporting it but making it appear delicate and unstable.

Maybe today we can cause some good to come of this machine, Hudson thought as he continued past the glowing white apparatus, to the research area.

A mother-of-pearl type of covering wrapped the entire sphere in order to provide a coating hard enough to take extreme pressure, but still capable of reflecting the energy bombarding it during the project. After a year of failure, the scientists discovered that diamonds - altered through a process of melting and molding - could be conformed to a covering that would provide adequate.

The only part of the machine not contained directly within the sphere was a high-intensity laser cannon. The cannon completed the operation of the apparatus and was Dr. Benjamin Keith's life's work. Fueled by Uranium 235, the activated laser could punch a hole in the moon and keep going.

The agent walked toward a group of men wearing suits. Their backs were to him so he couldn't recognize faces, but he knew suits weren't good. *On such a busy and important day, and we have governmental chaperones.* Hudson continued forward.

"Glad you could make it," Bob said as he ran out from a side office until he was within whispering distance. "We have some special guests."

Hudson stepped into the room with his best fake smile in place, but he was not prepared for the crowd inhabiting the small office. The sea of suits opened up and revealed President Hayden Christopher Langley sitting at a research table looking over schematics.

"Hudson, it's been a while. Glad to see you again," the President said as he stood and walked toward the shocked man.

"Mr. President, it is a surprise to see you again." Memories of the last mission flooded his mind along with warning bells about this powerful leader. "What brought *you* down here?"

The President walked past him and toward the machine. "When we had the incident six months ago, the only thing I've been able to think about is this day. Instead of causing harm, I believe this machine can do the world some good," he spoke as he raised his hands to the sphere.

He turned toward Hudson with excitement and anticipation, "Can you imagine? This machine might produce enough electricity to power the city."

"Sir, we can't promise that," Brad interjected. "We just want it to produce more than it uses."

"Bradley, that's what I like about you – always covering your bases." The President continued his speech. "Today, it might not power a city, but in the future." He stopped and looked around the building. After a complete scan of the facilities, he focused back on Hudson, lowered his eye brows, and dropped the pitch in his voice, "I just had to be here for this day."

The President turned toward Brad, "Are we ready to try this?" he asked with little excitement.

"Sure are. This is just going to be a simple test under low power. The scientists have been here for hours preparing," he gestured toward a glass room filled with people in white coats fifty feet away. "We'll start up the sphere, and instead of focusing the energy toward its collective converters which then power up its electrically hungry circuitry, we will redirect the power away so we can determine its output."

Hudson continued the overview reluctantly, "Mr. President, we power the fusion reactor for just over a billionth of a second, and we estimate that – in that short period of time – there should be enough power created to light a city block."

"Why has it taken so long to get to this point?" the President asked.

Brad jumped in, "Because this is the only fusion reactor in the world. We weren't sure it could be modified from its original intent. The science is complex. If Dr. Keith were here, he might have accomplished it in much less time, but the best minds that we were given had to go back and just understand the original design before they could try to modify it."

"It would be like bringing Edison in to reengineer the laptop. Edison was a very intelligent man, possibly the most advanced mind of his time. But, he wouldn't understand LCD screens, processors, hard drives, software and everything else. He would have to go back and study a hundred years of technology before he redesigning it. In this case, we were Edison. Dr. Keith was light years ahead of our best scientists."

"Yes, Hudson, the world is not the same without him," President Langley said with resignation as he patted the agent on the shoulder.

Hudson pulled away feeling cold.

"A young man wearing a lab coat ran into the room, "Sirs, I believe we're ready."

"Thank you," Hudson replied taking charge of the situation. "Men, let's go into the observation room," he said gesturing to another glass-covered space. The agent escorted the President and Secret Service agents into the room as Brad locked it.

"Here gentlemen, please wear these special goggles, unless you don't like your eyesight," Brad laughed. The Secret Service agents did not crack a smile.

Through an intercom, Brad spoke, "We're ready. Commence at will."

Words began to come through a loud speaker.

"Ten, nine, eight."

The machine began to hum.

"Seven, six, five," the computer counted down.

A smell started to form in the air reminding the men of a blown transformer attached to fluorescent lights.

"Four, three, two."

The laser below the machine came to life and a reddish-yellow aura was reflected out of the four tubes at the base of the apparatus.

"One."

A blue glow surrounded the vehicle and caused an immense electrical power that even the men within the rubber cordoned off room could feel through their bodies. Everyone shook from the tingling.

"Zero."

Light as intense as a super nova filled every crevice of the chamber causing the onlookers to shelter their eyes even with the thick dark goggles. Almost as quickly as it came, it was gone and the area returned to normal.

Seeing the researchers in the other room removing their goggles and scurrying around computer monitors, Hudson removed his protective eyewear and unlocked the door. He walked toward the scientists while Brad stayed with the guests.

After several minutes of talking with the experts, the agent returned to the observation room to find Brad with his large muscular arms crossed and rigid jaw set in pointed conversation with the President. Upon entering the room, they ceased their banter and turned their focus toward Hudson.

"Mr. President, it looks as though we were successful," he said with a smile.

"Great. Now what exactly is successful? What kind of energy was produced?" the President asked folding his arms.

"The first estimates are rough, sir," Hudson said pulling up a computer printout that he had been holding, "Exact numbers will be available in a few hours."

"Hudson, don't hem and haw. I'm not asking you to take this information to the Joint Chiefs. Just give me a ballpark."

"Well, sir, it took 15,000 kwh to start the initial reaction on the vehicle. However, the fusion reactor produced 1,200,000 kwh," he said reading the general information from the sheet.

"What does that mean?" he asked with a confused look.

"I would say that in that billionth of a second, we were able to produce enough energy to light the White House, Capitol Building, and all of the Smithsonians for close to six months."

Clapping his hands together, the President slapped both Brad and Hudson on the arm. “Great job, guys. That’s what I want to hear.” He smiled. “I want this presidency to be known as one that changed the world. A good way to start is to give the people cheap electricity.”

“Now, sir, we are years from bringing this to the market place,” the agent said trying to curb the President’s enthusiasm.

“Hudson, don’t rain on my parade,” the man said sternly. “I want this out in some kind of form within 18 months.”

Brad looked at his partner in confusion, “Sir, I don’t think that…”

“Men, I want it in 18 months,” he said signaling the end of the conversation. “Come on boys, call for the car. Let’s get back to the White House. What’s next on my agenda, Jack?” he asked the Secret Service agent while he opened the door and left the room.

Brad and Hudson watched the President as he rode the elevator up and left the building. It took them several minutes to grasp the mandate with which they were given. Brad broke the silence first. “You think it’s possible?”

Hudson broke from his stare, “There’s no way in the world. Somehow, I’m going to work it where you get blamed for it.”

His partner laughed, “Can I buy you something to drink?” he asked as they walked toward the concession machines.

After putting several dollars into the slot, Brad continued, “Hudson, how did you become in charge of this project?”

“Don’t I look smart enough?” he grinned.

“Sure, but don’t they usually have Ph.Ds over something like this? How did an ex-Secret Service agent become the head of a venture like this one?”

“I’d guess it’s because I’m the only government employee to have ever logged time in that contraption,” he said pointing to the still-steaming sphere in the middle of the room.

“What happened?” he asked, sitting in a chair and opening his soda.

“It’s classified, but needless to say, I’m glad that thing is mothballed. If it were used again, who knows what type of repercussions it would bring. Brad, you’ve only been here a few months. How did you get drafted into this dungeon of ours?”

“I don’t really know why they chose me. I was an instructor in the Army Rangers program,” he took a long drink of his soda. “I’d been doing it for approximately six years when I got a call from the Pentagon saying that they needed my help organizing a project.”

Hudson watched the man fidget in his chair.

"I don't have your engineering background. I went into the Army right out of high school."

The agent jumped in, "Did you have any field work? I mean, did they send you on any missions?"

"Sure, I was a mission leader in quite a few covert operations. We laser-marked areas for Air Force strikes, knocked off drug kingpins, and removed terrorists. Everything we did was under extreme pressure. I guess that's why they wanted me for this work. I can handle the problems and come up with a quick solution."

Hudson looked at the man who had to top 6"4" with his flat top. He could believe he would be a formidable foe. "Brad, you are very good at what you do. We couldn't have gotten as far as we had without your help. Many times I've thought you had ESP the way you would come in with an answer before the problem even occurred."

The large man smiled.

"The project is lucky to have your leadership skills. Whoever chose you chose the right man," Hudson said taking a long cold drink from his soda. His cell phone rang.

Pulling it from a clip on his belt, Hudson answered it as Brad looked on. "Hello, this is Hudson."

"Hello, Hudson, this is Thomas Patrick."

"Yes, yes, uh, Pastor, how are you?"

"I'm fine, Hudson. I'm sorry I'm calling you at work. I got your number from your wife, and she assured me that if you answered, it was alright to break into your day."

"She's right, Pastor. If I were busy, I would've called you back," he said putting down his drink. "How can I help you?"

"Hudson, I won't keep you long, but I was reading from my Bible this morning during my prayer time, and the Lord told me to pray for you."

The agent sat up and listened more intently. "What were you reading?"

"Well, my friend, I was in Matthew seven and when I got to the thirteenth verse, you immediately jumped to mind."

Hudson had learned to trust Dr. Patrick's teaching. In his early 60's, he was the perfect image of a Pastor. He was wise and had a thorough grasp of the scripture. In his presence many had been moved to "share" with him problems, blessings, and even life stories. This Pastor listened quietly and gave biblical answers that meant something. Nothing trite, nothing irresponsible ever escaped his lips. If Pastor Patrick felt called to speak with him, Hudson would listen.

"It was very odd, Hudson, I've never had such a strong impression from the Lord. He told me that I must pray for your next steps and for your safety," the older man said.

"Pastor, you have me kind of unnerved," Hudson added a chuckle just to keep things light as Brad looked on.

"Well, to put it bluntly, I'm unnerved. I have been praying intently for you for the last few hours."

"I don't have quick access to a Bible. Can you tell me what it said in Matthew seven?"

"Sure, now let me see. Ah, here it is. This is the tree and fruit passage. It says, 'Beware of false prophets, which come to you in sheep's clothing, but inwardly they are ravenous wolves. Ye shall know them by their fruits.' Now jumping on down to verse nineteen it continues, 'Every tree that brings not forth good fruit is hewn down, and cast into the fire. Wherefore by their fruits ye shall know them.'"

The older man stopped for a second, then resumed, "I don't know why the Lord has put you on my heart, and Hudson, I don't know what you are going to go through, but my friend, watch your step. Trust the Lord and let Him guide your path. This passage is telling me that there are those around you whom you cannot trust, and our Lord is always good to give us discernment. Hudson, follow His light."

There was silence on both ends. "Hudson, are you there?"

"Yes, yes, uh, Pastor, I'm here. I don't know what to say," the man said dumbfounded.

"Hudson, there isn't anything I expect you to say," the mentor added in warm soothing tones. "The Lord told me to pray for you, and I wanted to tell you that the Lord's will shall be accomplished. Trust in Him, and He will be glorified in the end."

"Well, thank you, Pastor," the agent mumbled.

"Hudson, can I pray for you right now?" the man said with intensity.

"Yes, uh, of course."

"Well, let's go to the Lord. Dear Lord, You are mighty. You are powerful, and only You are to be honored and glorified. We don't know what You have for Your servant Hudson, but we ask that You prepare him and make him wise. Your Word says that if we ask for wisdom, You will grant it liberally. That is what we seek for this man. Lord, we want Your wisdom for his path and decisions. Lord, we ask for Your protection on him and his family. Finally, we ask that his actions honor You in all that he does. Mighty God, we thank You for caring for us and we thank You for honoring us with Your attention. In Jesus' name, amen."

"Thank you, Pastor. I'm not sure what to do."

"My friend, God will tell you what to do when it happens. Just be pliable."

"Yes, sir."

"Hudson, I will continue to pray for you throughout the afternoon."

"Thank you for calling, and the prayers."

"It's my joy to intercede for you. Goodbye." The line went silent.

Hudson slowly put his phone away as he tried to make sense of the last few minutes.

"What's going on?" Brad asked.

"That was my Pastor, telling me that I need to be careful." He scrubbed his hands over his face.

"Ooh, that's spooky," his friend said making a scary sound and raising his arms.

Hudson waved him off. "It has me slightly unnerved."

"Well, don't worry. I got your back," the large man said looking at his watch. "Hudson, I need to get to an appointment."

"What kind of appointment?"

"I, uh, need to have a root canal. I've had trouble with a tooth in the back," he said pointing into his mouth.

"Yeah, I don't need to see it," the agent said backing in his seat.

"It'll take a few hours, but I'll be back later. By the way, congratulations."

"What do you mean?"

"We were successful. Cheap electricity in 18 months," he said with a smile as he started to walk away.

"We'll see," he replied as the technician entered the open air elevator.

Hudson watched the man rise to the top level. "Lord, what do You have in store?"

Brad disappeared from Hudson's sight and the agent sat back in his chair as he heard the outer door slam. *All I can do is sit back and wait for the waves to arrive.*

He took another sip from his drink knowing he had been in this place with God several times before. He was not sure whether he should be excited or terrified.

5 — JUNE 7, 1789

The man slowed the horse to a trot once the city came into view. The clock tower containing the famous Liberty Bell revealed that he had made it to the correct municipality, and by the newness of the buildings, he had to be in the right general time frame.

Passing Independence Hall and looking into the windows, the man wondered if George Washington might be sitting inside reading legislative documents. John Adams and Benjamin Franklin might even be discussing the future of the country at that moment. These were things the traveler could only imagine, but just being on the famous street made the last hour and a half trek worthwhile.

Upon arriving in the Philadelphia countryside, he knew he had to change into his new costume quickly. Entering early American aristocracy looking the 21st century covert operative that he was would definitely compromise his mission. He removed his boots, socks, cargo pants, supply belt and t-shirt. *I refuse to take off my boxers*, the man thought to himself. *I will not wear the thin baggy undergarments I was given.*

Taking a bag from the seat and opening it, he pulled the items out and started to put them on. He found a white linen shirt first, complete with 15 buttons and falling to his knees. The frilly part around his neck and the length of it made him wonder if it might be part of a woman's outfit stashed into his case by mistake.

Next, he found the silk stockings. As he held them in front of him toward the decaying sun, the operative hoped he could find a way to not wear them. He dropped the stockings on the ground and went back into the pack praying for long pants, the knee high breeches made it clear he would be wearing the stockings.

He picked the white stockings from the ground and pulled them over his feet and up past his knees. Unlike a woman's hose they lacked any form of stretchy material and would slip to his ankles without the breeches tightly buttoned just below the knee. The man pulled on the blue knee high breeches and buttoned them at the bottom.

Pulling out his black shoes, he looked for any sign of left or right, but found none. The shoes looked identical. He placed the sole of the shoe to his foot and found them to be generally the right size, but they were straight – with no curve whatsoever. The man forced them on and took a few steps. Content that they would stay on, he tucked in the knee length shirt, bloused it a bit to keep it from bunching at his backside and buttoned the pants.

Just like a vest, the brown waistcoat went easily over the long-sleeved shirt and he buttoned it up reluctantly. At 85 degrees, it was already warm in the Pennsylvania countryside, and the last article of clothing made him wilt just looking at it. The coat was a closely cut, knee length garment made of wool just like the pants.

"It seems as though the *men* would need the fainting couches with all of these clothes on," he mumbled to himself as he forced on the wig that gave him a low, brown pony tail proper for the time period. It also added yet another reason to be grateful for his own era of air conditioning, shorts, t-shirts, and flip-flops.

A blue felt three cornered hat and walnut cane finished the look.

"I can feel testosterone evaporating from my body," he complained has he looked himself over. "Time to go."

Pulling a goatskin bag from the vehicle and slinging it over his shoulder, he looked to the southeast and headed that direction. Following a 20-minute walk, the man found a farmhouse, borrowed a horse from the barn, and after quickly saddling it, he headed the final three miles into town.

Passing the Hall, he heard the bells ring out for eight o'clock. "Right on time," he mumbled as he continued east on Walnut street. The man had visited Philadelphia in *his* time and knew that the various trees lining the streets gave them their names. Walnuts bent over the road overhead and he passed Chestnut Street, noting the trees of that name lining the way.

The Second U.S. bank and St. Joseph's church appeared ahead of him and turning north on Third Street, the First U.S. bank came into view. He turned again onto Dock Street until he saw the building he had come so far to enter. Veering onto Logan's Alley, he found the City Tavern.

The City Tavern or Merchant's Coffee House, was the political, social, and business center of the new United States. Reformers such as Jefferson, Adams, Franklin, and Paul Revere all ate there. The Declaration of Independence and The Constitution both trace their roots back to friendly discussions over food and spirits consumed within its walls.

The five-story brick Federal design was considered the finest establishment of its kind in the colonies. In one room, a patron might hear a concert or an opera. In another, the latest political news would be discussed. Traders exchanged promissory notes, bills of exchange, and conducted all manner of business in spaces throughout the building. Just a few years earlier, George Washington had celebrated with over 250 bluebloods prior to his inauguration in New York City.

The man looked back at the tower of Independence Hall and laughed. *It's funny, that this is where the real power sits.* He dismounted the horse and threw the reigns over a pole sitting next to a water trough. The man checked his bag for its contents then walked under the awning and up the steps into the building.

Upon entering the room, he found the wood beamed establishment busy with activity. The smell of cedar planks, several dozen sweaty men, and the usual smells from a fireplace near the back gave the place a distinct rugged quality that he wasn't certain he appreciated. *These people need to stop wearing so much wool.*

Since he had not come through time and space to observe eighteenth century architecture and grooming habits, the traveler went to work looking for his target. Walking deeper into the institution, he found men around a simple bar talking and drinking. Others were meeting at tables playing chess or relaxing after a long day of legislation. No workmen were present, he noticed. Everyone appeared well-dressed, and clearly, in spite of the smell, this was where the aristocracy refreshed before going home to their families.

Finally, in a back corner, he found a man perusing papers over his dinner; a very small man, not taller than 5'5". He realized the man's size was a match for the one he was looking for. Moving closer, he glanced at the large parchment he held steady, writing with a quill and inkwell. Before the page moved, the man could see the words *Constitution* and *Amendments* in old English. He pulled up a chair across from the person so intent on working on his manuscript.

"Do you mind if I sit here?" the traveler said.

The older gray-haired man looked up from his work with a perplexed look, "Sir, I am deep in thought. Would that you excuse me to my work."

"I will be gone very shortly," he replied with a smile. "How is the beefsteak, I hear it is very good?" commenting on the remainder of the food on the table.

While writing without looking up, "Quite agreeable," the fastidiously dressed editor mumbled.

"How is the rum, do they water it down?" he asked as he removed the bag from his shoulder and placed it on the table.

Dropping his quill and releasing the paper, the man spoke out of frustration. "Sir, through your speech, it is quite apparent that Philadelphia is not your permanent residence. However, I am busy in thought and occupation. I must prepare for the work of the people and cannot…"

A large grin came over the visitor's face, "James, that is why I'm here."

"You are very forward. Have we had the honor of being introduced?" he queried out of confusion.

"Nope, but you are going to want to hear what I have to say." He pulled out a letter containing a wax seal on the front.

"What have you there?" James said looking at the letter as it was placed in front of him.

"Motivation. Please, open it," he replied gesturing to the letter.

He bristled and spoke in an irritated whisper, "It contains King George the Third's seal. I cannot." Looking around the room he glanced to see that he wasn't being watched. "It could be treason if I were to be connected to royal dispatch."

The man took the letter and pulled the string breaking the seal.

"Who are you that you would have kingly correspondence?"

"James, don't worry about me." He looked at the small man, "This letter is for you," placing the sheets before him he sat back in his chair.

The older man started reading the letter and began to turn pale. He looked around the room and read it again.

"So tell me, what do you think? Isn't it is nice to have him say all those kind and glowing words about you?" he gloated taking a drink of the man's rum.

"I…I...," he mumbled not able to finish his sentence.

"A father of our country and can't finish his sentence." Getting very serious, the traveler leaned closer to the older man. "That letter states that good King George III appreciates your help in trying to bring the country back to the crown and understands that even with your best efforts, you couldn't turn it back. So, he has land and plenty of money waiting for you in England when you decide to return. He will make you a national leader, and you will have a place in the House of Lords. There are other things in there, but you have the idea."

"A lie!" he said pounding his fists. The tavern looked over in his direction. Once again whispering, "I have had no dialogue with the crown."

"No, but this letter says that you have," picking the correspondence up he waved it carelessly.

"I have sacrificed a great deal for the colonies and will not turn against them."

The stranger took another drink from the man's rum, "James, if this letter or others get out…"

"What others?" he asked incredulously.

"As I said, if this letter or others get out, you would swing from the nearest tree, and your family and lineage would be shamed throughout American history. What do you think of when I say Benedict Arnold?"

"He was a treasonous pig," the older man said with disdain.

"That could be your name, and I wouldn't want that to happen."

"What is your involvement?" James questioned with eyebrows furrowed.

"James, I'm here to help you. I want to protect you and have a way for you to be cleared. I wouldn't want this letter," he said laying it back in front of the angry man, "to be at the General Assembly in the morning. Your amendments would be forgotten and your place in history would be lost."

"How do you know of my amendments? You are not part of a stately delegation," he grunted sitting back in his chair.

"I am very familiar with them. That is all that you need to know. James, we…"

"You are not a friend or acquaintance. Cease from calling me James," the small man spoke pointing a finger in his enemy's face.

"Fine. We want you to remove one line in one of your amendments. Just a few words, and this letter and all following correspondence will disappear."

The older man looked at the papers before him. "These twelve amendments are carefully worded. They are unchangeable," sitting back and crossing his arms.

"We want you to remove the words, 'Congress shall make no law respecting an establishment of religion, or prohibiting the free exercise thereof,' from your third amendment."

The older man looked down at his page. "I will not remove those words. I have retained the wording from the Virginia Declaration of Rights, the English Bill of Rights; works of the Age of Enlightenment where it references natural rights, and the Magna Carta. This country must not endorse a single religion as so many others have – leading them to the church institutionalized by the governing power!" he said through pursed lips.

"You must remove those words, and you will." Trying to think up a quick argument to soothe the man's conscience, he leaned back in this chair and continued. "Because that wording comes from many British documents, it looks as though we are trying to emulate them. Do we want our children and grandchildren to think that we fought a war, just to set up our government on the principles of the people we defeated? There is no logic in that."

"The Pilgrims sailed from the old country in search of religious freedom. We must ensure that through all generations," he added countering.

"Your buddy Alexander Hamilton is totally against a Bills of Rights. He said, 'Bills of rights are in their origin, stipulations between kings and their subjects, abridgments of prerogative in favor of privilege, reservations of rights not surrendered to the prince," he said quoting word for word.

"My colleague does not understand as I the gravity of our situation."

"You don't understand the gravity of this situation. You will remove the wording to protect the nation, or you will be hung for treason and your name and lineage disgraced. When you submit these tomorrow morning, you will have it without the words, 'Congress shall make no law respecting an establishment of religion, or prohibiting the free exercise thereof,'" he spat pointing to the words under his third amendment. "Do you understand?"

The man sat there motionless. "You will listen to my words, or tomorrow this letter and many more will be circulating throughout the Statehouse of the Province of Pennsylvania," he said pointing west. Leaning over the table and staring at the small man right in the eyes, "Do...you... understand?"

"I...I...uh...understand," he said with sweat running down his face.

"Good, then we are in agreement," he replied with a smile as he took a last drink of rum. "Oh, yeah. If I have to come back here again, you can guarantee that next time our meeting will include others whom you may be devoted to. And I won't be so cordial with them."

The older man sat motionless.

"And James, you need to dump *that* first amendment," he said pointing on the vellum paper as he started to stand. "It isn't going to be ratified. And, oh, yeah, that second of yours won't be ratified for over 200 years. Focus on three through twelve. Those are where you are going to stand out. That information is free and has nothing to do with our deal," he smiled as he ate a few raspberries from a dish near the poor man's plate.

He picked up the sack to leave. "You can keep the letter. The King was so impressed with you that he sealed two," he remarked as he pulled another from the sack. "Enjoy that one."

The older man turned pale as a ghost.

"Well, Mr. Madison, I need to go. I have enjoyed our chat and look forward to seeing what happens in the morning."

He threw the sack over his shoulder and turned to leave. Opening the door of the historic site, he gave one more look toward the back table to find him throwing the letter in the fireplace and wiping a tear from his eye.

"*Mission accomplished*," he thought to himself as he closed the door and headed off into the night.

6 — MONDAY, MID-MORNING

The large hallway directed Dr. Myers away from the Church History class and out through the tall double doors of Mullins Hall. The morning was clear and the sky blue, but something was not right. With his briefcase unfastened and stuffed under his arm the professor pulled out the book in question once again and thumbed through it as he walked.

"I must have missed it," he mumbled to himself as students moved out of his path. He read without looking up.

Heading south toward the majestic building called Norton Hall, the professor was not able – even after looking again – to find the information he had studied the night before.

"I know I read it in this book," he said out of frustration. Slamming the hardcover shut he wished his office were not seven minutes away. He picked up his pace.

Normally the trek across campus provided time to focus his thoughts on the next class or research project he was heading to. But not this day. The beauty of the courtyard ceased to soothe his troubled mind. He stopped and looked out, remembering the simplicity of earlier years; those days before he had seen so much of the past.

The open courtyard revealed students throwing a Frisbee or studying for the next exam. True, even though the professor enjoyed the student's life and had more degrees than pictures on his walls, he never wanted to go back to that time in his life. Still, something about the seminary brought tears to his eyes just now.

He looked over the future ministers making their way to class and thought of the adventures lying ahead of them. The excitement of God's call seemed so full of possibility in the past. He sighed and prayed those students' adventures were easier than the ones he had been through.

He opened the large doors and nearly ran up the stairs to his office. Entering the room to the Ancient studies faculty, he found the four doors within the office suite to have post-it notes littering the center glass. *I must be the first one here*, he thought as he smiled at the receptionist.

"Hello Betty, how are you?" asking as he walked right by.

"I'm fine Dr. Myers," the young woman in her early 20's said as she went back to the computer. *I wish she were taking Hebrew instead of her husband, she would probably be making a better grade*, he thought as he turned the key and entered his office.

Walking around the leather chairs reserved for guests and students, and passing the walls of bookshelves, he rounded the corner of the large wooden desk and started pulling books from the pile he left the night before. Normally, this man was immaculate. Everything was organized and in its place, but when he got the late night call, he worked until he felt prepared and was too tired to put everything back up. Dr. Myers was glad for once he had a pile of opened books on his desk, for it made the quick research easier.

After scanning each volume, the professor would throw it aside and pick up another. Each book had been left opened to the passage pertaining to the Jefferson letter and yet after reading through six different texts, not a single copy referenced the famed correspondence. He turned to his computer and awakened the screen. Getting on the internet, he typed in Danbury Baptists. A screen full of references came up on the Connecticut association but nothing about Jefferson. Next he typed in Danbury letter and nothing showed up on the screen. The professor became more frustrated and typed in Danbury, Baptists, Jefferson, and letter. After paging through the many articles and web sites associated with the search, not a single one referenced the information that he knew he had read the night before and had studied many times in his past.

The professor sat back in his chair and placed his hands over his head. "What has happened? Something's wrong because I'm not making this up." Thinking of somewhere else in his office the information could be contained, he continued to mumble, "Where could it be?"

"It looks like you've jumped out of one too many planes or come up from a dive too quickly and gotten the bends. It doesn't look good for a professor to talk to himself," a voice said waving his index finger and smiling.

"Morning Frank," Todd replied rocking in his chair.

Dr. Frank Rice was the Dean of students and an imposing figure at six foot two and around 350 pounds. He came from the old school of pastoring and going to as many houses for dinner as possible.

"Todd, I hear you cut your class early," the man said standing in the doorway.

"Yeah, Nathan asked me to teach for him this morning because he's out sick." The large man squeezed into one of the leather chairs. "I just got confused on a subject," he said spinning around in his chair and facing the older man.

"I was teaching on Jefferson and the Danbury Baptists, and then the information that I had studied disappeared from the book," he said forming his hands together on the desk and looking down.

The gray haired man spoke up, "Tell me about what you were teaching."

"Just the normal things. How Jefferson wrote a letter to the Baptists and that's where we get the phrase 'separation between church and state.'"

The man looked confused. "Separation between church and state?"

"Yes, I was telling them the story, and the information wasn't in the book and nobody seemed to know what I was talking about. I can understand not preparing for the lesson, but the students had no idea about what I was telling them."

"I'm not sure what you're talking about," Dr. Rice said fairly quietly.

"Frank, you know, the Jefferson letter. He told them the government had to stay out of religious affairs."

"I'm sorry Todd, this is the first time I've heard of this and my area of study was the Colonial Church."

Dr. Myers smirked, "Frank, are you trying to pull something over on me. I personally remember you referencing this in a chapel address you gave several years ago."

"Todd, you seem to be under pressure. You might have what Nathan came down with. Take the day off..."

"Frank, I don't need the day off. I feel fine. You don't remember this?"

"No, Todd, I don't. I wish it was actually written like that, because it might help the church today, but I don't know anything about it."

The young professor sat back in his chair and stared at the back wall.

"Todd, I have a meeting to get to," the large man said as he stood and straightened his coat and tie. "Take the day off, I'll bring someone in to fill in for your classes."

"Frank, I'm fine," Todd spoke with defiance.

"Take the day off," the man said with finality as he left the room. "I'll pray you get to feeling better."

Todd took off his coat, loosened his tie, and rolled up his sleeves. "I need to get to the library."

After the cryptic call from his Pastor, Hudson returned to his office. Normally, this would be an exciting time where he and the staff would take a few minutes to enjoy the success of their work. However, as he passed the control room, he left the scientists in their merrymaking. They deserved the few minutes of downtime for they had created energy; cheap, abundant and almost limitless energy.

Hudson mumbled, "Good job guys," as he headed off to the quietness of his office.

The agent's workspace was at the end of a simple white hallway. As he opened his door, he entered an area that was totally his own. There were action movie posters hanging on the walls, next to notes he tacked onto the drywall. He had brought in a piece of tacky carpeting to cover the white linoleum of the floor. His simple metal desk occupied the center of the room with an ancient couch sitting next to it – in case he had to catch up on his sleep after a long work session. Add a few metal filing cabinets, a telescoping chair, a lava light, and an 80's fountain that looked like liquid was flowing from a suspended soda can into a mug below, and the room was complete.

What the agent loved most about the personal space was his 'system.' Hudson's wife wouldn't let him leave "piles" – as she called them – around the house. Not that he was dirty. He just didn't think it was important to put things away, especially if he might get them back out in a day or so, or whenever.

When he accumulated effects at home, his wife quickly put them where they went. He could never forget the day she got into a cleaning fit and set off to work in the garage. There are still small grumble sessions in the Blackwell house over where his needle nose pliers disappeared to.

The agent considered himself extremely efficient as long as his system was in place. But he was the only one who understood his system, of course. So, when he moved into this office, he had made it a place of comfort. He could leave all of the piles that he wanted.

And that is exactly what he encountered when he opened the door.

After knocking down a few books in an attempt to open the door he finally got through.

"I need to put those up," he mumbled to himself as he went to his desk to find his Bible.

The book was resting in the center of his desk where he left it. After clearing the slinky, some loose papers, books and a remote control car from his desk, he made himself comfortable. He opened the Word to Matthew 7, thinking again how his Pastor had unnerved him. What was God trying to tell him through his friend and mentor?

Having read the passage many times and heard several sermons on the topic, he knew the "Tree and Fruit" section. However, he wanted to reread it again so the Lord might possibly reveal something else that he was to know.

After looking over verses 15-20, it was clear his Pastor was trying to warn him. The people he would come in contact with in the near future must be tested by the Spirit. Verse 15 was the clearest, stating that there will be those who look like one thing but are really another.

Sitting back in his chair and looking to the ceiling, Hudson tried to think through the people he knew. There was not anyone in his life he thought this could represent. Hudson was a friendly man but did not keep any more than a few close friends; people whom he had spent years with or those with which he had endured trials. Time and desperate situations reveal a person's character, and he would trust his life to the friends he kept. The agent moved forward and looked higher up in the chapter.

Moving up to verse 13, he noticed it says that one can only get into God's Kingdom through the narrow gate. *Is God trying to protect me through this information, or His Kingdom*, the man thought to himself. He moved down to verse 21 and read that not everyone who sounds religious is really godly.

Putting his Bible down, he placed his palms over his eyes and began to rub. "Lord, what are you trying to tell me?" The burden grew as his elbows found the desk and his shoulders sagged in spiritual exhaustion.

The professor ran over to the James Boyce Library, a large colonial brick building complete with bell tower and steeple that housed over a million items. As he opened the large white door, the man knew that if the information were available, it would be found among the miles of bookshelves.

Dr. Myers had spent years of his life within the thick walls of this building and so knew exactly where to head for early American historical writings. He first pulled out books on Jefferson. All were informative but revealed nothing on the topic of interest.

He then moved to the Baptist history section and looked for Danbury Baptists. After several exhaustive volumes had been thumbed through he came up with nothing about the letter they received from the President, he then went to information on the First Amendment to the Constitution. Pulling a few thick writings with him, he progressed over to a wooden table in the commons area.

The open area was available in most libraries; however Southern Seminary wanted to make it a total resource building. In addition to computer stations lined up on the tables, there were flat screen monitors hanging from the ceiling. The Seminary believed that a Minister who stayed up on current events was better able to prepare for the pulpit because he could bring in real life examples to lock in the points given from God's Word.

Todd's blood pressure was rising as he doubted his own sanity. "I know that I know this," he mumbled as he dropped the books on the table and pulled up a wooden chair.

Opening a text on the history of each constitutional amendment, he once again read the account as to why it was written, hoping to find a reference to the lost letter. Nothing in the readings or footnotes mentioned it. Book after book came up with the same outcome under the wording of the First Amendment, *"Congress shall make no law respecting an establishment of religion, or prohibiting the free exercise thereof; or abridging the freedom of speech."* Leaving the books opened, he sat back, propped up his feet on the table and looked up toward one of the screens.

The device was programmed to *FoxNews* and had the President apparently giving a speech to the press corp. "This can't be good," he mumbled as someone shushed him. Todd knew the President and held little trust in the man. Feeling his world falling apart, the professor added insult to injury and started reading what the President was saying on the closed captioning.

The President was just beginning his prepared speech. "Good Morning everyone," he said shuffling several pages.

Why isn't he using the teleprompter, the professor thought. *This must have been a last minute development.*

The President continued, "I want to thank you for assembling on such short notice," he said to the press with a smile then spoke looking to the camera, "America, our country has been under attack. No, there is no other nation warring against us, the fight is coming from within." Letting the words rest for a second, he looked back at his notes.

"For decades and possibly centuries, our nation has been at war with itself. We have pitted one religion against another. We have called those who follow a God as fundamentalists, or right-wing Christian conservatives. Those who aren't placed in that camp are called moderates or liberals. Add to this the difficulties this supposed Christian nation has had with other countries, especially those of our Arab friends the Muslims, and our nation has been fractured." He stopped once again.

Flipping pages he looked back up. "I don't want a divided nation. I don't want our people warring with each other. During my Presidency, I have tried to bring factions together and stop the separation. However, the religion issue has continued to divide us from the core.

Our nation must look compassionate to other countries. Our country must reach out to those people who are oppressed and relay the message they are welcome here – whether or not they are Christian, Muslim, Buddhist, or choose not to worship anything or anyone at all.

It is my desire to assuage the fear that other countries have because of the differences in our beliefs. Therefore, the office of the President will take over the leadership of religion within our country. All denominations, sects and beliefs will simply register with the government to ensure they are in compliance with new regulations set forth from this office."

"What?" Todd said out loud.

Placing his hand up he quieted the crowd, "Now understand you will continue to worship in the way that you have grown accustomed and in a way that is meaningful to you. However, by the Presidency taking over religious leadership, we will ensure a national standard and compassion toward other beliefs.

By doing this, Iran will not have to fear us as a nation opposed to their values and beliefs. Those in India will trust America more, and therefore feel free to open up new trade routes. China, and its government-controlled religion will be more able to open up dialogue on future events."

Todd mumbled, "He's enforcing his own act of supremacy like Henry the 8th."

"Shh," the librarian whispered.

Switching pages the leader continued, "I know that for many of you this will be a change. America never implicitly wrote anything in its Constitution or Bill of Rights about religion, so that people would always feel free to worship as they see fit."

Smiling into the camera, "Remember, the Pilgrims came over from our friends in England so that they could worship freely. That will not change, and in fact it will be more of a national creed because there will now be a governmental blessing on your belief."

"That's not legal!" Dr. Myers yelled.

A small older woman walked by, "Dr. Myers, please be quiet and take your feet down from the table. You need to set an example."

He took his feet down. "Did you hear that; it's not legal?"

The woman glared at him.

"It's not legal. The First Amendment prohibits that."

As he finished the last few words and looked toward the book, the world blurred. It was as if a jet flew by. A small band of blur sped through the room bringing a change with it. The professor's head was spinning because with the distortion came a thunderous crashing – like a small sonic boom. Shelves were in different places, people that were within the room disappeared and others reappeared. The color of the library was altered and Sandy, the woman who had been lecturing him about his feet was replaced by another woman whom he had never met.

The professor pulled his hands from his head trying to make sense of the change.

"Sir, are you alright? Dr. Myers, are you alright?" she said tapping him on the shoulder.

"Who are you?" he mumbled, not being able to focus.

"What, Dr. Myers?" the young woman said perplexed.

"Who are you?" he said trying to stand.

"It's me Angie. Angie Nelson. I'm in your Hebrew class."

"Thank…thank you," he mumbled not knowing who she was. "I'll be fine." She walked away in confusion.

Looking down at the books, the words had changed. The paragraphs were reordered and the examples and illustrations were in different places. Focusing on the First Amendment it read, *"Congress shall make no law abridging the freedom of speech, or of the press; or the right of the people to peaceably assemble, and to petition the government for a redress of grievances."*

The words were gone. The words stating that the government shall make no law *"respecting an establishment of religion, or prohibiting the free exercise thereof"* were gone. The world was different. The words were different. History had been changed.

The professor knew he was not losing his mind, and even though everything around him had been altered, somehow, he was the only one who knew the difference.

"I'm not losing my mind," he grumbled. Sitting back in his chair and taking in a few deep breaths he said, "I need to call Hudson."

7 — MONDAY, MID-MORNING

Hudson finished praying with no clarity or insight into what God had spoken through his pastor. Nothing came to mind, spoke to his heart or pointed his thoughts in any direction. Spiritually, he was coming up with one big blank.

Pulling the phone from his pocket, he pushed the first speed dial number and waited for her to pick up. Sometimes, her walk with the Lord seemed closer than his. At least, she often understood spiritual things before he did. Maybe she had some insight, but just a word from her today would ease his mind.

"Hey, Hudson. What's up?" she asked.

"Honey, can't a guy have a little bit of surprise in this era of technology? With that phone putting up every bit of information about me before I even get on the line, it's hard to be mysterious," he teased.

"What, were you trying to be my secret admirer?" came her coy response. "I can always turn off the display and let you call me back. I'll act surprised."

"Tempting. Actually, Babe, I need your help. Where are you?"

"I am on a school bus chaperoning Michael and 36 of his little friends to the Natural History Museum. Don't you just wish you could trade places?" she joked.

"No, I wouldn't want to take that honor from you. I love you too much," he retorted with a smile.

"Thanks. You said you needed something?"

Hudson pulled a pinch of metal shapes from the magnetic paper weight on the corner of his desk and let them shoot back onto the pile. "I just need your wisdom."

"What's going on?" she asked with concern over the sound of a bus full of kids yelling.

"I got a call from the Pastor."

"What did Dr. Patrick want," she asked with surprise.

"He in essence warned me about something that was coming, Honey."

Hudson took the next several minutes to bring his wife up on the talk he had with the Pastor and the verses he had researched.

"What do you think it means?"

"I was kind of hoping you could tell me," he quickly replied.

"Hudson, I know you already know this, but it sounds like we need to be wise and walk carefully. The Lord is trying to tell you something by alerting the Pastor. You know that I love you more than anything. You also know that I am with you no matter what. When this comes, we will go through it together."

"It's good to know you're on my side."

"So, have you prayed about this?"

"Yeah, Sweetie, I have."

"Well, then, just keep your eyes open."

"Of course I will, but I…" The phone went dead, the room blurred, and a sound much like a train rushing by coursed through the building. The sensation caused the agent to fall back in his chair and drop the phone due to the uncontrollable response of pulling his hands to his ears.

His head hurt and his ears rang, but he got up as quickly as possible to see what had happened. Snatching his phone, he ran from his office into the open chamber housing the sphere.

"Is everyone alright?" he yelled.

Suits and white coats came running from every part of the building to see why he was yelling.

"What happened, is everyone alright?" he shouted again.

A researcher was the first to arrive. "Hudson, did something happen?" he questioned looking around the room.

"What do you mean? Is anyone hurt?" he barked, realizing suddenly that he was still yelling.

"Hurt from what?" The white coat asked nervously.

"That boom, or earthquake. Was it related to the sphere?" He tilted his head to somehow shake the ringing in his ears and headed back into his office.

"Hudson, why were you so loud?"

Another white coated popped in.

"What sonic boom?"

"I didn't feel an earthquake," came the deeper voice of a suit just entering.

"Yeah, we don't have too many here in Virginia," a balding man with a clipboard stepped through the door with a smirk.

Hudson lowered his voice, but his hearing was still overpowered by the infernal ringing sound. "Something happened. It shook my office and, evidently, about made me deaf." He looked around, "Didn't anyone else feel that? Hear that?"

The scientists looked at each other in dismay and mumbled a unanimous no.

Suddenly uncertain about his own experience, he shook his head like that might change the reality before him. Something was off here. He just could not make it out yet.

"I want a complete diagnostic run on the sphere. There had to have been a localized disturbance, possibly aiming in the direction of my office from the machine. I want you to find out what caused it," he said with finality.

The white coats dispersed quickly and began muttering investigative assignments and theories. Hudson turned toward his desk, not liking that the anomaly had hung up on his wife. He pushed her speed dial. The display showed that the register was blank.

"I wonder if the surge fried the memory," he mumbled.

Manually inputting the number, the display showed it to be a non-existent phone number, a beeping sound blared through the speaker. Hudson tried the number again.

Maybe I put it in wrong, he thought.

The same results occurred.

"This can't be right," he said looking at the display. "Maybe this phone is totally gone."

He called his home number to see if the machine would pick up, so he could test whether it was working. The same information came up. Non-existent number and the incessant beeping.

The agent rubbed his temples and put the device back in his pocket, mentally making a note to pick up another one on the way home when it unexpectedly came to life. He answered without looking, just grateful to get his wife back on the line.

"Sorry we were cut off, Honey."

A familiar male voice registered over the line, "Hudson, I know that we have had some close calls in the past, but I would rather you not call me Honey."

"Todd, is that you?" he probed in confusion and embarrassment.

"Yep. It's me."

"I'm sorry, I thought you were my wife," he said walking around his office. "We were cut off for some reason, and I thought she was trying to call back. Todd, we've had some kind of incident here in the building, and I need to work on it. Can I call you back later?"

"Are you talking about the sonic boom? I don't know what else to call it."

"Did you feel it there?" Surprise colored his voice.

"Hudson, I think it was felt everywhere. Have you noticed anything odd since that time?" Todd left the library as he spoke and started toward his office.

"What do you mean by odd?" the man asked sitting back in his chair. "I've been in the manufacturing building all day."

"You know that I'm pretty level-headed, don't you?" he said sitting at a bench off the main quad. "I mean, we've been through a lot together, and I don't seem crazy to you, do I?"

"Todd, I trust you and your judgment. What happened?" he asked switching hands with the phone.

"Hudson, when the boom, or atmospheric blur, or pressure crash, whatever you want to call it occurred…" He stopped for a second.

"Come out with it. What happened?"

The words came out in a rush, "Everything changed."

"What do you mean, 'everything changed?'"

Looking around to make sure he was not being overheard, he spoke more quietly, "Everything changed. The room I was in changed. Things were in different places. People disappeared and others reappeared. A woman I've never seen before today says she's a student of mine."

The agent remained silent.

"Hudson, everything transformed. And have you seen the news today?" he asked starting to raise his voice.

"No, man, I've been doing tests."

"The President had a news conference this morning saying he is officially taking over the leadership of all religion within America," he gritted out the words.

"Well, that can't be. He was here this morning checking on our progress. He didn't seem like he had a speech that big to make. He would've been preparing for it."

"Well, he made the speech, and it looked like it was a last minute job."

"What do you mean?" he asked sitting forward in his chair.

"He used paper notes. He didn't use a prompter. A speech that big should have been prepared for weeks, yet he was fumbling through notes."

Hudson blinked. "I can't believe this."

"Well, believe it. The President is taking over religion."

"Todd, I'm not a Constitutional scholar, but isn't that against the law?"

"That's the other thing I haven't mentioned yet. The law's been changed."

"I hadn't heard about that. When did it happen?"

"This is the oddest part, but it looks like it changed during the phase boom thing. I know this sounds crazy, but I was researching the first amendment this morning and before the boom, one of our rights was that the government would stay out of religion, and after the boom, the wording was gone. The books changed. It was as if history was rewritten. I can't find anything about 'separation of church and state' in books, on the internet or by other scholars here at the university. Hudson, history has been rewritten."

"Todd, all we did was a power experiment here in the lab. We didn't do any leaping." Somehow guilt crept into the other emotions crowning his thoughts. "We've turned off the circuits that allow the sphere to leap. It is just a big generator now."

"I'm telling you the world is different. Somehow, someone has rewritten history, and it sounds like the President *is* aware of it."

"It just can't be. There's only one time machine, and I was here with it all morning," he said walking around his office.

"Hudson, I need to get off with you and call Aaliyah," he said starting toward his office. "I'm not crazy. Do some checking. We've seen firsthand the potential that machine has for destruction."

"I tell you it can't go anywhere! I disengaged the time circuits myself."

"Then someone has reengaged them or there's a twin somewhere. I'll call you soon," he said as he slapped the phone closed.

Hudson left his office and walked back into the open chamber. Staring at the large opalescent sphere sitting in the middle of the room he could not believe it had leaped. Not only that, but the hard connections wired into it from many spots around the walls and the constant scrutiny from security and scientists would make it impossible to commandeer.

"Do we have progress?" he queried a lab technician walking by.

"Sir, we haven't found anything out about the boom. We're still trying to corroborate your story," he said holding a clipboard.

"Peter, I want you to give me printouts on power usage within the building for the last 24 hours. If a light bulb went on within this facility, I want to know about it."

"Yes, Mr. Blackwell," he said starting toward the computer room.

Hudson moved toward a tool box adjacent to the vehicle. "If you've jumped, I'll find out."

Pulling some tools from the bench, he walked over toward the sphere. "Now, let's see if anyone has turned you back on."

—

The professor continued toward his office and called his wife. Dialing the number it took several seconds for her to pick up.

"Hello," she said with a strong Hebrew accent.

"How is my Jewish Princess this morning?"

"Todd, what happened?"

"My ears are still…what is the word…uh…"

"Ringing," he answered.

"Yes, my ears are ringing and my head hurts. What happened?"

"I'm working on it. I think it has to do with the sphere," he said with regret.

"Oh, no, Todd. I thought Hudson…broke…or take apart."

"Yes, Hudson said he dismantled it. I just called him."

"My Love," she began, "you and Hudson take me from a place of loneliness and sure death on that machine, and so for me it saved me. Through that machine, I met you, and fell in love. Our Lord blessed me through that, but it can hurt...many…people."

"Yes, Princess, it can. Have you seen the television today?"

"No, I am preparing for a lecture this afternoon. I have been studying all morning."

"Aaliyah, teaching a class on Jewish history can wait. The students could use a break. Someone is changing American history."

"No," she said with fear in her voice.

Todd made it to the doors of Norton Hall and stopped. "Princess, I was told to take the day off, so I'll be home shortly and will bring you up-to-date then."

"Todd, we have to know that the Lord already knows of what is taking place. Our God owns the… cattle on a thousand hills, so he will be… aware of someone trying to change the…what is it…direction of this Nation under God."

"Yes, I know."

"Hudson is very wise and loves our God. We must pray for him."

"I agree," he said as he sat on the steps looking out over the campus.

"Dear Lord, Jehovah Jireh, our Provider, we praise you," she started. "I thank You for my life, and for my husband. You give such great gifts because of your… deep love for us. My God, we pray right now You will be with Hudson as he tries to know what has happened. We ask… you guide his… steps and be his Jehovah Magen, his shield.

Lord, we pray You are blessed and that You are…exalted through all happening. And Lord, use us in a way that You see fit, so that You are glorified. We praise You and thank You. Amen."

"Thank you, Aaliyah, I should be home in a little while," he said standing and heading toward his car.

"I love you dearly."

"You know that I love you, I went through time to find you," he added.

"You are my hero. Goodbye."

"Bye," he said closing the phone. "Lord, please work this out. I feel in my spirit that it's going to get worse before it gets better – a lot worse."

Sighing he left the path and entered the parking lot.

8 — OCTOBER 30, 1517

"I need more time," the man mumbled out of frustration. "I don't feel prepared," he said as he climbed into the cockpit and brought the vehicle back to life.

"It has to be done," the mission coordinator answered.

"Why, Rex? We have all the time in the universe at our disposal." Knowing the name "Rex" bothered the tall thin man, the pilot made it the permanent nickname for him. "Why can't I wait a day and better prepare for the jump," he questioned, receiving the bag the man handed him.

"I'm told we go, so we go. And stop calling me Rex."

"I'm just paying respect to the leader around here," he said straightening up and saluting.

"Doctor is fine. Anyway, we have to go, and there isn't anything that we can do about it," he replied as he rifled through the sack. "Of course, I would like to let the machine rest a while. We don't know how all of these successive jumps will affect its performance."

He opened the mission supply bag, "You need to wear this hair piece."

"Not again," the pilot complained.

"Put it on. You know your target, and this will help you get in. You also have a black-hooded robe, cross, and sandals." Searching a moment he brought out one more item, "Oh yeah, a rope belt. Not much explanation needed there."

Black, piercing eyes met his.

"I don't like the quick turn around anymore than you do. We get paid – and paid well – to implement his plan." He grabbed a small leather case from the bag and flipping it open continued, "I think you know what to do with this."

"Yeah," the man said out of disgust. "I know what to do," he muttered.

"There's no way around it," he said leaning on the edge of the sphere. "All of the psychological profiles we've run on this character show that there is no way we can threaten, embarrass, harass or generally intimidate. This person is deeply convicted and immovable." The case slipped back into the bag, and he held it out for the other man to grasp it.

"We may be able to stop him for the time being, but he will eventually migrate back to his purpose." His eyes lowered as he spoke quietly, "So do your work and get out of there."

"I got it. Is there anything else?"

"We think we've found a good close spot to bring the vehicle to a rest. It'll be the middle of the night, and you shouldn't have to travel far to find your target."

"I've read the mission overview."

"Then, I think it's time to go," he said backing away.

"I'll see you soon," the pilot spoke as he pressed on the dash to lower the canopy.

After the top half of the sphere mated with the bottom half, the internal lights came to life revealing a backlit dash. The area in front of him was set up into four quadrants. The left two quadrants were relegated to time. One area was of the time you were leaving referenced by Greenwich Mean Time, then day, month, and year. The quadrant paired next to it was of the time the vehicle was to seek in the same delineations.

The other two right quadrants involved space. One determined the exact longitude, latitude and altitude the machine was leaving and the other noted the intended final destination.

The pilot touched the screen as checklists appeared before him on the display. He carried out the routine checks and belted himself into the left seat while stashing his bag under the right. Working his way through the lists he touched the screen to indicate completion. After several minutes of checks, a metallic voice came over the overhead speaker.

"It looks like everything is right in there, and we are getting all greens in here," Rex spoke from the control room within the large cavern.

"Ready in here."

"Okay, then sit back and let us do the driving."

The operative hated that line. For one thing, he did not like placing his life in other people's hands. For another, it sounded like some cheesy bus line advertisement. "Just get on with it," he grumbled.

"Here we go," the speaker vibrated before going silent.

The man pressed himself back into the seat and felt a surge of electricity course through his body as the inside lights dimmed. The vehicle took on more and more charge, turning the canopy translucent and allowing him to see the activity occurring within the room.

The man remembered as a child in science class, the teacher charging a Leyden Jar capacitor, and as the students got their hand within an inch of the metal covering, a blue spark would form. The electricity coursing through the room outside the sphere was on the magnitude of a million times stronger. Watching the scientists remember their eye covering in a flurry, he viewed electrical bolts bounce off of the rubber lined walls. Several strikes hitting hard enough to cause burn spots on their destination.

The charge within his body grew, making the leap now eminent. Doing what he could to keep his mouth from screaming, he saw the blue hue of the machine turn to a red hot glow. The temperature within the cabin grew as he closed his eyes and pressed his head tightly against the seat.

A millisecond later, the machine vanished, and the room went dark.

The total trip within the sphere was only 10.2 seconds, and after finding its destination, the vehicle's internal lights increased in illumination. The mechanism shut down.

Leaning forward, the operative looked over the blinking displays in the cockpit and found them registering the correct place and time. "It looks like we're here," he groused as he turned his head back and forth to minimize the stiffness from the short but bumpy ride.

After unbuckling himself, he stretched to the right and pressed the button that extended the telescopic canopy. The top half of the blue pearl rose as steam – which had permeated the space – began to fill the air inside the room he had landed in. Pulling the gun from his holster, he quickly waved the vapor away and checked the chamber.

The circular room surrounded by high stone walls appeared empty as the pilot pulled himself from the seat and jumped out of the cockpit. Still on guard, he scouted around the cavernous space. Wood planks covered the floor all the way to the stone walls that rose 25 feet where they formed a peak. Only cold and damp silence hung about the room, making the pilot more depressed than afraid. Still, he looked for the exit as quickly as possible and found the only way out to be a set of steps dropping from the floor on one side of the chamber next to an outer wall. Leaning over the opening, the traveler saw a circular staircase dropping at least 100 feet. From his vantage point he could see that no one was around below.

Walking over to the gothic wrought iron window, he looked out over the quaint countryside noticing no movement outside. The rampant thunder and lightning had forced even the most determined night owl inside. The plan to arrive in the middle of the night prevented exposure. The storm was just a lucky break that provided more coverage.

Feeling comfortable about his situation, he walked back to the sphere which was still steaming and hot to the touch and pulled his bag from under the seat and put on his current outfit. When he had completely changed clothes, he pulled on the skull cap to give him the appearance of baldness.

"The celibacy thing is bad enough, but they have to dress like this?" he grumbled. Pulling the leather case from the bag, he thrust it under his robe and started toward the hole in the floor that would take him from his lofty perch.

The operative climbed down eight stories, and made it to the ground floor silently where he slowly opened one of the large doors. Peering through the small crack he found the streets deserted.

The long wall of the building impressed him. Great ability and determination were required to build such a structure. "The Schlosskirche is a beautiful church. It's too bad that I'm about to stop the event that makes it famous." With a sigh, he headed out into the rain.

Walking the cobblestone streets among the formidable stone buildings gave him pause even more so in the heavy rain that fell, making him cold and wet.

Following a short ten minute walk, the soaked monk imposter found his final destination, the University of Wittenberg. A school only 15 years old by current standards, but one that had been closed down by Napoleon more than 200 years before the wet man's birth.

The multi-level stone structure was formidable, but because it was filled with religious students, it posed no real threat to him. "Nonetheless," he complained, "I wish they would have given me more time to plan this out."

Lighting struck overhead.

There were entrances on each side of the building. From a quick look at ancient plans of the structure, the operative remembered prayer rooms on the north and west sides – which would be filled 24 hours a day. There was a small chapel on the east side and most dormitory rooms were situated on the south. After a quick surveillance of the structure, and seeing only a few candles burning within the rooms, the man determined the south entrance would allow the fastest access to his mark and offer the fewest possible obstructions.

The large edifice stood like an imposing force above him as he turned the bulky lock. Heavy wood on well-oiled hinges slid open to allow his entry under the rock entrance.

Door after door passed by on the trek down the long stone hallway, and still he did not hear or see any movement. His destination would be on the second floor, so he continued toward the center of the dormitory until he found a grand staircase.

Beneath his weight, each wooden step raised a multitude of creaking and moaning sounds. Following a rise, a 180 degree turn and a second rise, the man found the floor to complete his mission. He spun south and saw a light on in the room at the end of the hall. The room he needed to enter.

Grabbing a pewter cup sitting outside one of the quarters and filling it with water from a container next to the stairs, he carried it toward the apartment. As the light under the door grew brighter with each passing step, the man straightened his wet robe and the cross hanging from his neck. He made sure his scalp cover was on and secure and pulled the leather case from under a pocket within his robe.

Once outside the room, he looked back down the hallway and found it empty. He opened the case and pulled out a syringe filled with a clear liquid. He was intentionally unaware of the composition of the liquid. He guessed the results of using it. Leaving the cap on the sharp end, he knocked on the door.

"*Ja*," came the reply.

The pilot cleared his throat. "*Es ist spät und ich habe gedacht, dass sie etwas wasser wollen würden*," he spoke in perfect German. (It is late and I thought that you would want some water.)

"*Vielen dank, dass nett ware*," (Thank you, that would be nice.) he replied as the man opened the door and entered the room.

The living space was small; approximately seven feet square. Within the room a fireplace glowed with burning embers. A narrow bed and a two foot square table with accompanying chair in which the man was presently sitting and working were also there.

On the table sat an inkwell and a large piece of paper in which the occupant was writing. The wording was Latin and the title was "Disputatio pro Declaratione Virtutis Indulgentiarum." This is what the traveler had come hundreds of years into the past to ensure was not distributed.

The operative continued the conversation. "Here is your water."

The man took the cup without looking up. "Blessings be on you for your thoughtfulness," he replied.

"What are you working on?" the wet man asked.

Finally looking up in surprise, "I am writing Albert, the Archbishop of Mainz and Magdeburg protesting the sales of indulgences." Starting to get angry, "John Tetzel the papal commissioner for indulgences in Germany has been raising funds for the renovation of St. Peter's Basilica in Rome. He has no right to offer repentance through a piece of paper. Tetzel has often said that, 'As soon as the coin in the coffer rings, the soul from purgatory springs.' I also deny the pope's right to grant pardons on God's behalf.

The only thing indulgences guarantee is an increase in profit and greed, because the pardon of the Church is in God's power alone. I will put up with it no longer.

Are you new to the University?" the real monk asked, suddenly somewhat confused.

"Yes, I am very new to the area," he replied pulling the syringe from under his sleeve and removing the cover.

"I must get back to my work," the man replied, "I must mail this in the morning and have another copy to place on the Castle Church door for open debate."

"That is why I am here," he said as the man continued writing. With a darker tone in his voice, "I must take that with me."

"I am sorry, but are you a courier?"

"No." He stopped his forward motion as he realized he was not finding an easy place to insert the syringe due to the thick robe. Finally, he plunged the short needle into the man's neck and emptied its contents. "That letter must not be seen."

The young man grabbed the back of his neck but immediately started to weaken in appearance.

The operative grabbed the letter and sat on the bed. Still speaking in fluent German he turned to the dying man. "You see, that letter will change the world as we know it."

A faint raspy voice came to life, "It is just a letter that I…I hope will…will bring people…closer…to God. We must stop…the…heresy and ungodly teachings."

"My friend, that letter does much more than that."

As the man slumped against the wall next to the desk, his eyes grew pale. "*Vater ergeben ihn* – Father, forgive him," he choked as his eyes closed then slipped from the chair to the floor.

The letter and the rest of the paper on the desk, he grabbed and flung into the fire, "Mr. Luther, I am well beyond forgiveness and your 95 theses are history."

He stepped over the man whose place in history was now removed and left the room closing the door behind him. Following a five minute run back to the Castle Church, he ascended to the top amid cracks of thunder, heavy rain and lightning strikes of a severety he had not seen but a few times in a lifetime.

Looking through the gothic window one last time he changed back into his dry clothes. "It seems like the heavens don't agree with my actions."

Placing everything back into the bag and stuffing it under the seat, he jumped into the machine and lowered the canopy. One minute later, the murderer and the sphere disappeared from the lofty space filling the tower with a light that would have been easily confused with lighting striking through a sky awash with rain.

9 — MONDAY, LATE MORNING

Spending the next hour opening panels and tracing fiber optic cable on the sphere produced no results. The disengaged circuitry was still severed with no indication it had ever been reconnected.

Hudson was lying on his back under the machine in dark blue slacks with his white shirt sleeves rolled up when Peter came back over with the information he had requested.

"Mr. Blackwell," a young MIT grad with a Masters in Theoretical Physics and a clipboard broke the silence.

The agent pushed back on the floor dolly and almost rolled into the poor fellow. "What did you find?" he asked dropping his tools and standing to look at the information.

"Just what we expected, sir," he stated matter-of-factly, pulling several papers out of his lab coat and laying them on a table a few feet away. "You can see the spikes on the X and Y axis are referencing power usage over time.

Hudson nodded in agreement.

Tracing his finger from left to right, "We see minimal power used within the building on Sunday, and that usage goes up early this morning when we all showed up to start preparing for the test."

"And here is where the test occurred," Hudson said pointing at the large spike on the graph.

"That's correct, sir. Nothing out of the ordinary. And sir, there was no latent surge or spike." Several more papers came forth from the clipboard. "That graph was power usage or input. I have several others showing the same information on different scales and divisions, but these graphs show particular output."

Hudson grabbed the papers and sat in a chair next to the table as the white coat fidgeted over his shoulder.

"Mr. Blackwell, you can see that the power the machine created went out at this point, and nothing has come out since," came his unsteady reply.

"Are you sure?"

"Very sure. Sir, I was only brought onto the project just recently," he lowered his voice in his earnest attempt at communication. "That machine is checked and double checked every few minutes. I have never known any project that required so many readings even when no tests are in progress.

I don't know what that thing was designed for. But I find the interior seating and dashboard perplexing for a generator."

Hudson just listened to him without trying to reveal his assumptions.

"To make a long story short, that *apparatus* has been dead since we turned it off over in the control room. No power has gone in, and none has come out."

The agent pulled the power usage graph back up from the pile of papers and found what he was looking for – the test spike. "Peter, is this a lot of power?"

"Yes, to get that thing humming, it takes a huge amount of power," he said in response.

"If we were to look at businesses, or industrial plants, or what have you, how many places in America could use that much power?" he asked.

"That much power usage in a billionth of a second? None sir." The poor man stuttered a moment in his qualification, "But, Mr. Blackwell, understand that some of the larger manufacturing plants, such as a steel plant or automotive facility might indeed use a large amount of energy such as this. But not in a billionth of a second. They would need continual power at a fairly constant rate."

"Pete, you have answered my questions. Thank you," the agent said, intending to end the conversation.

The young physicist started to walk back to his post, when Hudson called him back. "Pete."

"Yes," he said, lifting his eyebrows in anticipation.

"Pete, would it be possible to find other spikes like this?"

"Well, we can trace the building's usage, if that's what you're asking."

"No. Throughout, the U.S."

"That would be a large undertaking. Perhaps, with the right clearance, I could narrow the scope of our search."

Hudson pulled a pen from his from pocket and started writing on the power usage chart. "Peter, I want you to search for other spikes like this one – anywhere you can find them."

"Yes, sir."

"I think I can narrow your search," he said without looking up. "Focus your time on Maryland and Virginia. Now, Peter, the power usage won't look like this one," he said, pointing to the spike. "This one is brief and therefore sharp at the top. I need you to look for usage of the same magnitude, but lasting maybe 20 to 30 seconds. And the usage will come in pairs. Maybe a minute apart."

"Yes, Mr. Blackwell," he said starting off to work.

"I'm giving you my clearance, and it should open up information for you," he dropped back to his task once again. "Oh, by the way, keep this between us."

He nodded and left. Hudson sat back in his chair looking at the sphere. "Do you have a twin?"

Todd walked the full length of the parking lot to get to his car. The red 1969 Dodge Charger glowed at the end of the lot. The end of the lot for two reasons. One, it gave him a chance to process his day as he meandered toward it in the evening. Two, well, it kept his baby away from the ubiquitous door dings that happened near the front of the lot where busy students parked badly and swung things about in a hurry.

Usually, just taking out the keys for the drive home was always a joy. Today, was different. And not even 400 horsepower could make it better. It all came down to the machine – again.

Todd knew the threat posed by the device better than anyone other than Hudson and his own wife. The deadly, if not ingenious potential of the thing could cause much damage to history, to life, and our way of understanding it. His partner constantly monitored the creation, to prevent this, but in the wrong hands, time travel could destroy the very fabric of existence. He eased into the soft black leather seats and prayed his assumptions were wrong.

Turning the key, the large Hemi engine roared to life, and he thought back over some of the experiences that brought him and Hudson together just a year earlier. He remembered the agent walking into his office and telling a crazy story about the government designing a machine that could travel through time. He had not believed it until they were fleeing the campus with assassins hot on their heels.

One midnight flight on a government-owned Concorde later and they landed in Israel to find more guns, terrorists and that they were running for their lives. Getting shot and having to jump through time with a bullet in his shoulder was not part of his life's plan either, but their mission succeeded; their task to jump back to the first century and to apprehend a man determined to kill Jesus Christ before He went to the cross.

Todd looked over his shoulder and placed his car in reverse.

The only good from the whole experience belonged to bringing his now wife Aaliyah back to his time. As the fault for her attack and near death experience lay at his feet, they really had to option but to transport her with them and sort things out later.

The professor placed the vehicle in drive and turned to leave through the main campus gate. Memories flooded in. Visions of his Savior on the cross dying for him. Not a day passed without that powerful memory coming into his thoughts.

Pulling away from the campus, the red light forced him to stop.

His body could still feel the earthquakes and see the lightning as it struck across the sky in rebellion to what humanity was attempting to do to its Creator. Then the decision to take the beautiful dying woman from her time and deliver her to the future, to keep her from dying alone in the aftermath of Christ's death on the cross.

The man smiled as he looked at a picture of his beautiful wife taped to his dash.

"We made the right decision," he mumbled as if his friend was in the car.

The second mission rushed to his mind, again protecting the Savior at his birth. And yet he knew somehow, that the adventure and the struggle had been planned for him and Hudson, but especially for his wife who had found peace in understanding her past.

"Was it all just a dream?" he wondered aloud, and not for the first time.

Could he have really seen legions of angels or met Aaliyah's mother, or King Herod? He had been there, lived it, learned and grown in Christ through it all and yet, it all seemed surreal as time passed.

At the moment, he was glad he remembered. All of it. He had seen the hand of God at work in a way few throughout time ever would. "Lord, thank you for working it out. You are omnipotent, and I'm glad You're on my side," he praised and chuckled to himself as he pulled into traffic.

Turning from 7th street onto Broadway, he headed east toward highway 264, the ten minutes home seeming like an eternity tonight.

Suddenly, his eyes blurred, and he blinked hard to regain his vision and maintain control of the vehicle. A force blew through him with the power of a locomotive and the rest of the countryside shook with its power. The energy accompanying it felt stronger than before and the sonic boom nearly ruptured his ear drums.

Fighting instinct, he kept his right hand on the wheel as the left went to cover that ear and he thrust his right ear into his shoulder. The pain was indescribable as he jammed on the breaks.

The visual blur lasted for several seconds, and while his ears were ringing, his eyes focused on a world that was changing. Trees were disappearing leading to streets and houses. Homes that had been in the location for more than a century were being traded for strip malls and shopping centers. Broadway, which was a straight roadway, started to alter shape with curves and additional street lights. The world he had known was different.

The large two and a half ton vehicle screamed to a stop between lanes in the middle of a four lane highway. One car zoomed around him barely missing his right bumper as a second hit him dead on at close to 30 miles per hour forcing his head into the high seat behind him.

The impact thrust the vehicle into another lane of oncoming traffic, causing car after car to swerve from his location. Several missed him, but one hit the muscle car on the front right quarter panel shoving the vehicle back over ten feet and forcing his head into the steering wheel. Luckily he managed to protect his face, but he felt a warm liquid slip down from his forehead as he heard other cars crashing around him.

Once the demolition had stopped, Todd tried to open his door. With a large thrust from his shoulder, he was able to move the damaged metal enough to exit. The vehicle rested halfway between the oncoming and outgoing traffic.

Standing in the middle of the thoroughfare with his hand over the large cut above his eye, he could not believe what he was seeing. Had he not experienced this feeling just an hour before, he would have thought some type of trauma to the head was affecting his judgment. However, he knew that what he was seeing was accurate. Everything was different.

Turning his head slowly to avoid dizziness, he took in the street and the people coming from their cars and finding ways to help. Then he saw it. Something that he could not believe. Southern Seminary, an institution training people to do God's work in Louisville for well over a century, was gone. Norton Hall had disappeared. The educational buildings had vanished. The dormitories and school housing was no more. In its place were low income houses, a convenience store and a quick lube. In the blink of an eye, everything he knew was no more.

Standing in the middle of the street as steam poured from his once prized machine, and hearing people yelling and children crying, the bloody and confused man mumbled with tears running down his cheeks and a look of fear on his face, "Oh Lord, what do I do? Your people need your help."

Hudson watched Peter walk away as he sat at the table reading the variety of graphs prepared on power usage and production when the room blurred and the earth shook. The stool the agent was sitting on was not stable enough to control the spasm his body went into when the high decibelic crash occurred. He fell to the floor, flinging the papers all around him as he grabbed for his ears.

The intensity was larger and the pain greater than before. Either his body had sustained damaged from the previous occurrence or something was causing a bigger aftershock.

Several scientists ran over trying to help, but for the several seconds that the vibrations and shocks lasted, there was nothing they could do to help him. He balled up into a fetal position and grunted through the agony.

"Someone call a doctor," one man yelled.

As several men pulled out their cell phones, Hudson stopped them, "Did you feel that?"

They all looked at each other nervously.

"None of you felt that?" he asked seeing faces he had not seen before.

One man said no.

Hudson held out his hand. "Don't call a doctor," he yelled as he started to rise from the black rubber floor. "I'm fine." The agent was exhausted from the hurt he had just gone through.

"Please, everyone go back to your work," he stumbled to his desk trying not to go into some form of shock.

The men still had their phones to their ears.

Trying to stand up straight, he waived them off, "Put the phones away. I'll be fine."

One scientist picked up the chair as another brought a paper cup of water. Sitting in the seat he took a sip. He still did mot know what was happening.

"Guys, go back to work." The men slowly walked away not knowing what had happened.

Hudson looked at the machine. This was the second time he had been through the effect, and it was much stronger than the first. "I know you weren't involved," he muttered at the large contraption just ten feet away.

Looking back toward the control room, there were many people that were new. Faces that he had not seen before were now part of a team that he had hand chosen. In their concern for him, it seemed as though they knew him. But he had never seen them before.

"Todd was right. Things have changed," he said in a whisper as he looked over the room. "Lord, what is going on?" he prayed as he pulled his phone from his pocket.

Trying his wife's cell once again, the display and the audio tone relayed the information that there was no such number. He then dialed in his home number. The same response was offered.

He slammed the device down on the table causing looks from everyone within the building once again. "What is wrong? What's happening?" some asked.

Looking in the control room, he saw Peter once again. "Thank you Lord, he's still here.

Peter," he yelled gesturing toward himself. The man looked up. "I need that information right now, do you understand?" he said with a focus he had never used on an employee.

The young man nodded nervously as he ran back to his work station.

10 — MONDAY, NOON

Completed in 1908, Union Station is a triumph in engineering. The building, one of the nation's best monuments to the Beaux-Arts style of architecture still stands as a gateway to the Capital of the young nation.

Originally, the grand structure covered more than 200 acres and, with over 75 miles worth of track, was larger than any other train station in the world.

Currently, this building houses over 100 dining and shopping destinations, is the base of operations for Amtrak, welcoming 29 million visitors a year – many of whom come to the building simply for a quick lunch. At noon every Monday, Sara fit into that category.

Sara Brennen was in demand. Having spent time as a page in Washington during her upper teen years and then clerking through college, the woman graduated with enough savvy, brains and beauty to move right into assistant positions with higher-ups like high-powered Congressman and Senators.

Just looking at the 5'4" woman, no one would guess she has the ear of several Senators and most of the other assistants within several blocks of the Capital. Blue-eyed with blonde hair layered perfectly around her high cheek bones and over her shoulders Sara smiled genuinely at everyone she met, and, at 32 had enough confidence to command the respect she deserved from the people who naturally enjoyed her natural smile.

She had always thought it odd that her honesty had brought her the most attention in the marbled halls of politics. Honesty was unique. But unique often corresponded to being a coveted commodity in this city. Because of her desirability, she always had a job, even when Congressmen and Senators came and went.

At some point she had realized it. Everyone wants Sara on their roster.

White blouse, black pencil skirt and black heels – her uniform of choice for days like today – brought second looks from most men she passed, something she was accustomed to, but she headed to one of her favorite Station cafés undeterred.

Sara did not like being ogled in general, but would much rather have had the lookers be businessmen her own age than the aging politicians hanging around today, looking for another conquest. Nevertheless, fighting off significantly older men was something she had grown familiar with in Washington.

Lord Acton had it totally right in the young woman's eyes, "Power tends to corrupt; absolute power corrupts absolutely." So always being kind and taking more than one self-defense class kept the former gymnast well protected.

Normally, lunch was her time to get away. She invited friends from the building, usually Amy or Laura, to dine with her and catch up on the latest scandal or give wise council in each other's love lives. Since both had lunch meetings today, she headed to pick something up and find a quiet place to sit alone with her thoughts and a good book.

Finding her favored establishment, Café' Renoir', she headed up to the counter.

"Sara, good afternoon," the man said wearing an apron and a large smile.

"Hello, Remy, how are you?" she replied, eyes sparkling.

"I am great, now that you are here," the man said with a French accent. His large round face, bushy eyebrows and short crop of thinning hair made him homely by the world's standards, but his heart made him beautiful. "My darling, what would you have today?"

"I'm not sure. Why don't you surprise me?"

The man's face glowed. "That I shall do," he said as he turned to begin work.

The young woman sat at a table with a bent umbrella outside of the main doors of the restaurant. She liked watching the tourists. Born in the capital, she often took the grandeur of the city for granted. However, she loved seeing the families walking through the enormous structure.

It was easy to tell a tourist. Always a camera and a large number of bags, the latter she did not have an answer for. With all of the great sights in D.C., including the monuments and prodigious museums, the government buildings and National Archives, she often found tourists taking pictures of Starbucks or the Gap. The tourist moms frantically tried to keep their children close by. She thought of it like corralling turkeys. As soon as you got one in the right place, another one ran off.

As much as it was something that she joked about, secretly and down deep, she wanted that for her life. She wanted to try to round up the children. She wanted a man who would love her and provide for her. Even though it was out of date and light years away from her present situation, she wanted the picket fence, porch swing, and possibility of growing old with someone she loved and loved her back.

Sara would never let those aspirations out, even to her closest friends. Those kind of thoughts destroyed perfectly good career women. She still wanted that life. It just never appeared likely on her radar. Perhaps she kept the hope alive by coming to the Station and watching these families.

After several minutes of sitting and observing, she noticed Remy walking toward her with a smile and a lovely plate full of a delicious creation. Sara knew he did not give every customer this kind of attention, so she delighted in everything that he did for her.

"You must take a bite right now. I must know what you think," he commanded forming his words with care and waiting anxiously.

Sara picked up the elegant fork from the ornate glass dish and cut a small piece of the delicacy. After bringing it to her lips, her eyes closed and she made a 'yumm' sound.

"Remy, you have outdone yourself this time," she spoke smiling.

Clapping his hands together and laughing out loud, "I knew that my Sara would like it. There is nothing too good for my Sara."

"Oh, Remy you flatter me. If I were just five years older, I might chase after you," she said playfully.

"My dear, if you were five years older, you still might not be old enough to be my granddaughter. Then, there is my wife. She might not like losing her strong man Remy," he poked at his chest and then laughed, "She is a rather large woman and tends to be very jealous."

"Remy, what is this?" she questioned taking another bite.

"I shall call it,... Saraonsito," he smiled knowing she heard her name in it.

"It is just fantastic. I still don't know why you don't have your own restaurant on the Champs Elysees," taking another bite.

"My dear, if I did, then I would not be able to spend this time with you," he retorted heading back into the café.

Sara opened up her book and savored every bite of the delicious lunch.

Hudson went back to his office to hunt through files. As project director, he was given all of the documents and personal papers Dr. Keith had written before his death. After 15 minutes of searching, the agent found nothing.

At the moment, the weight of what he was looking at was lost on Hudson. The works of the late Dr. Keith, one of the most brilliant and creative thinkers of the last 200 years, were filled with the hand-scribblings of the genius invaluable to any scientist. Since they revealed nothing about a second sphere, they meant nothing to Hudson.

"Oh Lord, let me be wrong," he said out loud. A soft knock came from the door.

"Yes, come in."

The door opened slowly, and Peter stuck his head in.

"Open it up and come in," Hudson said gesturing. "What've you found?"

"Well, sir, nothing."

"Nothing, what do you mean nothing? Wasn't there any type of spike out there?"

"The problem is, we are locked out of any site that might give us that kind of information," he responded walking fully into the room and closing the door behind him.

"Locked out? We are the top of the food chain here. People get locked out from us, we don't get locked out from them," he spoke incredulously.

"That's what I thought. We can order movie tickets, or check the football stats, but we're locked out of anything having to do with a power grid."

The agent was stunned.

"I can't look at cooperatives, statewide companies, or anything having to do with electricity."

"Is that normal?" he asked rocking back in his chair and crossing his arms.

"No, frankly, it's not. This is not protected information. I can't even look at my electric bill for this month.

Thinking that it was just a local problem, I tapped into my home computer and tried searching from there. I came up with the same thing; roadblocks. I'm not a conspiracist, but I would say that information has been restricted by the government."

"Wow, my fears have to be true," he mumbled.

"What sir?"

"Nothing." Sitting up and waking his computer, Hudson started typing. "Peter, if we were to try to locate that machine out there another way, how would we do it?" pointing through his doorway to the pearlescent globe.

"I don't understand," he asked out of confusion.

"Please sit down," the agent said pointing to the chair. "We know that we can track the machine by power usage because it gobbles a lot of it when it runs. Would there be another way to track that generator by normal systems that are already in place?"

The man sat in the metal chair and thought for a second. "Sir, let's say that somehow, someone stole that machine out there. No, it might not work."

"Pete, tell me. We're friends here, and I need your expertise."

"Sir, if I were trying to track it, I'd use weather radar."

Hudson sat forward in his chair. "Why?"

"Well, we should be able to see it several ways. We could use satellite or Next Generation Radar; that is if the devices are looking in the right place at exactly the right time.

With a satellite traveling around the earth, it isn't taking pictures every second, but on a set schedule. And if the weather's good, the meteorologist might be testing the facilities or upgrading them…"

"Pete, just get to the point," he said with pleading eyes.

"Well, we know that one of the things NEXRAD measures is base reflectivity. Base Reflectivity basically corresponds to the amount of radiation that is scattered or reflected back to the radar by whatever targets are located in the radar beam at a given location. These targets can be hydrometeors such as snow or rain, et cetera, or other targets like birds, or planes and the like.

Satellites work the same way, except they can focus on the infrared spectrum.

Well, when that thing starts up, it goes through the spectrum of electromagnetic waves. There are some microwaves produced, as well as a boat load of infrared, UV and a small amount of X-rays. That is a nasty beast to be around when it is powering up."

Peter shook his head. "Anyway,… usually when the radar images come back, they're color-coded from say greens and blues all the way to the worst which is reds and purples. Anything past 75 DBZ is usually tagged as white because we don't have any weather that bad very often."

Hudson absorbed his every word thoughtfully.

"I can't say that I'm right, but I'd bet good money that if we could get a hold of some of those radar returns, we would find a nice white circle sitting right over this building."

"Pete, go and find the exact time when we powered up this morning," he said as the man ran from the office.

Hudson cued up the NOAA site as Peter ran back in the room. "Sir, it looks like it was 8:52 and 47 seconds."

With Peter walking around his desk, Hudson went to work. First he looked through the archives of the last few hours from the NEXRAD information. Nothing could be seen. The technology was so sophisticated, that it would obviously dump information it knew to be inaccurate or anomalous.

Then he pulled up the GOES satellites. America has two geosynchronous orbiting earth satellites. One called GOES East and the other GOES West. Tapping into the East archives, he started scanning the information from 8:52. Watching it the first time he and Peter saw nothing. Next, they zeroed in on D.C. and ran it again. As they got to 47 seconds, they saw the faintest of blips.

"Did you see that?" Hudson asked.

"It was sure quick, but that would make sense. The satellites don't have the ability to take pictures as fast as the machine powered up this morning. It might just look like a faint spot if the event and readings weren't coordinated."

They ran it again. "That's it!" Hudson yelled. "You couldn't lock us out of this," he mumbled. "Peter, get back to work. Use this information to start looking for another spot like that. Narrow your search to say a 50 mile circumference from here and search times to within the last few hours."

"Yes sir."

Hudson tried to contact his wife again; with the same result.

—

Sara relished every bite of lunch and was sure to give Remy a hug before she left. "Thank you for the lovely dish. You have made my day," she glowed.

"My dear, just your presence brightens my day. See you tomorrow."

"I'll be here," she smiled as she left the café.

He chuckled and yelled after her, "You are trying to make my wife jealous."

Exiting through the grand doors of the huge building, Sara thanked God for Remy. God had blessed her in so many ways and she never wanted to take it for granted.

She did not officially go to church. The National Church of America was her only choice, but she wanted a more personal relationship with her Creator. She remembered her parents saying over and over again that the government should have never gotten into the business of religion. Her mom spoke with fervency that…, *"A relationship with Christ should not be filtered through the Presidency. It's not how God set it out to be."*

Sara listened to her parent's personal teaching and accepted Christ as a young girl. She held their views tightly to herself.

Over the last several years as the President had grabbed more and more religious power, she was on the forefront of the wave against it. Using all of her contacts and influence, she tried to diminish the office's power, but to no avail. No one seemed to see the wrong in what was happening. Those who had no relationship with the Creator of the universe felt no concern for losing their rights to worship.

Now with rules about when people can go to the government church and regulations for worship, she had not entered a church door in over a year. Instead, she spent time reflecting on God's word each morning and night in her personal quiet time – reading from a version of the Bible not sanctioned by the government.

The path religion had taken hit her in the face twice a day. As she headed south on Delaware Avenue and walked several blocks back to the Russell Senate Building, to the west just three blocks stood one of the newest reminders of the state church.

A tall building with spires stretching to the sky had been erected several years ago as the National Cathedral, a building representing religion in America and the seat of its power. Having never entered the dark doors, Sara could not imagine the interior, but the outside did not look like what God would want for His people.

Granite walls soared into the sky ten stories with four towers, one on each corner rising another ten. Its gothic presence was a beauty of engineering but showed nothing of God's love or His sacrifice made through Christ Jesus, God the Son. There were no crosses adorning the building. Nowhere on the structure were there praying hands or Biblical inscriptions.

Chimes did not ring out great hymns of the past and the stained glass showed American historical scenes such as Washington crossing the Delaware not Jesus caring for the poor or healing lepers; something a church should display. The young woman had never been a part of formal religion, but she knew something was wrong about the building and its teachings.

Within a block of her destination a black stretch limousine stopped in front of her. A large man with a gun pointed at her slid from the car, "Hello Miss Brennen, you're coming with me."

Momentarily stunned, she shifted her weight improperly on her heals and twisted as she tried to turn and run. She felt her blouse rip across the shoulder as a grip like a vice prevented her escape, ripping buttons in the process. The hired muscle outweighed her by more than twice, and the disparity between their weights made her easy prey. Swinging her free arm and legs any way she could brought her into contact with the solid body slowing forcing her to the vehicle.

"You stop kicking, or I kill you here," he growled.

Knowing there was no way out of his clutches; she stopped resisting and willingly got into the back seat of the black vehicle. On a clear day, just a block from the leadership of America, Sara Brennen was taken. And no one cared to notice.

"I think I've found what you're looking for," Peter said throwing open the door to Hudson's office.

"What did you find?" the man asked looking up from his Bible.

Pile of papers in hand he shifted his weight, "Here is the NEXRAD data, and here is the satellite data," he said dropping them on his desk.

"What am I seeing?"

He placed his finger on a white spot on the page, "That's what you're trying to find."

Hudson leaned closer to the page, "That's us from this morning?" he asked distorting his face.

"No, it's not. We're located here," he pointed to a place several inches away. "An exact duplicate of what we did happened here. And it looks like it's transpired three times within the last 24 hours."

Hudson sat back in his seat not believing what he was seeing. "Where is this exactly?"

"I thought you would ask that. I've overlaid the longitude and latitude with a city map. Your bright light is coming from here, about ten miles away," he said once again pointing to the page.

With his eyes wide, the agent sat back in his seat. "Peter, I'm moving your clearance up to a G4. Everything we've discussed is top-secret, and if you breathe a word of what you know to anyone else, I might personally be hanging you from the highest tree. Do you understand?"

"Yes sir. It's our secret."

"Please leave me and go cover your steps. No one can know what you were doing, or why you were doing it."

The young man smiled and exited the room.

Hudson stood up and walked out of the office. "How ironic to have placed it there," he mumbled. "Lord, I need your guidance. It looks like I've been pulled in again." He entered the elevator to exit the building.

11 — MONDAY AFTERNOON

Hudson exited the back door of Cox Manufacturing to a different world; so dissimilar that it made him feel dizzy. Over the past two years as an employee of the government he had driven down the quiet residential streets to the facility hundreds of times. Each time he was surrounded by 40-year-old homes, some still inhabited by their original owners, and others overflowing with children and young couples just starting out.

The site for the nuclear facility was perfect – not necessarily for those in the neighborhood, but for the government and its desire to maintain secrecy. Because of the beautiful tree-lined streets, surrounded by curbs and sidewalks, no one would ever think that the simple commercial building could house such dangerous equipment.

Something had happened during the last four hours. The sonic phases had changed everything as he knew it.

Closing the back door behind him, he normally came to an eight-foot wooden plank fence separating the back of the building from two acres of unoccupied land. Past the land, nice two-story houses with swimming pools and trampolines could be viewed in the distance. Children could be heard playing and birds singing their songs to the neighborhood.

As he held the rail walking down the six steps to the parking lot level, his eyes could not fathom the change. The simple wooden fence had been replaced with chain link topped with razor wire. The open land had disappeared and metal buildings cramped the space forming an industrial park.

The agent started toward his car, and because of the height of the prefabricated buildings, could not see much. He did see men grinding fenders at what was evidently an auto repair shop. Off to the corner, another large broken down building sat with piles of old scrap metal out front, possibly a recycling company. Rounding the corner of the structure, Hudson's ears were filled with the sounds of metal crashing, classic rock from the radios of men working, and curses coming from the newly-formed alley behind the government facility.

"Oh, Lord, what has the world become?" he asked as he opened the door of his car.

As he started the minivan and put it in reverse, Bob screeched into the lot. Parking his car and running over to Hudson's driver's side window he asked, "Hey, Buddy, where are you going?"

"I, uh, I was going to run by the house. I forgot something," he replied.

"Well, then I'll go with you," he offered with a smile as he stood at the driver's door.

"No, Bob, it won't take thirty minutes. I don't need help."

"I have thirty minutes to spare. We can let the scientists take it for a while," Bob said trying to persuade the agent.

"No, man, I'm fine," he said not wanting to show his bewilderment over the events of the morning. "How did the root canal go?"

"Yeah. I waited in the lobby for several hours, can you believe that? They were so far behind they couldn't get me in," he answered looking at the agent. "What did you leave at home?"

"I think my sanity," the man mumbled as he put the car in drive and steered it through the opening in the chain link fence.

Bob watched the minivan drive away and then went into the building.

Todd sat in the back of the ambulance for close to 30 minutes before the medical personnel decided it was safe for him to leave. With a large cut and red lump on his head, the attendants thought he might have a concussion. His questions about sonic booms and changes in scenery did not help his situation. But he knew the only way he might escape a hospital visit was to play along and act "normal." Whatever that was in a world turning upside down.

Once he was released from the triage area, the professor was asked to answer questions for a good half hour from the Louisville police department. It had been longer than a decade since the last five car pileup in the southern city, and they wanted to ensure he was cited for every possible law he had broken.

Because the accident happened for no apparent reason, they scrutinized him more than normal for an auto accident. It was a clear day, ruling out any weather problems. The sun directly overhead precluded glare off of the glass. His Charger had been in pristine condition, so the possibility of mechanical error was minimal. The professor was in his 30's, and therefore some types of health problems such as heart attack or stroke were ruled out after the medical personnel released him.

Finally, after taking two breathalyzer tests, they found him to be totally sober without any alcoholic drink in his system.

There was a slight possibility that he had a reaction from some type of illegal drug he was taking. He told them he was a minister, and they dropped the option. In this altered reality, ministers were sanctioned by the state and therefore drug-tested weekly. Something he did not know at the time.

"Dr. Myers, why were you traveling in this part of the city?" a large black police Sergeant asked.

"I don't understand the question," he replied pressing on the white gauze covering his cut.

Very pointedly he rephrased the question. "Sir, our computers show you to live about ten miles south of here. They also show that you teach at the Louisville branch of the National seminary. That is about 12 miles from here. So, let me ask you again, why are you ten miles north of home?"

Knowing he could not tell the truth unless he wanted to go to a psych ward, he had to come up with something, "It, it was just, a nice day, and I wanted to go for a drive before teaching class. Mondays are very long days and I wanted to clear my head before the marathon of classes began." Pointing to his head, "I guess I didn't clear my head very well," he said with a faint laugh.

"Well, sir, we are citing you for each of the five cars. You are also responsible for any and all damages to city property." The officer handed him a ream of papers, "You will also need to pay all costs involved in the time and resources of the EMT's and Louisville Police Department."

Todd looked at the many tickets.

Turning to leave, the large man came back to offer one more bit of information. "Dr. Myers."

"Yes?" Todd said looking up from the papers.

"If I were you, I'd get a lawyer." Pointing to the chaos behind him, "These people aren't happy. Have a nice day," he spoke as he turned to walk toward a pair of policemen looking over the scene.

Sitting in the back of a squad car, Todd pulled out his phone and called his wife. After several rings, she quickly picked up.

"Todd, where have you...been?" she asked with her fluid Jewish accent. "I have been trying to call you since it...it happened. The boom, the sound. My husband, I look out the front and the back of our house, and all is different. The houses look, not the same. Our neighbors are gone..."

"My Princess, I know. Calm down, I don't know how, but it's going to be alright."

"Our Lord must take control!" she replied emphatically.

"Yes, Aaliyah, He must. However, right now I need you to come pick me up."

"Did something happen to your vehicle?" she asked.

"Yes, something did happen. Please come get me. You'll see me on Broadway. How are you feeling?"

"I feel like the baby is going to come sooner than…expected."

"I hope he waits until everything is corrected."

"He is going to come when the Lord is ready for him. I will leave immediately."

"Thank you, Princess," he said as he closed the phone.

Pulling up redial, Todd entered in Hudson's number again. "I sure hope he knows what's going on," he mumbled as the phone began to ring.

Hudson drove toward his house breaking every speed limit posted. Every mile he passed made his heart fall deeper into his stomach. Why had not he been able to reach her? His wife always answered the phone, no matter what was happening. In fact, this had even been a source of frustration between the two because Hudson often urged her to let the thing ring. "It is my phone, and I won't be a slave to it," she would often say.

Her sweet spirit and warm smile came into play as she got up each time and replied, "Honey, what if it's an emergency. You wouldn't want that on your conscience."

The agent always gave in, not because of her argument because there had never been a single emergency in their many years of marriage, but because of the way she would say it. So, for her to not pick up the phone was worrisome.

It could be that the museum required her to turn it off. He hoped that was it. Prayed it was.

As he drove on the highways speeding toward his house, he noticed that many things had remained unchanged. The Capitol area was unaltered, and so were many of the monuments. However, businesses, signs, housing editions, and even streets were altered. Taking in as many of the differences as possible, the agent thought about his wife and their first encounter.

He had met the blonde-haired beauty in High School and loved her at first sight. Hudson wrestled for the team in High School – the Fighting Trojans – and they had a pretty good record. Much of their success was because of Hudson, and he enjoyed the notoriety it gave him. Being right at six feet and weighing in at 210 pounds made him one of the larger guys on the team, and everyone enjoyed watching the heavy weights wrestle.

The night they met, Hudson was on the mat with Jack Johnson. The guy had a reputation for not using deodorant the day of the match and rubbing garlic all over his body, so his opponent's nose might force him to give up without a fight. Hudson did not give in that easily even though Jack's pungent plan had worked many times before with a roster full of other opponents.

As the two men went in and out of locks and holds, Hudson noticed a girl in the stands. He had never seen her before, so he presumed she must have been from the other school. She had thin Roman features, a beautifully innocent smile and bright wide eyes.

For an instant his mouth opened, and his eyes got stuck on the girl of his dreams. It was during that brief period of time that Jack rolled the love-struck wrestler, and Hudson began counting the ceiling lights. After a quick three-count, Hudson, the school favorite, was out and the aromatic opponent victorious.

It was not his best moment on the mat, but after the match he sought out the girl in the stands. Not being the smoothest guy around, he told her bluntly that he had lost the match because she distracted him. She quickly furrowed her brows and walked off. However, after a few hasty corrections to his insensitive statement, he got a date.

Their first date was not anything spectacular, the normal pizza and a movie, but it was the beginning of a romance that would not die. Hudson loved her beautiful blue eyes and her short but tight five-foot, four-inch frame. He enjoyed the way that she could speak for hours on whatever seemed to cross her mind. And most of all, he loved *her*. She had a zest for life that he did not have. She could talk about the beautiful night sky or a simple flower in someone's yard, and seemed to live life to the fullest. She gave Hudson a new and refreshing outlook. He was hooked from the beginning and stayed that way.

Turning onto his street, Hudson noticed much of it had not changed. The houses still looked similar with only subtle alterations like trim color and landscaping. Continuing forward, he saw his house and turned into the driveway.

"It's here," he said. "Thank you God."

Jumping from the car, he noticed the name Blackwell hanging from the mailbox, but saw other things that had changed. His two children Michael and Amy were notorious for leaving their toys out in the front yard. Even as he left this morning, there were bikes and trucks, even an old doll strewn about on the grass.

This always bothered Hudson because he wanted to present a well-ordered image to the neighbors. His wife would remind him that his children were more important than the image, and he always relented. Deep down, he still wanted a tidy yard.

"Maybe she had them clean it all up," he mumbled as he slowly walked toward the front door.

On the way toward the entrance, he did notice several changes. The yard that was usually beaten up from children's play was thick and lush with a nicely cut edge on it. Instead of the row of gardenias he had planted for his wife, there were several meticulously trimmed boxwoods in their place. The row of annuals she planted each year were replaced by a rock garden. The agent started to feel sick to his stomach.

As he stuck the key in the lock he did not see the window clings his wife bought for the children to place on the windows every holiday. There had been sombreros representing Cinco de Mayo. Shamrocks for St. Patrick's Day. He even remembered trees adorning his front glass for Arbor Day. The glass sparkled cleanly today with no decoration, even though Halloween was coming soon.

The lock turned, and the agent walked inside. Nothing inside looked anything like his family's home. Everything had changed. The soft red sofas his wife had chosen were now replaced with thick leather ones. White walls replaced the coordinating colors of his home. Hudson started jogging through the house, peering into every door and searching every room.

He found Amy's room first, but in place of the pink princess bed stood free weights and a treadmill. The P51 ceiling fan and space flight wall mural had disappeared in Michael's room, and in its place were an office with desk and filing cabinets. Frantic, the man ran to his bedroom. Ransacking the closet usually three-quarters filled with his wife's clothes, he found nothing but neatly arranged suits, a wall of men's shoes and drawers full of undershirts and socks.

Heading into the bathroom, he found no makeup or hair rollers, just various cologne bottles on the counter. His wife's notorious piles of clothing, worn or soon to be worn, were gone. The room was spotless. The way he would have left it – if he were not married.

The man went back downstairs trying to hold back the emotion. As he walked into the living room, he noticed pictures hanging on the wall that he had not seen initially. The photographs were of himself doing things; things that he had always dreamed of doing. One showed him riding a camel on the Giza Plateau with the pyramids in the background. Another of him on a mountain. It was a high mountain and the clouds were well below him.

"Where could this be?" he asked himself. After thinking of something that he always wanted to do, he muttered, "It has to be Everest. I always wanted to climb Everest."

The next picture was of a rafting experience between large cliffs, "Most likely the Colorado River through the Grand Canyon."

Walking numb to the next picture he saw himself piloting a hot air balloon. And finally, the last picture stood out of him on a large motorcycle, riding through a beautiful fall scene filled with bright red and yellow foliage. "I don't own a motorcycle," he muttered. Then he walked to the garage and opened the door. In place of his wife's minivan sat a sparkling, red Indian Chief. His spirits dropped. He assumed the pictures to be Vermont. Again, something that he always wanted to do.

Hudson ran from the house and drove the two miles to Abraham Lincoln Middle School. Running from the parking lot he went directly to the welcome desk.

An older lady, looked up from her papers, "Hello, may I help you?"

"Yes, I would like to know if the field trip has made it back yet," he said out of breath.

"Sir, I don't think we have a field trip out today."

"Yes, you do, my two children are on it. My wife was a chaperone. They were going to the Natural History Museum."

"I don't think so, but let me call." After a 30-second phone conversation, she replied. "Sir, we don't have any field trips scheduled today. The Principal confirms this."

Feeling his heart beating out of his chest and sweat dripping down his face he muttered hopefully, "Okay, then I need to take my children out of school early."

Turning toward her computer she typed the code to get to the proper screen, "What are their names?"

"Michael and Amy Blackwell."

The round gray haired woman typed in the names. "Sir, we don't have any children by that name."

"Blackwell. B…L…A…"

"Yes sir, I spelled the name correctly. Just like it sounds, Black…Well. There are no children here by that name."

Almost yelling and losing patience. "Look again."

She quickly typed in the name again. "Sir, there is no one here with that name. Maybe you got the wrong school. This is Lincoln. Maybe you wanted Fairmont, just a couple miles over."

Hudson turned with tears in his eyes and started to walk away.

"Sorry, sir," the woman said standing and watching in confusion as the man left the building.

The agent made it to his car and covered his face to hide the agony his heart felt. Tears formed before he could stop them.

"Lord, why?" he prayed. "My family is gone. My wife is gone. My children are gone. How could You let this happen? God I never cared about those other things. Everest, the motorcycle, the pyramids. You gave me so much more than those futile experiences. God, I want my family back. Lord, I need my family back. I need Your help," he cried as his phone rang.

Wiping his face on his sleeve and taking a couple quick breaths to regain composure, he pulled the phone from his pocket and answered. "This is Hudson."

"Hudson, it happened again," Todd said very excitedly. "Everything is different. The streets…the city. My Seminary is gone. I work for something called the National Seminary."

The agent listened quietly.

"Hudson, are you there? Did you hear me? Everything has been changed, and no one knows it but us."

Overcome with emotion, the agent started to cry uncontrollably.

"Hudson, what's wrong? Hey man, tell me. What's happened?" the professor said to his old partner.

"Todd, they're gone," he wept into the phone, his voice garbled with emotion.

"Who's gone, Hudson? Tell me what's going on?" Todd said forcefully, having never heard his partner cry even in the worst of situations.

"My wife, my kids. Sara, Michael and Amy. They're gone. It's as if they never existed," he said continuing to sob.

The professor sat silent for a second and then spoke, "I'm coming."

"What?" Hudson asked.

"I'm coming. I will be on the next plane to D.C."

"No, I'm fine."

"No, buddy, you're not. I'm coming to help you," his thought came as the only means to lighten the dreadful situation, "I seem to remember a certain agent needing my help before. Coming to my office and asking me to sneak him under the Temple Mount. I'm starting to feel like Superman."

Hudson chuckled.

"My friend, it was you who reminded me of God's greatness last time. I'm telling you that God is in control. And somehow, He *has* allowed this to happen. But you know what?"

"What?" Hudson asked.

"It doesn't mean that's how He wants it. And it doesn't mean that we can't jump in and help to make it right."

Starting to regain composure, the agent continued to listen.

"Hudson, I think the world needs a couple heroes to return it back to normal. Are you game?"

"Todd, I don't know what's happened. I don't know how this occurred."

"I asked – are you game? Are you up for the challenge God has before us?" he questioned forcefully.

Hudson sat quietly and thought about his family. He looked outside the car window at the children playing on the playground. He wanted them to have the history that God had created, not something man devised. "I'm game," he replied quietly.

"What was that? I didn't hear you," Todd shouted like a coach.

"I said, let's make it right," he burst out the words, feeling a sense of strength and determination.

"Okay. God, please be with us. We need Your direction and guidance. Please light the path we are to follow, and somehow, God be glorified through our actions," he prayed as Hudson shut his eyes.

"My friend, get back to work and do research. We need to find out what's happening."

"Got it."

"I'll see you in a few hours," the professor said.

"Thanks, Todd."

"Hey that's what friends are for," he said closing the line and dialing his wife.

Hudson put the phone away, started the car and headed back to Cox Manufacturing.

12 — MONDAY AFTERNOON

Hudson took his time getting back to the facility and drove by his house one last time – unreasonably hoping to see his kid's toys in the front yard, or his wife's begonias – but nothing had changed. The house that he and his wife had built and spent years together in was now a bachelor's pad.

Instead of taking the highway, the agent drove street to street. Once again, things had changed, but not everything. The layout of the thoroughfares remained the same, or he'd have lost his way from the get go. Still, it all looked unfamiliar.

Following a 40 minute tour to reacquaint himself with the area, he made it back to the lab to find Bob tinkering around under the sphere.

"Hello?" Hudson called, looking over the upper floor railing, "What's going on down there?"

Bob rolled the dolly out from beneath the vehicle as he called out, "Just trying to figure out what might be happening inside this thing."

Hudson entered the open air elevator and started down, "Bob, I'm checking some things and I need the panels left open."

"Did something go wrong that I don't know about?" he asked standing from the floor with tools still in hand.

With the scientists stopping their work to watch the conversation, Hudson chose his words carefully before stepping from the elevator, "No, everything went fine; I'm just doing my job, and checking on things."

"Hey buddy, we can't do further tests with the vehicle in pieces. We need to replace the panels."

"Leave them where they are," he walked past Bob and the large machine without looking over at them.

"Hudson, what's going on?" the man shouted as he dropped the tools on a table. He picked up a rag to wipe his hands.

"It's not your problem. Just leave everything where it is," Hudson called back before slamming the door.

The agent sat in his chair and awakened his computer. "Oh, Lord, let me find her," he mumbled as he started to type.

Opening a government search engine, he immediately put in his name, knowing his family would appear on the same screen. "Please, let them be there," he pleaded as the information came up.

All of Hudson's statistics were on the display: his age, weight, education, past occupations and present employment labeled as "Employee of the Department of Energy." In the columns labeled spouse and children, the word "none" was written in each one. The agent's heart sank.

Inputting his wife's name revealed nothing. The two other women in the city with her name proved to be the wrong people when the picture came upon the screen. Sitting back in his chair and wiping his eyes, Hudson was distraught.

"Lord, how can you give me these precious jewels, and then allow them to be taken away?" A knock reverberated through the door; the agent gave another wipe to his eyes and sat up straight. "Yes!" he barked.

Peeking around the opening, Bob looked through and knocked again. "You got a second?"

"No, man, I don't," he mumbled shuffling some papers on his desk.

Coming in the door anyway, he picked up a pair of hand grips from the top of a filing cabinet and gave them a squeeze, "Hey, buddy, what's going on? Are you alright?"

"Yeah, I'm fine. Just need some time to work things out," he said still typing into the computer.

"Hudson, when I was brought onto this project, it was to work beside you. From what I hear, you've encountered some kind of boom or booms this morning. And you've been acting kind of nuts, from what the scientists have been saying. Now you're performing unscheduled work on the sphere – work that may put us behind for the next test.

I would say that something is not fine," he sat in the chair and squeezed the grips rhythmically.

Leaning back, Hudson breathed deeply and clasped his hands behind his head, "Bob, have you noticed anything odd today?"

"You mean other than your sudden eccentricities?" he replied with a smile.

"Yeah, other than that," he said typing again into his computer.

"No, man, it's been a fairly normal day."

"Bob, what do you know about me? I mean, tell me about myself."

With a weird look on his face, "I'd say that you're a focused and motivated leader. You're an adventurer with all of those trips you take. You do fairly well with the ladies, and you're a good friend. What else do you want to know?"

With a sad look on his face, "That's enough." Hudson immediately leaned forward in his chair and looked at his computer.

"Why don't you take the rest of the day off? Go for a run, or find a climbing wall to tackle. You might've had some kind of response to the surge that none of the rest of us experienced," Bob sat forward in his chair and tapped on the lava lamp. "I can take it for a while."

With a large smile on his face, he looked over at Bob, "I think I might just do that," he said taking the sheet rolling out of his printer. After folding it and putting it into his pocket he stood and walked to the filing cabinet behind Bob.

"What are you working on my friend? You need to get home and rest."

Bending down to the drawer next to the floor, he looked at the titles on the edges and pulled out four composition notebooks.

"Why do you need Dr. Keith's notebooks?" he asked standing from his chair.

Hudson responded, "Just need to do some research."

"You know those books aren't supposed to leave this building?"

"So sue me," Hudson said as he headed out of the small room and toward the elevator.

Bob walked from the office and watched his friend rise on the elevator. A serious look came over his face as he caught a glimpse of him leaving through the security door. "I hope you know what you're getting into," he mumbled as he headed back into Hudson's office.

Todd walked to the back of the 767 and waited in front of one of the bathroom doors. He normally tried to book the seats that were farthest forward in the aircraft and usually on an aisle. The aisle allowed him to stretch out when no one was coming and the forward seats got the cleanest air. Well, the pilot's got the air right off the scrubbers, but at least he sat next in line; that is, when he got his choice of seating. Not today. He only prayed this trip did not end with some deadly disease he had no immunity to, newly created in the last restructuring of time. He could imagine viruses of all sorts that he had likely never been exposed to in this newer and more sinister time.

But when he had called the airlines, attempting to get to Washington as quickly as possible, there were only two seats left, and both were in the back.

The two step walk to the bathroom area was quick, but the wait still took several minutes. After a hairy overweight man opened the door and squeezed from the small sheet metal room, Todd pulled in a deep breath and rushed into the space.

Pulling his phone from his pocket, he retrieved Hudson's number. Normally he would never break FAA regulations by using a cell phone on a plane, but he needed quick access to his friend and hoped that in the 20 seconds he was in contact, the aircraft would stay in the air and on course.

After several rings, Hudson picked up. "Yeah," he said leaving the parking area of the government facility.

"Hudson, meet me out front of Reagan National at 4:15. That should give me enough time to get on the ground and run to the main exit. We're arriving at Gate 28."

"Great, I have it. 4:15. I'll be there."

"How are you doing, Hudson? Have you found out anything new?" he asked pulling his hair back and looking at a large lump on his forehead in the small mirror.

"I'm working on a lead now. Todd, I'm scared. I really don't know what's going on yet."

"God's going to get us through this. You know He doesn't want His world being changed, so He's going to have to tell us what to do to get it back. I better go; I can't hold my breath anymore. Be there at 4:15!"

"I'll be there," he said putting the phone back in his pocket. *What did he mean that he can't hold his breath anymore*? With a questioning look on his face, the agent headed toward his destination.

Todd closed the phone and burst from the small room. Looking at the hundreds of people jammed into the aluminum tube, he thought to himself, *all of our technology and we're still jammed in here like cattle.* He shook his head and sat back in his seat making sure he did not go into the bathroom again.

Driving through the Capital City at any time is slow going but for the agent it felt like a snail's crawl. Taking the 395 loop, he exited onto C Street and because of road construction was stuck for several minutes.

"Why do they have to be working now?" he complained. He tapped the folders beside him thoughtfully. Dr. Keith, the originator of the sphere program, kept every thought, every notation in college composition notebooks, and one went with him everywhere. When he was designing the sphere, several colleagues suggested he dictate them into a secure desktop computer so the information could be more easily organized. But, true to his old-fashioned ways, he believed paper to be where the real genius happened. After his death, all 68 handwritten books were left in Hudson's keeping.

Several honks later and feeling his blood pressure rising, he finally broke free from the congestion and turned left onto 1st street and again onto Constitution Avenue, he saw the Beaux Arts building at his right. The colonnades with the thirty-four Doric columns mirrored the Capitol's design making the large building easy to identify.

He steered into a restricted space in the big parking lot, just a few feet from the west entrance of the limestone and granite structure. Having a top level clearance gave the agent several perks, like parking near the door. *Ah, it's the little things in life, but at the moment, the little things are all I have,* he thought dismally.

Passing several pilasters on the sides of the structure, Hudson showed his identification at the door and quickly started down the long passage.

Having only been in the building a few times, Hudson found a legend approximately 20 feet down the marble hallway filled with nicely dressed men and women heading for various spots within the structure. He found the name he was looking for and headed for the second floor, suite number three.

Going east down the long hallway and dodging people coming in and out of offices, he finally came to the Rotunda. He passed the towering columns surrounding the domed room and glanced at the lone statue of Richard Russell Jr. in the center. Hudson ascended the wide stairs exiting the Rotunda and listened to passing people talking about everything from water conservation in Chicago to preservation of wetlands in Arizona.

I didn't know there were wetlands in Arizona, he thought to himself as he stepped onto the second floor. Hudson found the name he was looking for on a door overlooking the Rotunda in the Senate building, Senator Arlen Dupree.

Opening the door, the agent understood why a building that once held 96 Senators and 10 Committees now only held 28 Senators and 4 Committees. Arlen had at least 6 offices all to himself. Tearing down the walls and expanding his horizons, the Senator displayed his power in Washington with rich leathers, dark mahogany walls, and over-sized furniture. Obviously, this man from the large state of Texas wanted everyone to know it.

Going up to the assistant behind the desk, Hudson got right to the point. Quickly flashing his security badge he asked, "Is Sara Blackwell here?"

The woman in her early 20's answered quickly, "Sir, we have no one in this office by that name."

"Sara Blackwell. I read on the government website that she works here."

"No, sir, there is no one by that name," the woman replied with a smile.

"She is low 30's, bright blue eyes, light brownish blonde hair. Around five foot four."

The woman looked kind of confused. "That sounds like Sara Brennen?" she spoke questioningly.

"I'm sorry, that's right, Sara Brennen. Is she here?" he asked feeling nervous.

"No, she isn't back yet."

"When do you expect her back?" he asked fairly pointedly.

"She went to lunch, and I haven't seen her since. She may have had some last minute appointment to get to. Do you want me to leave your name and have her call you?" A large voice boomed from behind her.

"Michelle, get Senator Rollins on the horn," he shouted from around a meeting room door. "I got a bone to pick with him."

"Yes, Senator Dupree," she quickly replied dialing in numbers on the phone.

Arlen Dupree stepped into the room, filling the space with his Texas-sized presence. Ostrich boots and an 80x beaver Stetson cowboy hat made it difficult for anyone to miss him, especially in Washington. He was proud of the Lone Star State of his birth, and at 61 years of age he still broadcasted more grit than men half his age.

Senator Dupree had lived most of his life outside of Dallas and made his money the hard way. He had dug it out of the ground. He went to church each Sunday, despite plenty of disagreements with the church and its teachings.

"Hudson, is that you?" the man asked, offering a hand.

Shaking the Senator's hand he smiled passively, "Yes, sir, it is."

"Well what brings you to this neck of the woods?" he asked slapping the agent on the shoulder.

"I was just looking for Sara."

"Well, me too. If you find her let me know. She was supposed to brief me on some things after lunch." His eyes fell on the young woman on the phone, "Michelle, where is she?"

"I don't know sir," she answered shrugging.

"Get her on the horn too."

The red-headed woman dialed the number and, after several seconds, looked back at the Senator, "It went right to voice mail. Do you want me to leave a message?"

"Nah, she'll be in soon enough." He looked over at Hudson, "So what do you have going with Sara?"

"Well, uh…"

"You trying to take her out or something?" the man continued, nudging him in the side and lowering his voice, "She would be a great catch. Well worth the effort. She's a cutie."

"Yes, Senator, I know," he answered very quietly.

"Well, I better git. Michelle, did you get a hold of Rollins?"

"Uh, yes, sir. He will meet with you in ten minutes."

"Great work, honey." Stopping and looking at the man again, "Hudson, did you get that project of yours under control?"

"Well, uh…"

"You know I was against the whole idea. If you can get some cheap energy out of that thing, well, then I guess it will have turned out alright."

"We are still working on it," he said not really knowing how to answer.

"Hudson, you're a good man, and I trust you. If anyone can turn that evil contraption into something good, it's you. Always know that you can call on me."

"Thank you, Senator."

"I mean it," he said looking the agent in the eyes before closing the door behind him.

Hudson refocused his attention toward Michelle. "It's fairly important. I would normally stay, but I have to pick someone up at the airport. Would you have her call me when she gets in?"

She quickly jotted his number on a pad and nodded, "Sure, Mr. Blackwell."

The agent left the office suite with no more answers than when he came in.

13 — MONDAY, LATE AFTERNOON

The heavy feeling of sleep surrounded Sara as she struggled to pull herself up from where she lay. "What happened?" were the first words she uttered as she rubbed her temples trying to ease the throbbing in her head.

Sitting on the edge of the bed, she tried to focus on the room around her. *"Where am I?"* she thought. Gently she lowered her legs over the side and, wondering at her sudden dizziness and lack of balance, remained in her position a while longer.

Obviously this was not a hotel room. Someone might have worked hard to make her feel that way, but the space behind the bed lacked a headboard. Sara lifted her feet again onto the bed and leaned back against the wall. Cold, painted cement chilled her spine.

From what she could tell, Sara was in a large underground vault of some kind, possibly 50 feet long and over 30 feet wide. Along the twelve-foot ceiling overhead, aluminum piping ran back and forth, bringing ventilation and warmth. "*Thank goodness for that*," she breathed quietly.

Still not able to totally focus clearly, she closed her eyes and rolled to her side. With the motion came a groaning like the springs on a trampoline, telling her the bed was only a war-era cot covered with a mattress. At least the comforter under her cheek smelled nice and new and appeared to be of good quality.

A few deep breaths later Sara lifted her head and steadied herself, looking about the space. A desk with paper and a cup of blue pens stood next to the cot.

Slowly turning her head to minimize the pounding behind her eyes, she noticed a couch with a television across from her, next to a small fridge on top of a cabinet.

Forcing herself from the relative safety of the bed, Sara placed a hand to the wall and made her way around the room cautiously to find out if the refrigerator contained anything to revive her body; or at least her morale.

"Why do I feel like I've spent the night drinking?" This last thought was spoken aloud even as she questioned why she had said it – having never been drunk in her life.

Opening the fridge she found bottled water, several containers of various fruit juices and colas. She took a water and scanned the small appliance and the cabinet next to it for something to eat, but found nothing. At least the water felt cold as she took a long drink and let it revive her from the inside.

She meandered a little further and discovered a door. Turning the handle of the metal entrance, a loud creak revealed a small military-style bathroom. Very military.

A sink, a lavatory and a small shower head were all crowded into the tiny room. Figuring the corner was the shower, her next realization came that no curtain or towel offered any privacy. The drain in the floor provided an exit for the water, but no barriers prevented it from drenching everything in the room as it pounded off of the walls.

"I guess you have to cover the toilet paper if you plan on showering," she chortled with a nervous chuckle. Her quick wit always came out in difficult situations. Strong and determined woman though she was, something about the whole situation filled her with an uncharacteristic fear.

Still reeling with a heavy head, she backed out of the lesser space. The room that housed the quarters had two other doors. She found the closest exit sealed shut. Composed of thick metal, the door had been welded from the inside.

Turning and looking the 50 feet to the other side of the room, she saw another exit. It looked very much like the welded one behind her, but it had not been tampered with. Sara instinctively bolted forward to try it only to find herself on the floor the next instant with a pounding head.

"Ah, okay. Well," her words came through clenched teeth, "I should tell the management to put grips under the area rugs in here. They might just have a lawsuit on their hands if someone were to get *really* hurt." The sarcasm sounded bitter to her own ears. But she was so out of her comfort zone here. Apparently, the area rugs were intended to warm up the room by covering the concrete floor.

Clutching her head a moment before she made it to her knees, she finally covered the distance only to realize the door could not be opened from the inside. Pounding on the gray door, she called through it in exhaustion, "Let me out!"

The echo from the room and the decibels within her head made the sound excruciating. Her eyes closed against the pain, but she regained her determination and kept yelling and pounding. "Help! I'm in here. Someone let me out!"

After a minute of calling to apparently no one, she worked her way back to the bed. "How did I get here?" she asked tearfully, letting her head fall back onto the pillow. The young woman kicked off her shoes and tried to reconstruct her day. Thinking back to where everything went wrong, the clouds in her mind started to clear. Events appeared before her as if she were watching a tragic play.

She was back on Delaware street.

A large man jumped from the black vehicle, "Hello Miss Brennen, you're coming with me," he declared as he lifted a dark gun in her direction.

She tried to flee when the brute grabbed her shirt, ripped her blouse along the shoulder seam and popped several tiny buttons from the center of her blouse.

Feeling the gape in her white blouse, she fisted the fabric together and pulled her arms to her chest in an attempt to feel less vulnerable than she already was.

Fighting with everything she had, she knew there was no way out of his clutches. His next words made her situation clear. "You stop kicking, or I'll kill you here, I swear it," he growled as her elbow made contact with his left shoulder.

He shoved her into the long limousine as she started to reason with him. "I don't have much money, but I'll give you what I have if you'll let me reach my purse."

"I don't want or need your money."

She pulled back, her face stunned, "Then why are you doing this to me?" She made a one-handed move to close her gaping blouse as she held the other hand out at the gun pointing in her direction.

"I work for Senator Dupree. We are to have a meeting in five minutes, and when I come up missing, he'll have the whole town looking for me."

His chuckle mocked her, "I work for people bigger than Dupree, and I don't mean his size. As long as you don't cause any trouble, you won't get hurt. It's a real easy proposition."

"Why do they want me? I don't know anything that isn't general knowledge on the Hill. We're working on several bills, but nothing secretive." Now she was just trying not to cry.

"Sara, we don't want your information. We just want you,"

"You sound like you know me." His calm demeanor confused her.

"Have you seen me before?" he said with a smile.

She thought for a second, "No, I don't remember you. Have we met?"

"That machine's amazing," he mumbled. "Just sit back, we'll be there shortly."

The car wove its way past the Capitol and onto Pennsylvania Avenue. Passing the National Gallery of Art, the National Archives and the FBI building, Sara looked out, occasionally glancing back at the man watching her with the pointed gun. With the Department of Commerce on their left, the long dark limousine turned north onto 15th. The massive edifice of the Treasury Department Building loomed large before the stretch vehicle that then turned left once again onto Pennsylvania Avenue.

Sara looked nervously back at the man who had abducted her, "Where are we going?"

He just smiled, indicating that her best guess had become reality. Because of the terrorist bombings on the Murrah Federal Building in Oklahoma City, the Twin Towers in New York and the subsequent threats from any group desiring to make a point, Pennsylvania Avenue from 15th streets to 17h streets had been closed off for decades. With her vehicle gingerly making the turn onto the highly restricted streets, her destination must be the White House.

The black vehicle was quickly waved through the main gate and entered a tunnel on the west side of the building. Immediately, the vehicle took a sharp decline heading deep under the People's House.

Activating its lights, it turned left and stopped at a parking garage. An attendant opened the door, and her captor waved the gun in such a way that she knew it was time to exit the car.

If it were not for electric lights, the garage would have been totally dark. Off in the distance she saw two other Limousines, a Cadillac and a duplicate of the car she just arrived in. The only difference in the vehicles being that the other two had American flags sitting at all four corners. Moments before strong arms propelled her through a door behind her, she realized the car she had been in could have belonged to the Secret Service. In her bewildered state she had not noticed the POTUS symbols within the vehicle. The heavy door slammed behind her.

Ushered down a long white hallway with lights overhead every 15 feet, taking everything in now seemed mandatory. "Where are we going?" she asked trying to stay up with his large stride.

They came to a door on the right about 40 feet down the hallway and entered another corridor, walking another minute. At the end of the tunnel she found what looked to be a train station. Sara knew that it was not a Metro, but was very similar.

A single train car was sitting and waiting for the two with its doors open. The pristine vehicle was painted blue with gold striping and had the Presidential seal across its side. He dragged all 115 pounds of her over its threshold, and she wished for the first time that she had packed on weight at some point. After regaining her balance and looking up, she saw that the rail car had another occupant.

"Hello Sara," the man said calmly with a smile.

"Mr. President, uh, hello," she muttered straightening her blouse and holding it closed with her hand. "Why am I here?"

The machine left the station and started its trek.

"Sara, I first want to say that I'm sorry for all of this."

"'Sorry' is not going to cut it, Mr. President. If you wanted to meet with me, all you had to do was call."

"Yes. I regret that we had to go to this cloak and dagger approach, but, uh, well," looking at his hand, "everything came up rather quickly. There was no time to work this out without my friend here," he said gesturing to her captor.

Feeling the heat rising within her, the words tumbled out, "I have already asked this, but why am I here?"

The train car passed several stations and continued toward its destination.

"Mrs. Bl…, I mean Miss Brennen, I want you to know that you will be well taken care of. You will not be harmed."

"What do you mean that you will be taking good care of me? I can take very good care of myself. I want off of this train," she said as forcibly as she could.

Starting to stand, the large man pushed her back down. The President raised a hand at the guard, "It's alright."

"I want off of this train. Then, I'm going to go straight to Senator Dupree," she stared at the man in the suit across from her.

Sitting there quietly. "Sara, I regret this, but we have to keep you."

"Keep me?" she yelled. "I will not be staying here!"

"I'm sorry, but you must. I have important work to do and need you as collateral."

She looked at him curiously.

He continued while wringing his hands, "I just don't think that I can stop certain people's movements without you."

The train started to slow, and Sara's eyes grew wide. "Who can you stop by holding me? I'm single, and have two older parents. I don't even have a boyfriend. Who could you stop by holding me?" she asked.

He got a dark look on his face. "You have much more influence than you even know."

The train stopped at a dimly lit station and its doors opened to a grand hallway.

"I'm sorry, but you will be staying with us until I know that everything has worked out," he plastered on his patented smile, "Until it has worked out for the good of the nation."

Sara wiggled away from the monster behind her. But, the President waved his hand, effectively having her stopped by the arm when she jumped up. To his surprise she worked with his movements to turn him around, causing him to trip on his own foot caught in the way, then took the opportunity to kick him in the groin and bolt from his grasp.

"I refuse to along with this!" she yelled as the President backed up.

Sara ran from the train car down the long corridor. Her captor grunted and hobbled after her. He knew the woman to be intelligent and inventive but was not prepared for the low blow.

Frantically, the woman tried each door she came across. Most looked like they had not been opened for decades, but she gave them a tug anyway. Nothing broke free as she continued down the dark hallway. With the man regaining his stride he quickly bridged the gap between them.

Tears were running down her face as she pulled on each door in front of her, "Please open, Lord please let it open."

She tugged on another and nothing happened. Hearing his steps behind her, she grabbed the next one, and it opened to a staircase. Sara ran up the steps as quickly as her black pumps would allow her. Her legs were flying up the incline while the monstrous man was spanning two and three steps at a time. She knew if the tunnel did not end quickly, he would overtake her.

The steps seemed to go on forever and finally when she was almost out of breath, the tunnel ended, and she came to a door. She heard people on the other side. Lots of people. "Lord, let me out of this," she cried.

Pulling the door open just a few inches she saw where they had taken her. Then the door was forced shut, and she was sprayed in the face with a substance smelling like a bathroom cleaner. Her captor had caught her before she could escape.

Within seconds, she had lost the fight with consciousness. The man caught her fall and carried her over his shoulder like a sack of potatoes toward her dungeon.

Looking up at the ceiling, Sara started to cry. "Dear Lord, help me. I am so afraid."

Tears fell onto her thin pillow, but she refused to give in to the emotion.

"God, what have I done? Why would I be such a threat that the President should be worried?"

Noticing a large circular grate on the ceiling, she looked around the room. There was not enough furniture to stack for her to get to it, and then it looked to be bolted into the cement.

The young woman lay there trembling and afraid when a verse came to her mind. It was true that the government listed suggested readings for the state church, and that none of them were the Bible. But Sara continued to read her copy every morning. She knew God was more than the government wanted her to know about.

The verse that came to mind was Psalm 28:7. As she said it out loud she tried to make it personal and more meaningful for her situation. With tears in her eyes and a tremble in her voice she started to speak, "Lord, I know that you have heard the voice of my cries. You are my strength, and You are my shield. God, my heart trusts in You, and because of that, I shall thank You, even in my dungeon.

God, you know that I'm afraid, but I will trust in You."

Sara opened her eyes, and the room had not changed. She was still locked in the cold cement space, but she knew that she was not alone. Her God would protect her. She had to just be faithful.

Getting up from the bed and wiping her face with her hands she went to the fridge and opened a bottle of juice. Sitting at the small metal kitchen table, she tried to remember the last few seconds before she went unconscious.

Taking a sip she pondered that last moment, "What did I see? Where am I?"

She remembered voices and a statue of some kind. It was a big statue of a man standing tall with his arms down at his side. "Where have I seen that before?" she mumbled.

Being a resident of the capital city, she had not been to the many attractions that drew people from all over the United States, but she knew that she had seen that statue. She had only a glimpse of the area beyond the door, but she knew she had seen it.

Walking over to the 70's style couch she sat down. "Someone doesn't have very good taste in furniture," she said just to make herself feel better. Taking another sip, it finally hit her. "It was Jefferson. The Jefferson Memorial."

Looking around the room at the heavy cement complex, her eyes finally stared straight up at the circular grate as she muttered, "I'm under the Jefferson Memorial. I'm being kept in a shelter under the statue of Jefferson."

Sara felt better. It did not get her out of the memorial dungeon that she was locked in, but she felt that she had some type of control over the situation, even if it were just the knowledge of her location.

Another sip of cherry juice slid down her throat, "Now, I just need Prince Charming to ride in and save me."

She propped her feet up on the table and leaned back on the couch.

14 — MONDAY, LATE AFTERNOON

The Oval Office is the President's formal workspace. In this room, he conferred with heads of state, dignitaries, and staff. From the desk, he often addressed the American public through television.

For Bob, this office engendered fond memories and he held a respect for it like no other place on earth. He was accustomed to the original marble mantle from the Oval Office of 1909. Glancing up, he enjoyed seeing the Presidential Seal embossed into the ceiling.

Across the mantle, framed perfectly within the curved windows of the space, he saw the Resolute Desk – made from the timbers of the H.M.S. Resolute, the abandoned British ship discovered by an American vessel and returned to the Queen of England as a token of friendship and goodwill. When the ship was retired, Queen Victoria commissioned the Resolute Desk from its timbers and presented it to President Rutherford B. Hayes, in 1880. Many presidents since Hayes had made it their own. And Langley was no exception. Standing at attention behind it were two flags, the American and the Presidential.

Around the curved walls of the famous room hung pictures from American masters portraying events that changed the greatest nation's history. Within the recessed bookcases were gifts from other countries' leaders, historical pieces from great Americans and first edition books written by American authors.

Everything about the space had always drawn attention to America's greatness. All aspects of the office related to the strength, might, and wealth of history that come from the diverse people representing a nation focused on God-given liberty and the pursuit of happiness. As Bob found his customary chair, he noticed the room no longer radiated with that pride. The room was not the same as it was even 24 hours ago.

One of the first sights that overwhelmed the former Army Ranger was the lineup of national flags encircling the room, reminding all that America's greatness came from its rich immigrant background. The room spoke to the strength of a country exalted because of its diversity.

He looked to the ceiling and noticed the new Presidential Seal. For more than two centuries the hallmark had boasted a bald eagle in the center holding an olive branch with one foot and an arrow with the other, breathing from its mouth a banner with the written words *E. Plurbus*

Unum. Fifty stars had surrounded the words, "Seal of the President of the United States." No, this seal was different.

The center containing the eagle had not changed much, but the next ring from the center had a red background. Within it were various religious symbols. A cross, the Jewish star, the Egyptian Ankh and Eye of Horus, the Islamic Star and Crescent, a Yin Yang, the Mars and Venus symbols, the Masonic Compass, a Swastika, three strikes representing the Druid religion and a handful of other symbols that he had never seen. The seal was also engraved into the Resolute desk. He winced.

"This must have been in the works for a while. That carving took some time." Bob shook his head in silence.

Getting up from his seat he went to the recessed shelves and found pictures of the President leading various religious ceremonies. One appeared to be a mass wedding. Another seemed to be of him leading a Catholic Holy Service. The Ranger stood there amazed at what was different from when he was there just a few days earlier.

Pictures of American scenes had been replaced by world religious events throughout history. One showed tens of thousands of Muslims. Bob thought it might be the Hajj because he could see the Kah'ba in the center. Another was of the Wailing Wall surrounded by thousands of Jewish devotees.

While walking around the room he saw a picture of a Buddhist temple with Monks banging a large gong in the center. There were other paintings, but he had seen enough.

Heading back to his chair in front of the Desk he saw a third flag sitting behind the desk that had not been there before. Ambling around the massive desk, he grasped the lowest corner and held the red flag straight. It appeared to be a Presidential religious flag. In the center were the golden words "Supreme Religious Leader of America." Surrounding that was the same band he had seen in the Presidential Seal, containing the many religious symbols in silver.

"Jack, have this on my desk in 20 minutes." He heard a voice behind him.

"Yes, Your Excellency," a man replied as he shut the door.

The leader of the nation looked up as he entered the room. "Bob. I see you found my newest flag," the President said with a smile.

Bob walked back around and sat in his customary seat.

"So what do you think of the changes?"

"I can see that many things have been altered."

"That's what I call progress," he laughed putting his papers down and sitting in the large leather chair tucked under the Desk. "You are either moving forward or moving back. You can't just stay the same around here."

"As I look around this room, it's hard for me to see if we are moving forward or back," Bob said pointedly.

The President's eyebrows dropped, "What we are doing is for the better."

"I like your new outfit." Bob's tone begged to differ.

Taking off the thick satin band around his neck that held a medallion, the President threw it on the desk. "I need to wear it to keep the nation unified."

Bob leaned over the desk and picked it up, "What does this represent?"

"We are saying that we are globally unified. Our nation is tolerant to all others' religions and customs."

"I haven't spent a good amount of my life in the service of my country to say that we are no better than anyone else. America is the greatest nation on the earth, and I want everyone to know it," he grunted.

The President raised his hand, "Calm down Robert. When Mecca is no longer the center of Islam. When the Vatican's power is relocated to this great city. When the Jews come to America for pilgrimages." Getting up and looking out the window behind him, he spoke more quietly, "When Hinduism, Buddhism, and all of the other ism's around the world come to America to worship. When the Christians are no longer looking to a cross in Israel but leadership in D.C., then America will be great. That's what we're doing here."

Bob sat silently.

"This is about making America *the* greatest nation on the face of the earth!"

Bob quietly watched.

"What do you think of what we're trying to do? From the file we have on your background, I hear that you come from a very religious family. Wasn't your father a Pastor?" he asked standing in front of the window looking at the soldiers on the lawn.

Bob stood from his seat, "I don't like the personal questions. Yeah, my parents are religious. My father was and still is a pastor out in Kansas. He leads a little church of a hundred people and has for years. Mom supports him and they have always spent more time with that church than they ever did with me."

The President stood in his dark blue suit and red tie turning to watch the man.

"Dad would go to the hospitals to visit the sick when I was the star pitcher in a ballgame. He'd go on visitations to prospective members when I was home sick with the flu. We went on vacation to religious conferences. Can you believe that?" He stopped a moment before turning to look at the President.

"They never let me be me. The wanted me to be something that conformed with what a pastor's boy should be. Well, I wasn't that, and so I went into the Army as soon as I graduated High School, so I wouldn't be around to embarrass them anymore. Christianity is my parent's religion, not mine, so I don't care what you do with it."

"Good, well then we're agreed." He gestured to the seat in front of him, "Sit down, Robert, and bring me up-to-date with what happened on the jumps."

"Well, first off, I'm worn out. I need some down time."

The President sat and looked at him.

"Since last night, you've lived about 24 hours, well I've lived close to 40."

"How's that?" he asked.

"When I jump, they bring me back just a minute or so after I leave. So to you no additional time has taken place. However, in that minute of your time, I may have lived four or five hours to get the mission accomplished. I've accomplished three assignments since last night. I'm exhausted."

"Interesting, I hadn't thought of that. What else can you tell me?"

"I'd say that everything has gone off without a hitch. You're the one with the history books, but I've done everything you've asked. And I think the outcomes have been to your expectations."

"You have performed exceptionally." He started counting on his fingers. "By removing the Danbury Baptist Letter, we were able to take the words 'separation of church and state' out of the American vocabulary.

Then you motivated Madison to remove the first amendment, allowing the government to promote religion. By removing Luther, the protestant reformation was kept to a minimum allowing us to help align the remaining few "Christian" denominations. We no longer have the hundreds of versions of Christianity; Baptists, Methodists, Presbyterians, Church of Christs, the Evangelicals or Charismatics, etc. Just a few varieties which are now under one umbrella making them impotent and without the real power to evangelize. So far everything is going off like clockwork." The leader smiled.

He slid a file from the grand desk, "How has Hudson been taking this?"

"He's been upsetting the other scientists with stories of sonic booms and has been sending them on diagnostic checks. I think, that they think he's losing his mind. They tell me that he's been irritable and acting out of character."

"What do you mean by that?" he questioned, writing in the file.

"Hudson's a great guy. He's a focused leader, and everyone respects him. Beyond that, he cares about each person there. He knows about their families and is genuinely interested in every employee at the facility."

The President listened intently.

"However, everyone knows that something happened to him this afternoon. The researchers think that it has something to do with the phase shift or sonic boom that he's telling them about, but we know that it's something more. He's been demanding and impatient. Just a few hours ago, he stormed in and told me to stay away from the sphere. That's something I can't remember him ever doing."

"I can imagine him being upset with all that's going on. What else can you tell me about him," the leader asked with furrowed eye brows.

"He's snooping around."

"What do you mean?" the President asked sitting back in his chair.

"Like I said earlier, he has the scientists looking over the data a dozen different ways. I did see him talking with Peter, one of the newer researchers several times today."

"You did lock those computers out of any sites that might give them information on what we're doing, didn't you?" he asked rubbing his temples.

"As many as I could think of." Bob stood to walk over to a picture on a wall, "Langley, Hudson's smart. He may not have a Ph.D, but he is a very intelligent man. I've gone up against many people in my time in the service. Been sent all over the world undercover to take out opposition." He looked back at the President, "A person like Hudson makes me nervous."

"Why would that be?" the leader asked, sitting forward in his chair.

Bob moved toward the President. "Hudson is righteous and upright. He'll go into hell with a water pistol if he thinks that what he's doing is right. To add to that, his family's been taken away."

Looking right at the President he pointed, "He's cornered, and I think he's going to come out fighting. He's one of the few people who will want the world to be back the way it was."

Langley sat for a second to think the new development through. "Can we control him?" the President asked. "I guess a better question would be - can *you* control him?"

"Why can't you just have him put away somewhere?"

"It's not that easy," he responded. "Hudson's a leader on one of the most secret projects we have going. If he disappeared, we would definitely have trouble." Standing from his chair and walking around the desk, "No, he needs to continue acting like nothing has happened, and when his leads dry up, he'll give up."

"I hope it's that easy. He did leave with some books this afternoon."

"What books?"

"Some of Dr. Keith's writing pads. I looked on the list after Hudson left, and he took numbers 77-82."

"What do those books correspond to?" the President asked rather startled.

"They are the section on 'Ramifications of Time Travel.' He's trying to determine if the sphere was involved."

"What do you think he'll do when he discovers that it wasn't his sphere?"

"I'd bet that he'd start looking for another one," Bob answered quickly.

Sitting on the edge of his desk, he spoke quickly, "Then, we need to stay ahead of him. Robert, I have another jump for you to make."

"No, I need a break," he answered out of frustration.

"You must. One more jump, and you can take the night off."

"I'm exhausted," he grumbled sitting in the chair.

"We need to get these jumps behind us if Hudson is trailing." His urgency was palpable now.

"We can control him," the man responded waving his hands to dismiss the extra work.

"Robert, a few hard days, and you will sit on easy street with more money than you know what to do with. Plus, being the Secretary of Defense may not look too bad on a resume."

The tall athletic man looked up with renewed strength.

"When we have everything in place, I'll have control of the world's hearts. When that happens, I will be in charge of all aspects of government. Then I will need people around me whom I can trust."

The Ranger listened intently.

"You have proven yourself trustworthy. I can see you high up in the new world government."

With a smirk on his face, he gave in. "Give me the file."

The President walked around his desk and picked up the folder he was looking at earlier. "Our best researchers say that if we do it this way, we should get our desired outcome."

He opened the file containing maps, current historical contexts, principle characters, and his mission.

"Look that over, and then we need you to go," the man said obviously ending the meeting.

Standing from his chair still staring at the file, Robert followed the President to a private elevator hidden within a closet and he got in.

"Get to the site, and they'll have everything you need waiting for you," he said standing outside the elevator.

Closing the file, he looked up. "Don't forget what you have promised me."

One touch to the red button on the side would send Robert to a railway below the White House, "Don't worry," the President responded with a smile. Standing straight and looking up, he started to quote, "I think it was Alan Cohen who said, 'It takes a lot of courage to release the familiar and seemingly secure, to embrace the new. But there is no real security in what is no longer meaningful. There is more security in the adventurous and exciting, for in movement there is life, and in change there is power.'

Robert," he said with hesitation, "You and I will share that power." Reticent, "By the way, call me Supreme Excellency, Mr. President, or whatever other exalted title you can think of. If you call me Langley again, I will have to have your indiscretion corrected." The Leader's eyes were dark and focused.

After several seconds, the President slapped him on the arm, lifting the tension, "Now go and bring in the new world order."

The Ranger nodded and the doors closed.

15 — MONDAY, LATE AFTERNOON

The lift Bob had ridden down opened to the most technologically sophisticated mode of transportation yet. Walking directly from the closing doors of the elevator to the opened waiting entrance of the coach, the Ranger ambled in and sat on the luxuriously rich leather of this climate controlled ride. Having been preprogrammed to locate its next destination, the machine silently left the dock starting to pull additional gravity on the large man's frame.

Bob rode in silence through the tubes running underground beneath Washington. In the last 24 hours he had ridden this line again and again, but was still amazed at how quiet it was.

Since its development during World War I as a means of quick egress for the Commander in Chief, the underground rail system had morphed many times. Originally a simple steam locomotive, today the MagLev technology allowed him to sail above the guide rail by approximately 10 millimeters using magnetic fields. The rail itself now propelled the train by changing magnetic fields rather than having an onboard engine on the vehicle itself. No wheels grinding on the tracks. No bumps or shakes. No engine noise.

Being the size of an average travel trailer, the "train" as it was loosely called, had every possible amenity; a small kitchen, lavatory and the edge of technology in communication. It also contained meeting and sleeping areas making this an ideal tool for business, and comfortable for long stays.

Bob glanced to the front of the cabin and found the liquid crystal read out showing the train to be traveling at 132 miles per hour. Knowing he had just a few minutes to his destination, he opened the file and tried to absorb enough of his mission to get him through.

Scanning at the biographical information, he found the name Dr. John Rainolds; his next target. He had entered college at the age of thirteen, and, four years later, became a fellow at Corpus Christi College. By the age of 23 he was lecturing older students in Greek from the official podium of a full professor. Soon after completing his doctoral studies, the Queen of England appointed him to be a Royal Professor of Divinity in the University.

"This guy's smart," the man mumbled. Looking out through the front window of the train, he saw a small glow down the track. Feeling the deceleration begin, he knew he only had a few seconds left to pull in any last biographical data.

Perusing to the bottom of the document, he found several quotes which obviously summed up the man's brilliance. The first read, 'His memory was little less than miraculous. He could readily recite any material passage, on any page, column and paragraph of the numerous and voluminous works he had read.' The man was called, 'the very treasury of erudition,' and was spoken of as 'a living library, and a third university.'

As the train prepared to stop, it thrust the Ranger forward in his seat. Holding on to the armrest, he spoke, "This person is intelligent and a defender of the church, why would he be a target?"

The train shut down and the door opened to a large cavernous room filled with men in white jackets and clip boards running from place to place. Bob grabbed his folder and exited the train as the door shut and vehicle headed back the way it had come.

The brightness of the room surrounding him made him see spots on his eye lids. The 100 foot high walls sparkled with blinking white lights against shiny white paint. Only the back wall stood in contrast with a 50 foot black glass-covered observation room.

Continuing forward into the chamber, he saw the door titled "Preparation Room" and walked toward it. As he did, he passed the centerpiece of the large space – the sphere sitting in the middle of the room. This travel vehicle was very much like the one at Cox Manufacturing except that portions of it seemed to disappear as he walked by.

The lead scientist had said to not worry about the gaps that appeared to drift in and out of the large apparatus. He had been told several times that as parts of the sphere went out of space/time, they visually seemed to disappear. Even though in reality, they never left the building.

Staring at a cavernous hole forming in the side, he mumbled, "I don't want my body to start forming gaps like that."

But the newer version of the sphere had been enhanced so much that he was told any part of it may exist in many times at once. This machine was quicker and smoother than the old vehicle and gave more options for the traveler. Bob had never trekked in the original sphere, but could not believe the ride was worse than the moments he had been through in the "new and improved" version.

Opening the door, he stepped into the white-tiled preparation room to find his normal attendants. He liked to think of them as Thing One and Thing Two. They wore red suits; both had shaggy blonde hair and never stopped moving.

"Hey guys, it's time to start the party. I'm here," he announced to the men checking clothing hanging on a coat rack.

"Strip down," Jeff said without turning in his direction, "You need to get this on." Mike chimed in, "Hurry up, you don't have much time!"

"What are you talking about, just throw the stuff in the machine and let me go. I'll dress when I get there."

"We can't do that," Mike said flatly, still fussing with something on the costume hanger.

Jeff again, "They're putting you closer to your destination this time, and you need to have everything on when you get there."

"You won't have time to change clothes," Mike quickly added looking over a pair of boots he placed on the table in front of him.

Bob shot back, "Why do they need to get me that close? Just find a location a little farther out," he grumbled throwing the folder on the table for effect.

"It has something to do with it being in England in January," Jeff answered. "They need you to be dry and fresh. If you trek through two feet of snow for over a mile, you won't look like you're part of the Royal Ensemble."

Sighing, he started to strip down to his underwear. Seeing some loose undergarments, the Covert Op knew he was going to the 17th century. He pulled them on and then took the next stack from the focused attendants. The frilly white shirt and short bright red pants buttoned at the knee covered the under shirt, making all of the extra fabric uncomfortable to wear.

Tugging at some white stockings, the man's man grunted. Once again, he was given shoes that could be worn on either foot, and he finally pulled on a knee-length, red coat with gold piping.

A red hat with a turned up brim and a long thin polished maple wood cane finished the ensemble.

Mike pulled out a full length mirror on a stand for the seasoned military assassin to look at himself before he left the prep room.

"You look mah-velous," Jeff acted out with a smirk.

The soldier's expression dropped. "I look like one of the three musketeers," Bob yelled. "Who would have ever dressed like this on purpose?"

Mike answered, "We did a lot of research. This is what the elite wore in England during the time you will be entering. You look the part."

Jeff agreed with a nod, "Oh by the way, put this on."

The operative spun the large piece of fabric over his shoulders and spoke, "I look foolish and feel my testosterone dropping by the minute," he remarked picking up the file from the table and attempting to storm out the door.

Thing One and Thing Two glanced at each other with satisfaction as the door closed on the cape Bob was wearing. Feeling his temperature rise, he reopened the door to the snickering of his assistants. "And why would they have ever worn a cape?" he asked pulling at the large garment and leaving the room.

Departing the prep room, he once again entered the cavernous space housing the sphere. To the left were several tables where scientists could be found looking over data and discussing the events of the day. Pulling up a chair on the end, he removed what appeared to be a map of England from perhaps a few hundred years ago. A large circle was drawn with a yellow highlighter, and the words Hampton Court were written upon it.

He guessed that to be his location. Scanning through the dossier, he found a sheet with information about the site.

"Just give me the important information guys. I don't need a Ph.D. dissertation," he mumbled looking for the most basic of data.

After thumbing through the few pages on Hampton Court, he found it to have been the home of many monarchs of England including Henry VIII, Edward I, Mary I, and Elizabeth I. He would be there when James I, VI was reigning over England.

"James I, VI. What does that mean?" he complained.

Looking up the information, he found out that James was the first King of England with the name James but the sixth King of Scotland with that name.

"King of both countries, huh?"

A sheet titled "Historical Context" informed him that about the time James ascended the throne, the Roman Catholics had hopes he would favor their form of worship as his mother was the Romanist Mary, Queen of Scots. They arranged for a petition on their behalf be sent from the King of France to the new English King.

Bob discovered that on the other side were the Puritans. They rallied a petition signed by ten percent of all the clergy in England; thus equaling one thousand signatures. It was called the Millenary Petition. *That would explain the name*, he thought. This group hoped the King would favor a reform of the Church of England for James had been brought up in the Scots Kirk – a church in Scotland.

Starting to feel hot in the clothing he was wearing, he opened a few buttons and continued his analysis. Because of the trouble both sides of the religious aisles were causing in England, James I decided to have a conference and work out the difficulties. The 'black death' was beginning to ravage England, so the King decided Hampton Court would be the best place to hold the gathering as it was 15 miles southwest of London just along the river Thames.

Getting bored with the history lesson, Bob blurted out, "Who cares?"

"The President does," a man said walking toward him.

"Sorry Doc." Bob stood as the genius behind the sphere walked into the room. "How can any of this affect what we do today? Some conference over 400 years ago involving people in England?"

"Evidently you haven't read far enough. Are you ready, Robert?" the man asked. "Our people have been working overtime to ensure you perform your missions flawlessly."

Moving toward the sphere with Bob following he continued, "I've been worried that there would be problems with the vehicle with as many jumps as we've made in the last 24 hours. However, everything seems to be running perfectly."

"That's good to hear. It's my neck on the line," the large man responded.

"You are the one piloting the vehicle, however, everyone's neck is on the line if you or I screw up," he retorted looking directly at the man in the eyes. "We are all in this together, and each person here can help take responsibility for the mission."

He started to point at people around the room, "If he didn't find the correct location site, you would appear inside some mountain somewhere. If she didn't do the research on the precise time period, your mission would be meaningless," he gestured toward the control room. "If those people weren't totally sure that this vehicle was safe, you could quite literally disappear into oblivion. And those employees research props like you're wearing now, but that group runs the software that makes everything happen."

"Alright, already! I got it," Bob shouted.

"Do you? Just to add one more person to the list. If I didn't design this thing, you would still be in the Army crawling through swamps trying to take out some third world leader."

The shorter scientist pointed up into Bob's face, "So the next time you think you are in this by yourself, get rid of all of the self-absorption and look around for a second. Many others are toiling behind the scenes to give you the ability to travel through the centuries and take all the glory."

"I understand," Bob murmured, not exactly out of humility, but exhaustion.

"I hope so. Now, are you ready to go?"

"Yeah, I guess so. I still don't know why I am doing this."

Touching his hand on a pad outside of the sphere, the canopy of the large vehicle raised. "Get in. You'll have a few seconds to look the file over while we're powering up."

He climbed the steps on the outside of the vehicle and worked his way over the edge where he found his position and started to strap in.

The Doctor looked at his watch, "You will leave in the next few minutes. We are scheduled for 4:53 eastern time, and has been the case, you will arrive back in our time two minutes later. That is, after you have fulfilled your mission.

"You know that you push this area here on the dash, and it will return you to this time. You have all of the time in the world while you are there to get your mission fulfilled, but you will be returning to this day and time. Two minutes after you leave."

"I hate that. I may go through six hours, but it has only been two minutes for you."

"That is one of the problems with time travel," the project designer said with a smile.

"On our end, this vehicle is in a cyclic loop. The machine is acting like a… a yoyo. Think of it this way, once it leaves, it goes to its destination and then comes immediately back."

"How can that be, I may have been gone for years?" the man asked.

"There are books filled with equations to explain why, but think of that yoyo again. While it is going down it is spinning. That spinning is covering a lot of ground even though the yoyo may only move 10 or 12 inches. It is in those rotations that you have all of the time in the universe.

We could talk about this all day but you have a mission to fulfill. Get your work done and bring the machine back to me unharmed."

"Ai, Ai, Captain," he responded with a salute.

Placing his hand over the side panel once again, the canopy started to lower.

"Everyone out of the staging area!" the leader yelled. "One minute to jump!"

The room quickly started to empty as each technician found their designated spot.

Bob looked over the folder once again and found his connection. Finally understanding why he was to intervene, he sat back and pressed his head to the back of the seat. "Here we go again," he ground out through gritted teeth.

The room went dark except for the blinking lights on the walls which became increasingly active. A charge ran through his body, and the smell of ozone brought the mental preparedness he had been trained with. Nine... eight. . .seven. . .just a few seconds before he leaped.

With a bluish glow, the room lit up again, not because of the many lights recessed into the walls but because of the shear electrical energy the vehicle was absorbing. The machine grunted to life with a vibration that coursed through the cockpit. Pain spiraled into his gut until Bob thought he could not take the assault on his senses another second.

Instantaneously, the machine disappeared and the room returned to normal.

16 — JANUARY 15, 1604

The sphere bumped around for close to 20 seconds before it came to rest. Bob sat back, tired and sore from being shaken again and again for what his reality knew to be several days. He spent a solid minute attempting to regain his focus prior to leaving the cramped sanctuary. The new world outside would not embrace his next mission, that was for sure.

"I don't remember this thing being that violent last time." The seat creaked a bit as he sat forward to stretch his shoulders. Following a few deep breaths and some quiet meditation, the Ranger drew on his U.S. Army training for the edge he needed now. Something akin to a soldier heading off to war.

Bob was well aware that each mission was its own personal combat. Because of the unique infiltration he was required to undertake, the man had to use all of his training and much of his intuition to ensure the objectives were met. His Commander-in-Chief had chosen him to make the specific timeline changes on behalf of his country, and he was not going to let the greatest nation on the face of the earth down.

The canopy broke its pressurized seal and began to rise, an audible hiss and steam filling the chamber. Now a lone musketeer, Bob fanned his hands in an attempt to dissipate the gas and peered out at the world before him.

A gust of cold air shocked him into his new reality. His natural body heat, combined with the heavy layers of fabric he had been wearing in the cockpit had made his trip a smothering sauna-like experience. The vehicle had oxygen monitoring, but nothing controlling the temperature. Since the technicians had not been too quick in sending the machine off, the cockpit had produced enough heat to cause a lesser man to pass out. Something Bob had come close to experiencing a time or two. Even though the cold was expected, the first assault of it nearly made him shriek.

"A clear night sky, light wind and snow on the ground. The temperature must be in the 20's. It's certainly below freezing." He noted that the sweat drops on his face had begun to freeze.

Looking around, he noticed what appeared to be a frozen lake encircled with stones and lines of flower beds well-dusted with snow. There were rows of eight foot hedges and off to his left, a massive complex of buildings all glowing with chandeliers filled with candles.

"A quarter of a mile to the main building," he said sizing up his situation. "It looks like we're resting in a summer garden." He thought a moment. "A nice place to hide something in winter. No one's going to be out here tonight." He pulled himself from the craft and eased himself over the side. The moment his feet hit the ground they swished out from under him, and he came down hard on his backside.

Melting snow revealed a circle approximately 50 feet in diameter formed by the heat of the sphere. As it cooled, it was beginning to refreeze into a circular ice rink of sorts.

The Ranger slipped several more times and cursed under his breath before he regained his footing and eased out of the circle.

As he righted himself, the world around him came into focus. There were only two ways out from where he stood between the hedge rows, with neither exit closer to the main building than the other. Bob looked at the sheet detailing the complex and location of the mark. Content his questions were answered; he picked up his bag of equipment and headed for the closest exit.

After a few minutes and about 25 turns later, he realized his mistake. The thought struck his exhausted mind like a blow. "I'm in a maze. And I should have expected this."

The hedge maze had originally been intended for entertainment. Something Bob could not bring himself to comprehend tonight. He reversed his course and walked the length of the garden toward the other exit. Which also opened to a maze. A secondary one. After several expletives, he headed back to the sphere to see if there was a quick solution for the predicament he was in.

Mazes such as the one had been widely used for those temporarily imprisoned during summer games. Rulers of the day would start each player at different entrances and see who made it to the reception area first; often while the monarchs watched from the palace above. The winner might get some type of jewelry or just be titled "King of Festivities." In times past it had been a way for the common man to see one of his own invited to a king's reception. Off-times the winner would normally be allowed to wear strands of jewelry and be given a king's feast for a day.

"I don't have time for fun and games," he swore as he leafed through the folder full of papers lying on the passenger's seat of the sphere. "Where is it? There has to be something with the solution to this maze."

As he threw paper after paper on the floor of the sphere, he finally found one with an aerial photo of the grounds. Placing his finger on the picture representing the building in front of him, he located his present spot. Turning his body toward the pond and orienting the picture, he quickly worked his way out of the solution. Both exits seemed to have routes that were equally long, however the way to his left would get him to the main road more quickly; the way in which he would get into the castle.

"If this maze has changed over the last several hundred years, I'll kill whoever chose this spot for me when I get back. I swear it," he fumed as he started once again toward the first opening; slipping several times before he got there.

Twenty minutes later after dredging through now a foot of deep snow, and often taking wrong turns and finding subtle changes in the maze, he was freed from the labyrinth and made his way to the only road into the palace. "I swore they said they were going to keep me from dredging through snow," he cursed.

Staying behind trees to ensure he was not detected, the Army Ranger looked over the massive buildings for a possible way into the complex. Knowing his mark would be located within the center structure, he focused his attentions there.

The main entry to Hampton Court was a large iron gate that would be raised to allow carriages through. The walls appeared to be over ten feet thick, and there were four guards protecting the entrance. As he squinted along the length of the building there were four more sentries standing erect in front. Because his present location was at an angle to the palace, he could see two more guards along the side of the building, and he guessed that the other end had a matching pair.

Moving his eyes up the corner he saw two archers along the top. Obviously, they would be the most accurate marksmen of the King and could be deadly over several hundred feet. Scanning the woods he found himself in, he guessed there to be several soldiers roaming the grounds as an offensive form of defense. He could not be sure that his instincts were correct, but he would have people combing the woods if he were in charge of security.

Except for the archers on top of the building, all of the soldiers carried curved swords several feet in length. Even a time traveler with 21st century weapons could not compete with so many obstacles. And those were only the ones he could see.

There would be no storming the castle. He would have to find a more subtle way in.

But, as he could not immediately see another entrance into the fortress, the traveler had another problem. His mission was to remove John Rainolds without killing him. The idea was that his death would elevate him to a martyr and provoke an even greater following of his work. But if he were disgraced somehow, those working with him would do all possible to stay away from any ideas he was championing.

With the soldier's hands and feet starting to ache from the cold, his attentions were drawn to sounds coming from down the long tree-lined road leading to the castle gate.

"What's this?" he whispered as he hid behind a bush along the dark route.

The sound became clearer, and Bob was able to see two orange-colored lights coming his way.

"A carriage." Straining to see up the road, the traveler made out two horses and a single driver. "A closed carriage," he mumbled.

As the transportation came into view, the coat of arms on the side announced it as one of the King's coaches likely carrying a guest who required no security coming for the festivities on the following day.

"Lucky break." He smiled a moment before raising himself to run forward and crouch in the snow-covered culvert next to the main road. Bob remained motionless until the carriage rolled past then pulled himself up onto the weapons compartment kept on the back. Looking through the shutter-like window covering, he found a single man in the compartment. The man's head rested inches in front of the blinds, and the Ranger knew that he only had a few seconds to react before they would be at the castle.

With a quick action, he lifted the shutter, and as the man turned toward the sudden rush of cold air, Bob reached in and twisted the man's neck, causing him to fall lifeless to the floor. Then he climbed up over the top of the gold and black carriage and went for the driver.

But the alert driver had seen his assailant coming and stopped the horses in their trot. Trying to get the long sword out of its scabbard proved impossible before Bob was on him.

With one large jump, the Ranger dragged the man off the carriage and they fell to the ground. With the traveler holding onto him, the men rolled several times before the driver's body came to rest on a large rock on the side of the road. A dark flow came from his head, and his eyes stared off into the night. Bob drug the small man to the carriage and threw him in the back. After a quick change of clothes into the drivers tight uniform, he took the reins of the carriage and turned it around. He now knew how he would fulfill his mission.

After dumping the bodies in a ravine alongside the road and making a trip into a busy district of London, Bob returned the carriage back to the same spot close to two hours later. Knowing nothing about the driver he replaced, he lifting his scarf over his face and placed his hand under his coat to gain a solid grip on the gun under his belt. The silencer could drop the gate guard without much attention, but would only gain him a few seconds. He had to be wise in his approach. The horses continued forward.

When the carriage was within a hundred feet of the iron gate, the guards came to life. As Bob feigned a cough to ensure he would not have to speak, the men started to raise the entrance. Evidently, the coat of arms on the side of the vehicle was all that was necessary to gain admittance to the castle. If the Ranger were in charge of security he would have never let anyone in without a thorough screening. He got lucky. Again.

Moving under the large arch, the driver found himself inside a great courtyard. There were many entry points, but he needed only one; that to his left. Steering the horses toward it, he brought the carriage gently to a stop in front of the large double doors.

Bob looked to the stars and realized it was after eleven o'clock. Because of this, most of the castle was quiet. He found no guards inside the courtyard and so stepped down from the driver's seat and opened the side carriage door.

Two pairs of eyes blinked at him. "Remain here. I shall escort you up in just a few minutes. Remain quiet." A quiet giggle slipped from the cabin before he closed the door and walked up the steps to the guest residence.

History dictated that Dr. John Rainolds' room while at the castle was on the first level. As he walked down the hallway filled with coats of arms, and covered with rich wood grains, he hoped his instincts were right.

Because of the lack of electric light, people during these centuries generally were up when the sun was up and went to bed when it went down. During the winter months, people would stay up with candlelight several hours later; however, he assumed his mark should have been asleep for over an hour by now.

Arriving at the large entryway of this pivotal man in history, he placed his ear to the wood. The soldier heard nothing. Seeing no illumination below the door, he believed Rainolds to be asleep. He pulled a tool from under his belt and worked the ancient lock. It clicked, revealing he had access to the dark space. Looking up and down the hallway, he then quietly slid behind the door.

The room opened into a mini-suite. Presently standing in the receiving room, there were two other doors that would lead to the bedroom. Both were carved ornately and gilded. Walking toward one entrance, he slowly opened it and found a closet containing the Doctor's outer garments. Bob looked over his shoulder to the other door and quickly breached the gap. Placing his ear to the ornately decorated piece of wood, he heard snoring on the other side.

Pulling a Ziploc bag from his pants containing white powder, he opened it. Knowing that he could not use very much or he would kill the man, he stuck his second and third finger in the bag covering them with powder and walked into the chamber.

John Rainolds was sound asleep, so his work was very quick. Silently moving toward the four poster bed covered in curtains, he placed his fingers containing the powder over the man's mouth and his nose. He wiped the powder liberally over both openings.

The 52-year-old man quickly awakened but by the time he sat up in bed, the substance which had entered his nasal passages and had been absorbed through his mouth was beginning to take effect.

"Who art thou?" the gray haired man asked with a slight slur in his speech.

Sitting in a gold leafed high back chair, "My friend, consider me your entertainment director."

The man tried to move but found difficulty controlling his body. He rolled to the side of his bed and attempted to grab his night coat. "What evil hast thou beset upon me? My movements are…challenging."

"Don't worry, you'll be feeling fine in the morning."

Not being able to stand, he sat back on the bed. "Why are thou here? How have I offended thee?"

"My friend, I'd rather not be here. Believe it or not, I have come a very long way to see you."

The man tried to focus but was having difficulty keeping his eyes on the Ranger. "Why…, why, would…"

"I know what you want to ask. Why would I be in England to see you? Well, believe it or not, you are going to affect a very powerful country some 400 years from now."

"How?" his speech labored.

"Tomorrow morning when you meet with King James, you will offer him a simple idea, one that he hadn't thought of until you mentioned it, and one that we can't have you say."

"Wha...?" he stopped trying to speak.

"Evidently, you suggest that the King authorize a new version of the Bible. We will call it the King James Version. I think you in England will call it the Authorized Version. Just semantics," he stood and paused to look at himself in a long mirror.

"Anyway, we can't have one version of the Bible gaining prominence. There are a handful of versions right now: Tyndale, Wycliffe are just a couple. The one version *you* inspire," he said walking to look over the man lying on his back, "Helps to remove dissension between the different religious sects. And that's something we can't have. We need the fighting between the groups because that keeps the Christian denominations weak and segmented. If they're grumbling with each other, they can't be focused on doing 'God's work,'" he said with air quotes.

"We need Christianity impotent and disjointed. In essence, in the future, we will bring them together the way that *we* want, but we can't have you helping us now." He removed the night coat Dr. John Rainolds had half managed to put on and lifted the man's legs back up on the bed.

"I could have easily killed you, but I have a far more pleasant fate waiting for you. Or at least it would be for me. I'm not so sure you'll appreciate the gift I'm giving you." Standing tall, "Several hours ago, I took a ride out to the Ratcliffe Highway." The man's eyes grew wide. "Yeah, I thought you would know what that means. For enough money, a man can find all kinds of companionship down by the waterfront. Anyway, I've brought you a couple of the most beautiful Venetians a man could want. I could have fetched a few Flemish; they say they are experts in their field. But then, the Venetians, they say, are for the aristocracy. You should be proud that I hold you in such high regard. So, enjoy the night," he remarked taking one last look in the mirror, "Compliments of the U.S. government."

Bob left the room and found the waiting coach. He opened the door, "Ladies, here is enough money for a month," he said handing them a bag of gold pieces. The women grew more excited in their apparel not fit for the locale they found themselves in. "Don't feel like you need to rush, and give the good man a night he won't forget." He smiled and led the women to the room.

Several minutes later, Bob got back up on the carriage and headed for the main gate exit. Before heading through the cavernous opening, he stopped the stage next to one of the main guardsmen.

"Sir, I believe that something nefarious is occurring in Dr. Rainolds' room. There was much noise resonating from the hall." The soldier ran toward the room and Bob whipped the horses causing them to run from the castle.

Several minutes later, the Ranger was back in the sphere, having accomplished his mission. Dr. John Rainolds, the church leader who had advised Queen Elizabeth, and who suggested King James authorize a new version of the Bible was discovered with two prostitutes in the King's residence. He was stripped of his religious titles, lost all credibility, and died a year later a pauper in the streets.

The night lit up with a flash of light, and the sphere was gone.

17 — MONDAY EVENING

The distance – as the crow flies – from the Russell Senate building to Reagan National Airport spanned a few miles across the Potomac River Bridge, but it took Hudson 45 minutes to accomplish. With the downtown construction, school buses filled with children on field trips, and the masses of people trying to leave the city after a long day at work, the agent was late to meet the professor at the airport.

Rounding the corner to the arrivals gate, Hudson found his friend standing next to a cement column talking to a man with a briefcase. Todd shook the man's hand and walked over to the car as Hudson got out to greet him.

"Hello, friend, it's been too long." Hudson clasped the man in a quick hug.

"I'm just sorry we have to get together under these circumstances."

"Yeah." Hudson lowered his head a moment. "Do you have any bags?"

"Nope, there wasn't enough time. I'll buy what I need."

Hudson slapped him on the shoulder. "I'll take care of you. I'm bound to have something you can wear."

"I'm sure it'll all work out. But you do know we have totally different styles, right?" The professor slowly looked over the much taller agent and laughed as they left in the minivan out of the airport exit.

"How are you, Hudson?"

"I'll make it."

"What've you found out?" Todd activated the onboard computer.

"As I told you, my wife no longer exists. I found Sara, but she's still using her maiden name."

"I'm so sorry Hudson," He watched the larger man's forearm muscles ripple as he squeezed the steering wheel.

"She's the advisor to Senator Dupree. Evidently, she's very influential throughout Washington. She always did love politics." Tears pooled in his eyes and spilled as he blinked. "She's probably happier without me. Now she can achieve all of the goals that she couldn't while we were married."

"Don't go there. You two were meant to be together and you will be again."

Hudson wiped his face.

"Todd, my kids are gone. It's only been a few hours since I left this morning, and I already miss them. They are my true… my true… joy." Sobs wracked his frame even as he focused on the road ahead.

"God's not going to let this go unchecked," the professor said trying to encourage his friend.

"How do you know? God has allowed this to happen. He could have easily stopped in before it began."

"You're right," Todd replied as Hudson looked over at him in confusion. "You're right." The professor continued scanning through screens on the computer.

"What do you mean, I'm right? You're the seminary professor. Tell me why God would allow this to happen," The steering wheel rattled when he punched it.

"I can't answer that," Todd responded calmly. "God does His own thing. What I do know is that all things work together for our good, and that He'll be glorified through this. Do you think God wanted this to happen? I mean do you think this is His plan for you, this country? Or even the world?"

"I wouldn't think so."

"Well, then we have to believe that He's going to make it right."

"That sounds a little simplistic," he shot back. "You haven't lost anyone."

Todd felt Hudson's pain radiating from him in waves, and his compassion for the man grew. *God, give me the words.* "No, Hudson, for some reason my wife is still here. I don't know why she was unaffected. And we don't know how these changes are happening, really. The next change might affect my family too."

"I'm sorry."

"You don't need to apologize. I know you're hurting, but understand, it's going to be alright."

"I hope so," Hudson's answer was weak.

"Hey man, let's pray that God works this out."

Todd closed his eyes as Hudson continued to drive, and he prayed for the next several minutes asking God to give them strength and to direct their paths. He asked that the Lord restore the timeline and somehow His kingdom be blessed through the efforts.

"And Lord, restore our faith. Give us an unshakeable faith so that we can understand the meaning of Hebrews 11:1. That faith is the substance of things hoped for, the evidence of things not seen. Lord, we can't see the end, but we hope for total restoration. We are believing in Your name that it will happen. And when it does, we ask that You get the glory. Mighty God, we pray this in Your name, Amen."

Both men looked up, and Todd smiled at his friend as an explosion that could not be imagined reverberated through the vehicle. Pain coursed through their bodies and the crash of thunder they heard seemed to tear through their ear drums.

Todd hugged the dash as Hudson tried to resist the urge to hold his head through the pain. The car headed at top speed toward the Potomac River crossing. *A crash at this speed could kill us and send this vehicle into the rushing water below,* Hudson thought clearly through the pain.

Before they could hit the moving sidebar, the professor put his hand on the wheel to help steady them. During the phase shift, they passed through other vehicles, saw buildings disappear and others reappear in their place and even noticed potholes take their spots on smooth concrete.

Grunting as if they were in jet fighters exceeding 4 G's, Hudson yelled at his friend over the tremendous noise in his head, "When's it going to stop?" Hudson tried to pull the car to the side of the road.

"I don't know!" His partner yelled back. "This is longer and stronger than the others." A semi disappeared in front of them. "Watch out!" The professor yelled as a dump truck seemed to appear within the space of the engine compartment."

Slamming on the breaks and pulling the vehicle to the side, their car drove through a camper appearing on the side of the road.

Todd looked back, "Wow!"

Hudson watched the large machine take shape through his rear view mirror as the minivan came to an abrupt halt in the gravel on the side of the road. Material variations took place everywhere simultaneously. Vehicles appeared and disappeared at random. Trees vanished and new roads appeared through the congested thoroughfare.

Looking across the river inside the beltway, buildings began to change – their variations of bright colors fading to a dull cream. The white granite of the Washington D.C. mall now covered most of the city. No longer kept sacred for the Capital building, White House, and Monuments, the whole city gleamed with the white façade.

"What happened?" Todd pointed toward the hub of the metropolis.

"It looks like government buildings now take up the whole area. Maybe the entire city. There are more national buildings," Hudson replied getting his focus back.

"Buddy, that was the worst surge yet. It took over a minute to complete."

"Todd, the incursions someone is making are affecting the timeline much more completely. Whatever they're doing is disturbing or changing more of the nation, if not the world, each time they jump."

"What do you think they've done? Get us a place to park out of the way so we can research where they might be heading."

Hudson pulled the vehicle back into traffic and found a convenience store parking lot where they could sit and think.

With a shaky hand due to the onslaught on his senses, Todd started working the minivan's computer.

"It looks to me that the first real jump had to be with the letter to the Danbury Baptists. I was right there when it happened, and saw my notes disappear." Following several searches, "See, there's nothing there about it."

"You called me during the second boom," Hudson added unbuckling his seatbelt, opening his door and standing alongside the automobile.

"Yeah, yeah, I remember. I'd guess someone goofed with the Constitution. That should be the First Amendment." Todd's hands flew across the computer.

"What did you find?" Hudson questioned walking around the car looking for damage.

"It's just as I thought. There isn't anything about Congress not making laws to respect an establishment of religion. It looks like whoever's doing this wants to change the religious practices of the American people." Opening his door, the professor looked over at Hudson as he stretched in the parking lot. "Why would someone want to affect religion?"

"A person's ideals are powerful," he mumbled rising from a deep knee bend. "A true follower of Christ would never change their principles, they'd rather die. But if they never hear about Jesus and His offer of salvation?"

"You're saying, the best way to enslave a people is to remove their God," he asked incredulously.

Hudson finished, "And maybe offer them a new one. What else have you found?"

"Let me just look up churches in the D.C. area. If someone's messing with religion, the churches will show it." He fumbled through several screens when he finally glanced up. Hudson was standing alongside the automobile.

"All I can find are National Church this and National Assembly that. There are plenty of churches, but there aren't any denominations." Looking over a few more screens he muttered as he read. "Martin Luther helped to bring about the Reformation to get us away from the possible evils of one dominant teaching coming from the church. There should be dozens of denominations." After a few more seconds he looked up. "And I can't find Martin Luther anywhere."

Hudson walked around and sat back in the driver's seat, "So, essentially, they've removed him to ensure one major church?" He thought about that a moment. "Well that should mean there's only the Catholic Church or a church like it. Is this National Church, the Catholic Church?"

Todd looked over the tenants listed on the first church he could find with the name national. "Nothing here is Catholic. No Christ, Sacraments, or rites. This seems more like a philosophical bag of mish-mash. It speaks of self-realization classes, how-to workshops on being great citizens…"

"What did happen to the universal church?" Hudson asked.

Todd continued to type looking through historical information. "It seems that they're still alive in small pockets around the world, yet have no real influence in America." His eyes scanned screen after screen. "Evidently the church followed normal history, and in 1964 allowed for the vernacular to be used."

Hudson looked confused.

"They gave the opportunity to hear the Mass in the people's common tongue and not Latin." Hitting several other tabs, "It looks like there was no consensus on what Bible to use. Parish fought parish, cathedral fought cathedral. Huh."

"What is it, Todd?"

"Well, where's the King James? The Catholics would have created a Bible in contrast to the King James Version and its required use in the Anglican Church. That's what they should have used and referenced in Mass. Without the King James there would be no impetus to create their own common language version. I'm looking that up."

Sitting in his chair and gazing out the window, Hudson's heart sank thinking about his family.

"No, there's no King James version. Without that unifying force of one main Bible, many churches will rise up with their own interpretations. The King James Version made the Catholic Church create their own version thus giving one Bible to read from. Other traditional churches would have accepted the King James as their choice for Bible. Each major group had their own focus all from the creation of the one translation.

Everyone reading from the same version will cut down on differences in subtle theology. Evidently, they didn't have that, and therefore fought among themselves. This splintered the church and made them all run in their own directions. Rome couldn't keep everything together and, in a country like America, image is everything. Their image became one of in-fighting. The church became weak and insignificant and people left it."

Hudson played with his keys, "So they've taken God from the people and offered them a highly organized government-led belief system with no fighting."

The professor added, "I'd imagine they offer tax incentives for followers and probably make it a requirement their bosses give them time off for the self-help of the national religion." Looking out the window, "Hudson, without Christ there is no hope. Who would want to do this?"

"Todd, we know the only person with the ability to make this happen is the President. It was him who sent the Senator back to Israel during Christ's birth and probably sent Clark back before Christ's crucifixion. Who knows, he probably put the hit out on Dr. Keith."

Glancing back toward Hudson, "Why would he want to do this?"

"He's a megalomaniac. He wants to control the world. It isn't enough that he's President of the greatest nation on earth; he has to rule the people completely. From the beginning, the sphere project has been about taking over the world. I thought it was about righting potential wrongs, but it was all about power."

Interrupting, "But you told me the sphere wasn't involved."

"No it wasn't, at least not the one I manage. However, I think there's another one, and it's more powerful."

"What do you mean? How can it be more powerful?" Todd asked incredulously.

"The sphere I use has to have a recharge time or there is a potential for it exploding. If it jumps too many times within a 24 hour period, it will drain the backup cells causing the potential for a containment breach. The fusion reaction within the cells is controlled by the generators and has a backup, the power cells. Without a power source, the fusion reaction will become uncontrollable and thus takeout miles of real estate.

"This other sphere must be a better design. It has jumped at least four times within the last 24 hours."

"You still haven't told me how you know there is another sphere."

Bringing out maps, Hudson opened one up. "Here is where I think the other sphere is."

Tracing his finger over the map and showing the movement of the land.

"But that looks like downtown Washington!"

"To be more precise, I'd say it's right under the Washington Monument."

"There's no irony lost on that choice. The current President trying to become greater than our first."

"It's also very close to the building that houses the President. I'd bet he has an underground connection between the highly visible edifices. Maybe some kind of rail system."

"Hudson, this isn't fighting with Roman soldiers, or first century weapons. This is beyond us."

"It may be beyond us," Hudson said turning forward in his seat, "But it isn't beyond God. Let's go downtown."

The men closed their doors and left the lot.

18 — MONDAY EVENING

"Are you sure this isn't too much make-up?" The President looked into a hand mirror.

"It's perfect, Your Excellency," Philippe responded with a smile. "We are adding a little color to your face to give you that healthy sun-glowed look." The delicate sponge he held dabbed at a tiny spot of imperfection.

"It seems too dark," the leader grunted.

"The bright camera lights will wash you out, just trust me."

"Philippe, what do you think of his new gown?" Remi asked holding it high.

"Oh, I am so moved." Hands clasped to his heart dramatically. "I've never seen you do better work."

"Well, I didn't have much time, but I have been thinking about this for a very long time. I am so blessed that our religious leader would ask me."

President Langley smiled. "Remi, it is perfect. It looks strong, yet religious. It should exude power, but still appear comforting. I love the way you worked the national seal subtly into the cloth. Nice touch."

Remi bowed keeping the garment from hitting the ground.

Philippe jumped in after fixing one last blotch on the leader's neck. "You are finished."

John Costall, the President's Chief of Staff opened the door to the private room and entered. "Sir, here it is. We have your speech completed. It's short and to the point – just like you asked. I hope you like it. We were given so little time to write it, we've no luxury for any edits or changes."

The President grabbed the tablet.

"And here is the other work. We're ready to send it out when you tell us," he finished handing the man another tablet.

Langley took a little over a minute tabbing through the contents of the handheld device, then looked at his Chief of Staff. "This better do what I want it to do." His eyes were cold with his intent.

"Y-yes sir, uh, Your Excellency. Understood. It's what you asked for." Costall bowed and then retreated.

The director quietly popped his head through the closing door, "Five minutes, Sir."

"Remi," the President smiled, "I need to get into this new apparel."

The young man smiled, handing the leader the first part of the ensemble. "You will shine like the stars in the sky."

Hudson pulled his cell phone from his pocket and dialed Senator Dupree's office. After several rings, it was answered.

"Senator Dupree's office, this is Michelle."

"Michelle, this is Hudson Blackwell…"

"Yes, agent, I remember. How can I help you?"

"I was wondering if Sara Blackw… Brennen was in?"

"No sir, she isn't. She never came back from lunch."

"Is that normal for her?" He knew Sara would never intentionally worry anyone.

"Well, Sir, it isn't. She always calls when she's changing her schedule. In fact, she missed several meetings this afternoon."

"Has someone tried to contact her?" His concern rose.

"Oh yes, I tried to get in touch with her several times, but she never answered. To be honest, I'm a little worried," Michelle's voice dropped.

"Okay, Michelle, can you have the Senator make a few inquiries? Have some of your security people check on her. Ping her phone or have people run by her house."

"I will talk with Senator Dupree, but I'm sure he'll get on this quickly. He's asked several times about her. Um, why are you so concerned, Sir?"

He stumbled through his thoughts to come up with an answer, "She's… supposed…to have brought me up on a bill coming up for a vote involving the project I'm working on. We're on hold until she gets in touch with me."

"Yes, well, okay," the woman innocently answered.

"Thanks Michelle, will you call me when you know something?" Hudson asked.

"I have your number and will contact you the moment I hear anything. Goodbye."

The line went dead and Hudson placed the phone back in his pocket.

"So what was that all about?" Todd questioned upon seeing Hudson's expression.

"Sara's disappeared."

"So she's alive after the last blast?" Todd added.

"Yes. She's still not married to me, but she hasn't disappeared from the city. She works for Senator Dupree."

"That sounds like her. She wouldn't work for someone who wasn't a good man." Todd knew his attempt to brighten the situation would fall on deaf ears.

"Dupree is a good man, but it looks like Sara has disappeared. No one has seen her all day."

"Do you think that's a coincidence or is there more to this?" Todd spoke with concern.

"At this point, nothing is coincidence. I'm not sure why anyone would involve her unless it was to slow me." Just talking it through focused Hudson's thoughts. "There are only a few people on earth that might know what's happening. Because we have been through this several times, we would know how to right it. By taking Sara, they might be trying to control me."

"Do we know how to make this right?" Todd asked. Watching all the newly-marbled buildings pass by as he was a little uncertain.

"We will have to find this second sphere, and neutralize it. Then we go back and stop them before they can start," he spoke with a finality in his voice.

"Where are we heading?" His concern for his quiet friend changed to worry.

"We're going to the Mall. I haven't been to the Washington Monument in a while."

Sara prayed for well over an hour after the being locked in by her captors. She couldn't get it out of her mind what the President had said.

"'*I don't think I can stop certain people's movements without you,*'" she mumbled to herself. "What could that mean? My parents are political nobodies. He couldn't be speaking of them." She paced the room.

Continuing to think out loud, she wondered "Why would Senator Dupree be affected by me?"

She knew the Senator would do anything for her, but what could she be involved with that the President would need leverage against her Senator. She was not part of any project big enough to involve the White House, just FDA projects, parks projects and the like. There was not anything that could involve the White House.

Sara went over to the fridge and pulled out bottled water, opening it, she began to talk to herself again.

"It's obvious the Senator's always at odds with the White House because of their differing political views, but they're amicable. They have an ongoing slow burn that's expected. There's no way it could be Dupree. Even the President knows, you don't threaten a Senator, because if you're found out, you will go to jail."

Walking over to a small recliner, she sat down pulling her legs underneath herself.

"What could be bigger than Dupree? If he doesn't want me because of the Senator then there must be something bigger he's using me to get to."

Still confused, Sara drank the water and fell asleep, not understanding her situation yet, but knowing her God would take care of her.

~

The President walked by many staff on his way to the White House Press Room – his long train trailing behind him. Hearing the quiet mumbles and "Ahs" of the workers made him hold back a grin. As they cleared his path and bowed before him, he appreciated the distance he had come in such a short few months. Although his address remained 1600 Pennsylvania Avenue, his platform had been elevated exponentially.

When he first began his Presidency, he wanted to do what many Presidents had done or tried to do; make the world a better place. He sought to help the poor, stop world hunger, bring countries together through diplomacy and common goals, but he soon realized how impossible that dream really was.

Knowing how many Presidents had been through the euphoria of helping the world and the disillusionment of understanding the lack of power to do so, he had resigned himself to his fate. He would have to bring the Congress and Senate together and hope they guided the country the way he wanted. Realistically, he had known that would never happen.

Langley was resigned to be a lame duck President. He realized that becoming President added substantial weight to his life's worth, yet he yearned for more. He wanted historians to speak of his name with dignity and admiration, not just refer to him as a footnote in history.

Resigning himself to his lot, the leader started working both sides to play the middle. It was slow going but eventually, he was able to get minor things accomplished. He did not cure world hunger, but he believed there were fewer starving children in America. He was not able to eradicate all disease, but he had helped several countries with small outbreaks of deadly virus.

Hayden Christopher Langley was not a bad President, just not a great one. He would never be remembered like Washington who sacrificed everything to build a fledgling nation. Of course he was no Jefferson, or Lincoln. He could not be a Roosevelt or a Kennedy because there was no war, and he obviously did not want to be murdered. The thought made the man shudder as he walked the hallway.

Because of the politics of the time, President Langley was destined to be one of many; Until the day Benjamin Keith came to his office.

"Sir, here are your notes, if you need them," an aide said as he walked beside. "The prompters are working fine, but it is nice to have a backup."

"Very good," the leader said as he held them with his free hand.

His thoughts faded back to turning down the Dr.'s request for a meeting initially. Only after several months of appeals had he relented ten minutes of his time.

In one short meeting, that physics genius brought him a hope, a future, and - more importantly - a legacy. Dr. Keith gave him the opportunity to do more than any single President had ever done. He could possibly change history and form a new future; one that would be better for America, and one that would be better for himself.

As he grew closer to the meeting room, more people began to congregate. Passing the aids in the hallway, Langley heard the adulations of his work thus far. Some would say, "Your Excellency," while others would say, "Your Grace." One man said, "You can change the world, thank you!" And the now-religious leader smiled not acknowledging his fans as he continued toward his destiny.

The first meeting with Dr. Benjamin Keith had been surreal to the world leader. Many people enter through the curved doors of the Oval Office with requests for aid, or assistance. Some even offer solutions to a present problem within the world, yet none had ever told the President they could remove all of the world's problems.

Even when Dr. Keith said it, the President has been suspicious. Phrases like that generally resulted in the visitor's removal from the Office. But Dr. Keith had quickly added one thing. *"I know how to manipulate time."*

"You know how to do what?" the President had sat on the couch in the center of the room with his tea as the man started to pace.

"I know how to manipulate time. I mean, I think I know how to manipulate time. I've spent my life working on the equations, and I believe with enough power, we can enter another time period, possibly with the potential to change events, or right wrongs."

The five foot ten inch man pulled on the slacks of his suit as he sat grabbing a file from his briefcase. "This is proof." He handed the paper to the President.

"Uh, Dr. Keith was it?"

"Yes, Benjamin Keith," he replied with excitement.

Pulling the page before his eyes he stated his thought bluntly. "I don't know what this means."

With excitement, the scientist sat next to the President, "Those are the equations that prove this is possible."

"So you have no evidence for this technology except some equations?" the President asked incredulously.

"Sir, you wouldn't have allowed me in your office unless you knew my credentials. You know I have a Ph.D. in physics from Oxford. I've worked with some of the world's most renowned physicists, scientists, and engineers."

The President nodded.

"You also know that I work for a military contractor, and we have produced some very, well, terrible weapons for your Presidency."

Standing and walking over to the Resolute desk, the President leaned against it and crossed his arms, "Dr. Keith, this is not a military presidency. We pay for your expertise so that we can keep peace."

Understanding he upset the world leader, the scientist stood and walked the room. "I appreciate that and would never insult you; I'm just trying to say that this government has used me quite extensively for defensive weapons, when your presidency could use a few offensive."

"Offensive?" the President asked after taking in his last few words.

"Yes sir. We don't have to wait for people to go against us."

Coming back to his senses he waved the paper around, "These are just equations, how do I know they work?"

"Well, Sir, I've sent very small things into the future."

The leader's mouth dropped.

"Yes Sir, as I said, our problem is power. We need a lot of it to make a 'jump,'" the physicist said with hand quotes. "At our facilities, we only have so much power that can be allocated at any one time without closing down the plant. So, I've had to work at night or on the weekends. I've had several successful jumps and have proven that bio-matter will not be destroyed through this process."

"So how much bio-matter did you send?"

"About a microgram." Putting his hand out he tried to slow the leader's thought process. "I understand you'll scoff at that amount, but we were able

to send it one minute into the future. It disappeared, and then reappeared one minute later, totally intact and unaffected by the 'ride' it went through."

"Let's say, this is possible," the President muttered reluctantly, "What do you need from me."

Stopping the pacing he looked the leader in the eyes, "As I've said, it's all about power, and if we had more, and I mean a lot more, we could do it right."

He listened intently and then walked around the large 19th century desk and sat in his chair, "So you need access to large amounts of energy?"

"Yes sir, we would need our own power plant or the ability to build our own fusion generators," the scientist replied walking toward the desk and standing on the great seal design in the carpet.

"That's all you need?"

"Well, sir, I'd need a place to work, a hand-picked staff, top level clearance, and all of this would need to be kept secret."

"Secret! Why would it need to be secret?" he asked putting down a cup he pulled from the desk.

The scientist started to pace again, "What if the military were in charge of this work, which branch would get it, and would they turn it into a weapon of some sort? Their goals are much different than mine.

What if this project were placed under the EPA, would we ever build anything because of the regulations involved? I can't have OSHA involved in this. We are braving a new world. New worlds are never made with health and safety regulations.

I can't have this audited by the IRS or any of the accounting offices in Washington because this is going to require a lot of money. I mean, it will take many zeros placed after the numbers to get close to the price of this project.

I don't want the Congress involved in this because they'll take all of my time reporting to them on my progress. Or even worse, they'll try to shut it down depending upon who's in power.

Sir, I'm trying to be as open and honest as I can with you. We would need only a few people in-the-know on this project. I believe you and I are like-minded. I don't want to use this as a weapon, just as a safeguard in case someone does something to hurt our country."

The scientist got more animated as the President watched quietly, "What if a rogue nation deploys a weapon against us? With this technology, we can go back and remove the weapon before it's ever invented."

The President nodded.

"Let's say, a coup takes place in the world allowing a new Dictator to gain power, and we find out that he's killing many of his people. What would we

do now? We'd send over a few planes or involve some elite team to try to take him out. This could lead to war, or at the minimum would result in the loss of life from our brave military men or innocents in the area.

With my technology, we just stop the coup before it begins. We could also go back and help him have a better childhood, or keep him from getting beaten up in the school yard which turns him into a tyrant. I don't know. Whatever we do, it's safer and can result in a much better world that is guided by our morals and ethics. Essentially, everyone wins.

So, once again, this is too big to be controlled by a bureaucracy. I'd need your guidance and a few Senators, maybe a General or two. But we're in charge," he pointed to the President and himself, "They wouldn't be."

The President stood, "Do you think this is possible?"

"Yes Sir, I know it is," Dr. Keith smiled.

"Well then, let me mull this over and get back with you."

"Thank you for your time sir. If you allow this project, I will offer you a Presidency that will be remembered through the ages."

The President came back to his senses as he stopped before the door to the press briefing room. *That man did it. And today it begins,* he thought to himself.

"Are you ready, Sir?" his Chief of Staff asked.

"I've waited my whole life for this moment. Let's make history."

The door opened and he entered the room to great applause.

19 — MONDAY EVENING

The President walked into the Press Room to hear the mumbling of a hundred voices. Members of the journalistic community huddled in clusters, others hunched over laptops, while a few stood isolated – phoning their various networks and publications. At the splendorous entry presented before them, the room went suddenly quiet. All waited until the grand master of the room had settled into his position behind the podium before erupting into a standing ovation. All stood. All cheered, no matter the political bent of the journalists and producers.

Hayden Langley had been in this room numerous times to answer questions with this group, but had never received the applause he thought was due his position and political record. Today was his day.

Normally he carried off the role of his office in the signature blue suit and red tie. It had become customary before he was President and would have continued on after him. All that had now changed, and his fresh apparel better fit his position.

The alteration was simple – yet glorious. He still wore a white French cut shirt buttoned at the neck with black slacks. And black patent leather lace-ups still covered his feet. The new design centered on the jacket. It had been replaced with a gown-like design in the form of a Papal or a Doctoral robe.

The President believed his position required a look that everyone would know to be one of power so he had a floor length robe with train designed. Made of black satin, the robe bore the new emblem of the United States embossed subtly in the fabric. Dark red piping edged along the dangling sleeves and continued up and around the neck.

He now carried a staff in his right hand in addition to the gold medallion hanging about his neck. This gold rod stood over six feet in height, and had what appeared to be a world with an open book facing forward.

Walking slowly for effect, Hayden Christopher Langley arrived at the podium. As an assistant took his staff, the man gave several more seconds before he tried to quell the applause.

"Thank you, my friends. Thank you." He extended his palm toward the small crowd.

The adulation continued.

"Please everyone, be seated."

The cheers barely diminished.

"Thank you, please be seated. I must get on with this important information."

The Press Corp began to take their places and, after another ten to fifteen seconds, the room was quiet enough to hear a pin drop.

He breathed in majestically, "I have called this special conference to announce exciting new opportunities for the United States of America and the world."

He paused. "Because of the importance of what will be said tonight, I have accessed the White House Channel from every electronic device, ensuring that all within the borders of this country – and many around the world – have the ability to hear what will be said. So, all cell phones, tablets, vehicle displays, and televisions will now be coming on – even if turned off – to ensure all citizens know of the blessings ahead."

Hudson and Todd had made it to the Washington Monument and were attempting to find a parking place when the in-dash display stopped presenting engine data and revealed a screen with the words, "A Message from the Supreme Leader."

"What's happening? Who's the Supreme Leader?" The professor balked.

"I don't know," Hudson said as he turned a corner to find a parking lot with a few places empty.

The screen showed the President wearing his gaudy attire.

"Is that Langley?" Todd yelled. "What's he wearing… and when did he become the Supreme Leader?"

Both men pulled their phones from their pockets and looked at each other.

"I didn't know the government could access our private displays." Both Todd and Hudson's phones came to life showing the same images appearing in front of them.

"It looks like more has changed than just the timeline," the agent mumbled. "I saw him just this morning, and he didn't look like that."

The professor laughed, "He looks like he's a wannabe Pope."

"That may be exactly what he wants to be," Hudson replied matter-of-factly.

"This is going to be good," Todd said with a sigh.

Sara was awakened to the television coming to life. Having just napped for an hour or so she was groggy but knew if the machine was turning on, then it must be a message from the White House. Understanding the man who would be on the set was also the man who had abducted her; she regained her focus quickly and sat up in her chair.

The world leader straightened his papers, looked forward, and began his speech.

"My subjects, fellow countrymen, and friends. I want to thank you for the time you are offering me tonight. I will only commandeer your devices when I believe it extremely necessary, and tonight is one of those rare instances.

To begin, our relationship with the world is still strong. Our allies are completely dedicated to our causes and any skirmishes within creation are under my control and will not affect your safety or prosperity. You have my word on that." The man offered a determined face for the camera.

"What has brought me to you tonight is our future; yours, mine and our countries'. You see, I believe our Republic has been good, but it has the ability to be a shining light the world can see and emulate. We can have an unbreakable bond which will occur within this, the greatest country on the face of the earth.

Before this abundant nation began, a man named Columbus sailed the ocean blue, in 1492. He believed he had a vision from God and sought to discover a land mass in the name of God and King.

A group of Pilgrims sat foot on Plymouth Rock looking for religious freedom. They were Puritan by faith but desired to worship God in the way they chose. They selected not compulsory worship from the Monarchs of Europe but free expression of their beliefs.

Many within religious circles will say our first President George Washington was Christian by faith. They will quote John Adams with statements like, 'The general principles on which the fathers achieved independence were the general principles of Christianity. I will avow that I then believed, and now believe, that those general principles of

Christianity are as eternal and immutable as the existence and attributes of God.'" He looked to the camera for affect.

"These theologians will debate on whether Thomas Jefferson was just a deist and believed in Christ or if Benjamin Franklin had any real faith at all.

Other historians will look to men like Abraham Lincoln whom they will argue, freed the slaves because of his religious upbringing and background, and not some moral or ethical code instilled in him from birth.

Was Eisenhower a great military leader and President because of his natural talents and abilities? Or because of statements like this? 'Before all else, we seek, upon our common labor as a nation, the blessings of Almighty God.'

Did President Reagan bring down the Iron Curtain because of his trust in God? Or because he was a superb diplomat?"

The President became more focused and stern. "These same religious philosophers will look to some of the world's greatest scientists and thinkers and ignore and disrespect their ideas because they don't have any religious affiliation, or one that fits with their paradigm.

Darwin offered man the knowledge of his existence, yet he is attacked by those who believe in love and compassion.

Great men like Francis Crick who helped discover the DNA molecule, Sigmund Freud, the Father of Psychoanalysis, Alfred Nobel whose endowment supports scientific research, or Alfred Kinsey who permitted us to understand human sexuality, are all dragged through the mud or maligned by those who add nothing to society but hate – all the while saying they are doing it in the name of love."

His long fingers pointed at the camera, "Is a man evil, if he does not believe in 'God'? Should a man or woman who is bettering his world be limited by the labor of those who can turn a people against him?

Should a nationality be sanctioned or minimalized because they believe in a different god or multiple gods? Should other great nations be trivialized or considered backward because they believe in a dissimilar path to heaven?" he spoke gaining momentum.

"Are we to believe that our friends in the Middle East are malevolent because they do not worship like a segment of America? Should they not be given the same respect and honor as any other belief system with which man can put forth to offer peace and contentment?

I want to put an end to the hatred!" He pounded the room with his voice and the podium with his fist. "I want to put an end to discrimination no matter the form. And it seems the form is with respect to religion. As a country we are better than this, and I – as your Supreme Leader –expect more.

My highest responsibility is that of your safety and prosperity. I take this mandate very seriously," he calmed and paused for a few seconds. "It is my opinion that the greatest threat to man's safety is... religion.

This country is not 'Christian' and never has been. What has formed this nation and made it last for these hundreds of years is our compassion for humanity and our innate desire to reach for the stars.

Religion has caused more accumulated pain, suffering, and loss of life than any single personal desire. The agony of the crusades, the forfeiture of life through terrorism, the conquering of nations in the name of God has destroyed civilizations, and instigated countless millions of people to lose their lives and freedom.

Even today in a time of peace, there are small sects left that will isolate themselves away from the world or attack the reputations of those who do not believe as they do.

It is my belief the Pilgrims should have stayed and used their talents to grow their home countries rather than cowardly leave and take their beliefs to a continent not prepared to defend against it.

Men like Washington, Lincoln, and Reagan were great, not because of a belief system they held too tightly, but because of their willful determination and desire for justice.

This nation is no better or more exalted because of a so-called 'Christian' history than any other population on earth. In fact, we are isolated and hated by many other peoples because of our historical belief system.

We were attacked on 9/11, not because of our knowledge of math and science, but because of our hatred of those who were not Christian. We have received suicide bombers in populated areas, not because we produce food for the world, but because we have a religious air of superiority. To ensure our freedom and protection, we must let loose the antiquated – and embrace the future. Our future is in independence of thought.

The Renaissance brought Europe from the Dark Ages into a period of knowledge, art, and beauty. I see America going through the same kind of metamorphosis. If we can remove the shackles of ancient tradition and embrace and foster understanding and respect for all peoples we will be a better nation than we have ever been before."

His eyes found the camera. "It is time for me to take action. Former leaders have had the same opportunity afforded to me but refused to act and therefore nurtured bigotry. Today, I will start this nation anew," he spoke quietly.

"The National Church has been alive and well for years now, but has not had the attendance necessary to ensure its strength and capacity to impact lives. I will offer Americans benefits for attending church.

For every citizen showing membership at a National Church, the government will reduce your tax rate by five percent. If your presence is above 80 percent a year, that burden will be lowered by 10 percent.

All tithes given to these churches will be taken from your income so that once again, your tax responsibility is lowered." His big smile lit the screen. "There are financial benefits to church.

In addition to this, psychologists and psychiatrists will be part of the staff of these facilities. In the past, ministers would help you discuss your problems, but rarely had enough education to get you through them. They offered religious platitudes that left you with marginal hope and nothing else.

With trained personnel on staff, all of your personal snags can be worked through, and these professional's time will be paid for by the state. We will also have pharmacists dedicated to each church with a well-equipped dispensary to ensure you walk out with the medications you need. The cost for these will also come at a reduced cost for members-in-good-standing with the church.

Each facility will have people in place to work through any situation you might have ranging from where to find affordable housing, to help with your taxes. Church will become a one stop shop for any and every occasion life offers.

Finally, and what I personally believe to be most exciting, I will individually offer the words of wisdom each week. I will guide you through encouragements about patriotism, citizenship, life betterment issues and world news and information relevant to you today. It will be encouraging, informative, and will help jumpstart your week."

The pasted smile dropped and his eyebrows lowered. "With all of the good, there is always a little pain. To safeguard the growth of the National Church, all other denominations and religions will now be made…illegal.

I understand that for many of you, this will cause grief and concern, yet understand the new church will embrace the good of each of your creeds. Qualities like self-respect, sacrifice, and love will be promoted each week either in the sermon or within the lessons written for small groups. So, your distinction will be added to the collective to make… everyone better.

All seminaries, home churches, denominational buildings, individual churches, or land and property owned by religions organizations are now assets of the Federal Government. These resources will either be turned into new National Churches, used for the churches, or will be sold off with the proceeds going to support the ministry of the National Church. Nothing will be wasted, and everything will be utilized for your benefit.

For those within the work of the ministry, we have good news. You can join the National Church and use your talents to make it greater. We need your leadership to bring your present congregations into the new 'fold' of the church. For each of those willing to cross over, all of your present benefits will stay in place, including a ten percent increase in pay and retirement benefits.

It is clear you will need training to see what the new religion looks like, but that will be taken care of by the state, so do not worry about the cost. If you choose to become new ministers with us, your future is bright."

His smile dropped. "However, if you resist this change, your days ahead are not as bright. You may of course find a new vocation and become a good member of the National Church. But if you decide to go underground and begin cell churches teaching old and outdated philosophies, we will find you." He pointed at the camera.

"There is a $5000 reward from this point on for anyone informing the Government about those teaching bigotry and philosophy not sanctioned by the state. These citizen informers will be pillars for all of us to emulate and – even though it may be difficult – it is for the betterment of society and the world.

Also, anyone found teaching a viewpoint apart from that of the state whether minister or individual, your possessions will be taken, and you will be sent to a place where you can learn the blessings of collectivism." The President allowed his words to sink in.

"Let me be perfectly clear, if you teach about Jesus, or any figure normally associated with an historical religion, you will be held in contempt. Whether you are trying to indoctrinate a group of people or just telling your children stories at bedtime, this will be seen as a federal offense. It is essential to ensure everyone within this country comprehends the seriousness of teaching intolerance and hatred. These attitudes will not be stomached any longer.

Presently, the National Guard is being sent to churches throughout the country to guarantee full compliance. Please do not be concerned if you see military vehicles in residential neighborhoods. They are there for your safety.

Soldiers will be going to the houses of present ministers and pastors to help with their transition. It is my desire they quickly understand the benefits for them if they comply, yet there will be a select few who resist. They will be purged from the community. Once again, do not be fearful if this happens around you.

I also want to ask you to not help the remaining members of the family. Their slight suffering will aid in bringing the minister back into compliance with the new codes of the state. So do not give financial assistance in the form of money, food, or general aid.

In conclusion, this is a brave new world. For those who have been hurt by the 'church,' this is your time to know that it will not ever happen again. So get back into National fellowship this weekend. For some of you this is a sad day, but it does not have to stay that way. You will be blessed by the state and the support I offer you each week.

It is my prayer that this transition be quick, and that by the weekend, most of those in disagreement with the new policies be discovered and aided in their transformation. I am not naïve and comprehend that full compliance will take time. Your help in this matter will make this much quicker.

As your religious leader, I look forward to leading you in a way that will draw you closer to me. I have sacrificed my life for years in the work of public servanthood. I pray my sacrifice will ensure your future salvation.

Thank you for your time. I now bless the United States of America."

20 — MONDAY EVENING

The screen in the minivan returned to its normal function as Todd and Hudson sat in silence looking at the Washington Monument. The beautiful, white obelisk designed to remind Americans of their first and greatest President had grown dull and dark.

Never before, in all of the difficult places the men had found themselves had they felt so hopeless and without possibilities.

"Was that a joke?" Todd broke the quiet. "I mean, that was a skit by some comedy troop, or something, right?"

Hudson turned the vehicle off, "No, that was real."

"He can't do that. It isn't possible. Our Constitution has rules against it," the professor said with passion.

"He can, and he did!" the agent yelled back. "He's won."

"Hudson, don't say that. We can work this out."

"He's essentially rewritten everything in this country about religion. He's set himself up as a god. He has the power of the nation behind him and a vehicle that can be utilized to ensure nothing happens to him. He's won!" The agent ended with finality.

Opening the door to his vehicle, the professor stepped out and walked over to a bench next to the parking lot, leaving his friend in the drivers' seat. The sky was clear and, from his viewpoint, he could see each of the monuments as well as the Capitol building.

The work day had ended and only an occasional car moved down the main streets of the Mall. Todd zipped up his jacket and looked over at the White House.

The house where the President sat was lit up bright white. Even from the long distance, the observer could see people moving about and cars leaving the grounds. The press conference was over now, the reporters were moving on their way as if nothing at all threatened their way of life. Did they have any idea of the ramifications connected to the short speech they just sat through? The professor was tired and despondent.

"How can You let this happen, God?" He listened to the sound of the wind sweeping across the open area before speaking again. "How can you let this happen? Has this nation grown so far from You that You would allow it to be taken by the enemy?"

From across the way he heard the waterfalls of the World War II Memorial. It soothed his mind, but not his breaking heart. "Is there nothing left of this country that You would redeem? Are we so far gone that we can't be brought back?"

Looking past to the Lincoln Memorial, Todd saw Honest Abe carefully watching all the happenings of the most powerful city in the world. "What would you do? You liberated the slaves with the Emancipation Proclamation. You freed thousands and, less than 200 years later, our President is enslaving every citizen of this country." He looked over at the White House again.

Glancing over his shoulder, Todd saw the flags encircling the Washington Monument. The professor, who had taken students to this city many times, had a bad feeling in his stomach. "What do we do, God? Hudson and I have nothing with which to solve this, and he has all of the power.

Are You content that Your church has been made illegal? This country, one that was founded on people with a desire to worship You freely, is now making that very action a capital offense." He sat there quietly for a while.

"Your ministers are being rounded up unless they give up the calling You've given them. God, I've trained these people for years, many of them may be my students...or could have been my students in another time line," his voice dropped off.

"I don't know which way is up," Todd walked around the bench and leaned against its back as he faced the Capitol building.

Hudson came up in front of him – pointing up. "That way is up," Hudson joked as he walked around the seat and leaned on the back with him.

Todd laughed and shook his head, "I think you know what I mean. Hudson, how can he do this?"

"He's a megalomaniac," Hudson replied flatly. "The first time we went back to stop Clark, we both knew there was a larger power behind him. We thought it was the Senator."

"Well, it was," Todd answered.

"Sure, but there's always a bigger fish. We wanted Senator Hughes to be the mastermind, but the project was too big and too expensive for one man to have that much influence."

Todd nodded.

"When we went back the second time to stop Hughes, he made it extremely clear the President was the one who spurred him on to his acts of vengeance," Hudson finished.

"But why is he now moving? It's been six months since we came back. Why did he not just kick you out of the project and use the original sphere?" the professor added.

"When we came back the last time, we left the vehicle at my cabin. Because of all that was involved in moving it back to the manufacturing site, many people knew about a project that was supposed to be top-secret. The cat was out of the bag, one might say, so I guess he tried to make it look like nothing was going on while he built another one. He turned mine into some large generator while he worked elsewhere."

Todd put his hands in his pockets, "How could he build another one in six months? I mean, I thought this thing was extremely complicated. I never met Dr. Keith, but from what you've said, he was light years ahead of any other physicist around. How did this guy do it in six months without anyone dissecting the one you've got? Did they ever have research teams in there?"

Hudson answered, "No. Never."

"Didn't you tell me, you have all of his journals? Are his specs in there?"

"Yes, he didn't keep much on computer, it was all handwritten or in his head," he answered.

"If Dr. Keith was killed six months ago, how did that man," he pointed toward the White House, "make another one?" Todd started to pace.

"You know, I've been thinking about that. What concerns me is that this one seems to be better than the original. Our sphere can't jump that often, it needs time for a recharge. This one has moved several times in a day."

"How did he do it?"

"He'd need Dr. Keith," the agent answered.

Both men looked at each other.

Todd asked the question both were thinking, "Could Dr. Keith be alive?"

"That's impossible," thinking for a second, "Well, anyway, I don't know how. Dr. Keith was killed by Clark. I was on the scene and saw him dead," Hudson responded sadly. "He was shot through the head. He was dead." With regret, "There was no doubt about it."

"Can there be something about this timeline that could've changed that?"

"I'm not a particle physicist. I don't understand the timeline or how it works. I didn't think going through time was possible until we did it. So who knows?"

The professor started to regroup. "Let's back up for a second. Hudson, why are we the only ones who know about the other timelines? This entire world went through a change, yet we seem to be the only ones who see the deviations. Aaliyah also understands the alterations or differences in the U.S. before the booms, and she was only here a few months."

"I've read most of Ben's journals," Hudson walked toward the mound where the Washington Monument sat, "And there were a few writings on what might happen to the person who went through the jumps." Looking at Todd he thought aloud, "I mean a small amount, just a couple paragraphs. I don't know if he really knew. They were more like stray thoughts in his writings."

The professor listened intently.

"In his meanderings, he seemed to think that the person who goes in the sphere will remember only his timeline and not the new one. That person will be shielded from the memory wiping conundrum of a new timeline and might only know of what happened before they left."

Todd jumping in, "So essentially they'll be surprised at everything that happens because of their work. They change the timeline, and they don't get to enjoy its benefits."

"Yeah, something like that."

"We affected things in ancient Israel, and yet nothing really happened here," Todd interjected.

"Sure, Dr. Myers, but they were minor things."

Todd chuckled at the way Hudson used his surname. He tended to do that when he got in analytical mode.

"Sure, nothing really happened, because we didn't do anything that might affect the timeline. We removed Clark, but he was one man from our time. So we just stopped what he might have done in the future – which at that point was unwritten.

We brought back Aaliyah, but she was essentially a nobody with no future. I'm not wanting to hurt you, but you understand when we found her, she was essentially going to die. She was an outcast from society and had no way of supporting herself. So when you look at it, there was no real future to affect for her. We practically gave her a future." He put his hands on his friend's shoulder, "You do know how I love Aaliyah? And I'm so excited that you two are expecting a baby."

"Hudson, you don't have to be gentle with me. Aaliyah is my joy, and I understand her life just as much as you do. We've been through too much for you to get to me."

Hudson smiled.

"But what about Senator Hughes and Aaliyah's mother?"

"Same kind of thing. Hughes was from our time, and therefore hadn't had his future written, whereas Aaliyah's mother was a woman who wouldn't affect much. She was just a poor worker in Israel.

If we were to have changed Herod's life, or dealt with the disciples, I can guarantee America would have looked much different when we got back. But we didn't, so our work was minimal with reference to the timeline.

The guy who's busy now is changing huge things. These alterations are affecting everyone in America and spots within the world. That's why the booms."

"So, we know the other time – the original timeline – because we have been 'through time?'" the man asked.

"That's the best way to put it. At least if Dr. Keith's correct."

The men arrived at the great circle encompassing the largest of the Washington monuments. They found one of the granite benches and sat on it.

Todd looked up seeing the lights at the top of the obelisk. "Getting back to an earlier question, can Dr. Keith be alive? It looks like the designer was right, and we're unaffected because of our work in the past. Could they have gone back and taken him before he was shot?"

"I don't think so. At that point, we have a paradox. We know they didn't use my sphere to get him, so they would've had to go back in the new sphere, the one we think he created, to find him. They would have then used his expertise to create the sphere they find him with. Who knows, but I think it has to do with the changes to the timeline. Somehow in their jumps, he was never killed and never worked on the sphere project that I'm a part of. Or, at least we worked together, and at some point he was taken off the project to work on the other. I don't know."

"Why don't you look him up?" Todd asked sarcastically.

"Okay, let's see."

Hudson pulled out his cell phone and started touching on the glass screen.

"What are you doing?" the professor asked.

"I'm looking him up. I'm accessing my desk computer which allows me entrance into locked files because of my clearance." He pressed a few more buttons. "Someone like Dr. Keith is going to be unlisted and essentially protected from contact by the average person. I should be able to see if he's still is alive."

Several minutes passed in silence as the men watched a small screen, waiting for it to answer their question.

"Well, I looked up newspapers on the day he died, and there was nothing about his being killed. I then queried whether there was another sphere or project like it in the government database. Of course, nothing showed up. The only project I can find like ours, is ours, yet it has been lowered from top secret to just secret. I guess because it is a generator now and not a time vehicle.

There is a B. Keith who lives in D.C. that's on the government roles, and he seems to have the same type background, but the data is very cryptic. It looks like the info's been altered to make the person appear less important than he is."

"So is he alive or isn't he?" Todd was getting frustrated.

"Let me see if I can get his address."

Another minute passed before Hudson looked up, "He's alive and he lives exactly where he did." Hudson responded fairly surprised then pointed beyond the Capitol, "He lives a few streets from the Supreme Court."

"That's only about two miles from here, what are we waiting for?"

Todd headed back toward the car as Hudson looked over at the White House. Quietly he breathed a newly determined vow. "I'll have my wife and family back. And your end will be coming soon." Hudson followed Todd down.

—

Sara watched the television grow dark. She pulled a blanket over her shoulders as she backed farther into the overstuffed chair. "Oh, what are you doing?" the tired and scared woman asked of the world leader. "How can you hurt so many people?"

As tears started running down her cheeks, she closed her eyes and prayed. "Lord, please protect Your people. Lord, this nation needs help. We are so far gone."

She pulled the blanket up even higher as if that would protect her from the trouble the world was in.

"My God, why am I involved in this? I'm no threat to him. I just go to work and go home. I have no real life of my own, not that I wouldn't want one.

Oh God, it feels like I've missed out on so much. While my friends got married, I just dug deeper into my career. I'm so tired."

She cried. "I want the picket fence, the two kids, and the husband who loves me. I've enjoyed my life, but I feel like I've missed the real joys that You offer.

I've spent my life working on bills that don't matter, legislation that will be changed by the next leader, and seen the selfishness in politics. I'm just worn out," she repeated.

"God, if you get me out of here, I'll focus more on You. I love You, but I know I've put myself ahead of Your desire. God, will I get another chance?"

She wiped at the tears falling down her cheeks, "God, will this nation get another chance. I've watched this man over the last few years take more and more power, and no one has questioned him. Is there anyone to stand up to him? Anyone who will set this right? Are we destined to be a godless nation?

I know that I've not been the person I should have been, but I promise from this point on to follow You more closely. If you get me out of this, I will be what you've called me to be. I will never go to the National Church and will never worship at the altar of Langley."

Feeling more strength and conviction, "Lord, You are Yahweh God, and You alone are the true God. There is no one who can take Your place, and You will be seen high and lifted up."

Standing, she began pacing, "No matter what they may do to me, I will proclaim Your name. I will worship you as I've never done before, and I'll give my life – if you require it – so that You are seen as God on high. This man cannot beat You, and he will be shown as small and weak."

A smile came on the woman's face, "Lord, thank You for this trial, and I promise to make my life a blessing for you."

The woman prayed out loud for everyone to hear, quoting scripture as she went. With every word spoken, she became stronger and more prepared for what or who was coming. This small woman knew that God was not finished with her.

In truth, He was about to use her in a way she could never imagine.

In her present physical situation, Sara Brennen was a captive in an underground room. The walls were gray, the furniture spartan, and the exits locked. Yet her spirit soared beyond the cement walls she was detained in. She communed with the Lord, and the Holy Spirit empowered her. It was because of this that she was strengthened beyond her own capacity. Her frame was slight, but her God was immense, and therefore she was unstoppable.

Sara talked with her Maker for a while before she fell asleep in total peace.

21 — MONDAY LATE EVENING

The minivan turned onto A Street revealing a row of 19th century brick townhouses lit up by retrofitted antique gas lamps. Both sides of the street were immaculate with well-educated upwardly mobile people walking hand-in-hand or jogging with their dogs. Carved doors and trim painted in unique colors marked the neighborhood as having a well-coordinated HOA, while colonial stars or metal eagle accents spoke of an historical pride.

The vehicle slowed in front of one of the homes.

"Is this it?" Todd asked, looking at a beautiful two story red brick building with bright white trim.

"It's the home he had before, I mean in the other time frame. Before he was killed." His eyes scoured the brick street, "It looks somewhat like it did before, with subtle changes here and there. The agent pulled up behind a Mercedes S-Class and turned off the minivan.

Stepping out from the driver's seat, Hudson stopped and looked up at the beautiful home as he closed the car's door. The professor rounded the corner of the vehicle and glanced over at his friend, "What's going on? Are you alright?"

Hudson hesitated. "I haven't been here since he was killed. That was six months ago."

"I'm sorry," his friend added, "You need me to go up to the door?"

"Todd, this is where it all began. The last time I drove here, my life was simpler. Buddy, your life was simpler. When I last came here there was no time machine traveling the world, no retreats to the past, and no world leader wanting more power. How the world has changed in six months. It just doesn't seem fair."

"Who's to say life's fair? The Lord never said life was fair. He just said that He would help us get through the difficult times. You remember the verse in Joshua, 'Be strong and courageous. Don't be frightened or dismayed, for the Lord your God is with you wherever you go.'" He leaned against the car next to Hudson. "Yes, it's been tough and we've been beaten up and dragged through time, but we've been blessed to see what we've seen."

Hudson continued to look forward.

"We've seen our Savior dying for us. We were there after He was born. Do you remember the night the skies filled with angels? I tell you, if it all ended tonight, I'm with Paul when he said, 'I want to know Christ, and the power of his resurrection, and the participation in his sufferings, becoming like him in death.' We've been there and know what that looks like. We also know that if God has called us to this work, He will allow us to finish it."

"Yes, we have some memories, but I'll be glad when it's over," Hudson said flatly. "I don't want to be here, and I don't feel good about it."

"If that man's in there, he's the only one who can bring your wife back. Is she worth it?"

"Of course she is," Hudson replied looking at his friend.

"Then let's get everything back," Todd said, punching Hudson in the arm.

Hudson opened the door to the vehicle and pulled his semi-automatic from the glove box.

"What's going on?" Todd asked.

Tucking the weapon in his belt, "We need to be ready."

They walked up to the large white door and knocked.

The President left the Press Room handing his staff to an aid and throwing the robe to a makeup person. It took him several minutes to make it across the White House to the Oval Office.

Putting his feet up on the iconic desk Hayden Langley took out a Cuban cigar and lit it. Even though it was taboo to smoke in the famous room because of the history there and the priceless paintings on the wall, the leader felt he deserved it. Leaning back in the plush leather chair, he laughed.

"I did it," he chuckled loud and strong. "I am the most powerful man this country has ever known." Puffing on the cigar, he sat up straight again and pulled out a decanter filled with Scotch from a hidden compartment in the wall.

Grabbing a crystal glass, he poured an inch of the caramel-colored liquid into it. "Nothing can stop me." He took a drink.

"Ah, that's good." He sat back again in his chair. "This country is mine. Freedom now belongs to me alone, and nothing can get in my way."

Laughing again he thought about how easy it had been. Twenty-four hours earlier, he was just a President fighting to get things done. Now, he was the religious leader to over 400 million people – including all of the

Senators and Congressmen. He knew they would do anything he asked them to because he was their conduit to comfort, peace and, well, even heaven – not that he believed in such a place.

The thought came logically, and he sat up to think it through. "If I can control this country, can I not do the same with the world?"

Thinking to himself, he had brought together one country under one governmental religion. Yet, he knew the world still had many other beliefs that would eventually find their way back to his nation, weakening his position.

He reflected on the many skirmishes around the world caused by religious extremism. If he could stop those, many people would have more prosperous lives. Yet his musings did not stop there. He knew if he were their leader, he could enforce his belief system, ensuring peace on the planet. With one set of ethics and morality, the world would become a place of harmony allowing each man the ability to better himself how he sees fit.

There was a knock on the door.

"Yes," the President yelled with frustration at being interrupted in his thoughts.

John Costall, the President's Chief of Staff, put his head around the door. "Sir, I am sorry to interrupt you but I believe this is important."

Sitting up in his chair, he put his cigar in an ashtray and waved him in. "Yes, come."

The man walked in with a paper in his hand. "You asked me to alert you if anyone inquired into this person. Well, it looks like someone has."

"When did this happen?" looking at the paper.

"About an hour ago. He tried several channels to find Dr. Keith, and it appears he knows where he lives."

"Yes, where else would he live? That is, if he were truly alive."

"Yes, Sir." He allowed the leader to look over the paper. "Sir, I placed a trace on Hudson's car, and it is presently in front of Dr. Keith's house."

Speaking quietly to himself, "So, Hudson, you've finally put it together."

"What, Sir?" John asked.

"Nothing." Standing and walking toward the center of the room. "John, send some of our men over there and have them arrest Hudson."

"Yes, Sir."

"John, if he resists, they are cleared to use deadly force. This Republic must stand, and I will not have anyone compromising this great nation or our set of beliefs. The Jefferson Protocol will continue."

"Uh, yes Sir, I'll tell them," he answered nervously.

"Also, John, would you get Bob for me. I have one more… quick task for him."

Backing out of the room, "I will have him here within the hour." The door closed behind him.

Walking over to the large oval windows, the President looked out. "Hudson, you will not stop me. You've slowed me in the past, but I'm too powerful now. We've made too much headway for you to even think about righting it."

Picking up the glass of Scotch, he poured another then drew on his cigar, "Hudson, you can play nicely, and I will let you sit this out with your wife, or I will just remove you from the equation. Either way, you will not cease this movement of enlightenment for all people."

The man blew a smoke ring, sat back in his chair and placed his feet up on the desk.

The men walked up to the door and Hudson rang the bell. With no response, the agent rang it again.

Todd walked over to a large front window and looked inside. "It looks quiet. No lights are on, and I don't see any movement."

The agent marched back on the brick path leading to the door and pulled up a loose brick. Todd looked on. Pulling a key from the hole, "Looks like nothing has changed."

"How did you know where that was?" Todd questioned.

"I've worked over here many times, and Dr. Keith told me how to get in."

Approaching the door, he turned the lock and opened it to the sound of an inside alarm beeping. Hudson input several numbers, and the alarm went off. "It looks like he hasn't changed his code."

Todd smiled.

"The alarm was set for 'Away' so no one is home," The agent said as he turned on the lights.

"What's happened here?" Todd questioned seeing the room in a shambles.

"It looks like someone was hunting for something."

Feeling himself sink in the plush Oriental rug, Todd passed the overstuffed leather chairs and went to the cherry wood book cases. Bending down and going through the books all over the floor, the professor could tell Dr. Keith had good taste. He found classics from Shakespeare to Chaucer. The professor touched first editions of Tom Sawyer and the Great Gatsby.

"Wow, this guy has a collection. What I wouldn't give for some of these books."

Walking over to the fireplace he noticed a painting on the ground, "Is this a Picasso?"

"Yeah, he never really liked it, but it was a great discussion piece at dinner parties."

"It kind of looks like he isn't dead," Todd said. "Someone wants something he has or knows."

The professor continued to walk from room to room. In the kitchen he looked in the fridge, "Hudson, this fridge is totally cleared out. It's as clean as if it were new."

"Could the change in the time line have brought him back?" Hudson searched the room feeling more optimistic.

Stepping over the drawers in the floor and emptied cabinets with cans littering the counters, "What were they looking for?"

Yelling back, "Todd, I don't know, but I know where to find it."

Coming back through the kitchen, the professor made his way into the main room to find Hudson coming down the stairs.

"Anything or anyone up there?"

"Nope, the place is empty, but if they were looking for something, they wouldn't have found it."

Todd asked, "Why is that?"

"Because nobody's better at hiding than a physicist."

The agent crossed the room to the light switch next to the front door and flipped it up and down at certain intervals. "Look at that," Hudson pointed to a previously blank wall.

"Whoa, where did that come from?" Todd smiled.

An area in a painted sheetrock wall from the floor to about three feet up immediately revealed a hidden safe.

Todd walked around looking at the hole, "Are those holographic projectors in the ceiling?" pointing up.

"Yes. They look like speakers but paint a faux finish on the wall in all directions. That way, if they're blocked from one angle, another will take over."

"I guess that is about as good a hiding place as you can find. Someone rummaging around won't think anything is hidden behind a straight flat wall."

"That's the idea." Hudson went over to the safe. "Dr. Keith and I worked very closely I helped him set up his pass codes."

After inputting numbers on the key pad, the safe clicked. Hudson turned the arm, and the door opened. Beginning to look through the contents, a sound was heard out front.

"Hudson, did you hear that?"

"Yeah, sounds like we have company." Putting everything back in the safe and closing the door, the agent went back over to the light switch and started up the hologram. Then they ran over to the window in a side room.

"I only see two coming out of the car."

"Sure," Hudson responded, "But those are Secret Service; I know them. You can also tell by the cheap dark suits. They're here because of the President. He must know we're on to him."

Seeing the agents pulling out their guns, "Hudson what are we going to do?"

Hudson grabbed for his Glock and chambered it, "We're not going to be taken in. That's for sure. The President will bury us so deep; we'll never see the light of day. We're the only ones who know what's happened and can stop him. Stay here."

Hudson ran behind the door as the men slowly opened it. Todd watched from around a wall in another room.

Peeking around the corner, "Hudson, are you here?" the voice spoke.

Another man added, "Hudson, we just want to talk with you. It's Steve and I."

The men entered the room as Hudson closed the door behind them; weapon drawn. "Hello, Steve and Brad, please put your guns on the ground."

The men looked around. Seeing Hudson's 45 pointed at them, they put their hands up. "Hudson you won't shoot us. We worked together."

"Guys, that was another time and another place, drop the weapons."

Yelling, "Drop the weapons!"

The men slowly complied.

"Put your hands on the back of your neck and back against the wall over there," Hudson pointed with the gun. "Todd, come around here and tie our friends up."

The professor pulled of a couple of the heavy rope drapery ties and walked toward the men.

As Todd got closer to the taller one he knocked the professor to the ground as his partner grabbed for the backup gun on his ankle.

"Don't do it," Hudson yelled.

The man pulled the small weapon anyway and rolled – preparing to shoot.

"No Brad!" Hudson shot the man in the side, stopping his movement.

Steve tried to grab Todd, but the professor was not going to have any on it. A well-practiced front kick to the head and jabs to the sternum gave the larger man more trouble than he was ready for from the seminary professor.

The Secret Service Agent grabbed him and put him in a headlock. As the smaller professor tried to get out of the hold, Steve spoke, "Hudson, drop your gun or I'll kill him."

"Hudson, I've got this," Todd grunted while forcing his heel into the man's instep.

"Steve, let him go. We are not going anywhere with you," Hudson growled.

Brad started to move on the floor. Hudson knew that he had two uncontrollable situations in the room. If Steve was serious, he could kill Todd. Secret Service agents trained for years for such a position. The agent also saw the man's partner moving behind.

"Brad, stop moving. Steve, let him go." Hudson yelled with authority.

Todd continued to keep the man from getting a choke hold, but he was held fast. Punch after punch to Steve's side and multiple back kicks to the groin and shins were not enough for the large man to drop his prey.

After yelling again, Hudson saw Brad pull a gun around his partner and prepare to shoot. At that same time, Todd was able to get his leg behind Steve's, causing him to fall to the side.

"No," Hudson yelled at Brad

Brad's gun went off, and Hudson was not able to stop the chain of events. As Steve fell, he dropped into the path of his partner's shot and was wounded in the lower back. Immediately the man released Todd – rolling onto the floor as the professor fell onto Brad punching him in the head and knocking him out.

Hudson grabbed for his friend. "Are you alright?"

"Sure, I told you I had him. The question is, are they going to be alright?"

Steve was writhing in pain. Looking his former friend over, "He's going to need to get to a hospital pretty quick. He's taken a shot through the kidney. Brad's in worse condition. He's taken one just off center in the stomach. We'll call 911 as we leave." Hudson grabbed Brad's phone from his suit coat and input the code normal to the agency. The phone came to life, so he put it in his pocket to use later.

Running over to the wall, Hudson opened the safe again with the holographic disguise still on. The door appeared through the image and the agent pulled all of the contents out. There were journals, a Walther semi-automatic, some gold coins, a small zipper pouch, and around $30,000 in cash.

"We'll take it all."

Walking back to Steve he lifted the man's head, "Where's Sara Brennen? Tell me, where have you taken Sara?"

"Steve fought to speak, "Jefferson Mem...." The man went limp.

Hudson knew what that meant and walked out the door with Todd in tow.

"Jefferson, what's that mean?"

"We'll find out soon enough."

They walked up to the minivan, and Hudson got in.

"We have a problem," Todd said. "They sliced the back tire."

The agent got out and ran around to look at it.

Quickly thinking, "Well let's go in style." The agent opened a zipper bag he had pulled from the safe and found a fob with a Mercedes emblem on it. Pushing the button, the vehicle came to life, unlocked the doors, and turned on the lights.

"I think they have Dr. Keith just like they have my Sara. If Dr. Keith has been taken, he'd hope I'd get to him anyway I could, and would let me use anything he has to do it." The agent pulled the maps from the minivan and closed the door. Looking over at Todd, "Let's go."

Running to get in the passenger seat, "Hudson, you know they aren't just looking for us now because we might know too much. We've shot two Secret Service Agents." He closed the passenger door.

"Yeah, I know, but if we can right this, it will all be erased."

The Mercedes sped off down the street.

22 — MONDAY LATE EVENING

The trendy DC neighborhood faded behind them as Hudson called 911 from his cell.

"Two Secret Service agents are down on A Street, just up from the Supreme Court. You will find them at Dr. Benjamin Keith's home, fourth house on the left. Each has been shot."

The operator spoke, "We're sending an ambulance. Sir, what's your name, and are you helping with their wounds?"

The agent rolled down the window and threw the phone from the car.

"They should be alright," he said to Todd.

"Hudson, what did he mean back there about the Jefferson Memorial?" The professor moved his arm, working out the pain brought on by another skirmish. "That's a public memorial that's open to the air. Hundreds of visitors go by there a day."

Looking over at his friend for a moment he sighed and drove through the narrow streets, "Are you alright? You did pretty well back there."

"Yeah, I'll be fine. Just over-extended my arm. Getting a black belt in several martial arts always felt like a hobby until I got to know you."

Hudson pointed to the dash, "Todd, take that paper and open it." Todd obeyed and unfolded it. "That map shows the energy spikes that could have been caused by another sphere. At least, that's what I think it's showing."

"It's pretty crude, but what you can see is the bright spot in the middle."

The professor jumped in, "Yeah, you said that's the Washington Monument."

"Yes, GPS coordinates show that bright spot to be the Monument. But what's interesting are the four other white areas on the map."

"Yes, they're not as bright but still stand out on the page."

"I think they're conduits to the sphere; or the lab where the sphere is kept."

"I've been to D.C. many times. Looking at these straight coordinates – that would put these other lights at the White House, Lincoln Memorial, Jefferson Memorial, and the Capitol."

"You're right," the agent responded, as he turned the corner in front of the Supreme Court.

Todd looked up from the map, "Are you saying they have underground bunkers attached to the memorials?"

"We know the Metro runs underneath Washington moving tens of thousands of people each day. Why wouldn't there be a separate rail system, maybe one just for the President?"

Passing the Supreme Court, the Capitol came into view. Its bold, white columns lit up like a shining example for the world to see. Yet Hudson's stomach grew troubled looking at it.

The agent refocused and continued, "There've been rumors in Washington for decades about secret passages to get the President out. What if some rogue country decided to take the White House? There needed to be a way to get the President as far away as possible. And fast. An underground rail system would do that."

The professor looked at the large white building as they passed it.

"I think those white spots, essentially making a cross on the page, are the exit points for the energy dissipating through the channels that a rail system would run.

If I could've expanded the scale on the map, we probably would have seen every possible exit on that secret rail system heading as far as Maryland or Virginia.

I bet some third world country would pay dearly for the information we discovered by accident."

"But what about the memorials? I've been to each of them. There isn't anything there. There are small offices off to the side but no place to keep someone for a lengthy stay."

"Who's to say? All a visitor sees is what's on top. They could've very easily constructed bunkers underneath for any number of reasons when they were built. Each of those memorials are like fortresses, I bet they have Sara under Jefferson in some sort of makeshift prison."

Todd was thinking the problem through, "Why not just arrest her for some trumped up charge? The President could have her locked away pretty easily. Why put Sara in a secret bunker?"

"He's beyond power at this point. This is his game, and he's going to control all of the pieces. He knows that I'll be coming and could be the only one to reverse what he's done. She's collateral, and he's going to keep her close."

They passed the Air and Space Museum and were driving alongside the main mall. "In a few minutes we'll be at the memorial, look on the map to see if you can locate any spots that might look like an entry into the underground system," Hudson said as he watched over his shoulder for the police.

Noticing his partner on alert Todd questioned him, "How long until they come for us?"

"Well, the good thing is they won't be looking for *us*."

"What do you mean?"

"At this point, they don't know you're here. They're only looking for me." He thought for a second, "And from the wounds our buddies had back there, they won't be talking anytime soon. They're probably both going in for immediate surgery."

"I need to pray for them," Todd said, "They were just doing their job."

"Sure, they were both good men. I didn't work with either of them directly, but knew of them, and they were both dedicated to their jobs."

They drove in silence for a few blocks.

"Anyway, within the hour, they'll have analyzed the 911 recording and will put out an all-points bulletin for me. When the President finds out about his men, he'll start hunting me down before that. We have a couple hours at most to find Sara."

"Well, two hours are better than none," Todd said jokingly.

Getting more serious, Hudson looked at his friend during a red light. "Todd, if they get me, you'll be the only one who knows what's happened. It'll be up to you to make it right. They can't get us both, or there's no way to correct his plan."

"I got it, man," Todd replied, "but it isn't going to come to that. As we say in the church game, 'If God appoints, He'll anoint.' At this point, God is all we have, so He'll have to use us to do something we don't know how to do. It's up to Him to use our little scrawny selves to solve this monumental problem." Starting to chuckle, "Well your little scrawny self, I've been in the gym a lot lately."

Hudson put the first smile on Todd had seen since entering Washington. "When we get out of this thing, we're going to go to the gym and see who's stronger."

"You're on," Todd laughed.

Pulling up to the Jefferson Memorial, the professor viewed the large colonnade and portico of the domed white granite building. It was all lit up as Jefferson gazed across the Tidal Basin at his former home the White House.

"You know," Todd asked, "I don't think whoever built this place liked Jefferson."

"What are you talking about?"

Hudson parked the car between other vehicles in a small lot up the street from the building.

"That memorial," pointing at the edifice, "Was supposed to have been put on the fast track when Franklin Roosevelt, a big fan of Jefferson wanted a monument to his favorite President. They already had a spot picked out for another memorial, and it was on the south side of the basin. So that all sounds good, but look at where it is. It's way out of the way. You can walk all the way from the Lincoln Memorial to the Capitol easier than getting to this monument."

Hudson listened vaguely to where the story was going.

"I've been to this city a dozen times and have tried to start the walking trek to this memorial a handful of times – never actually making it because it's so far away. Everything else is on the Mall, from the Smithsonians to the war memorials, to a hundred other statues. This place is work to get to.

Jefferson was one of the founding fathers. He authored the Declaration of Independence. He was the third President of the United States, made the Louisiana Purchase and sent out Louis and Clark. This guy should be up there next to Washington," pointing at the obelisk across the Tidal Basin.

"So once again, even though they say they liked Jefferson when they built this place, I think they really despised him to put him so far off the beaten path."

"Huh," was all the agent could say.

"But back on to bigger problems," Todd continued, "I think there's some kind of access just northwest of here," he said pointing over the agent's shoulder.

Looking at the map with him he agreed, "Todd, I think you're right. It's a small hot spot almost like an opening or access point. The energy is so powerful when the sphere charges that it will search for any way to be vented to the atmosphere. Let's go."

The men left the vehicle and walked the three blocks toward the Lincoln Memorial. The temperature was in the 40's but the cold did not stop the men. Hudson would have searched for his wife no matter the temperature and was not going to stop until she was safe.

After eyeing the area over thoroughly he wondered, "Where's the access spot? There's nothing here?"

"It has to be here, let's look again. You go that way, and I'll go this way."

The men separated for several minutes when Todd spoke out, "Hudson, over here," he spoke with a loud whisper. "I've got it."

The agent ran over to find Todd on his knees in a grouping of boxwoods. "It's not been used for a while. The hedge roots have grown into the grating, but it looks like a way in." Turning his phone he lighted the area, "I don't see any rail system, but it is a passageway that seems to lead toward the memorial. It could just be a storm drain sending water to the Tidal Basin."

"No, this is it. The energy of the sphere wouldn't be released through a channel that wasn't connected directly back to the lab area. This has to lead to the main underground passage. Can you get it up?"

Todd pulled on the grate. "Nope, it's secure." His eyes glanced up, "Buddy, what's to keep them from coming immediately once we open this? I've heard stories that even the sewer systems in D.C. are wired with audio and video."

"They could come quickly, but I don't think they have this end of it wired up. Let's think through this," they lowered themselves, squatting toward the ground. "I know the security measures of the White House because I was in the Secret Service, and none of this was here in the old timeline. There was no underground system that I knew about – always rumors but no real proof. There weren't any bunkers under the memorials that I knew about for sure. So we have to believe that this came about after they started messing with the time line. Maybe they finally finished the project that was started earlier. Who knows? There may have always been bunkers under the memorials and access between them, but they now connected it for use by the President.

Even though this has only been a day or so for us, they would have been working on it in the other timeline; or this timeline for several years. This type of a system is hard to build and takes lots of money and time. So from the looks of this grate, they haven't been on this end of it yet."

Looking the area over for people watching he turned back, "I think we're safe for a while in the tunnels."

"I'll have to trust you," Todd replied as both men started tugging on the large grate.

They jerked and heaved, but it wasn't moving.

Scraping the leaves and dirt way from one corner, Todd found a large screw. "They have this thing screwed down." The professor pulled out his small Swiss army knife and opened the screwdriver attached.

"Hudson, would Dr. Keith keep anything in the car. My phone's going to go dead soon enough, and we will need light, and possibly a crow bar."

"You work the screws, and I'll go check the car."

Todd was on the last screw when Hudson returned.

"You have to love an anal retentive scientist," Hudson said with a smile. "He had a crank charge flashlight, a handful of flares, some rope, a basic tool set, and some energy bars."

"Was he expecting to be stranded for weeks?" Todd asked with a smile.

"Dr. Keith was always prepared. And for us, that's a good thing."

"Give me one of those bars?" the professor asked.

"You get one when we get in the hole." Hudson pulled out a large screw driver from a bag and placed it under one end of the grate. The large metal covering moved as Todd pulled on it at the same time.

Dragging it to the side, Hudson looked around again. Because it was now after ten, the area was fairly quiet except for the occasional vehicle. However, because their view was blocked by the hedges, the men felt fairly safe. Bending down, he cranked the flashlight a few times and when the light came on, Hudson stuck his head in the hole.

Shining the light both directions, the agent spoke, "It looks like an air shaft. This is just a thin passageway that doesn't seem to end. Below it is a cement floor that I'd guess is the main rail system."

"So now what?"

Hudson sat up next to the hole, "We go. I know this connects to the main passage because the energy was released through this point. So, we can be sure they connect. How far down the line, I don't know."

"You sure this is the only way? This reminds me of another small passageway where we were dragging my wife through the underground tunnels of the Temple Mount. That doesn't bring back good memories. Torrential rains, earthquakes, and my wife on the verge of death." Tod started to pace, "And I don't really like small spaces."

Hudson smiling, "I didn't know you were scared of small spaces."

"Who said anything about scared? I just don't like them."

"Todd, it's a beautiful night in Washington, and your wife is in Louisville safe and secure. You remember that we got her out of there, and everything worked out just right."

"I know all of that, but bad memories are hard to get over."

"Sure, all of life is a bad memory right now."

"What do we need?"

"If we can bring it all, let's do it."

The men then fastened as many of the tools as possible around themselves, stuffing much of it in their pockets.

"Hudson, once we enter that culvert, there is no going back. We are all in."

"Yeah, I know."

"Well, let's pray God guides."

"Good idea."

The men sat next to the opened hole and closed their eyes. Todd spoke out loud. "Father, we thank You for Your blessings. We thank You for our families. We thank You for our timeline.

Lord, we don't know why this has happened or why You want to use us to solve this problem, but we are willing and your servants. Please guide us and direct us. Please solve our problems before we get there, and most importantly, Lord, be glorified through our work. We say this in Your Son's name, Jesus. Amen."

Both men looked up at each other. "Let's do this," Hudson said. "I want my wife back."

The large man crawled into the hole and started inching toward the Jefferson Memorial, pointing the flashlight in front of him.

Todd inched in last, opened an energy bar and took a bite. "Anything's good when you're hungry," he mumbled. After a few seconds, he lowered the grate over the hole behind them and followed his partner into the darkness.

23 — MONDAY NEAR MIDNIGHT

The President was in the White House library watching men mentally spar over a dozen opened books.

"We can't do it that way," one man said.

"It'll all work out if we meet with the delegation at this time," another said pointing at a history book.

"I think we can solve it by simply removing this figure," a third man said.

The President jumped into the discussion. "We can't remove him, or the timeline will be extremely affected. You know that. Can he be pressured or threatened?"

"I don't think so," the original man said. "All computer simulations say he won't break."

"Computer simulations are only so good," one man said, running his fingers through his hair.

"Sure, but they've been pretty close so far," another retorted.

"We just can't go back there with that many countries involved. There are just too many variables," the third spoke out of frustration.

As they bickered around an endless sea of reports, a man who had remained quiet for a while removed his glasses and interrupted, "Guys, let's regroup. Maybe we're going about this all wrong."

The President looked up. "How so?"

"We know what our end goal is, and we're looking at this timeframe to make it happen," he pointed at a spot on a six foot role of paper covered with world events in the format of a timeline. Moving a bit to the right a few years, "What if we just go back here and offer a different kind of help?"

"Continue," the President said.

Standing and walking the room, "We know America is already in each of these places working, so what if we just ensure the help keeps them dedicated to our goals."

The leader's smile broadened, "I like it. It won't really affect the timeline but will ensure loyalty."

A knock came on the large mahogany door.

"Yes," the President said looking up, "What is it?"

John Costall opened the door, not expecting to see a room full of people, "Sir, I have Bob, and if you have a moment, I can bring him in," he said with some insecurity.

Walking across the room he sat in an overstuffed leather chair, "Yes, John, have him come in."

Looking to the previous occupants within the room, "Men I have a meeting. We go with Dr. Guerrero's idea. Have it ready within the hour. That will be all."

Several looked confused where others felt the problem was solved. They quickly took their books, maps, and timelines, and left through a side door – quibbling as they went.

The Chief of Staff directed Bob to a side chair next to the President where he sat down.

"Sir, there is one other thing. It's about some of the loose ends we were working on."

He waved him over, "John, come in. You are my Chief of Staff, and if you're talking about Hudson, then Bob is already involved in this problem."

"Are you sure, sir?"

"Yes, John, get it out," the President barked with impatience.

Bob looked up at the Chief of Staff with a grin.

The trusted staffer spoke nervously, "Well, he got away."

"What do you mean, he got away? We knew exactly where he was and sent men over to get him."

Bob laughed as the President looked over with frustration.

"Yes, we sent over two of your agents, and he got away."

"Did he leave before they got there?"

"No, he shot them."

The President stood up and walked along the long book shelves. "Hudson shot them? I can't believe that. He's supposed to be a Christian man." He air-quoted the word Christian. "Why would he shoot them? How did he shoot them?"

John trying to answer, "He didn't shoot them both. It looks like he shot one of them and the other evidently shot his partner in the back. We're trying to reconstruct the last hour or so to find out exactly what happened."

Bob put his hand over his face and chuckled.

"What's so funny?" the President asked with a tinge of embarrassment.

"It's not really humorous," Bob answered. "It's just that you can't predict Hudson. He's very well trained, and extremely intelligent. He's also in great shape."

"We had two men there," the President said, "How could he have overtaken them?"

"We don't know exactly," the Chief of Staff said sheepishly.

Bob jumped back into the conversation, "You have his wife – or the woman who was his wife. Hudson won't stop until he finds her. You essentially have a caged animal. He *will* attack. Hudson's family was everything to him. Because the timeline has been changed, he's not married and has no children. You have one angry man there."

"Well, this needs to be dealt with," the President said flatly.

"Sir, there is one more thing," John mentioned.

The President looked over at him.

"We believe there is someone with him."

"How do you know this?"

"Evidently, the agents slashed Hudson's tire, and he had to take another vehicle. When we searched his van we found a small bag with some clothing in it. It held a flight ticket stub showing the person had come in this afternoon.

It was just a stub, so it didn't have a name, but we're running all of the backgrounds on the passengers that came in on that flight."

The President picked up a wine glass and took a drink. "John there's no need to spend all of that time. The person you're looking for would be Dr. Todd Myers. He's the only other person who would know what's going on.

He probably went through the changes and called Hudson about them. The rest is a quick flight ticket and two men shot at Keith's house."

"Changes, sir, what changes?" John asked.

Bob looked up wondering how the world leader would answer.

"Don't worry about it. Just focus all of our resources on finding these two men."

"Yes, sir. Is that all?" John asked ready to leave.

"Yes, and this time don't underestimate our problem."

"Yes, sir," John said bowing out of the room.

The President sat back down.

"Speaking of changes," Bob said, "I'm having trouble keeping up with everything that's being affected. Streets, buildings, people, and governmental agencies are all different."

The leader just listened.

"Also, I seem to be having physical effects from this. I'm shaking occasionally and have a constant ringing in my ears."

"Bob, every time you jump, I go through a sonic boom, but the ends justify the means. Niccolo Machiavelli couldn't have been more accurate.

This world needs these changes. All this will result in a world of peaceful, easy-to-control people who have a sense of fulfillment."

Pacing the room, he fingered the binders of the ancient books, "We are changing the world to make it better," he pointed at Bob and himself. "We must cause a little pain to ensure a better future for everyone.

It does grieve me that Hudson's life has been changed. Because he's traveled in time, he's actually aware of the changes. He was a good agent and has worked hard for this country, but he is a minor bit of collateral damage in comparison to the monumental life changes that will occur for hundreds of millions of people."

"Yeah, about that," Bob jumped in. "My parents called me seeing if there was anything I could do." The world leader listened. "Well, they're part of that collateral damage. They are essentially afraid for their lives."

Stopping his movement, the President looked over at Bob, "Why would they be afraid? They don't know of the changes that have occurred to the timeline."

"No, it's nothing like that."

"Oh," President Langley understood, "Your parents were ministers, weren't they?"

"Yes sir, they were."

"They heard the speech this evening, didn't they?"

"Yes," Bob answered, "And evidently, being a minister is now illegal. I'm sorry, but I was sleeping during your speech. No offense."

"None taken, Bob. You've worked very hard lately."

The man crossed his legs and listened.

"You didn't hear the speech, but they can continue to minister. In fact, I hope they do."

Bob got a puzzled look on his face.

"They just need to follow the lead of the state, and minister according to the new way. We will take care of them very well if they follow the new outlines and agenda for a greater country. I can move them up in the State Church if they want to have a position of power. Would your father like to be a bishop or a cardinal in the new church?"

Bob fidgeted in his seat, "You don't know my parents very well. They are dedicated to Jesus."

The leader looked up at a bust of Napoleon sitting on a column.

"They loved Jesus so much that they essentially forgot they had a son."

The President was beginning to see Bob's motivation for being so willing to make religious changes in the timeline, and turned to look at him.

"All my father has ever had in his life is Jesus. He never played ball with me, was at the hospital with someone when I had a school function, and would spend hours working on a sermon without asking about my day.

He has preached for God for 30 years, and you'll never get him to cross over."

Lowering himself onto an 18th century end table the President looked at Bob, and spoke softly. "Bob, you are part of something much bigger than Jesus here. Your continued loyalty is making a friend in me that will never be forgotten. I'll not turn my back on you or reject you.

We're doing something unlimited, and the world is better because of you. I'm sorry that your parents believe in an antiquated system. I have never believed in a God and look where I am. I am the most important person in the world. I am proof that God does not make your life easier. But believing in Him limits your ability to make free choices. These outdated laws and the Judeo-Christian ethic have ended."

He patted him on the leg, "I'll do my best to ensure they're given time to come over to this side. After this is over, I'll allow you time to go back home and see if you can show them the benefits of the new life-changing system we have in place here.

Who knows, maybe when your father sees the new religion, he'll understand that true joy is family and home. When one stops worrying about the future or another life after death, they can focus better on the here and now. He'll see what he's missed, and you'll have time to make a new and better relationship with him. This is why we're doing what we're doing."

The President began walking again. "Bob, Stephen Hawking once said, 'There is no heaven or afterlife for broken down computers; that is a fairy story for people who are afraid of the dark.' We, Bob, have but one life and must live it to the fullest. We have the here and now, and I need you and your parents to help usher in that new philosophy. We can make this world a utopia if we can remove these unnecessary and even dangerous ideas from the people."

He moved his hands in continuous circles, "We've evolved after all of these billions of years to have the ability to travel through time and to correct mistakes of the past. Have you really thought about that?" The President became more animated. "We can travel to times and experience sights and sounds that the world still thinks are gone forever. We can experience beauty by watching Michelangelo create the Sistine Chapel. We can go to the library at Alexandria and research, or just sit in on a lesson with Plato."

He became more serious, "Or we can help people when they have no idea of an apocalypse coming. What if we could evacuate the people of Pompeii before Vesuvius blew. Or make steaks out of Mrs. O'Leary's cow before it starts the Chicago fire." The leader laughed, and Bob became more comfortable.

"What if we could stop some of the events before the World Wars began? Or maybe we just correct rogue thought; those thoughts that are pervasive and deep-seated. We need to squash all racism before it begins. There is no place for bigotry in America. Yet one of the greatest errors was to allow religion to flourish." The man stopped and looked at a painting by Monet hanging on the wall.

"It has caused more pain than any other single thing in history. Religious belief systems have kept the world in war for millennia, and it is time for it to stop." He pounded a table next to him.

"We're stopping all of that and offering true hope and peace. There is no place in America for this type of thinking. If I have my way, there will be no place in the world for it either."

Bob nodded, and the President sighed to lighten the tension. "Your parents will come around. They will see the benefits of where I'm taking them. Where *we're* taking them."

"I'm just not sure," Bob replied.

The President took on a fatherly tone, "Friend, you just need to trust me, and you need to stay focused." He walked over to the table with a bottle of wine, "Do you want me to pour you a glass?"

"No. Thank you," the man answered.

"Bob, I need you for one more jump. This will be the one to ensure this world is safe and permanently secure from this type of fanaticism."

Bob stood and threw his arms in the air. "No, not right now. I'm having physical affects from these rapid jumps."

"You're going to be fine. You look perfectly healthy. I know you're tired and needing a break, but you're the only one to do it."

"I thought I was getting a break."

The sincerity in his face was heart-rending. "Bob, we aren't finished. There are millions more people who need the hope that America now has. I promise, after this you'll get a break. I'll send you on the best vacation you could imagine. Find some friend to take with you and party on an unlimited budget, but now, Soldier, your Commander-in-Chief needs you."

"I just don't know if I have it in me. I'm afraid to make a mistake."

"Don't worry. No one is more focused than you are, and that is why we chose you." Walking over he patted the man on the shoulder, "Don't worry, if you mess it up, we can go back and fix it." The President laughed.

Turning and warming his shaking hands in front of the large pink granite fireplace, "Where do you want me to go?"

The President stood next to him with his arm around his shoulder in front of the roaring fire. "Let's have a drink, and we'll talk about it."

24 — TUESDAY, VERY EARLY MORNING, OCTOBER 17

Hudson knew very quickly the difficulty with their trek would be the illumination. Hudson had to crank the flashlight every few minutes. Worst case they would always have light with enough turning of the handle.

"What do you see up there?" Todd asked seeing only a faint glow in front of him.

"Yeah, not much," the agent answered pulling himself through the narrow channel feeling his belt buckle scratch the floor.

"I want you to know that you're going to be replacing my shoes when we're all done with this. I just bought these Italian loafers," the professor laughed scraping through behind his partner.

"I'll put it on the expense report." Hudson lurched to the left and slammed against the side of the tunnel.

"What is it? What happened?" the doctor asked.

"Nothing but a rat." He pushed forward again. "But a big rat."

"Is it coming toward me? I don't like rats."

"I think you've been through worse," the agent replied sarcastically. "We have a lot of debris in this tunnel. I know it's the ventilation for the rail system below, but it looks like it's had some overflow from the Tidal Basin or just heavy rain flow. They need to clean it out."

"If we find Sara, we might want to stop by and freshen up. We're going to be a mess," Todd added.

"We will find her," Hudson said flatly.

"You're right, we will."

The men continued crawling slowly for another twenty minutes stopping to charge the flashlight every forty feet or so. Knowing they were trapped with nowhere else to go but forward gave both men cause for concern. If there were security measures in this tunnel, they could easily be locked off on both ends with no one finding their remains for many years.

"What would you be doing right now if you weren't in this timeline?" Todd asked hearing his voice echo.

"It's one in the morning! I'd be asleep with my beautiful wife."

"Yeah, I guess it was an obvious answer, but it does make you appreciate what you don't have, doesn't it?"

"Yes, I guess it does. Sometimes the best thing in the world is just resting next to the one you love. If the Lord allows us to right all of this, I won't take that for granted again."

"We're going to get it back the way the Lord wants," the professor said assuring his friend.

They crawled for another fifty feet when Hudson stopped.

"What is it?"

"We've come to the end of the line. There's an iron grate with a lock on it."

"Huh. We don't have a pry bar or anything we can pull with."

"No, we have some rope, but not enough room to get any leverage."

"You can't shoot it out can you?" Todd asked nervously

"No, we could be hit by the ricochet." Thinking for a second, "Todd can you reach into my bag and pull out one of those flares?"

"It sounds like it's going to get warm in here," he spoke stretching over his partner's back and into the satchel he was carrying.

"There's no other way. Those things burn around 2500 degrees Fahrenheit and should melt through this lock."

Todd set the road flare into the hand reaching back in the dark, "If I remember my chemistry classes, it's going to be close. I think steel melts at around 2500 degrees," Todd mumbled.

"It's all we've got. This should be a fairly controlled fire, so I'm going to hold it on the lock until it gets soft. You know it's going to get bright so close your eyes until they adjust."

"I understand," he said pulling a long screwdriver from his pocket. "When it gets soft you should be able to pry it with this." The professor threw the tool up where Hudson was working.

"Good." He pulled the flashlight back to an area near his waist and directed it toward the lock, "Are you ready?"

"Yep," the professor said closing his eyes.

Immediately, the small space was filled with a red light bright enough to cause blindness. Hudson had his eyes closed just long enough to allow his vision to adjust from the dark to the dangerously bright and then went to work. As he held the hot end to the lock, he watched the metal turn red within the first minute. Several minutes later it appeared to be contorting in shape.

"How much longer?" Todd asked over the sound of the torch.

"We're almost there." Hudson began prying on the lock. A minute later, it started to stretch and tear along the shackle, so he could work it away from the grate. "We're in." Using the long screwdriver, he pried the grill open and poked his head through the opening. "We have good news and bad news."

"Why can't it only be good news?" Todd laughed.

"This opens up to a large tunnel below, but it's a 40 foot drop."

"Well, I guess it's good Dr. Keith had this paracord in his trunk," Todd said pulling it from Hudson's bag and tossing it up to his partner.

"The man was ready for anything. Hold my legs."

Leaning over the edge of the drop, Hudson couldn't see anything in either direction. Feeling safe the tunnel was empty, he dropped the flare to the bottom of the chasm. What appeared to be train tracks - possibly maglev tracks – appeared in the light below. Whatever it was, it was secret and few people knew about it.

Pulling himself back into the air channel, he unrolled the cord and fed it through the grate and then dropped it into the chasm – ensuring both ends went to the ground. "We're going to have to go out of this hole upside down. I also want to take this cord with us, so you're going down on both lines. Just pull it through when you finish, and I'll see you at the bottom."

"Don't worry about me," the man said with an echo.

Hudson grabbed onto the thin cord and fell through the hole. After 20 seconds of hand over hand he was on the bottom, and he quickly ran against a wall and looked in both directions for anyone who might be coming. Seeing nothing, he went back to the light of the flare.

"It's alright." He gazed up. "Come on down."

Todd fell out of the hole head first but righted himself quickly and looked like a pro falling down the rope. Pulling the cord through, he quickly gathered it around his arm and then placed it over his neck to carry. "You ready?"

The track ran in two directions, but the men knew that the southerly one would lead toward the Jefferson Memorial.

"Yeah, but if I'm right, we'll encounter some resistance in another 500 feet or so. If they have Sara in there, she'll be protected by at least one guard." Hudson checked his weapon to ensure it was chambered and ready.

"One guard shouldn't be that much of a challenge."

"If they knew Sara, they'd be smart to put more than that. She may be small, but she has tiny little fists of fury."

Todd laughed as the men snuck along the western wall away from the flare and without a flashlight. Walking as quietly as possible they heard the rumbling of the passageways but knew it was just echoes from equipment moving through some other channel miles away. Eventually, they were far enough from the distant red flare that the tunnel became almost totally dark.

After some distance of walking with both hands along the wall, they saw what appeared to be light and the tunnel curving to the left. As they snuck slowly forward, they viewed a subway-type stop. The exit was nicely tiled, had sitting chairs outside of two regal wooden doors with the crest of the President of the United States embossed in the wood. The new crest made the men shiver. This exit even had the words 'Jefferson Memorial' above the doors in gold.

"I think we've found what we're looking for," Todd whispered.

They moved closer, and not seeing any resistance at the outer entries, they progressed cautiously, stepping up on the landing.

Hudson spoke quietly, "If we encounter any resistance, it'll be on the other side of those doors. So just play along." Hudson put everything securely in his pack and in his pockets except for his weapon.

"What are you about to do?"

Hudson grabbed Todd around the neck and pointed his gun at his head. "Open up the door," he yelled.

Todd complied nervously.

Once inside they found two men dressed in suits. These agents immediately stood from their chairs that were situated on either side of a door along one wall.

"What is it?" one man yelled, trying to pull a gun from his pocket.

"I found this man walking through the tunnels on my midnight check," Hudson said with authority. "Lock him up while I go back and check the tunnels out."

"Who are you?" the other man asked walking toward Hudson.

Pulling his Secret Service ID, "I'm Hudson Blackwell, and am responsible for midnight searches of the tunnels. You've never met me because I've never found anyone until tonight."

Todd had his arms behind him as if they were handcuffed.

The two men looked at each other. "I don't know anything about midnight searches," one man said to the other.

"Me either. Let me call on this." The man lowered his weapon to grab for his walkie.

"Well, it's good I'm here. Who knows where this man could have gotten without me finding him first."

At that, Hudson threw Todd toward the man not holding a gun while Hudson pointed his weapon at the man with his weapon almost back in his pocket. "Drop it," Hudson yelled as Todd gave a roundhouse to the other man knocking him out.

The agent with the weapon was uncertain and had his semi-automatic pointed back at Hudson.

The men were locked motionless, when Hudson spoke again, "I'll not say it again, drop your weapon," then Hudson shot the man in the leg while the professor kicked the weapon from his hand. Todd pulled the cord from around his neck and cut pieces off to hog tie the men. Hudson checked on the wound and knew that the man would be fine with a few weeks away from work.

"Be glad, I'm giving you a vacation and possibly a medal," Hudson mumbled finishing the knots and taking the weapons from the men.

When both men were incapacitated, Hudson took out their phones and smashed them with the butt of his gun. "I can guarantee they change guards every few hours, they'll be fine until then." He looked at Todd. He also looked at the door behind them. "She has to be in there."

Pulling keys from one of the man's pocket, Hudson, unlocked the deadbolt, slowly opening the door into the room. Once it was ajar, he peeked his head into the area and a second later, fell to the ground with a large thud.

"Hudson!" Todd yelled, kicking the door open to find Sara standing over his partner. An old-fashioned tea kettle in hand.

Holding the container, she backed away, "What happened out there?" She had a funny look on her face. "I told you, I want to go home. I'll hit the next one of you that gets close to me if you don't let me go."

Leaning down over his partner, Todd held his hand forward, "Sara, we're the good guys," he tried to calm her nerves. "You could have killed him!"

"Well, I still might if you guys mess with me again," she said nervously.

"We're here to help. We are rescuing you." He tried to speak clearly.

"How do I know that? I was taken and placed in this jail for no reason, and how do I know you aren't going to take me somewhere else against my will?"

"Well, I can guarantee we're going to take you somewhere else, but it's for your good. We want your…we only want to help you…Do you even know who this guy is?"

Hudson began to moan and hold his head.

"No, why should I? He probably works for the President who brought me here."

"Well, Sara, I can't deny that. He works for the President, but he didn't bring you here, and at this point has gone to a lot of trouble to get you out. Hey, buddy, are you alright?"

"Ugh, my head hurts."

Helping him from the ground, Todd walked Hudson over to a chair to try to allow him to regain his wits. Sara still had her kettle but backed away from them into a corner.

"What was that gunshot?" Sara asked.

"Well, we had to make a point out there. But don't worry, no one is going to die."

"Good," Sara responded.

"Hi, honey," Hudson smiled not really knowing where he was.

Sara just looked nervously on. "Why did he call me 'honey?' I am no one's honey, and I don't play any games like that. If you think I'm going to have to repay you somehow because of what you have done here…"

Todd stopped her mid-sentence and slowed her forward movement, "No, Sara," He lifted his hands in surrender for lack of a better idea. "We don't expect anything out of you. Hudson's just a bit mixed up now. Why don't you let me have the tea pot?" He was able to work it away from her, and she backed once again into the corner.

Still on high alert and emotionally spent, she started to cry. Which caused Hudson to stand up – still not realizing fully his current circumstance. "Honey, don't cry. It's going to be fine."

"Hudson, you'd better remember we're in a different timeline fast," Todd scolded the wounded man.

Rubbing his head a moment, he started to remember the situation. "Oh yeah." He scanned around, "We don't know when the replacements are going to show up, so we'd better work our way out of here." His focus shifted back to Sara. Gazing at her, Hudson's heart softened. Shaking his head, he put himself back into the charade. "You need to come with us."

"I don't know you. Why would I go with you?"

"Because we are the only ones that can get you your true life back."

Todd looked at his friend, and his heart broke.

Extending his hand Hudson walked toward her, "Sara, you need to trust me, because I would never hurt you. I only want your best."

She looked at him and then extended her hand. "Okay, but I'm watching you."

"I hope you do. Todd let's get out of here."

Walking out into the area where the men were still tied on the ground, Hudson bent over and spoke to one of them. "Where is Dr. Keith?"

He looked up, "Who?"

"Dr. Benjamin Keith. I know you know all about the project. Where is the designer?"

"A long way from here. You'll never get in there."

Hudson stood, "I know where he is. Let's go."

He pulled the downed agent's guns from a corner, put one in his belt, and gave one to Todd. "When we head through these doors, we may encounter some resistance," he said pointing toward a large set of doors on another wall. "Don't worry about shooting. If we can get this right, all of this will be erased except what we remember."

Todd looked up and armed his weapon.

Looking at Sara he spoke more kindly, "Stay close, and we'll get you to safety."

She nodded as Hudson and Todd took the lead. Opening the doors they entered what looked like a Park Ranger's office. Taking a strategic stance, the men relaxed only after they cleared the room.

"If they aren't watching here, we may look like guests at the monument. Be ready for anything," Hudson said to his partner.

"We're almost out," he comforted Sara.

She smiled nervously.

Opening the door from the office led the men into the grand dome and – right in front of them – the 19 foot statue of Thomas Jefferson. Keeping their weapons in pockets, the men tried to walk quietly through the monument. At the entrance and facing the Tidal Basin was a man who obviously knew something was not going right. Hudson yelled, "Go."

Todd took off through the back with Sara in tow. Hudson covered the rear as the obvious Secret Service agent ran up from behind with his weapon drawn. "Stop," he yelled and then fired in their direction.

A divot was taken out of the granite next to Hudson. Dodging, he immediately fired his weapon back striking the approaching man in the chest. Falling as a lump on the ground, Hudson knew that most likely the man would not make it. It grieved him, but he had never asked for any of this. He was content with his life and just wanted to live it out with his family. He had been thrown into it because of a president bent on total power.

Hudson wanted to curse because of the injustice of a lost life – one the leader of the nation would not value or see as important. The saddened agent said a quick prayer and followed Todd and Sara off into the dark night, hoping for an end to a problem they knew was just beginning.

25 — JUNE 4, 1947, EVENING

Bob sighed with relief when the hissing sound indicated the short trip was over. All the earlier trips had involved longer and more grueling rides, but because the vehicle was only sent less than a century into the past – and just a hop and a skip from Washington – it was relatively quick and painless.

Steam filled the vacuum of the cockpit then quickly dissipated. Looking at the date and coordinates he realized that he should be within a block or two of his destination. He unbuckled his safety belt, stretched his long legs over the lower edge and found the foot peg to lower his worn body to the earth; once again in another time.

On the ground, he reached and picked up the dossier once again. The man he had to convince was not known for compromise, nor would he be easy to influence. Bob sighed again as he formulated a new approach. He read through the talking points, gathered his tools, and took a khaki-colored cap from the seat – arranging it correctly on his head.

As a military man for years, he did not like impersonating an officer of a rank higher that what he had earned. He had respect for the uniform and the men who had worn it before him. But for the next hour, he would act as an Army Lieutenant Colonel.

The short-sleeved, khaki shirt and matching dress pants were both well-pressed. Rows of ribbons decorated his left shoulder, and patent leather shoes and a highly polished black belt finished off his look. The impersonation bothered him. He would have to accept it as part of his mission and continue on.

Of all the people he had encountered in his recent time jumps, this man would be the most awe inspiring – a hero of sorts. Being the first five star General and called the General of the Armies, and yet being the first career soldier to receive the Nobel Peace Prize, this would be a day Bob would remember the rest of his life. Too bad he had to meet the man under these circumstances. Picking up his briefcase, he began the walk down the quiet street toward the Dodona house.

Passing the hundred year old homes in Leesburg Virginia, Bob took in the beauty of the large oaks and the striking examples of Federal architecture. Many of them looked like *Tara* from *Gone with the Wind.*

After a short three block walk, the military man found the residence. Four pillars held up the portico of the Leesburg, Virginia home named for the Greek oracle, Dodona. Evidently, the owner's wife named it because the oak trees surrounding the home reminded her of the story of the Oracle who spoke from a circle of oaks in ancient Greece. Soon enough, Bob found himself on the glowing red brick porch not yet ready to meet this great man.

Taking a cleansing breath, he stood to his full height and knocked on the front door. A woman in her 60's appeared.

"Hello, Lt. Colonel, how may I help you?" Her warm southern accent flowed like melted butter over biscuits.

"Hello ma'am," he said, assuming the woman was Katherine, the General's wife. "May I speak with your husband?"

"Sir, you know it is very late."

"Yes ma'am, I do, but I have important business that can't wait."

"The General is resting. He has a very important meeting in the morning."

"Oh yes, I know. That's why I'm here. When he hears the information I have for him, he'll want to speak with me."

"Please come in," the woman said opening the door wide and gesturing him through.

Stepping inside, he followed her to a sitting room off to the right, "Please wait here, he will be with you in a few minutes."

Bob walked the room, which appeared to be a library, and looked at the shelves filled with military history and strategy. He found various medals in presentation boxes, swords, and a host of pistols and rifles from numerous areas of the world and eras of history. Third Reich pistols and Samurai swords from Japan. Bob realized they must have been collected from a war that barely ended two years earlier – at least in this timeline.

Immersed in military history at that moment, he was unaware that he was being watched.

"Lt. Colonel," came a loud voice from the hallway beyond. "Why have you interrupted my time away from work?" The 67 year old man obviously felt put out.

Clearing his throat, Bob stood straight and saluted, "General Marshall, I'm here with important information about your meeting tomorrow, sir."

"There's nothing you can say that I don't already know," the military leader said walking into the room. "What is your name, officer, I don't recognize you?" the man asked sitting in a simple side chair.

"Robert Welsley, sir. I'm from a think tank of sorts within the Defense Department."

"There is no such thing. I'm the General of the Armies and know all that goes on there. Who are you?"

Bob knew he had to be frank with the tough military leader. Opening his briefcase he pulled out a file. "Sir, tomorrow you will be drawing up a contract called the European Recovery Program. Sir, we need you to be ready to, let's say, add to it."

"How do you know about what we're doing?" anger tinged the older man's voice as he stood.

Rising with him, Bob responded, "Sir, please don't get angry. If you will allow me, I will completely explain myself and why it's important that you listen." He handed the man the file, "Please look this over."

General Marshall sat and opened the manila folder. After several minutes of reading, he looked up. "What is this? I mean how can you have this? We haven't even written this yet. We will begin the process tomorrow morning. Who are you?"

"Sir, I am American and am here for the good of the country."

"I was with the President Truman this morning. He didn't speak of any of this."

"My President was explicit that I speak with you."

"What?"

"Sir, what you have in your hand is what – in my time – will be called the Marshall Plan."

"Marshall Plan. Your time?" he said, putting the paper on the table next to his chair. "Why would it have my name on it?"

"I know you'll have a lot of questions. Please allow me to explain."

The older man slowed his breathing and spoke with a more focused voice. "You have just a few minutes to get to the point, Lt. Colonel."

Starting to walk the simple wooden floor covered with a basic rug, Bob began to make his case. "The Marshall Plan sounds like a good idea, and for a while it will be. You just ended the war and want to ensure the weakened nations aren't taken over by communism, so America will help them get strong economies to ensure they stay with capitalism. You are trying to make allies in the future, not future communists."

The man watched him with a determined focus.

"However, during this transition, the communists – specifically the Russians – are gobbling up countries. Albania, Czechoslovakia, Hungary, Latvia, and many others have already been taken over by Russia. In my time, this causes great trouble."

"In your time. What does that mean?"

Bob pulled a 3D tablet from his briefcase, "Let me show you." He turned it on and placed it in the hands of the man who had never seen such technology – and would not for close to a century.

A video came to life filled with images of George Marshall and his committee working on the multi-national treaty. Pictures of reconstruction happening in various countries around the world were also included. Then the pictures go from black and white to color and then in three dimensions showing turmoil around the world in the future timeline. Wars were occurring, people were being beheaded, and mass killings were shown in numerous areas around the globe. In addition, various religious sects appeared and their fanatical beliefs were illustrated through the death and destruction they wrought. After four minutes, the video ended. The old man looked up at Bob, now looking much older than his 67 years.

"What have you shown me? What is this thing?" he spoke quietly, turning it in his hands.

"It is a tool that everyone will have in my time. It's loaded up with just about all of the information possible. You can search anything that has happened or will happen until my time. Is there something else you want to see?"

"No," he placed the small device back in the man's hands.

"There were pictures in there of me doing things I haven't done. Work in countries I know nothing about."

Bob pulled up his chair in front of the General and sat back in it. "Sir, I am from the future. About a century in the future to be exact. We have the ability to travel time and correct problems of the past.

My President desires a more peaceful and controllable world. Take the world you have now and offer each country the ability to destroy other countries 100 times over, and you'll see the problems we have in the future. We must bring them together," pacing the room.

"Sir, we can't have any more of these nations go their own way. America must govern them. We need a world organized by the values and ethics of this great country."

"But our focus is to ensure the postwar countries return to a strong and beneficial state. Everything we are about is ensuring sovereignty to the nations that we just conquered," the older man barked.

"Yes, my President understands this. Yet, because of these nations' diversity and individualism, there is no unity in the future. Each has their own focus and that eventually rips the world apart.

The President in my timeline believes the only way to ensure a strong future America is to make the weak countries that you are about to help, come under the umbrella of the U.S. with the end product being – they become annexed by us. They must remain weak, so that together we all become strong." He stopped walking. "You need to guarantee they eventually really want the power of the U.S. and its protection."

"That would make us no better than Russia," the man stood raising his voice.

"No sir, we are always better. What could be more advantageous for countries like Germany, Greece, Austria, or Turkey than to become American? They can keep their individualism but must be under our umbrella; possibly like Puerto Rico and Guam are today. That ensures they are with us in the difficult world ahead."

Shaking his head back and forth, the leader of men frowned, "I just don't know."

Pacing again, "Sir, you have fought well with the various areas of government to ensure men like Patton, MacArthur, and Nimitz could fight a war and win it. It will not help their memory to have the half of a million American sons that were lost, die for nothing if the future isn't as safe as the world is now.

We also need you to add China to the list of countries you bail out."

"China. They aren't even part of this."

"Yes, sir, you're right, but they need to be. They will eventually become the most powerful economy on the face of the earth. When they begin to build up their military, there is nothing else the world can do but watch. So bring them to the table and find a way to tuck them under the umbrella with all of the other allied countries. America needs to become one big nation."

Looking dumbfounded and off-kilter the general shrugged. "How can I do this? Many of us are working together on this project."

"Roosevelt and Truman couldn't fight this war without you. Their own memoirs say that. You can do great things if you try." He sat down again. "Let me be honest. We don't really know how this is going to work out. We, in the future understand there are many variables that are involved in this. But if we don't try, it is a greater failure.

If you can only get a few countries to become part of the United States, then we are stronger in the future and can add to the earth's unity and peace. Let alone if you do what we saw you do in World War Two."

Knowing he had done all he could to convince the man, he picked up his briefcase. "General, I am going to leave that tablet with you. You have twelve hours until it renders itself useless, but until tomorrow morning you can look through the history of America. See our future and the Presidents that help get us there. You can experience our ups and downs. Just push that little round button on front and ask it a question. It will take you to anything you could want to know about.

Please understand that it has to self-destruct because we can't allow the secrets of the future to get out. But it is important for you to see what's coming if you don't act now.

You must know how important what you do tomorrow is for our,... for America's future. If you fail, America will not have the influence it needs in the dangerous world ahead."

At that, the man headed for the door. "I'll let myself out. Good night, General."

Walking out onto the front porch, Bob could see the faint color of the tablet glowing through the front window as the powerful man started watching the events that would take place in a time in which he would never live. The General's eyes were wide and his face drawn in grief and uncertainty.

The traveler knew his message was made clear.

He began to whistle as he walked down the long path toward the sphere. Another mission completed. At long last, he could enjoy a well-deserved vacation.

26 — TUESDAY, VERY EARLY MORNING

Making their way back to the Mercedes Sedan, Hudson opened the passenger door for Sara and allowed her to sit while Todd jumped into the back seat from the driver's side. Running around the front of the car, Hudson remote started the vehicle, sat in the driver's seat, and headed southeast on East Basin Road passing the monument. Seeing commotion inside, the agent understood his window to leave the city would be short, so he found an entrance onto highway 1 and drove toward Alexandria.

"Where are we going?" Sara asked nervously.

"We're getting out of the city," Hudson said as he looked over his shoulder after crossing the Potomac.

"I thought you were taking me home," she sounded frantic and began to pull at the lock on the door.

"Sara, it's the only way – you have to trust us," Todd said leaning forward in his seat.

"I want out! Leave me here, let me out," she yelled trying to figure out how to unlock the door.

"Honey, relax," Hudson put his hand on her forearm.

She pulled her arm away. "Don't call me honey. You don't know me." She inched farther to the right in her seat.

"I'm sorry," Hudson said, "We're here for your safety. I wish you knew what we've been through to find you."

The professor leaned back in his seat and watched the difficult interchange.

"I'm only here to ensure you get back to your life. I hope you know that I'll do everything to get you back to the life you had before all of this craziness."

She continued to look out the passenger window.

"Sara, please trust me," Hudson asked, trying to drive fast enough to get out of the city but not get pulled over for excessive speed.

The woman's demeanor relaxed a bit but she stayed to the right of her seat. After a few minutes Todd broke into the awkward silence. "Hudson, it's been a long time since I ate. What about splurging for a burger?" he said, pulling up between the seats, "What about you Sara, would you like something to eat?"

"Yes, that would be nice," she said quietly still looking outside.

"Okay then," Hudson said.

The vehicle quietly drove for another twenty minutes passing Alexandria and heading west on Highway 95 when Hudson steered into an all-night pancake house. After parking the Mercedes on the side of the building behind other cars, Hudson cracked the hood.

"Is there something wrong with the car?" Todd asked.

"Maybe. If those chasing us have discovered we took Keith's ride, they've probably contacted Mercedes with the proper permits to get access to this vehicle's tracking device."

Sara looked on.

"It usually took a couple hours to get a permit for a company to release private information on a specific vehicle. I had to do it several times when I worked for the bureau." He pulled out a pocket knife," If you add that to the time for them to determine we have his car –they'll start tracking us pretty quickly. I want to slow them down."

After finding the place he was looking for on the driver's side of the engine he cut several wires. Closing the hood, he walked over and opened Sara's door. "I cut the cell and the internal GPS connection. Unless they happen to see this midnight black Mercedes as they pass us, we should have more ability to get down the road without problems." Reaching out his hand, he helped the young woman from the vehicle as Todd followed from the back seat.

Walking around the structure and to the front door, Hudson allowed Sara and Todd into the older building filled with truckers and those who worked the third shift of some industrial plant in Virginia. A woman with a simple dress and apron greeted them in a rush, "Darlins just find a seat."

Hudson sought out a booth next to a window facing the front of the building. With this simple vantage point, he could react quickly, heading out the back if trouble arose. Todd sat in the booth first, leaving Sara looking at him as if she should have been seated before him. The professor's ploy worked when Hudson sat next to her on the outside. He grinned.

"So what's good?" Todd said prying apart the syrup-sticky menu.

Sara glanced at the laminated pages without speaking.

"They have whole grain pancakes if you want those," Hudson offered to Sara, "they're on page two. You can probably get those with a side of fruit."

Sara looked over at him.

"It isn't my normal routine to eat at three in the morning, but a big omelet might hit the spot," the professor added.

"Yeah, I may do steak and eggs," the agent added.

A stocky woman in normal diner apparel came up and asked, "Do you know what you want?" She looked intently with pen and pad.

The professor answered first, "May I have the California omelet and a *Coke*?"

Sara then spoke quietly, "May I have the whole grain pancakes with butter..."

Then Sara and Hudson spoke at the same time, "On the side."

She looked at him in confusion.

Todd tried to help with the awkwardness, "Everyone wants that on the side. Right?" Looking up at the waitress, he added, "Put my butter on the side too."

The woman looked at him like he had grown a third head. Surely he was not expecting butter on his California omelet.

Hudson jumped in quickly, "Do you have green tea?"

"Sure, honey," the woman added.

"Why don't you get a pot for me." Looking over at Sara, "Do you want some green tea?'

"What's going on here?" Sara asked.

Todd interrupted, "Green tea helps to calm nerves. Hudson knows all about calming damsels in distress. I mean, people in distress. You know, with his job. Never mind."

The waitress looked impatient and a bit confused with pencil tapping on her ordering pad.

"Well, it just seems that Hudson here knows all of my favorite things," Sara said slapping her menu down and looking put out.

Hudson kicked his friend under the table, "Just a good guess," staring down his partner before finishing his order, "Steak and eggs, please, and make that one check. Thank you."

There were several minutes of silence before Sara spoke to Todd, "Tell me about your wife. I see you have a wedding ring."

"She's great. We've only been married about five months."

"What is she like?" the woman asked.

"Her name is Aaliyah, and she's Jewish. I, uh, met her," Hudson looked up curiously, "In Israel, after a recent project. She's beautiful, strong, and treats me like a king."

"Aaliyah is a sweet lady. It's amazing how this guy got so lucky," Hudson added.

"What do you mean by that?" Todd joked. "I'd say she's pretty lucky to have me. "Well, she did save my life, so I'm lucky to have her too."

"Saved your life?" Sara questioned.

"Yeah, this guy here got me shot," he offered, poking at Hudson.

"I didn't get him shot. He was running ahead of me, and I couldn't get him to stop," Hudson said with a laugh.

"Well, anyway, I wasn't going to make it, and she used old fashioned remedies on me to bring me back to health. Her company wasn't bad either. After that, it was love at first sight. Well love at first sight after I woke up from almost being dead."

"Yeah, but you have to give me credit for introducing you to Aaliyah," Hudson added.

"From what I remember you telling me, you essentially fell through her front door."

"Well, I found her in spite of how it happened."

Chuckling, Todd went on, "I guess I need to give you the credit. In a roundabout way, at least."

Smiling, Hudson looked at Sara, "Sara, tell us about yourself. What have you been doing all of these years?"

Sara looked at him awkwardly.

"I mean, what do you do?" he corrected himself.

"I work for Senator Dupree. I'm one of his aides," she spoke cautiously.

"What was your major in college?" Hudson asked.

"I have an English degree, but I became a temp for Congress every summer, and that's how I got to know the Senator. I do a lot of his writing and proofing. He has me reading bills and even asks for my opinions."

Looking at both men she held up her fingers in scout's honor, "But understand I don't tell him how to vote. He always does what he believes."

The men laughed.

"We figured that, Sara," the professor said.

"What about your personal life. Are you married?" Hudson asked nervously.

Sticking her fourth finger out, she admitted, "Nope, I'm single."

Todd looked over at Hudson and tried to hold back a smile. The agent kicked him under the table making the various types of syrup rattle in their containers.

"I'm sorry, I accidentally bumped the table," Hudson mumbled. "Why haven't you ever been married?"

"Well, not that it's your business, I've wanted a family, but the right man just never came. So, I just focused on my career." Sadness colored her voice, "But I've met many great people through my work."

Todd jumped in, "I'm sure you have. It must be exciting doing what you do."

"Most of the time it's relatively uninteresting work. But then there's that five percent that makes up for it."

Hudson could not help himself, "Do you have any hobbies?"

"I like to exercise – anything from yoga to running. I also like to cook. I read quite a bit and someday I'd like to travel. Maybe see the world. I meet and work with these fascinating people each day, and I've never really been anywhere outside of Washington. There is just so much out there that I would love to just sit and experience. Sitting on the Piazza in Venice and drinking a cappuccino, or riding a camel to see the pyramids."

"You always liked an adventure," Hudson's own voice caught him by surprise, but he corrected himself quickly, "I mean your job is adventure enough, let alone adding to it."

The professor looked at his friend as if to say, 'good save.'

"No, I want to live, and it feels like I've been on a bookshelf just waiting."

"How are your parents?" the agent asked.

"Well, they're sweet people. Why do you ask?"

Todd responded, "Well, we're just getting to know you."

"They're getting close to retirement. And…"

"What is your relationship with the Lord?" Todd broke in and changed the direction of the conversation.

Sara looked stunned and whispered, "You heard that the President made that kind of talk illegal."

"Believe me, we really don't care what the President wants. We know that he took you, and we will be dealing with him soon enough," Hudson spoke.

Both men became hardened in their stare as if they were in total control.

"I love the Lord, and Jesus is my Savior," she then said without reservation.

"What about your parents?" Hudson asked.

"They're going to be very scared. I watched the President's speech this evening, and if they saw it, well, they're going to be nervous about the future. If you know my Dad, he tells everyone about Christ. It's just part of his life, and I fear he'd rather go to jail than keep quiet about his Savior."

"He's a good man," Hudson added.

"He is a very good man, and I'm afraid for their future. He's not an old man, but he's not young either. The stress will age him beyond his years."

The professor spoke, "We're going to get this corrected if we can." Pointing at Hudson and himself, "We both love the Lord and want the world returned to what it was before all of these changes."

"Who are you that you can get the President to alter his direction? He's been slowly modifying legislation and the focus of the country for years."

"Well, it's not been that long for us," Todd mumbled.

"Let's just say, we know how to get the problem solved if we can find one man," the agent said passing the plates the waitress dropped on the table.

Todd offered, "Can I pray for dinner, or is it breakfast? Either way."

Everyone smiled.

"Dear Lord, thank you for this simple meal. Thank you for allowing us to find Sara, and let us correct – through Your power – all of the wrong that's occurred. We say all of this in Jesus' name, amen."

Each tore into their meals. Within ten minutes, everything on the men's plates was eaten. Sara offered one of her pancakes to Hudson, who ate it without reservation. The rest of her fruit she offered to Todd.

After a few more minutes, Hudson spoke, "Sara, I know you're nervous. But you're going to need to come with us for a day or two."

"What? But why?" she replied getting anxious.

With Todd looking on, the agent continued, "We want you back to your life as much as you do, but we can't let those men take you again. I'm afraid they won't be as nice the next time. Just give us a day or two, and we will keep you safe. Then you can go back to what you were doing before all of this."

"I don't have anything with me."

"Hudson has plenty of cash," Todd added. "I'm sure he'll get anything you need."

"Where are we going?" she asked.

"We have a drive ahead of us. We'll need to find a place to rest, we need to pick up some supplies, and then we'll start out fresh in the morning. We'll probably be there by tomorrow evening. I know you'll love the location, though."

Hudson was pulling out some cash when Todd spoke again, "Hudson, do you hear that?"

Immediately his eyebrows dropped, "Not again. Hold on."

This boom was much stronger than any of the others. Before the surge began piercing through their minds, the men watched what appeared to be a tidal wave coming toward the diner through the front window. The ground was rolling and contorting as the wave pushed through the countryside.

Even though it was in the middle of the night, an electrical glow accompanying the surge made it clear that this wave was changing all it touched. Roads were heading off in different directions. Buildings were removed while others replaced them. Forests were swapped with industrial areas and road signs changed color and even language. Just before the wave hit the restaurant, Hudson grabbed Sara and held her tight. Todd held his ears and tried to keep from shaking.

As the men contorted and twisted, grunting to the pain their bodies were enduring, Sara tried to remove herself from Hudson's tight grip. She knew he was trying to protect her but had no idea from what.

The men continued to writhe and Sara saw Todd's right ear begin to bleed. Even though she could tell Hudson was hurting, he held her gently. Surprisingly, she did not feel awkward at all. Instead she prayed for the men she had only met just hours before.

As the surge traveled through the building, Hudson watched it change from a simple gravel parking lot to one filled with gas pumps and semi-trailers. The pancake house was transformed into an all-night fuel station with attached restaurant.

The deafening sound wave passed through them as they struggled to keep quiet and deal with the pain. As it continued on past, the new norm in the restaurant gave them a moment to regain composure and take in the full brunt of what had happened.

Seeing blood on his hands, Todd raised a water glass and used it for his reflection. Discovering that his ear was bleeding, he knew he had possibly ruptured an eardrum and had some difficulty hearing as he had before.

"Todd, you alright?" Hudson asked releasing Sara.

"I can't hear that well, but should be fine. What about you?"

"Just a big headache," he muttered looking around and seeing people in the corners eyeing them. "Sara, what happened?"

She was nervous about what she saw, "You two just started shaking and obviously felt pain at the same time," she offered Todd napkins for the blood.

"Did you see anything change?"

"What do you mean change? You two went through something, but that's all that happened."

"Hudson, why is she still here with us? We know he made a big leap that time, but she's still here?"

"It looks like we're connected. I don't understand it, but somehow the Lord won't allow us to be separated. Are you going to be alright?"

"Yeah, let's go. We need to find out what happened, and how the world is affected."

Growling, Hudson stood, "We are going to stop this." The agent threw some bills on the table. "Are you ready, Sara?"

With her eyes as large as saucers, "I don't know. I guess so."

Looking at her intently and with compassion Hudson spoke softly, "It's going to be fine. You need to trust us. We will explain in time."

Todd was already up and heading out the door.

Sara took the agent's hand, "Okay, I trust you." Standing she walked in front of him and through the main exit.

Hudson just looked over the room, "Lord, please let us make it right before it's too far gone to correct." He followed them out into the dark night not knowing what they would encounter down the road.

27 — TUESDAY, VERY EARLY MORNING

President Langley gripped his head and fell to the floor, writhing in pain. An involuntary scream brought the Secret Service agents into the room immediately, unaware of the time change ripping through the People's House. Fearing a seizure, they started to call for the White House medical personnel.

"Stop!" Still breathing heavily, President Langley recovered enough to lift his hand in a halting gesture.

After the boom swept through the space, the man, obviously in pain, came back to his senses and calmed the agents, "I'm fine men, just had a bad cramp from exercising this evening."

"Sir, we must bring in a doctor," one agent said.

He stood to his feet and smiled, "No thanks. A little bit of pain never hurt anyone. I'm better than ever." He adjusted his night clothes. "Go back to your posts. That's an order. But again, thank you for the prompt response."

The President saluted them loosely as they nervously left the room. He then went to an overstuffed leather chair in the corner and tried to regain his composure. The last time-incursion was a large one, and after downing a glass of scotch and sitting several minutes, the leader opened up his laptop sitting on the end table next to him.

Pressing the power button, he remembered his first experience in the sphere. Even though no one would have recognized any changes after that leap, it had certainly impacted the world in a more substantial way than Bob's last jump. The screen came to life, and Hayden Langley remembered his anger at Hudson's second return from Israel.

"How dare he try to keep that machine from me," he growled under his breath. He had just discovered Hudson's apparent deception by landing it in the woods at Hudson's own cabin.

He smirked, "That just ensured I'll get it back – and that much more quickly."

A semi and some agents with a top secret clearance had it returned to the lab within 24 hours. That night, the leader went to the secret facility forcing everyone to leave while he spent time with the machine that had given him so much trouble.

He knew there would be no way he could use the apparatus after tomorrow because every scientists attached to the project would practically inspect the thing with a microscope. He only had this one opportunity to gain from it. A machine with so much potential would not help him if he could not use it for his own purposes.

Walking around the apparatus he pondered what could give him the most benefit. If he only had one jump, where would he go that would impact his future the greatest? It was like being offered only one wish. One wish was good, but it would not be enough. Of course, everyone knew that if you only had one wish, you should use it for more wishes. So as he continued to pace, the question became, how could he get more wishes?

He spoke out loud, "I need another sphere. One no one knows about." Stopping in his tracks, he wondered, "How do I get another sphere when the designer died months ago?"

Looking up, the leader saw a date and time painted on the wall, indicating the day of the first successful jump. It was not a large step, but one that proved the technology successful. And one that would prove to be greater than the one taken on the moon. Yet that life-changing moment was not performed by the designer because he was killed before the jump occurred.

He started moving again, "What if I brought Keith back? What if I saved him before he was killed, he would do just about anything for me. Then he could build another sphere, one that no one knew about. I could change the world." His voice rose, "I could correct any problem that occurred in the past. I could make the world what I want it to be. It could be a planet focused on the morals and ideals of the greatest nation on the face of the earth."

Thinking for several more minutes and feeling confident about his decision, the man walked up to the sphere and typed his presidential code in the keypad below the hand recognition location; knowing the vehicle would not acknowledge his print in its accessible pilots list. Instantly, the top half of the machine raised, and he climbed into it. Recognizing the time and coordinate areas on the dash, he oriented himself with the simplicity of the vehicle.

There were essentially two areas on the dash; one referencing where he was in time and location and one indicating where he would go. Being an intelligent man, he learned the touch screen system fairly quickly. He then looked at drop down menus, one containing a block of possible locations in longitude and latitudinal coordinates. He chose the White House back lawn; an area that was concealed from the public. Then he set the date to the evening of the day before Dr. Benjamin Keith was killed. The date on the wall helped with that.

Locking in the present location and time in the computer, so he could come back to it, the leader then found the area on the dash that would close the sphere. The top of the vehicle began to lower. Buckling himself up, the President sat back in the seat and saw a button blinking with the word EXECUTE. Looking over the console once more, and finding everything in order, he laughed to himself, "I'll need to change the date on the wall, because I'll beat that first attempt by a full day." He then touched the screen in half excitement and half terror, when the machine began to heat up. After a quick flash of light, the vehicle's top half began to rise again.

The leader cursed, "What's wrong. What else needs to be done?" Thinking through the screens on the console, he did not look out from the machine for several seconds. When he did, he noticed that he was surrounded on one side by large trees and the other side, the end of the White House.

"It worked." Feeling the cool breeze surround him, he knew he did not have much time. Quickly, he ran to the motor pool where a driver was reading a magazine. Recognizing the President, he quickly stood at attention. "Sir, how may I help you?"

"I need you to take me across town."

"Sir, the Secret Service wasn't alerted that you would be going anywhere."

"A last minute trip. Have a few men follow behind in another car."

"Yes, sir," the driver said as he went over to the intercom, and a dozen men ran down a side stairwell.

The head of the agency came up to the leader, "Sir, you were just in your quarters. How did you get down here?"

"Never mind. I need to make a quick run. Do not alert anyone else about my movements. Do you understand?"

"Yes, sir."

"Keep everyone else on their positions. Make sure no one leaves their assigned positions and ensure all outside patrols stay at the outer fence." The leader had to keep the Secret Service away from the sphere and allow the other President actually asleep on the second floor from getting wind of what was happening. "Do you understand?"

"Yes, sir. I can make that happen."

"Let's go."

After a short drive, both limousines arrived at the home of Dr. Keith. Getting out Langley spoke very clearly, "Everyone stay here."

Taking a defensive position, the men encircled the home.

Knocking on the entrance, lights came on within the home. When the door opened, a man in a nice bathrobe spoke, "Mr. President, how many I help you – especially at this time of the night?" He rubbed his eyes. "You know we have the test in the morning."

"Ben, it's about that. I need you to come with me."

"Sir, is there a problem?"

"Yes, there is. I fear for your safety."

The well-kept man awakened quickly. "My safety?"

"Yes, if you don't come with me, you may be killed."

Getting nervous, he weighed what to do, "Okay, let me get a few things."

"There's no time. I'll have everything you need brought for you."

The men walked to the second limousine, and the President directed Dr. Keith to be seated inside. Pulling the agent in charge to the back of the vehicle, the President spoke quietly, "Tom, I want this man taken to Green One immediately."

"Sir, that place hasn't been in play for decades."

"I know that, but everything is still there and can be retrofitted with current technology in just a few weeks. I'll be sending you a file within the next day or so. You're to fulfill everything written there. No one else is to know."

The man was taken aback.

"I will give you account numbers for the funding, and names of scientists who can help Dr. Keith with this new project. Are you staying up with me?"

"Uh, yes, sir. I guess so."

Focusing right in the man's eyes, he spoke clearly, "You are more important to me than just about anyone else at this point. So, don't forget what I'm telling you."

"No, sir, I won't."

"I need you to find a Navy SEAL or Army Ranger who can be the director for the mission. You choose him. Just ensure he's strong, loyal, and will give his life for the sake of the country and this endeavor. I will remind you of this in the file I'll be sending."

"Yes, sir."

"Once again, Tom, I've watched you for a while and know you can make this happen. Please don't let me down. This is for national security and the future of this country. If you fail, the nation will fall."

"I will do my best."

"I need better than your best. I need you to do it."

"I'll die trying."

"Finally, and this is the most awkward request. You will never come to me about anything with respect to this project. I will only come to you." The President had to ensure the current President; his earlier self was not involved.

"Do you understand? You will never come to me about any of this. If I need you I will come to you but you are to implement my plan when I send it whether or not I speak with you again for six months or so."

Standing there with his mouth open, the man was clearly shaken.

"There is no negotiating about this. Do not come to me! Just fulfill the instructions."

"Yes, sir," Tom said meekly.

"Get it done, Tom. I need you. Now take him to Green One immediately."

"Tonight, sir? None of this is scheduled."

"Right now. I will return with the other vehicle and get that file ready for you."

The agent returned to the passenger side of the limousine and told the driver to head immediately to Green One. Then the door closed.

The President watched the armored vehicle leave and sat in the back of the first limousine. "To the White House."

Leaving the townhouse, Hayden Langley was back in the motor pool of the People's House within a few minutes. Telling everyone to get back to their posts, he headed out to the sphere housed at the end of the large building. After reversing the coordinates on the console, and buckling his seatbelt, he was back in the lab within a few seconds as if nothing had ever happened.

The top of the sphere rose, and he left the vehicle on that night so many months ago.

He made one more jump a few hours after putting the file together, but never needed to get back in it again. Yet the few leaps he had made between future and past allowed him and four other people to know of the events that had changed; Hudson Blackwell, Todd Myers, Aaliyah that woman from the past, and Bob.

Bob, he knew he could trust; the other three would need to be dealt with.

The computer had booted up and his focus changed from where the world was a few months earlier to the results of all his hard work.

Knowing the most recent sonic boom was Bob completing his latest assignment, the Leader of the Free World did what millions of other Americans do each day; he searched the net.

He initially went to history sites determining what happened after WWII. There were changes, some good and some not so good.

Langley quickly discovered to his pleasure that he was the leader of a nation much larger than it once was. The United States of America now totaled 59 states and many more territories than it had ever had. Several European countries like France and Germany were now part of the fold and several South American countries also. "How did they get with us?" the man mused with a chuckle.

The problems were that even though some of China was now American, most of it went to Russia. After looking at a map of the earth, he discovered that the world was essentially split up four ways. American was the first, being the largest country with Russia following quickly behind in population and land mass. There were then many of the Muslim areas that had united to become an Islamic State. Finally there were the few countries scattered throughout the globe that no one cared enough to fight over.

Standing and walking over to his robe, the man knew he had much to catch up on before the new day started. He would go to the Oval Office and skim over daily memorandums to discover problems within the world. He would have to continue his search to find all the changes his efforts had caused throughout the globe.

He felt good about his work. The new day looked to be a promising one. Indeed, he was now a much more powerful man in the world. After tying his robe, he left his private residence and headed downstairs.

Hudson, Todd, and Sara found a second rate hotel called the Patriot's Motorway Motel. Each were given their own room comprised of a bed, which had not been changed in who knows when, a shower filled with mildew, and carpet that you would not want to walk on barefoot.

Even though the walls were paper thin, and his wife was in the next room having no idea of their having ever been married, he fell asleep relatively quickly. All night he woke up with fitful dreams.

Reality melted in his dreams, creating a dystopian world where the agent was attempting to take back a treasure. It was his. One that he had rightfully earned and sacrificed for, but one he could not get possession of. The thief who had stolen the article stood head and shoulders taller than he and fought with greater cunning. This man was more powerful and had limitless wealth. In his dream, Hudson continued to come at the man without a break, giving him everything he had. Fight after fight, day after day, the opponent was not to be stopped, and Hudson eventually stayed down knowing his energies were fruitless.

And then his opponent laughed.

The villain pulled his trophy from a shelf behind him and held it aloft – enjoying its beauty. He shined it and smiled, and all Hudson could do was to watch from a distance. Turning the trophy around, he showed it to the beaten agent. "You're not capable of getting it back. It isn't in you to have it again. And even if it were," He looked at it closely again, "It will never be the same because I have reshaped it."

He held it out toward Hudson. The agent realized immediately that it was his wife carved into marble. But along with her usual sweetness and optimistic smile, loneliness mixed with hopelessness shined through her marble eyes. Hudson stood up ready to fight again when the enemy put her in a safe that appeared on the wall. Hudson called out, and then awakened, sitting up in a cold sweat.

"Oh, Lord, give me strength," he said out of breath. "I am so lost, and I need Your guidance and strength." He stood up and went over to the sink, looking in the mirror. His reflection had aged beyond his 36 years. At the peak of health, he looked pale, haggard, and had deep circles under his eyes. He splashed water on his face, wiped off the sweat and went back to bed.

Falling back down on the sheets, he turned on his side and pulled over a pillow that would have been his wife's and hugged it close. "Please Lord, let me have my wife back," he prayed as he laid there over the next few hours remembering everything he could about their lives. He missed his children. In his current timeline, they would never be born.

After the replacements at the Jefferson Memorial found their comrades down, they immediately sent word to the White House. It was five in the morning when the President was awakened.

Several rings on the phone did not get a response from the private residence. Eventually, the head of security went upstairs to share the bad news himself. Knocking on the door, the man was startled when the President opened it quickly while tying his robe.

"This had better be good. I've been working much of the night and am only getting a little sleep," the leader spat.

"Yes sir, it is. Our men at Jefferson Station were found tied up this morning. One was shot in the leg. He's going to be alri…"

"Who did it?" Langley asked no longer in a morning haze.

"They didn't get any names, but they took Sara."

The leader picked up a vase from an end table next to the door and threw it across the room. "How difficult is it for you to keep that one small woman contained? I told you someone might try to get her!" he growled.

"Yes, sir, we know. I'm sorry. We had every access point covered along the railway. There was no way he could have gotten in."

"Well, he did, so your security measures weren't enough. Was it two men who took Sara?"

"Yes, I believe so. One was a little over six feet, and the other just under. That's all we know."

"Todd and Hudson," he mumbled. "No matter. They can't run forever. Start tracking them."

"We've been working on that. We think he is in Dr. Benjamin Keith's Mercedes, and we had a good fix until the beacon in the car went dead. We'll get them."

"Do you know where they're heading?" the leader asked scratching his head.

"They asked where Dr. Keith was. One of our tied up agents said he wanted to know where the scientist was being held."

That made him nervous. "Did he tell him?"

"No, he kept the location to himself."

Leaving the doorway, the President began to pace the elegantly decorated room. "It's doubtful he'll know where to find him, but alert the agents at Green One that there's a possibility of some visitors."

"Yes sir, will do."

"Find out where those men entered the railway line and lock it off. There should be no access to that Top-Secret facility."

The agent nodded.

"And find that car. I want those people in this house within 24 hours."

"Here, sir?" the agent asked in confusion.

He walked back toward the door, "I want them here, right here in front of me. I want to see their faces when I tell them they've failed to stop the progress in America."

The agent backed away.

He began to raise his voice, "I want them here, within 24 hours. Do you understand?" yelling.

"Yes, sir, I do," the agent stammered.

The leader slammed the door, and the agent ran downstairs to formulate a plan to find three people in a sea of 450 million.

28 — TUESDAY, 12 HOURS LATER, VERY LATE EVENING

"Hello, Dr. Keith. There isn't any time. The sphere has been compromised, and the world is at stake. I need you to come with me now!" Hudson said, looking over the fairly upscale apartment filled with fine furnishings, thick carpet, and works of art on the walls.

The doctor put his tea cup down, "Compromised?" he asked questioningly. Walking up to the agent he enveloped him in a grand hug. "Hudson, it is so good to see you. What do you mean, compromised? And why are you in a tuxedo coming through the vents?"

"You have no idea how good it is for me to see you," the agent smiled and hugged him back, then shrugged looking at his garb. "Long story."

"They've been protecting me here for so long," the scientists said. "I didn't think I'd ever be able to leave."

"First things first. Were you taken the night before our first jump was scheduled?"

"Yes, the President said my life was at stake, and they've been protecting me here ever since."

"They aren't protecting you – they're using you. What have you been working on?"

"I've essentially designed another sphere that's more advanced. They said the first had flaws and couldn't be used."

"They've been lying to you for months. The good news is, your creation worked."

Taking Hudson at his word, Dr. Keith began removing his robe and putting on some slacks when he stopped in his tracks, "It worked? It really worked? How do you know?" He looked up at Hudson. "You said that's the good news. What is the bad news?"

"Yes, Dr. Keith, I've been to the past many times, and it's worked flawlessly."

"I can't believe it worked," he smiled as he pulled a sweater over his t-shirt. "I was told that they have yet to try the technology."

"Did you say you've been working on a second sphere?" Hudson asked looking around the room for cameras and exits.

"They told me the first sphere had been sabotaged. To continue the project, we had to start over. I've been sending unmanned jumps with perfect results. But recently, the sphere has shown odd readings, as if it had been traveling to places without our direction. Our first jump is supposed to be a few months from now, but with these readings now, I'm uncertain."

"Dr. Keith, you asked what the bad news is. Those readings are from jumps being made when you are not there to supervise. Both spheres work well. But these jumps they've been making - they've essentially ruined the world with that second sphere. Everything changed, and the President altered the country to give him all the power. And now, well, the map of the world is very different than it was just two days ago."

Air hissed from his lungs as he sat down in a leather Chesterfield chair, now speechless.

Hudson pressed a hand to his shoulder, "Ben, I don't want to upset you, but I need you to make this thing right."

Dumbfounded he raised his head. "Right. How can I make it right? I didn't even know anything was wrong." Standing and walking to the closet he picked up some shoes, "I've not noticed any changes in the world. I watch the news and know of all of the events in the world."

Hudson interrupted, "Do you remember your theory that if a person has been through time, then they are essentially locked to their original timeframe?"

The man nodded to the question, "Yes," he spoke uncertainly. Sitting once again he pulled on his loafers.

"You said that person would remember the world in his timeline and could recognize any changes that might have taken place."

"Sure. But it was just a theory. It was just an idea I had that came when I was showering one day."

"It's more than a theory. I can recognize every alteration as it happens in the world. My family's been destroyed. All Christians are essentially running for their lives because of the sphere."

"I'm sorry, Hudson. I didn't know," his voice broke, realizing his responsibility. "I was told it didn't work."

"Yeah, well."

"It's hurt your family?" the man asked softly.

"Yes, Ben, my wife doesn't know me, and I no longer have children because I've *now* never been married."

Dr. Keith jumped up. "No, no, no! This was never to be used this way. It was to help and not hurt."

"Absolute power corrupts absolutely," Hudson said. "We don't have time to wrestle with this. I know you feel responsible, but you're innocent in all of this. We just need to correct it and put it back."

"Put the world back? What a statement." His hands moved erratically, "That's like putting the evils back into Pandora's Box. It can't be done," he paced. "Oh, what have I done? How could I have been so lied to?"

"Dr. Keith, we have no time for this."

That brought him around to his senses, "Yes, you're right." He looked at the clock, "So, essentially I've been imprisoned through a lie to get me to create a machine someone can use for their own selfish purposes?"

"That would be in in a nutshell," Hudson answered.

He looked toward the main door, "They'll be checking in within the next few minutes."

Hudson glanced around the room. "Do they do serious checks? Looking in closets and such?"

"No, they just look over the room, but that grate falling from the ceiling will indicate problems," he was pointing up.

Pulling a chair over, the man stood on it and lifted himself half into the opening speaking into the vent. "Give me a few minutes, and I'll be back. We have an inspection to deal with first."

Dr. Myers responded, "Okay, but make it quick."

Hudson replaced the grate and put the chair back in its place. "Do you have guards outside your residence?"

"Yes, someone is always seated at the outside door."

"So, we can't get out through there?"

"No, it's a labyrinth down here. You know they designed it to house hundreds of people, and it's a large facility. Without a map, it would be difficult to find your way around down here."

"Well, then we'll go back up."

There was a knocking on the door, "Dr. Keith, are you ready for me to secure your room?" the man asked.

"Just a minute," Ben yelled.

Pulling up his slacks above his knees and taking his robe from the bed, the scientist threw it on, "Hudson, get in the closet." He kicked off his shoes.

The agent ran over and closed the closet door behind him.

Working his way to the door, Ben welcomed the Secret Service agent, "Hello, David, how are you this evening?" he said nervously.

"I'm fine, sir. Are you alright in there?"

"Of course," Ben was looking around the door. "I am really tired tonight. All is well in here, so I don't need a security check this evening. Thank you," he tried to close the door.

"Sir, it is my duty to check your room each night, you know that," putting his foot in the door and stopping its movement.

"David, I'm in the middle of quite a few things and just want a little privacy."

"I'll be quick and leave you to your work," he said as if he was not going to take no for an answer. Pushing the door open he walked in, beginning his search around the room. "Have you seen or heard anything odd this evening?"

"No, David, it has been quiet as usual. I just have a mathematical equation bumping around in my head, and I need silence and time for a resolution to come to me. Should I be expecting some activity?" he asked trying to get information.

"No, Dr. Keith, just normal precautions. We want to keep you safe," he said looking through the kitchen. "Do you need anything from the store?"

"No, nothing."

The agent walked into the living room and checked the coat closet.

"Wow, you are being extra thorough this evening. Normally, you don't check the closets," he raised his voice a little so Hudson could hear.

"Just doing my job." Glancing into the bedroom the man seemed content with his search. "Well, everything looks good here."

"Thank you, David. I appreciate your concern for me."

"Anytime," he replied as he started for the front door. With the scientist in his lead almost to the apartment exit, the agent saw a pants leg fall from under the man's robe and stopped.

"Are you dressed, Dr. Keith?" he asked suspiciously.

Knowing he couldn't hide it, he forced the other leg down. "Truthfully, I wanted to take a walk through the halls tonight to think. Even if it meant bribing Joey outside the door with the promise of a time jump sometime after its completion."

"You're fully dressed and yet you put on a robe. What's going on here?"

"Nothing agent, just...," he watched as the agent made his way into the bedroom.

He looked under the bed, behind the curtains and eventually went to the closet. "Are you hiding something?"

Opening the closet, the agent with the linebacker build opened the closet door.

An unexpected right jab struck his face. He fell backward as Hudson jumped on him and the men tumbled to the floor.

Trying to pull his weapon, Hudson would not allow him access to the gun held on his hip, so he kicked and punched trying to remove the traveler from on top of him but, Hudson would not let him free.

David hit Hudson in the face, effectively removing him from his chest. Those two seconds of fog were enough to get him on his feet and reach for his gun. Hudson stood with his hands in the air.

David reached for his phone to alert the unit when Dr. Keith came up from behind and crunched the back of his skull with a leaded-glass vase full of daisies. The man dropped like a rock as water and flowers splashed all over the ground.

Taking the man's gun and putting it in his pocket Hudson looked directly at the doctor, "Get me something to tie him up with."

Dr. Keith ran to the kitchen and found some duct tape. Bringing it back, the agent tied the guard up, so he could not work his way loose.

"Is anyone else coming tonight?"

"No, he's the last, but I think he makes a report in to his supervisor after his rounds. We may have 20 minutes before he's noticed as being absent."

"Okay, go and lock the front door and put a chair under the knob."

The man took off the robe, put on his shoes and jogged to the front door.

"Do you have anything important pertaining to the project we need to bring?" Hudson asked, dragging the unconscious body to the far side of the bed.

"All of my journals," he replied.

"If you have a backpack or something, put them in there. We've got to get going."

The man ran to his recliner and turned it over. He removed the bottom and pulled out the journals.

Hudson watched the activity, "Why did you hide them?"

"I guess the only person I've ever really trusted is you, Hudson." He put the thin books in a backpack and placed it on his shoulders. "I'm ready."

Hudson tugged the chair back over and opened the grate. Reaching up in the hole, he found the rope and pulled it through. "Are you two ready up there?" the agent called.

"We're tied off up here," Dr. Myers responded. "We don't have the ability to pull you up, there just isn't the room in this little closet."

"Keith, are you still in pretty good shape?" Hudson asked with a smile.

"I'm only 46, and they let me workout to keep myself from going crazy locked up in here. I suppose I can climb a rope with the best of them."

"Okay then, you're first."

Hudson jumped down from the chair and Ben took his place. Pulling himself up through the large opening he found the passageway. It was not totally vertical, and that helped with diminishing some of his weight. Still, with no room for pulling and pushing, the climb was a challenge.

Hudson watched him disappear into the darkness above before he began his ascent. Seeing the once dead scientist disappear into the closet with his friends made him relax just for a second. After several minutes the man made it to the glow of the opening at the entrance to the shaft.

Even though he was worn out, his muscles pushed on and he pulled himself up through the shaft until he saw Todd's hand reach out and pull him through.

"One, big, happy family," the professor remarked at seeing everyone together in the small closet. He dusted off the agent. "The party is still raging in there so you and Sara can join the fray only to make a grand exit."

The scientist regained his breath from the climb and went over and hugged Sara. "Sara, it is so good to see you again. Thank you for coming to get me."

"Sure, sir, but I don't think we've met before."

Todd looked at Hudson and whispered, "How does he know her but she doesn't know him?"

Sara looked over at Todd.

Dr. Keith jumped in having overheard the professor. "Interesting, it's as if all the work I've done on the sphere may have affected my perspective of time in some ways. Somehow, when we worked together, Hudson, and you were married, that is the only reality I can recall. Yet in her timeframe, she's never been married. Interesting. So, I know her, but she doesn't know me."

Todd and Hudson were totally silent as Sara got wide eyes.

"Did I say something wrong?" Dr. Keith asked.

"What do you mean we were married? I've never been married. And what is this about a timeframe? What's going on here?"

"I'm sorry, Hudson, I thought she knew," the scientist said regretfully dropping off in volume.

Hudson took Sara's arm. "Are you ready for one more dance? You do look beautiful." Turning to look at the other men, "You have 15 minutes to make it to the car."

"We'll be there," Todd replied quietly.

Sara put her arm in his and noticed the sad look Hudson was trying to hide. He opened the door, and they left.

"Here, get under this cart." The scientist squeezed onto the lower level of the food cart and Todd threw a tablecloth over it. "Don't get out until we get to the car."

"Will do." Poking his head out, he looked up from the cart, "I'm sorry for telling Sara. I thought she knew."

"She had to have known something. Now she does for sure. It's all right. God works everything out for the good of those who love him."

Todd retrieved his waiter uniform, and put it back on. He tried to straighten it, but as he only had to pull it off for a few hundred feet he let it go.

He inhaled deeply, then released it and opened the door. Pushing the cart out of the room, he headed toward the 12 foot doors which exited to the grand ballroom. As he was pushing, he saw Hudson and Sara going through one last dance. The orchestra was rich and the female performer was singing the song, *For Sentimental Reasons.* Many of the words were so true for his friend who now had to gain back the love of the woman he had been married to for years. And he had no relationship to start from.

I love you, and you alone were meant for me, please give your loving heart to me, and say we'll never part. The words echoed gracefully across the gala.

The cart exited the room and the men headed down the main hallway.

29 — TUESDAY, VERY LATE EVENING

I think of you every morning...

Gowns spun around the parquet floor highly adorned as the colored lighting enhanced the warm romantic mood. The orchestra swelled as Hudson held Sara in the center of the dance floor. Above them, a mirrored ball reflected the light onto the walls in a million different patterns. He pulled her closer and moved into the dance.

Dream of you every night...

There was not much time to enjoy a moment with her. Everything hinged on their escape. But he had lost so much with her. Memories he knew so well she would never remember again. He wanted to regain what he had lost, if only for a few minutes. His thumbs caressed her waist of their own volition.

Sara lifted her eyes to his for a second. Instead of shifting out of his grip, she simply looked over his shoulder into the distance.

"What did he mean?" she asked swaying in time with his movements.

"What did who mean?" Hudson asked.

"What did that man mean?" He heard the tremors in her voice and felt for her.

"Sara, it's nothing. He's just a crazy scientist."

"I don't know you very well, but I know you're not telling me everything." She looked up at him again. "Your eyes tell me everything. It's just that – it's like there's something I don't know. Somehow I trust you, and I never trust easily."

He forced his gaze away from hers and she lifted her hand to bring his face back to her own.

"Sara, let's just finish the dance and get out of here. We need to not look suspicious."

Darling, I'm never lonely...

"That man knew me," she spoke softly. By the look of him, he knew me well, and I should have known him."

Hudson remained silent and looked ahead.

"But I don't know him." The uncertainty and break in her voice matched the same in his heart. "He said something about a timeframe." Her fingers drew his face back to her own again. "What does that man do? Tell me, Hudson." All fear of him evaporated from her face, and she gave him a warm smile with a lift of her eyebrows.

Recognizing he could not lie to her he answered, "Sara, Dr. Keith is probably the world's top scientist in theoretical physics."

"What does that mean?"

"Dr. Keith deals in the impossible," he answered.

*Whenever you are in sight...*The singer held the tone over before she began the next line.

"What's impossible? Don't be so cryptic."

"Ben has worked out formulas to understand time."

They continued to sway back and forth, and Sara asked her next question.

"What about time? How it works?"

Hudson looked down at her and loved her more. He treasured her small nose, blue eyes, blond flowing hair, and her inquisitive mind.

"Well, he understands time travel."

Her body stopped as the agent kept her moving. "But time travel is impossible," insecurity edged into her tone again.

He moved his hand to the middle of her back, "I thought so as well, until he proved it to me."

I love you... for sentimental reasons...

Moving in tandem, he spun her around the floor to prevent any tears provoked by the mood. They swayed in silence for several moments before she spoke again.

For whatever reason, she placed her head on his shoulder, her trust making it harder for him to think. "So then, why are we here? Why is he important? And you've never made any sense of why I'm here, for that matter."

"He's going to help us get your life back."

"But what do I have to do with time travel? Why do we need time travel," she mocked. "A scientist to get me back to my job with the Senator? How can he stop the President?"

Hudson, pulled her face toward his, "Sara, the life you are living now, is not the one you were destined to have."

"What does that mean? I'm doing what I'm supposed to do," she answered in confusion.

Couples twirled next to them.

"You've spoken to Todd and me about feeling like you've missed out on some things. Things that you should have had yet don't," the agent asked trying to be clear but finding that impossible at the moment.

"Sure, but who doesn't have regrets. Everyone has things they wish they could have done."

"Those regrets are for what you had. For things that were taken from you. The things you want to do are the things you have done in your original life."

"How do you know what I should have had?" She spoke indignantly, but fortunately well within a whisper. "Who are you to tell me what my life should be? I'm grateful for you and Todd rescuing me, but you know very little about me."

"Sara, why did the President take you?" he asked quietly.

"I still don't know. I'm just an aid to a Senator. I'm not important."

"Sara, you're everything. You are so important."

"What makes me so important?"

Looking up and around the room, his mind stumbled to find the words. "You were collateral to keep me from getting Dr. Keith."

"Why would I be collateral for a scientist I don't know?"

"You are very important. Todd and I, and maybe the President and his agent are the only four people on earth who know the way everything should be. Sara, this world should not be the way it is."

She looked up at him in the dark with a puzzled look on her face.

He continued, "There are only 50 states in the United States."

"No, there are a lot more..."

"No, there should only be 50. We don't have provinces in Europe. The President shouldn't be a religious leader."

"He's always been a religio..."

"No, he hasn't. This has all happened within the last few days. He should not look like a Pope and have influence over man's relationship with God."

I hope you do believe me...

"Two days ago, he was just a political leader. The world was simpler, and there were securities in the constitution keeping the government from getting involved in religion.

I know I may sound crazy, but you must believe me. Todd and I have seen time travel firsthand and understand the pain that it can cause.

This President has either gone back himself or sent someone back to change certain points in history to make himself more powerful. He has removed religious events from history; events that helped to form our original timeline. These events helped to make America strong and free and a nation that honors the Lord Jesus Christ – at least it was for many years. Now everything is messed up. Americans are now vassals of the President and must do what he chooses and believe what he tells them to."

"*If this is true*, what does this have to do with me?" she asked nervously.

"Sara, your kidnapping was to keep me from correcting everything." He would have to be more clear, "Do your parents still live in Virginia?"

"Yes, but what does that have…"

"Do they still live in that colonial two-story, and does their home still back up to rolling hills?"

"Yes," her eyes became bigger. "What does that have to do with anyth..?"

"Your dad is outgoing and always has a good joke. He loves the Lord and will always bring God up in conversation."

"Yes, but the President is trying to put a stop to that. I fear he won't stop telling about Christ."

"No, I don't think he will. Your mom is fairly proper, and makes a great carrot cake."

"If you're an agent, you could look those types of things up, right?" She looked away.

I've given you my heart… The interlude began.

"Sara, I don't want to really get into this."

"No, you've freed me from an underground prison, dragged me into West Virginia, helped me to break into a hotel to free some scientist and now we're dancing. This is not a normal day for me. So tell me why I'm involved."

Looking her in the eyes he gave up. "Okay. You love poetry by Blake and Browning. You listen to Christian music, but alone, you often go classical. You love to draw but believe your sketches are too elongated.

You are very organized but things tend to end up in piles," he smiled. "You are energized by people and would have someone over every night for dinner if you could.

Your favorite flowers are gardenias."

The interlude ended and the final chorus began. *I love you for sentimental reasons...*

Sara's eyes were very wide, and she stared into Hudson's face.

"You love to exercise and excel in yoga. You had braces when you were twelve and were the captain of the cheer squad in High School."

I hope you do believe me...

"Sara, you have a scar on your left outer thigh from a fall doing a... a scorpion at extension, or something like that." The small woman rubbed her leg with her hand at his words.

"Hudson, what does all of this have to do with me?" she trembled slightly in his arms.

She had to know. There was no way around it. "Sara, you were taken to keep me from working on the truth. You were kidnapped to stop me."

"How could I stop you?" She halted her question as she remembered what Dr. Keith said earlier.

I've given you my heart… The orchestra began to conclude the song.

"Sara, the President thought he could control me by taking you, but all it did was make me that much more determined."

He exhaled heavily then looked into her eyes directly. "Honey," a single tear slipped down his face. "I love you, and, until a few days ago you were my wife. Then everything changed. I would go to the ends of the earth to find you, and I will do everything I can to get our life back."

She let her hands slide from his shoulders and wriggled from his grasp. "Oh no. No, I've never been married."

"In this timeline you haven't, but in the true one, you have."

"I don't know you. You're trying to confuse me," she started to shake as she backed away.

"Sweetie, it's going to be fine. Don't be afraid. Let's get out of here."

"I'm not going anywhere with you," her voice was raising and couples around were beginning to look their way.

He tried to touch her and comfort her, but she pulled away.

"I don't know who you are, but, but… You need to stay away from me."

She turned toward the exit behind them.

"Sara," he sighed as he attempted to follow her unobtrusively.

As the orchestra began the next song and the people continued dancing, Hudson made it to the exit and grabbed Sara's hand. "I'm sorry for upsetting you." She stopped her movement. "Just another day or so, and I will return you to your Senate job. But I want to ensure you are safe before I do that."

She looked up at him, still shaken, "Okay," she said quietly. "I do know you are trying to protect me. If you were going to try something it would have been at that awful motel back there."

At Sara's last word, the overhead lights in the ballroom all blinked to life and men at the back of the space came through the doors with semi-automatic weapons drawn.

The women in the room started to scream as Hudson realized the depth of the problem. Looking back in the room he spoke to Sara, "We've got to go now."

All energy zapped from her, Sara held his hand tightly and allowed him to take her arm as they ran down the hallway toward the exit.

Hudson pulled his gun, "You remember where the car is parked?" he asked starting to get out of breath.

"Yes, I think so," she answered trying to keep up with him in her high heels.

"If we get separated, you make it to the car and tell Todd to leave this place immediately."

"No, I won't. You're going with me."

Looking over his shoulder and seeing men running down the hallway, he pointed his weapon back at them, and they broke off behind columns. Within several seconds, gunfire began that was pointed in their direction.

Running as fast as possible, Hudson got behind Sara and shot back at the men. They were at the exit and rounded the corner toward the vehicle as bullets whizzed past the agent's head.

"Come on Sara, faster," he yelled looking back and firing trying to ensure the men would not exit the building.

"I'm going as fast as I can. It had to be men who designed high heels, because they're not good for anything other than beauty."

"Well, they are good for that," he smirked as she laughed through a stumble.

The building lit up like a county fair and much of the countryside was lit as well as the parking lot and all of the attached buildings.

With the added light, Hudson could see men coming around the building. They were just 100 feet from the car when they saw the vehicle light up and leave the space. Driving toward them, both the front and back passenger doors flew open. Todd was in the driver's seat, "Come on you two, the clock is ringing midnight."

Dr. Keith sat in the back and pulled Sara in as Hudson closed the door. The agent jumped in the front and yelled, "Go."

The Mercedes leaped forward, covering the distance to the main gated entrance in just a few seconds. Before they could make it, twelve-inch diameter steel poles began to rise from the ground at the gate, effectively blocking it like any Governmental facility in Washington.

"We can't go through that," yelled Hudson.

Everyone lurched in the back seat as the professor turned the vehicle the other way.

Hudson was craning his neck to see if there was a second exit, but found poles rising from every road leaving the main parking areas. "Turn back around," he called.

Todd turned the vehicle as a few bullets hit the trunk.

"Hudson, is this my car?" Dr. Keith asked incredulously.

"Yeah. Sorry, doc."

A few more bullets zoomed past leaving sparks on the pavement.

"Where to?" Todd asked with both hands on the wheel as if driving in a Bond movie.

Pointing to the right, "The gate has bushes on the sides of it. Jump the curve and run through them. There should be enough room to get through without hitting the trees."

Instantly, the vehicle jumped the curb and headed for the edge of the archway.

"They don't have those poles in the bushes do they?"

"I guess we'll find out."

Todd looked over at his partner with doubt as another bullet hit the trunk. Dr. Keith covered Sara as she leaned her head down in the seat.

"Is everyone alright back there?" Hudson yelled.

"Yes, just get us out of here," Sara mumbled into her dress.

Sirens at the facility began to whine throughout the countryside as the vehicle hit the bushes. Scraping both sides of the expensive machine and taking off the mirrors, the car squeezed through between the trees and the gate.

Finding the main road, they jumped the curb again leaving the grass as the professor floored the now-battered piece of German engineering. All four wheels were still intact and the engine purred like a sewing machine.

Hudson looked back over his shoulder seeing men going in all directions. Some were running back toward the facility while others were at the gate trying to get it to retract. Knowing it usually took five minutes in a lock-down scenario for the equipment to be reset, he spoke, "Todd, get us down the road as fast as you can."

"I'm doing everything possible."

"We're going to have people following very soon. I won't be surprised if they have a helicopter."

"Great. You know the only way out of here is this two lane road. If they want to, they can just block it off somewhere ahead."

Querying the phone's GPS, Hudson scrolled through several pages until he found another route.

"Todd, take the second left. It will probably be rough and slow going, but we can meet up with a major road in maybe 20 miles."

"Will do," he answered leaning forward in his seat trying to find a dirt road in the dark.

"Dr. Keith, are you still with us?"

"Yes, Hudson, I am fine. Thank you for getting me out of there."

"Sara, what about you?" he said putting his hand on her knee around the seat.

"I'm not hurt." She put her hand on top of Hudson's as she leaned back in the seat and shut her eyes.

The agent just kept it there as Todd turned the vehicle onto a dirt road in the middle of West Virginia.

30 — TUESDAY, VERY LATE EVENING

The President, clad in a tuxedo, relaxed in a side room sipping a 1953 Hine 250 Cognac with his bowtie loose. After enduring a White House soiree, a few of the remaining attendees - mostly dignitaries and ambassadors, stood in his presence, obviously doing all in their power to impress the world leader. Their conversation had just begun to bore the President when John Costall knocked on the door.

"Come in," President Langley growled through a Cuban cigar.

Smoke and the smell of alcohol stung the nostrils of the Chief of Staff as he entered through the large mahogany door.

"Sir, do you have a few minutes?" he said knowing his information would upset the powerful man.

"Come back in a little while." The President replied. In the background, laughter erupted over a private joke in the corner.

John just looked at the man sitting in the large fauteuil chair, "It is important."

"Okay. It had better be," he said rising and putting out his cigar in an ashtray resting on a nesting table. He downed the rest of his cognac and led the Chief of Staff down the hall to his private office.

John had only been in the private space a few times, and the stark contrast to the rest of the rooms within the people's house always shocked him. Even though the desk was the one used by F.D.R., it was covered with various office toys and a lava lamp. The many books on shelves were interspersed with trinkets, gizmos and mementos that were important to the world figure. Costall wanted out as quickly as possible.

The world leader sat as he spoke, "What's going on?"

"There was a break-in at Green One," the staffer said waiting for the words to fly.

"Don't tell me they're still on the loose," he said sitting up in his chair.

"This just happened a few minutes ago, so we are still receiving the intel, but I think… they are."

The man sat in silence.

"Our men have been going over recorded video of the facility, and it looks like you were right, Hudson is working with Dr. Myers."

He continued to stare straight at him.

John pulled a paper from his pocket to break the man's focus, "Uh, it says here that Sara was with them."

"How'd they get in?" he growled. "Why weren't they picked up by credit card usage or something, anything?"

"Hudson evidently used cash, and they had some kind of a ruse about Sara being pregnant. Whatever happened, the person checking them in allowed them into a room. We saw that Todd came up through a back door."

"How could that happen?" he pounded the desk. "What else?"

"Dr. Myers found some wait staff apparel. The other two went to the ballroom in formal wear, evidently purchased at the shop there. And again, with cash. They apparently climbed down a ventilation shaft in a closet off the ballroom to find Dr. Keith," the man kept his eyes on his paper.

"Did they find Keith?" his eyes became narrow slits.

"Yes, sir, they evidently overtook a guard and climbed back up through the shaft." Clearing his throat he added, "All four made it to the car and somehow got away from the compound after much gunfire and destruction of property. It's going to be difficult calming all of the wealthy and influential people that were witness to what the Secret Service were involved in."

"So where are they now?"

"They're heading on the only road away from the Greenbrier; east toward Virginia."

Standing from his chair, he walked around the desk, "Now listen to me."

The man shook his head, "I want them caught. I want them stopped. At this point, I don't care if they're dead or alive. They'll not affect the way I've put this nation together. Do you understand that?"

"Yes."

He poked the man on his chest, "I want all resources on this – police, state police, the Secret Service, and the National Guard if need be. Bring in helicopters and tanks if required, but I expect them to be stopped."

Anxious, he started to pace the room, "They're now too powerful. If they have Keith, then they have everything. The person who designed the spheres is the one who can shut them down and possibly reverse everything I've put together."

Coming back to look John right in the eyes, "They'll go no farther, even if that means we launch a missile to stop them. Do you understand? You are cleared to do whatever it takes to halt their progress."

"Sir, there are quite a few farms in the area. What will those people think, seeing a military build-up in their front yard?"

"We'll pay them off when it's over. Just stop them." He yelled, "Stop them! Go, and do it!"

John backed away and left the leader in his office.

Hayden Christopher Langley fingered a treasure from his shelf only a moment before he crushed it and threw the pieces across the room. "He will not stop me."

~

"Can you hit a few more ditches?" Hudson asked as everyone was being thrown around the vehicle.

"Hey, you sent us on this dirt road. I only have one headlight, and this Mercedes' suspension is for the Autobahn – not dirt roads in West Virginia. We're not in an SUV." He had both hands on the wheel turning left and right to keep from hitting more holes. "Where are we going? This vehicle isn't going to last long on these backways."

"We'll drive it until it won't go anymore," the agent shot back.

Keith poked his head between the two front seats. "Hudson, are those my journals up there?" The notebooks protruded from the bag on the dash.

"Yes, Ben, I grabbed them from your house," Hudson replied.

The scientist's mind started to turn. "Hudson, do we have a laptop on board with a roaming Wi-Fi connection?"

"Yeah, this one should do." Pulling one up from his floorboard he opened it and waited for it to boot. "It has a satellite connection. Why do you need it?"

"I'm just curious about something," the man said with reservation.

Hudson handed the laptop between the seats.

"Let me have those books if you can," the scientist added.

The agent pulled the books from a backpack. Dr. Keith looked through the journals with his finger going across the pages. After he found what he was looking for, he began typing on the computer.

"Where are we going, man?" Todd asked quietly as the car bumped back and forth. "You know the President has probably every person in America who owns a gun after us. The Army, Navy, Air Force, Marines... If we were near the water he'd probably have the Coast Guard firing on us." The car lurched to the left and then back.

"Yeah, I know. I'm not sure how we get out of this. This road will protect us for a while because they'll expect us on the main highway. But it won't take them long to get choppers in the air, and then we're sunk."

"We need to pray," the seminary professor reminded them.

"I agree," Sara approved. "May I, Hudson?"

"It would be a blessing," Hudson smiled.

The scientist kept plugging away on the computer.

"I hope you don't mind if I keep my eyes open," Todd added sarcastically.

Hudson chuckled as she shook her head vigorously. "Please do!"

Sara bowed her head in the vehicle as it continued to careen left and right and they bounced in their seats. "Dear Lord, we need You," Sara started. "We have no idea what to do and are at the end of our rope, so we need You to make a way. We're doing everything we can to honor You with our lives, but it seems people are working against that. Lord, we just want to show the world that You are all-powerful and that You love us. So give us a miracle. Quickly. In Jesus name we praise You. Amen."

Hudson and Todd said a hearty Amen, and then the vehicle hit a large rock sending the car off the road. Forcing it back up onto the dirt, the professor knew something was damaged but found no other option than to push it forward.

The machine growled and squeaked as it moved more slowly toward their only exit from the area.

"Bingo!" Dr. Keith yelled.

"What's bingo?" Hudson asked.

Clapping his hands, "Do you want a quicker exit out of here?" the man in the backseat asked.

"Sure, but how are you going to do that?" Todd replied.

With the screen glowing in his face he looked up, "Hudson you said the original sphere was never damaged, and that it worked perfectly."

"Yes, sadly enough, but it did everything you designed. Why?"

"Several days before I was taken, and supposedly *protected* by the President, I did some extra work on that sphere."

Hudson and Sara listened intently as Todd continued to watch for holes in the road.

"What extra work? I knew everything you did on that machine," Hudson asked.

"Hudson, I implicitly trust you and would have told you about the changes. But they took me that evening. There wasn't any time to tell you about the backdoor I put in it."

"What does this mean?"

"It means I can access it here and now."

"No, that's impossible," Hudson sighed at the unrealistic thought. "Recently, the President forced us to turn it into a makeshift power plant. There was no way we could have used it when we left."

"Power plant, how did that work?"

"I'll bring you up later, but back to what you were saying."

"Oh yeah, there was no way you could have known about it, but I always had a loaded program that I could access, to force it back to its original parameters.

I was concerned about someone using this for reasons other than good, so I have always had a method to access it and hide it if need be. I'm glad I don't trust anyone, or I wouldn't have put this backdoor access in."

"So what are you telling us, Dr. Keith?" Sara asked.

"Well, I have already corrected everything your husband, I mean Hudson,… I'm sorry," he said looking at her.

"It's all right, just get us out of here."

"Alright. I have reformatted the computer and returned it back to its original specifications, and I can bring it here if you want."

"What?" Everyone yelled over the loud sound of the road beneath the car.

He laughed. "This is so exciting. Hudson you said it actually does what I designed it to do?"

"Yes, sir. You're brilliant – almost too brilliant."

"To think my life's effort actually worked," he was giddy. "But I digress. If you want that thing to land on the roof, I can put it there. It might be better if we stopped, so I could get precise longitude and latitude."

"Todd, let's pull over," Hudson remarked to his partner.

The Mercedes came to a stop on the side of the road as Dr. Keith got out with computer in hand. The other three occupants followed.

Walking around a moment to orient the computer, the scientist came back and placed it on the trunk and continued to work. "Guys, this should only take a few seconds. Because it isn't traveling through time but just trans-locating, it will be instantaneous when I push the EXECUTE button. Give me another minute."

Everyone watched in rapt attention as the man furiously plugged in the laptop. Looking up in the night sky, they found all the constellations visible. Sara, beginning to feel the chill in the cool night air shivered and wrapped her arms around herself. Cautiously, Hudson came up alongside her and held her close to keep her warm. She did not resist but snuggled in tight.

Dr. Keith stopped typing. "Are you ready?"

The three started backing away.

"If I've done this right, it should end up behind us about a hundred feet." Looking over his calculations again, "Yeah a hundred feet that way," he pointed behind him. "Here goes, now cover your eyes because it's going to get real bright."

Hands over her eyes already, Sara twisted into Hudson as he covered his face with one hand and placed the other on the back of Sara's head. Todd turned the other way, and Dr. Keith continued to monitor the action on the laptop.

He pressed EXECUTE. Several seconds passed and nothing happened.

"What's going on? I thought I..."

Before he could finish his sentence, the vehicle that had caused so much trouble in the past, appeared in a flash of light and a surge of power. The countryside was bathed in illumination for hundreds of feet. Like a Tesla coil, the trees had tendrils of electricity wrapping around them close to 50 feet away. A small fire was started off to the south.

The weary refugees could feel the hot energy wave that accompanied its entrance, and ozone permeated the air. As quickly as they came, all of the effects were over and everyone looked behind them to see the vehicle slightly glowing, covered in steam with the top half rising, and evidently prepared to jump again.

"I did it!" Dr. Keith exclaimed. "I can't believe I really did it." Clapping his hands, he walked toward the engineering marvel of his own creation.

Todd stamped out the fire it had started, and Sara opened her eyes to see the thing that had so affected her life – but that she had no reference for.

"What's that?" She asked staying in Hudson's arms.

"That's what's going to get us out of this mess."

Dr. Keith ran over to the machine and looked inside. "It actually works. I can't believe it."

Hudson released Sara reluctantly and walked over to the elated doctor, patting him on the back in a moment of joy he had thought was lost forever. "I wish you could have seen it originally when we made the first leap. It was a Neil Armstrong moment."

"Wow, I just can't believe it works. I've conquered the time barrier."

Having put the fire out, Todd joined them. "Dr. Keith, you have definitely changed the world," he replied, almost sarcastically.

The good doctor appeared unaffected by the remark, "Now, how are you involved in all of this? Are you a scientist also?" Ben asked the professor.

"Nope, I have a Ph.D. in Theology. I'm a seminary professor."

"Have you traveled in my design?"

"Yep, I've been all over."

Confused, he looked to Hudson for answers, "How does a seminary professor get into a vehicle like this?" Dr. Keith asked.

Wanting to answer that, Hudson stopped him with an arm extended.

"Let's not worry about that now. Needless to say, he can run it just as well as we can," Hudson smiled.

Dr. Keith went back to thinking about his vehicle.

The steam was beginning to dissipate when Todd spoke again. "So where do we go?"

Everyone got silent.

"I don't know, I didn't expect this," Hudson muttered the thought as he made his way back to Sara. She willingly moved again into his warmth.

"We can go anywhere now that we have it here," Dr. Keith replied.

"We don't have much time. The solar flare this thing sent off is going to bring the world to our location. At any moment. Dr. Keith, can you find the other sphere?"

He thought for a few seconds, "I can set this laptop to search for it, but I can't find it unless it jumps. Once that happens, we will have its every move," the scientist answered.

"So, then can you get us into the underground tunnels under D.C.?" Hudson ran back to the car and pulled out a map from under the seat. "Here is where we need to be," he said, pointing at a spot on the large paper.

"What data do you have other than this? I've never heard of these tunnels," Dr. Keith queried uncertainly. "These aren't the Metro tunnels are they?"

"No, these are secret underpasses, and I don't have much info on them."

"Hudson, do you hear that?" Todd asked looking down the dirt road they had driven.

"Hear what?"

Everyone got quite and looked behind them.

"Somebody's coming. They're far away, but it sounds like a large group." Sara added.

"She's right, we don't have much time," Todd jumped with anxiety in his voice.

"Ben, do your best and get us there," Hudson said quickly.

"I don't know the exact location. I don't know the elevation. If we get this wrong, then we'll materialize into a wall," the scientist shot back.

Sara inhaled nervously and tucked her head into Hudson.

Todd aimed his whole arm toward the oncoming armada, "Do you want to go back to the Greenbrier?"

The man typed furiously as Hudson climbed in first, then helped Sara into the vehicle and onto his lap – the most logical space in the two-seater-and-room-for luggage vehicle.

"Is this going to work?" she whispered.

He laughed for the first time in days. "It's not as smooth as the Mercedes, but you can go through time in it. So we give up a few of the creature comforts for its performance."

She sighed and did her best to simply look forward.

Todd climbed in next and sat between the seats. "I wonder if there's a world record for how many people you can stuff into a time machine." He laughed.

Sara and Hudson did not think his joke so humorous.

Climbing in slowly, Dr. Keith spoke, "On the next version of this we need an easier way to get in."

"Sure," Hudson answered, "Just get us out of here."

"Another version of this thing. We don't need the ones we've got," Todd grumbled.

Hudson tapped his leg to keep him from starting a fight.

Sitting in the seat, Dr. Keith kept inputting information. The readouts on the dash of the vehicle changed to correlate to the time, location, and altitude of the required jump. Hudson could see that they would be traveling in present time to an area around the National Mall. He saw the elevation as a negative 25 feet.

"After a quick research of the distance subway tunnels run below the surface, I think I have it right." The scientist said looking at everyone… "But I can't be sure."

"I'll take your guess over most people's facts any day," Hudson responded.

Hearing the vehicles closing in enough to feel the rumble through the earth, Professor Myers retracted the top of the sphere as several cars came to a screeching halt behind them.

"Time to go," Hudson yelled.

"Are you sure?" Ben asked.

"Yeah, push the button!" Todd barked.

Hearing military personnel cocking their weapons and yelling, "Get out of the vehicle," Hudson held Sara tighter.

"Let's go!" Hudson and Todd yelled.

At that, Dr. Keith pushed the ENTER button on his laptop and forced himself into his seat. Immediately, the machine began to heat up and glow.

"Get out of the vehicle, or we will open fire," someone called from the outside.

"Don't worry, the voltage traveling through the outer shell will protect us," the scientist yelled over the roar of the machine. No one felt any safer.

Gunfire ricocheted off the shielding of the sphere. No bullets made it through the aura surrounding the vehicle.

Energy coursed through their bones and the vehicle whined eerily until they were nearly to the breaking point. Then it happened.

The sphere vanished in a flash that threw everyone standing outside nearly 100 feet away and even overturned one Humvee parked behind.

The West Virginia countryside was once again quiet and dark.

31 — WEDNESDAY, VERY EARLY MORNING

Every manhole cover within a half mile of the sphere's landing site blew off in a flash of light. The access points to the secret tunnel system lit up like search lights, causing a half dozen early morning accidents in the capital city.

Uncertain of the exact elevation, the doctor monitored and corrected the sphere's trajectory in the last millisecond – jostling all of its occupants around the small space. Had he not added that specific subroutine at the last minute, the vehicle would have dropped four additional feet due to the miscalculation in negative elevation, ensuring the destruction of the scientific marvel.

Once it came to rest, the top half of the sphere started to rise as the cockpit filled with steam – powering down and preparing for another jump.

Hudson spoke first to Sara, "Are you alright?"

"Yes, I think so," she said cautiously.

"I'm alive," the professor added trying to stretch out of his squeezed space.

Dr. Keith waited for several seconds before he chimed in, "Did we make it?"

"Yes, Ben. It looks like we did," Hudson responded.

"We really made it? We translocated across country?" he spoke quietly, not believing what had happened.

Todd crawled across the scientist on his way back to solid ground, "Yeah, we're here. Wherever here is." He looked around.

"Everything will be different. No more need for planes and trains. Eventually, we won't need cars. We can go around the world instantly. Can you imagine that?" the designer continued with excitement.

"Whoa, let's slow down. We can worry about the future tomorrow. Right now, I want to fix the past. Dr. Keith, do you know exactly where we are?" Hudson asked.

The scientist looked about in a daze over what he had accomplished.

The agent spoke again, "Dr. Keith, where are we?"

"Oh, yeah," he popped open the laptop to see a screen with a blinking dot. "We are essentially where you asked to be. Right here," he pointed.

The agent looked at the dot and found their location to be just a bit west of the Washington Monument.

"Which direction are we facing?" Hudson asked again.

"The sphere is designed to face toward the most open space." The scientist looked down the long tunnel designed for a secret rail system. "That way is west," he pointed.

"So we need to go behind us. Todd what do you see?" asking his partner.

The professor ran into the dark a short distance and came back. "It looks like an empty tunnel. Nothing moving that I can tell."

"Well, they'll be coming soon. I'm sure we made a grand entrance." Hudson jumped out of the vehicle and looked at the scientist, "Ben, I need you to take this machine out of here and get Sara to safety," he said as he pulled his weapon.

Sara began to look nervous, "What do you mean, take me to safety? You're the one who got me to safety. I'm staying as close to you as I can."

"No way, honey… I mean Sara," he corrected himself. "You need to go. It isn't safe here, and my top goal is to ensure your protection."

"Well, I'm not going," she flounced out of the machine in her gown and stood her ground.

"And I'm not going either," Dr. Keith added. "If they have adulterated my technology for their own desires, I'm going to be there to shut it down."

Hudson knew a lost battle when he saw one, "I really need you two to go," he tried to direct Sara back up into the vehicle.

Sara swatted his hands and stood next to him, "I'm going with you."

"I should have known you wouldn't listen," the agent said with frustration.

"What's that supposed to mean?" she asked, incensed.

He mumbled his response, "I've lived with you for a long time."

Todd laughed and Sara spoke again, "What did you say?"

"Nothing important," he said more clearly.

Dr. Keith came from the vehicle with his laptop. "Hudson, I have perfect reception in here. It's like this entire tunnel system is designed to ensure data communication." He turned around with the laptop in his hand seeing if the reception would change.

Todd answered. "I wouldn't doubt it if this is the President's rail system. He has to be accessible even if he's down here."

"I have a complete connection to the sphere even down here," he looked at the laptop. As if getting a great idea, he started poking on the screen of his watch, "You know what; I could probably sync the program to my watch. It has an active wireless connection and can interact with the net and perform basic inputs on programs." He went through several screens on the small display on his arm and then tapped on the laptop to connect them wirelessly.

"Sounds like a good idea, Doc," Todd added as he looked up and down the rail system. "The more options the better."

"I have a basic sync now. Back to the original question, do you want me to send the sphere somewhere else? I can ensure they won't get to it."

"That's probably a good idea. Can we get it back pretty quickly," Hudson asked.

"I've already added several subroutines," he patted the sphere. At the punch of a button it'll appear within 20 feet of us."

"Sounds good, get rid of it – since none of you will listen to me and get back in it and go," Hudson retorted.

"So where are we going?" Sara took his arm as if they were going on a picnic.

Hudson was about to answer when Todd jumped in. "This reminds me of a great Bible story about a guy and some large hungry animals."

"Daniel," Sara answered.

"Yeah, honey, you're right," Hudson said quietly as he pulled her tight. "We are most definitely going into the lion's den. Guys, it's all about the next few minutes, and not to be a downer, but we aren't prepared for the force the President is going to have amassed to protect this facility."

Sara spoke up, "Then we need to pray. We know God is more powerful. He *will* cause us to succeed."

"Amen," Todd added.

Hudson began to pray as Todd and Sara bowed with him. Dr. Keith looked on. He was a man of science and his faith was what he could see and touch. But, since he knew the odds were stacked against them – even though he had never thought much about God or the afterlife – during this prayer, he found himself hoping there was a Being bigger than himself to help them through the difficulties ahead. Halfway through the prayer, he closed his eyes.

It was after two in the morning when John Costall went to the White House personal. Wearing some sweats, a t-shirt and a jacket he had left his home and broken every speed limit in town. He figured breaking the White House dress code would pale in comparison to the news he carried.

Waking President Langley was the last thing he wanted to do – especially after the bad news he had relayed several hours earlier. This was part of his job, no matter the ramifications.

He knocked on the door. He heard no movement from the other side, so he tapped on the door a bit harder. Then came the grumblings of the man he waited to see.

"What is it?" came the voice from the other side of the door.

"I have information you need to hear," the Chief of Staff spoke to the paneling on the door.

The locked started to click and turn and the President appeared in his silk robe. He just stared at the man.

"Mr. President, we have a problem."

"Why is that all I ever hear? Why can't I hear that everything is under control?" the President derided.

"I'm sorry sir but there was a large EM spike in your private tunnels," John said looking at some papers in his hand.

"What does that mean?"

"There are only a few things on earth that could put out the electromagnetic field we discovered just forty minutes ago in your tunnel. A nuclear reactor would fill the requirements.

I don't know much about the secret project you've been working on in the tunnels or across town at Cox Manufacturing but you mentioned it as a new type of energy source. I had security check on the Cox site and they said the apparatus was gone." Speaking with regret, "Evidently it has disappeared."

"Gone, what do you mean gone?" the leader stood with his mouth open.

"Again, you haven't brought me up on this project other than the fact that you're working on something – but it isn't there anymore. I was told there's a big open hole where it previously stood this morning. Did your men move it to the tunnels with the other project? Are you working on both of them there?

I just thought you needed to know about this energy spike because many of the scientists for the NSA have been trying to get to you."

"What happened in West Virginia?" he asked flatly, changing the subject as he backed into the residence and began putting on jeans and a sweatshirt with the new religious logo on it.

"Yes, sir, it seems there's quite a bit of confusion about that." He cleared his throat as he followed the leader in. "Our forces were just about to apprehend the group when there was a blinding light and a huge surge of pressure. Evidently, a handful of men are pretty broken up – several are headed to the hospital."

The world leader slipped into some leather loafers and pulled on his presidential jacket.

John continued, "Interestingly enough, the blinding light of West Virginia occurred just a millisecond or so before the surge in the tunnels." John was no idiot. He knew something more existed here than the President was willing to say, "Do you think there is any correlation to the two events?"

President Langley left the residence in silence as the Chief of Staff closed the door behind him.

The Chief of Staff pulled a sheet from his file. "I had the NSA check on the blinding light phenomenon. The EM spike in West Virginia is virtually identical to the one occurring under DC, and almost instantaneous."

They ran down several floors until they found the basement.

"What else do you know, John?"

The man was trying to keep up as they entered the underground White House railway. Seeing the maglev train sitting there, Langley entered the vehicle. John stayed out on the platform.

"I know that each of those power surges was large enough that, if an auto mechanic had a volt meter out, it probably blew the fuse." He sobered, "Mr. President, Supreme Leader, even our enemies will know about this. Every satellite in space will have picked this up. We have a publicity mess and possible security risk."

Langley pointed his fingers, "Take care of this. Make up whatever story you need for it to disappear. Tell the foreign leaders we had a breach at a coal plant in West Virginia, and it blew some transformers in DC."

"Sir, they know where all of our plants are. There's no way they'll believe…"

"I don't care what you say, just give me time to get this sorted out," he pushed a button closing the doors on the vehicle, leaving the Chief of Staff with a publicity mess. Washington Memorial," the President spoke as the train immediately left the station.

The machine smoothly and evenly rose to a speed of over 100 kilometers per hour before arriving at the station just a mere 43 seconds later. The doors opened to a cacophony of sights and sounds.

The Leader was unprepared for what his eyes revealed. Just about every person on the staff was at their station running through programs and yelling across the room at other scientists. No one saw him enter.

After several seconds of observation the Supreme Leader yelled, "What is going on here?"

The room became silent and everyone stood at attention. A tall man named Nicholas approached the President. "Sir, we didn't expect you."

"Nick, why wouldn't you expect me? It sounds like we have a Level One emergency."

"Well, yes sir, there has been a breach in the system."

"Let me see if I can guess what's happened. The sphere at Cox Manufacturing has been commandeered and landed in West Virginia, then just a short distance from here in the tunnel system. Am I right?"

The man was dumbfounded. "We came to the same conclusion just a few minutes ago. Who could have taken it?"

"I have my ideas."

"Sir, there was no way it could have been commandeered. We don't know how it was accessed."

"Keith had a back door somehow he never told us about." He looked at the second sphere through tall glass windows, "I want that one locked off. Take it off the grid. I don't want him getting to that one also. If he takes it, we're sunk."

"Yes sir," he answered taking notes.

"What else has happened?"

"Well, our security force is low because it was sent to West Virginia. But we sent some men to the place of the incursion but no one was there and the sphere was gone. We found a second EM surge five minutes after the initial one which probably means those who took it, left with it."

"I wouldn't bet on it. What does all of the electronic security show in the tunnels?" he queried walking toward the glass and gazing at the sphere that was larger than the original and had a blue topaz color to it under the lights.

"Those tunnels were never designed to have such a vehicle landing in them. All of the circuits to the security are blown out so we can't see anything in there."

"So, we could have a herd of elephants in there and never know?"

"Pretty much, sir."

"Okay, here's what we do. Get all of the security to the tunnels. If there is someone in there, I want them found and brought to me." He pointed at the machine, "Lock it off. I don't want it disappearing. Have you found the original vehicle?" changing the subject.

"No we're still searching for it. The data is coming in slowly. It looks like it was landed in several locations, kind of like hiding funds by sending them through multiple banks. We've seen hits in the middle of the Pacific, the top of Everest, the jungles of South America and even one in space. If Dr. Keith's involved, we may never find it; at least not in time to shut it down."

"Okay. Do what I've asked. Also find Bob. We may need him here."

The man took the notes. "Anything else?"

"That's enough for now," he grumbled as his focus went back to the world-changing machine. Nicholas bowed and started giving directions to the other technologists.

Langley stared at the equipment before him; a science that allowed him to craft the world into what he desired. With a few more jumps into the past, he could be an uncontested world leader.

If he only had more time! The paradox of the situation was not lost on him. He could not stop Hudson without knowing where he was going next, thus making the machine before him useless without the agent revealing his plan.

"Hudson, it's coming to the end," he spoke under his breath. "We've been at odds for a while now, but I will finish this."

The leader opened the doors to the room covered in lead and electrical absorbing materials and walked in, leaving the dissonance of mission control behind him as the doors sealed shut.

32 — WEDNESDAY, EARLY MORNING

The vacuum caused by the sphere's exit sucked the wind from the tunnel with a loud whooshing sound. The accompanying rush of pressure sent them flat against the wall of the maintenance closet they had discovered just in time.

"The vehicle's departure causes an area of high pressure around its epicenter when it jumps from an open space and then a vacuum when it leaves," the good doctor had explained just before sending the machine into flight. "It will only bring about a surge of ten feet. However, in this enclosed tunnel system, the force might well kill us."

Had they not found that protection, they would have been sucked a hundred feet down the maglev tunnel.

Even in the closet each felt the wind knocked out of them. Hudson had wrapped his arms around Sara and pressed her to the wall, but she still slumped forward as he released her.

"Sara, are you alright?" Hudson asked.

She rose looking dizzy, and spent a few moments catching her breath. "Just a little winded. I'll be fine"

Hudson supported her gently, making small circles with his hand on her back, until she looked more stable.

"Doc, you need to make that machine a bit more subtle," Todd smirked.

Dr. Keith rose from his crouching position, "I just. Well, I can't believe it works. This is the most elated I've felt since, well, ever."

"There's no time for that now. We've once again made our positions known to anyone who was looking," Todd noted bringing everyone back to their situation.

"Todd's right," Hudson added. "We don't have time to live in the moment. If everyone's fine, we need to start moving."

Everyone nodded in agreement.

"Sara," he spoke as she looked up. "I want you to stay close to me," he popped the clip into his weapon and looked down into her eyes. "I only have a few shots. Let's hope we don't need them. Just…," he stumbled on his thought. "Just don't leave my side."

Hudson glanced over at Todd, "Hey buddy, can you run up the line about a hundred yards and see what's ahead? I'll stay with the group."

"Will do," the professor affirmed, looking both ways in the tunnel before heading up the track.

Dr. Keith opened his laptop to determine the sphere's last location as he sat pecking away at it, mumbling as he typed.

Sara grabbed Hudson's arm, getting his attention. "So, how long were we married?" she asked quietly.

"Sara, we really don't need to think about that right now," Hudson answered dismissively.

"How long?" she pulled him down and looked him in the eyes.

"Thirteen years."

Sara exhaled heavily as if the wind was taken out of her again. "Thirteen years? Thirteen years that I know nothing about."

"I know this is difficult. But right now, we need to focus on the here and now." Hudson responded.

"Were we happy?"

"Ah, Sara, let's not get into this."

"Answer my question," she returned with focus.

"It was a joy and a blessing. The time we...of our... marriage were the best years of my life."

She could tell he meant what he said, and looked down at her feet now out of her heels and resting on the cold floor of the tunnel. "How did we meet?"

Hudson smiled and then laughed, "Well, the first time I saw you, I was on my back in a wrestling match. You made me lose that day to an ugly, sweaty and less savvy opponent."

Her mouth dropped in disgust.

He sighed before finishing his thought, "I thought you were so beautiful that I totally forget about the man trying to pin me to the mat."

She formed a grin and sat on a stack of boxes next to him. "Did I, or did we,...this seems so crazy,...did we go to church?"

He sat next to her, "Oh yeah, we were in church every Sunday. The Lord is what rooted our lives. You led our home through grace and godliness and God blessed us because of it. Much of what I am is what you helped to make me. That is why I believe the Lord has used Todd and me the way he has. I am a better man because of you."

She smiled again. "What did our house look like?"

"I'd say it was perfect. A two story colonial with flower beds filled with roses and gardenias."

"Oh, I love gardenias."

"I know. Sara, our life was picture-perfect. You were the ultimate wife and a patient and loving mothe...," Hudson knew he had gone too far.

Her face went solemn, "We had, I mean, have children?"

"Sara, why don't we get ready to move."

"No, tell me."

"Yes, Michael, eight, and Amy, ten."

Tears formed in her eyes. "Where are they now?"

There was a long break. Hudson was forced to think about his loss, "Well, because everything has been changed, we never got married and... they were never born."

She stood up and started to get upset as Dr. Keith broke his attention from the screen. "I don't know anything about any of this, and yet I feel responsible."

The agent heaved himself up feeling the weight of the world on his shoulders and pulled Sara back into his arms to comfort her, "This isn't your problem."

"No, it's mine," the scientist broke in with regret.

"I was so focused on my place in history that I didn't think about the ramifications of what I was doing." Shaking his head, he sighed. "I really thought they would do what they said, and protect and help people with it."

"It was just too tempting and easy. Don't worry, Doctor; I just need you to think about setting everything right."

The man focused on the computer again.

"Sara, our children were beautiful and we had a perfect life, but you aren't guilty of any of this. If we can correct the problem, then we'll have that life back."

"But I liked my life...this life. Sure, everything you spoke of sounds like a perfect dream, but it is just a dream to me. It's not anything I know or remember or..."

"I understand."

"In my life, I'm busy and work with powerful people, I have a future..." She turned her face into his chest and broke down in his arms. "Hudson I feel like a fish out of water. I don't know where I'm supposed to be. Am I an aid to a Senator or your wife and Michael and Amy's mother?"

"Let's just think about the place we're in right now," he hugged her as she cried. Head dropping onto hers, Hudson's tears fell into her hair.

The scientist, weighted by the responsibility he finally understood, watched the couple hold one another up. This thing he had created had changed millions if not billions of lives for the worse.

Hearing a few steps running down the tunnel, Hudson pulled his gun and pointed it toward the opening of the room.

With his hands up, Todd spoke breathlessly, "Hey, it's just me."

The agent returned his weapon to his belt. "What did you find?"

"Yeah, there's another platform like the one we found at the Jefferson Memorial. It's about three blocks up." He put both hands on his knees and sucked in some air. "I ran all the way."

"You need to be in better shape," Hudson poked trying to get a rise out of his friend.

"Hey, I'm in great shape. I'd probably be doing better if I could get some sleep, a nice meal, and be with Aaliyah for a long while." Standing up he regained his wind, "Every time I go anywhere with you, you mess up my world," he laughed. "Anyway, the Washington Memorial platform is well-guarded. No way are we getting in there with just one gun and a couple of bullets."

"What do you suggest?" Hudson asked, still holding Sara. "Is there any other way around the subway entrance?"

"I don't know. A few hundred feet up there are large breaks in the wall."

Dr. Keith interjected, "What do they look like?"

"Large. They're probably six feet high and have louvers over them."

"That's it, Dr. Myers. That's how we get in," Ben finished.

Everyone looked at him.

"It's part of the design. We know that a room underground can't take the pressure differential formed when the sphere jumps in time."

Hudson interrupted, "But Cox Manufacturing doesn't have six foot air chambers."

"No, we have a diffusion system there, but that building isn't underground. This place needed a way to vent the pressure without blowing out a length of the tunnel. Those louvers as Dr. Myers said are direct air shafts to the sphere. We have six of them running in different directions venting to either the surface or a couple running into the tunnels."

"We follow that vent, and it will take us directly to the room it is housed." Todd added.

"Sounds too easy," Sara spoke quietly, still wiping her eyes on the edge of her dress.

"Well, it is unless someone tries to jump in the sphere. If they do, we'll probably be killed," he said without emotion.

"Sara, you really need to stay here," Hudson asked her again.

"Nope, I'm going with you."

He heaved a sigh, "It was worth a try."

"Hudson, you said I need to focus on returning the world back to the way it was," Dr. Keith said.

"Yes, this is not how it's supposed to be."

"Well, after working through this, there are only a few things I can think of that would restore it."

All three waited for his answer.

"We could stop whoever traveled back in time at each jump before he ever makes the changes. But we would have to fix them in reverse order. The last jump would be the first we try to stop. If we moved out of order and fixed the second jump first for example, everything else would be changed because of it, and it wouldn't correct the initial problem."

"That makes sense," Hudson affirmed.

"And to do that, we'd need to know exactly what happened, and I don't think we know precisely what they did."

"You're right," Todd filled in. "We generally know where they hit, but not exactly."

"Well, that wouldn't help us," the scientist mused. "There's a second option. We stop the person who made the jumps early in his life."

"Sure, but if we do that, the President will just find someone else."

"Well, then we could stop him before he makes this project his own personal toy."

With regret the agent added, "Yes, that's an alternative."

"Finally, you could go back and stop me before I design this thing," Ben said with regret, knowing his part in the situation.

Asking an awkward question, Todd grinned, "So we go back in your time machine to stop you from building the time machine we go back in."

"I don't have all of the answers," said Dr. Keith, slightly perturbed. "There are conundrums in time travel. Anyway, it would *probably* work."

"About that," Hudson stopped the philosophical debate. "There are some things I need to tell you about the past, Dr. Keith. Things that will affect your… *life*."

"What things?"

A sound was heard in the tunnel.

"Quiet!" Hudson whispered.

The professor and the agent flanked the doorway and moved quickly into the darkness leaving Sara and Ben wide-eyed.

After a minute or so of grunts and an outcry or two, Todd and Hudson came back in with two men in headlocks. Throwing the strangers onto their backs they pinned them to the ground.

"Hudson, there's no way you'll get much further," said the first man.

"Marc," Hudson answered the older agent, "We're going to stop the President. I know most of your force is in West Virginia, so you're poorly staffed here. We'll make it."

"Hudson, you used to be a great agent."

"I'm still a great agent. The motto of the Secret Service is 'Worthy of Trust and Confidence.' We protect the President. Sadly enough, this time, I'm protecting him from himself." Looking over at his partner, "Todd do we have anything to lock these men up with?"

"I'm on it. I found some electrical wire in one of these lockers. It should do."

Hudson and Todd tied them up where they were not going to get loose.

"Marc, you probably won't say, but it's worth a shot. How many more men are in this tunnel?"

"All of them," he cornered Hudson with his smile.

"We need to get going. If these guys are patrolling, there'll be more."

"Todd, you're right."

Sara saw some cuts on Hudson's hands, "Oh, you're bleeding! Are you alright?" She asked as she lifted the hem of her dress and dabbed at the small wounds.

"I'll be fine. Sara. I'm okay, really." She looked up just then and he grasped her smaller hands in his larger rough ones for a moment.

"Hudson, you said something about needing to tell me something," the scientist voice broke the mood.

Hudson's countenance dropped, "Ben, we have to be very careful in how we correct the past."

"Why's that?"

Static broke through one of the two-way radios Todd appropriated from the captured agents. The professor listened closely.

"Hudson, these guys are supposed to check in. If these guys are Marc and Steve they're late in reporting."

"That's a problem," Hudson shot back. "They only have one minute to reply in an emergency situation like this before reinforcements are sent out."

"Let's whisper that we can't talk right now, or something like that."

"No, they have a code they must respond with, and we don't know it. We need to get going." He looked at Dr. Keith. "I'll tell you later."

Ben took the man's intense look in stride considering the situation, but tucked away the knowledge that it was no little thing he had to share later.

Taking the men's weapons, Hudson put one in his waist and gave one to Todd who did the same.

"Is everyone ready?" the agent asked, hugging Sara close once more.

Ben answered first, "As ready as ever."

"Lead us Captain," Todd said trying to break the tension.

Sara looked Hudson in the eyes, "I'll go anywhere you ask. Somehow, I know you'll take care of me."

The agent kissed her on the forehead, "Then let's get to that air shaft."

Hudson left the room with Sara holding onto his hand. Ben followed closely behind with Todd being the last to leave the room. Looking at the men tied up in the corner, he just smiled. "Guys, if everything goes right, you'll not remember any of this." He laughed a tired laugh, and followed his team out into the dark tunnel.

33 — WEDNESDAY, EARLY MORNING

Sara followed Hudson closely through the dark tunnels and watched his every movement. A tighter grip on her hand alerted her to stop short behind him and almost do a face plant into his back. She caught herself just in time and stood stock still awaiting his next move.

The heat from his back and her own warm breath against it produced both a claustrophobic awareness and a deep attraction to this guardian of hers.

Being taken care of was not new to Sara. She loved her parents and understood that they would have given anything for her protection while in their care. But she had not felt cherished like that since childhood – until Hudson. Every movement seemed to be in regard to her welfare.

They turned a corner and he pushed her behind him, looking for agents patrolling. At every curb or track line, he would slow down to ensure she did not fall or damage her shins. Several times he held back to be certain she could keep up even though he would have been safer if he had left her behind.

Looking up at the man before her as he checked a corner, she knew she admired him. More than mere admiration, it was respect, appreciation, and that new awareness. She could see how she could have fallen in love with him in another life. He was strong, tall, warm, kind, protective… everything a woman could want. And this man had loved her for many years. Loved her still. And that's where the claustrophobia came in.

It was such a crazy world she was in. Hudson had been married for over a decade to another woman. Even though that woman was her, it still felt awkward – wrong. Worse yet, Sara was beginning to feel affection and a longing for a man who was married. Could it be possible that she was the same woman in both timelines? None of it meshed with life as she knew it.

That other Sara had been formed by high school experiences and dating Hudson through college. She would understand the sacrifice and years of patience that came with being a wife and mother. This Sara had none of that. In her world, she had spent time on nothing but her career and her future. She worked in government and thought about bills and laws, not homework and dinner. Could Hudson love her the way he loved the other Sara?

Was that even a question she cared about? Did she want a relationship? Well, if she were to be honest, the answer would be yes. She had longed to care for someone special. Children were a part of her life that she knew she had overlooked. Just going out on a simple date was something in her timeline she did not have time for. And the man in front of her was in essence trying to right everything that was wrong with the world to get her back. She was drawn even closer to him even though she knew very little about him.

But how much did she need to know? People had been married for thousands of years through arranged marriages. She supposed she could be, or perhaps stay, married to him quite easily, but did she want that?

Drawn further into the dark tunnel behind the man of her thoughts, she became more confused with each question. She wanted love – and marriage – but was not certain that love would, or even should be with Hudson. What would that do to him?

What if they were not able to correct the world and reset it back to Hudson's timeline, and she just did not want a relationship with him? What would it do to the man dragging her through the tunnel? Would it destroy him? Would he be able to live without her? The questions mounted.

Continuing the frenetic line of reasoning, she wondered if she were happy in the other timeline. He had said that they had been so, and certainly his trekking through time and all of this mess just to find her proved his veracity. If Hudson were able to correct everything, would she remember any of her present life? And if she did, would she want to move into the role of being a wife to this man and mother to children she had never known? Sara hesitated in the run.

Feeling her tug behind him, Hudson looked back, "Sara, are you alright?"

"Yes, I'm fine," she whispered. "Just getting tired."

"Do you need to rest?"

"No, let's get this done," she said wiping perspiration from her brow.

Hudson smiled and continued forward with her hand in his.

Sara began to feel bad about herself. "*Even when I'm thinking of leaving him, he still thinks about me*," she tried to hold back tears. "*I don't deserve this kind of love*," she thought.

Nothing made sense anymore, and the further they went the more confused she became. Everything that had happened today seemed to be about her. The questions that loomed large in her mind became the tipping point of her thoughts.

Would Hudson have worked so hard to right this world if he had not been married to me – or the other Sara? Is all his effort about saving the country or just getting his wife back? Me back? Even as she struggled in her cumbersome attire to keep up the pace of the men around her she knew the answer to her questions.

Hudson had done all of this to get her back. He might have worked to save the timeline on some level, if she were already safe and still his. But deep inside her Sara realized his love for her went far deeper than any love she had ever thought possible. And then she wondered, *Could I ever love him as much as he loves me? Or Sara?* They came to a crossroads and paused, allowing her to touch the back of his hand as he held her other tightly. *He's a good and true man. I can't imagine being loved by him, deserving him.* At that final thought, she wept.

Hudson turned at the sound. "Sara, are you alright?" He whispered.

She looked up into his face in the darkness, overwhelmed by all her thoughts, "I can't do this," she spoke plainly.

Everyone stopped and looked at her with raised eyebrows.

"You can't do what Sara?" Hudson asked gently, trying to look up and down the tunnel unobtrusively.

"I can't be everything you want me to be."

"Huh?" his head whipped around to face her. "What?"

"I can't be a wife, or a mother. I don't know how. I don't even know you. I don't know our children. I'm not sure how to be a mom. And what about my job?"

"Honey, um," he continued to scan the space ahead of them. "We just need to get to the access point," he tried to pull her forward.

She would not budge, "You don't understand. You couldn't. I have the world on my shoulders right now. I'm…I'm overwhelmed."

It occurred to Hudson much later that the effects of the time jump had produced a similar emotional reaction in Aaliyah months before. At the moment, his concern for their safety trumped any other understanding of the woman's emotional state. "Well, you don't need to be, let's worry about some of this after we get into a better more secure position…"

"That's how it always is, isn't it? None of you know what I'm going through here," she sobbed. Sara was beginning to lose it in the tunnels.

Todd made the connection the other man was missing and gently removed her hand from Hudson's now utterly confused grip. "Sara, why don't we talk for a second," Todd asked. "Tell me what you're going through. I'm a good listener."

They moved away from the two men who now sat down, dumbfounded, in the tunnel.

"It sounds like you've been working through your situation. Is that right?" Todd asked.

"I just can't be what he wants me to be."

"What is it he wants you to be?" Todd probed with care.

"He wants me to be a wife and a mother. To take care of him and lead a family." He could see the emotion building in her eyes and was reminded of Aaliyah standing on a hospital bed, waving a bedpan around and yelling at the nurses in Hebrew. "Well, I don't know how to do those things!" she finished.

Todd just smiled. "No, I'd imagine you don't."

"And to add to it, I don't know if I want to. I have a pretty good job that keeps me very busy," she added with confidence.

"I'm sure you do," he said, using affirmation to draw her mind from the emotion.

"I like my life. Who are any of you to take me from everything I know? Sure, this world *could* be better, but it's all I know."

"Yes, I agree," Todd said looking at the men standing under a dim lamp.

"All I'm saying is that I can't guarantee anything."

"I'd say that's a fair assurance."

She sat there looking at him. "Well, aren't you supposed to encourage me some way? That's what pastors usually do isn't it?"

"Yeah, maybe, but sometimes we just listen."

Her strong confident demeanor suddenly broke and she dropped her head onto his shoulder, sobbing into his coat. "Todd, what do I do?"

He patted her on the back and whispered in her ear, "It's going to be alright. The Lord will be with you through all of this and more." He hugged her tight for another moment.

"I just don't have any more strength," she stood straight.

"I know you're tired," he smiled slowly, taking the opportunity to examine her pupils in the darkness.

"How can you be so confident?" she queried.

"Because I know you much more than you do, evidently," he replied with confidence.

She looked at him confused.

"Sara, you are one of the most intelligent and strongest women I've ever met."

"We just met a day ago," she replied, confused.

"Sure, in this timeline. But you are the same throughout both. You're just as beautiful, witty, smart as the woman in the other timeline, and your determination and confidence matches the other Sara's exactly. You are no different." A moment later he thought of something. "Let me tell you a story about yourself. Maybe it'll give you a bit more strength."

Hudson shrugged his shoulders in front of him pointing at his wrist, and Todd put a palm up asking for another minute.

"We really met six months ago." The thought made him pause. "It seems like a thousand years ago. You know it's amazing how people come together through difficult times."

She listened.

"When Hudson and I returned from our first jump, we were pretty broken. We had seen more than anyone should ever see or experience. I'd been shot; Hudson had managed to save everyone and was worn out. To add to that, I came back with a woman I loved, but she was on the edge of death. Let me tell you, it was a difficult time."

Sara's big blue eyes glowed in the tunnel.

"We were then sent back immediately into that crazy world again. For one week, we ran for our lives and came back with no reserves. But Sara, if it weren't for you, we wouldn't have made it."

She looked at him curiously.

"Sara, it was you who restored Hudson. He had no joy left. He saw the world as ugly and fractured. He is a good man, but even good men can become hardened and dark when they see so much evil. That was Hudson. You brought him back.

Sara, it was you who healed me. I didn't want to go back into the ministry. I'd seen God do great things around us, but I knew my weaknesses and didn't want to face them any longer. I was ready to give up, but you encouraged me and quoted scripture after scripture to me. If it weren't for you, I wouldn't be in a church or teaching at seminary today."

Her eyes grew wide and she stood a bit straighter wiping a few tears away.

"Finally, Sara, you essentially gave me my wife. When Aaliyah came back from Israel, she bordered on psychotic and knew absolutely nothing. No English, American customs, for that sake, she didn't know how to cook, or even how to turn on a light in a room."

"She didn't know how to turn on a light?" Sara asked flabbergasted wiping a few more tears from her cheek.

"That's a long story. But no, she didn't know anything. I mean anything," he got a bit dramatic. "Anyway, you were there with her in the hospital. You took her into your home before we were married and spent time each day teaching her the things she didn't know; which was essentially everything. You took her through the New Testament and allowed her to know Christ much deeper than she did.

You taught her to dress and to walk and to carry herself in contemporary society as a grace-filled woman." He laughed. "Sara, you even taught her English.

Without you, I wouldn't have my Aaliyah whom I love very much. You gave me my wife. My life. In a few months I'll have my first child."

She smiled.

Getting a smirk on his face, "Well, okay, that's one thing we didn't need your help with. We figured that out on our own."

She laughed out loud as Hudson and Ben looked nervous in the dim light.

He chuckled with her. "Sara, I know you're scared. I know you're uncertain about the future, or the past, or even where you are right now."

She nodded.

"But there are several things I know. First, the Lord will get you through this."

She stood a little taller and inhaled deeply at the Truth spoken.

"The second thing is that you are strong. And you are a godly woman. And you are going to make it through this.

Hudson isn't asking anything of you. I know him very well. Yes, he loves you, but most importantly, he wants the best for you. If this was to end and you had no feelings for him, it would make him sad, but he loves you enough to let you live your life.

I'd imagine he'd try to get to know you though. He's pretty determined. You may have a lot of flowers and candy sent to you. Or something. At least I hope he'd do things like that."

She smiled.

He continued his thoughts, "Let's not worry about the future. The present has enough troubles of its own." He wiped the last tear from her cheek. "Are you going to make it? You better?"

"Yes, I'm better," she said hugging him.

"What do you say we get going again?"

"Okay."

They turned and looked at Hudson and Ben who had perplexed looks on their faces.

"Do you think I've made them nervous?" she asked with a bit of uncertainty to Todd.

"Yeah, but I think they'll make it. I can guarantee you've had Hudson confused a time or two in the past."

"Oh, you know it. If he's married to me, he's going to always be guessing what's coming next."

"I have no doubt," they walked over to the men.

"Is everything back on track?" Ben asked cautiously.

"Everything was always on track," the professor responded winking at Sara.

She grinned. "Of course it is. Let's get that circle, or machine, or whatever you call it. Where's this exhaust pipe we need to find?" Sara questioned innocently.

Hudson grinned and stuck out his hand. She put her hand in his and they continued down the dark tunnel as if nothing had ever happened. Ben had no idea what had transpired but followed closely behind. Todd held back in the rear and observed his friends walking hand in hand.

He said a quick prayer as he saw Sara looking up at Hudson. She was not watching him because she wanted to know where to go, but because she wanted to know who he was. From his position in the back, Todd knew she was trying to read or know the real man. She wanted understand deeply and sincerely who he was. The small woman that they had spent so much time and effort to rescue was the one who had rescued them many times in the past. Todd admired the woman.

He prayed quietly out loud, "Lord, please be with her. Give her peace, confidence, and strength. Let her know who she is in You, and maybe she can know who she is in this world."

The man smiled as he looked back for anyone approaching and then took his place behind Ben.

34 — WEDNESDAY, EARLY MORNING

"That's it," Ben shouted as he ran ahead. "This set of louvers should take us right to the room where they house the second sphere."

They had arrived at an opening covered with three vertical slats. Individually, each slat extended four feet and were two feet high. Their design allowed them to stay closed until a burst of pressure caused them to open up enough to let the air through. Each blind weighed about 30 pounds and could be pulled open with little effort.

"So we just walk in there, and we'll find the sphere?" Todd asked.

Looking at him Ben responded, "Yes, it's about that easy. No one is supposed to have access to these tunnels, so I wouldn't imagine they have to worry about people coming through this specific access.

Those vents leading topside may have a grating on them, but these shouldn't need it with the security they have down here."

Todd frowned in confusion, "It just seems like it ought to be harder than that. I mean, my tax dollars aren't being spent very well if we've only encountered 2 agents, and those were easy to tie up."

Hudson jumped in, "To be honest, the sphere cost close to a trillion. I'd say that's where your money went."

"A trillion, and all it has caused is problems," Todd looked at Ben. "Sorry, Ben. It *is* genius technology."

"No need to apologize. Just because you can dream it, doesn't mean you should build it."

Everyone nodded.

"Hudson, are we ready?" Ben asked.

"Yeah," he said tugging on the middle louver. "Sara, you go first, and I'll come in behind you."

Sara looked down at her voluminous skirt, then back up at him with an eyebrow cocked. Hudson shrugged and let a slow smile crawl across his face. Sighing, but realizing there was no other way, she gathered her dress about her as best she could in all modestly and ducked into the two foot opening at her waist. Hudson followed closely behind.

Once everyone was in, Hudson pulled out his phone and turned on the flashlight app. It was just as the doctor said, a simple straight shot meandering through the underground area of the National Mall. They had gone a hundred feet when they saw a second set of louvers with light coming from the other side.

Hudson put a finger up to his lips as he creeped up to the wall and slightly lifted a louver. Scanning the bright room, he saw the sphere as Ben had indicated. The room appeared to be empty. The mission control section adjacent to it swirled with activity, but the machine was in a hibernation mode with no apparent power charging it up.

Crawling back, he said to the group, "Yep, it's there. But, Ben what have you done?"

The scientist looked perplexed. "What do you mean?"

"That one is bigger than ours. It has a blue hue to it and seems to be powered differently."

"Oh yes, it's quite dissimilar," he said as they crouched in the exhaust tube. "It's much larger. We wanted to be able to bring something back from the past, so we have storage space and a rear set of seats."

Hudson looked on.

"We also powered it differently. *Your* sphere is laser powered but stores just enough energy for a few jumps. It really depends on how far you're traveling as to how many. That one," he pointed toward the louver, "Is fusion powered. It can translocate for twenty-plus years before we need to change the power cells. It's far superior to the original."

"Why all the upgrades?" Todd asked.

"Because we had unlimited funds. The first sphere, Hudson, your machine had governmental oversight which means we had to beg, borrow, and steal billions to get it finished. That one in there, I was told had no fiscal restrictions. If I could dream it, they would build it." Smiling, "I even think I put a few drink holders in there." He laughed.

Everyone else stood there stoically.

He continued, "That one is superior in every way."

Rubbing his head, "So, how do we stop it?"

Dr. Keith became very sober. "Well, I haven't really thought that through." Sitting down in the vent he opened up his laptop. After a minute or so he spoke quietly, "Hudson, I can get remote access of that sphere if you can get it to ping me."

"How do I do that?" He asked incredulously.

"It will take all four of us to open the sphere. Normally there's a palm print access or a keypad number. Well, none of us have entrée to the sphere, so we don't know the seven digit access. Besides, none of our palm prints will admit us. However, there is a remote access meant for the tech guys to be able to get into it to work on it. A small button sits under each strut and, if pressed, pops the top on the sphere. Once that happens, just run it through a dummy cycle, and I'll be able to lock onto it. I'll quickly change the passcodes, so that it'll take them a decade to get them."

"All four of us? Is there a way I can reach two of the buttons? I don't want Sara out there," Hudson responded flatly.

"On the old sphere yes, but this one is bigger. The legs are close to seven feet apart. You're a big man, but not that big. It'll take all four of us."

"How else can we get this thing?" the agent questioned.

"Hudson, if that's how we do it, then we do it," Sara said confidently.

"No, I don't want you out there. If they get us, you can still get away through these tunnels."

"No, my place is here with you. We're going in there to finish this, so no one is ever hurt again."

"Sara, it's not going to happen!" He realized his emotions were nearer the surface than usual, but could not for the life of him understand her at the moment.

"Yes, Hudson it is. I'm going with you. You aren't leaving me." She looked away and folded her arms as if everything had been said.

"Aah," he grumbled. "Why don't I feel like I'm in charge here?"

She did not respond.

Frustrated, he directed his attention to the other men. "Okay, here's what we're going to do. Ben and Sara will be through last and will go to the closest struts on the sphere. Todd and I will run around it to the other side. Ben, get that computer ready." It was not a request.

"I'm already on it. You push those buttons, and in an instant, the program I've written will change all the codes."

"Is everyone ready? Sara are you sure?"

"I am," she put her hand on his face.

Everyone else agreed.

The agent pulled out his weapon. "Well, let's go," Hudson said as he opened the louver and jumped into the room – weapon forward.

The President was pleased to see Bob walk through the front doors. "Bob, thank you for coming."

"Did I have much of a choice? A dozen men came to my home and essentially told me there was a national emergency."

"I'm not sure it's a national emergency, but an emergency, nonetheless." His face fell as he gave the bad news, "Hudson's in the tunnels somewhere."

"How did that happen? It's a fortress in there."

"He flew,...if that's the word, flew the sphere in there."

"What sphere? The Cox vehicle is essentially in moth balls. We turned it into a nuclear generator."

"He has Dr. Keith."

"Dr. Keith is guarded by an army," he shot back.

"I know, stop stating the obvious. Needless to say, everyone is loose, and they're coming here to correct everything you did."

Bob started to pace. "Where are they now?"

"We don't know exactly. The sphere disappeared, so they could be in it. Or they could have sent the sphere ahead and are still in the subway system. We have people searching but haven't found anything yet."

"Okay, why do you need me?"

A man bumped into Bob wearing a white coat like the hundred other men at terminals within the room.

"Where do you think Hudson is?"

"How am I supposed to know?" Bob shrugged.

"You've spent months with him. You'll know him better than anyone else."

"If Hudson thinks this is the place to make corrections, he'll come here. Hudson's pretty focused and predictable. He'll always try to do what's right."

The President started to pace the pristine floor, "Well, I can't have that. We're trying to make a great world, and we must protect it at all costs." Looking at Bob with his arms crossed, "You need to make another jump."

"No, there's no time," he backed away.

"This will be an easy one. I need you to go back to the day before yesterday and stop Hudson. It would be a quick trip with no real planning."

"You want me to arrest him?"

"No, I want him dead."

Bob looked pained. "I will not kill Hudson!" his voiced raised.

The President pressed a palm at him, "Quiet down. You're here because you have the ability to solve problems, and this," he pointed off down the tunnels, "is what I need you to do."

"Hudson's a friend. He's been extremely good to me."

"I can be better. I have power and prestige to give. I'm the main religious leader and the most powerful man on earth and can make your life very pleasant. Do you want land, or money? Do you want companionship? I can take care of you, if you take care of me. I remember those who sacrifice for me and their country."

The man just looked at him.

"Bob, you're a military man and, because of that, I need you to come to the aid of your countrymen."

"I didn't come prepared for a jump. I don't have supplies or my weapon."

The President pulled a large semi-automatic from his belt and handed it to Bob. "Will this do?"

Todd and Hudson rounded the corner to the sphere and slid underneath it. From their vantage point they were able to see Sara scurry through the hole in a sea of red taffeta and Ben follow closely behind. A few seconds later, everyone was in place.

Ben moved slowly and methodically to show everyone where to find the button. Right behind the strut on the base of the sphere was a small door about the size of a hand. He pulled on a locking bolt and it dropped, revealing a few controls.

"It's the orange button labeled *ACCESS*," he whispered.

After he was sure everyone was prepared, Hudson whispered, "On three. One, two, three," everyone pressed their button.

Immediately a sound of pressure releasing almost like air brakes on a semi was heard. The machine began to vibrate and several of the elements beneath the vehicle started to blink and glow. Everyone scurried from below the machine.

Todd, Sara, and Ben grouped together near the exit while the designer ran through programs waiting for the computer to recognize the sphere. Hudson jumped into the cockpit and scrolled through windows searching for access to the clearing or 'dummy' cycle.

"Follow me over here, this man will tell you when and where you will arrive," the President said wondering why Bob was looking at the sphere and not him.

"What's happening in there?" the military man said pointing to the room containing the sphere.

The President looked around to see the vehicle opening. "What's happening to the machine?" he yelled.

A hundred scientists craned their heads toward the large windows.

The President and Bob ran to the central windows looking into the room and saw Hudson at the panel.

The world leader smiled as he casually opened the door to the chamber housing the time vehicle. Bob followed him in weapon still in hand.

"Well, hello, Hudson."

The agent did not look up.

"You've sure kept many of us busy."

The man remained focused on his work.

"And who's that over there in the corner? That lovely lady must me Miss Brennen. It is Miss, isn't it?"

Hudson did not react to the obvious jab.

"It looks like our resident theologian is here. Dr. Myers, welcome. It must be a blessing to be in the same room with the god of this age. I can give you an interview to take back to your class if you would like."

Todd just glared him down.

"Last but not least, it's our own version of a present day Lazarus. Dr. Keith what do you think? Are you proud of your work?" The President gestured around the room and to mission control as if a presenter on a game show.

He continued to work.

"Hudson, Ben, stop your efforts. It's not going to work."

Neither of them ceased their plan.

"When you accessed the Cox sphere, I had the men here break any possibility of a remote connection. Your little computer isn't going to commandeer *my* machine."

Hudson looked up and Ben lowered his device.

"Now, it seems that I have your attention. Hudson, why don't you come on down from there? No amount of tapping is going to make that thing work. And the rest of you, come on out here into the open. You're not going to be able to leave through that little vent, so you might as well just come on over."

No one moved.

The President grabbed the .45 semi-automatic from Bob's hand and pointed it at Hudson. "I said I want everyone to come over here. I've been patient, but I'm losing that tolerance quickly."

"Do what he says," Hudson spoke slowly.

"Thank you, my friend. I don't want to execute anyone, at least not this morning. We may have a few later on today, but they will be great examples for the world. Those illustrations will show everyone what happens to those who go against the nation and its direction."

The team of four knew he was talking about them. Hudson had no doubt that he would make a public example out of each one. A man with this kind of power was capable of just about anything.

The agent knew the Lord had to help them or their efforts would be in vain, and they would die having not completed their mission. Silently he prayed for wisdom.

35 — WEDNESDAY, EARLY MORNING

"Are you saying we're the traitors? Mr. President, or Supreme Leader Man, or Dream Weaver, or whatever you're calling yourself these days. We're the ones attempting to *rescue* America. To take back what you've lost!" Hudson yelled as he climbed down from the sphere.

"We're trying to uphold America's foundations as a country under God. To bring her back to who she was supposed to be – how the founding fathers saw her. You've destroyed everything this nation has worked so hard to become – in just a few days!"

The Supreme Leader laughed out loud. "What? I've recreated it. Redesigned it for the good of all!"

"For the good of all?" Sara responded sarcastically. "You've removed all freedom given by God, and made this land into a perverted version of itself. Your own, little, fantasy land. America was dedicated to God from the very beginning, in much the same way Israel's first temple was – as a place to worship Yahweh, the one, true God. It's neither right nor possible for you to remove that from these people." She stopped for only a moment, "And I have a feeling, God is about to resolve the problem you've created."

"God? There is no God. I'm god. I am the only real deity here on earth. This nation is under one true god, and that god is me. So everyone can continue to worship as they always have, knowing that I will – and have already been – their savior."

Todd stage-whispered to Sara, "He's beginning to sound like an Old Testament Pharaoh. And I seem to recall how God destroyed everything Pharaoh believed in pretty handily through the plagues."

"Those are myths and legends from the past. The only god you need to see is the one before you."

Sara took a step toward him before Dr. Keith pulled her back, "I'm sorry, but you are not God in any kind of a way. You've used the minds of others to manipulate a system in order to elevate yourself." She shrugged Dr. Keith off her arm, and took a deep breath.

"I, for one, am not bowing down or praying to you. You are no God. My God, Christ Jesus saved me. You can do nothing but hurt and destroy."

"Sara," the Supreme Leader pinched the bridge of his nose and closed his eyes as he leaned onto the wall behind him. "I'm being very patient." He turned to Dr. Keith. "What about you, Lazarus? Do you have anything to add?"

"Why do you keep calling me 'Lazarus'?"

"Oh, haven't you told him?" he asked, looking at Hudson. "Well, Dr. Keith, I really am literally *your* god. Essentially, I brought you back to life," he waved off any speech on the doctor's part as he spoke. "No thanks are necessary. Well, just a little thanks wouldn't be frowned upon."

Benjamin Keith turned to Hudson now to his left. "Hudson, what does he mean, *brought back to life*?" he asked.

"I told you there was something I had to explain about changing the new timeline back."

The genius looked perplexed.

"Dr. Keith, in my timeline…," the words stuck in Hudson's throat. "In my timeline…you died."

"Died! I never died."

"You did," Hudson replied with solemnity.

The designer just looked at him in confusion.

"Someone killed you. I was there, and saw them remove your body. Somehow, he," he said, pointing toward the President, "sent someone back to rescue you before you were killed."

"Like I said, no need for thanks," the President offered with a smile. "And the aid that plucked you out of the jaws of death is my trusty colleague, Bob. Wave, Bob."

Hudson finally took his eyes off of the leader to see his former employee Bob standing there with him. Instantly, the agent understood what was happening and connected all of the dots created from the last few days.

"When were you going to tell me about this, Hudson?"

The agent broke his thoughts and looked over at Ben, "When I had time. I started to back in the maintenance shed."

Dr. Keith began to pace a small figure eight as he always had in his problem-solving mode. "This can change everything. If I correct the timeline, then I die."

Sara touched his arm and effectively stopped his movement, then placed her hand on his back, apparently in prayer for the man.

Todd interjected, "Ben, we've seen how time travel isn't always cut and dried. There are ways we can fix it where you might live."

"I'm living on borrowed time. I shouldn't be here."

"Not in my new timeline, Ben. You see all of the good you've been able to do so far. Can you imagine what grand creations you'll devise? You'll have as much power as God ever had. Besides, your options include the illustrious choice of death," he paused for effect, "Or living the life of a king with the power of a god. As your savior, I'm the one with the greatest gift to bestow. And remember, you owe me your life."

The blistering dilemma before the doctor stilled the hearts of each of them. It was Sara who broke the silence, "He doesn't owe you anything." She turned back toward the President and watched Mission control behind him running around in an uncontrolled frenzy on the other side of the glass.

Todd picked up where she stopped. "Ben, Jesus is the only one who can bring salvation. Somehow, this guy snatched you before you were murdered, but he's going to expect indentured service for his so-called gift, and as for the things you might create – well, you've seen the results of the genius invention we all call the sphere. And, as he said, you *owe* him, so he *owns* you. What kind of life would that be, really? Dr. Keith, Jesus doesn't want anything like that. Jesus came to give you life and give it more abundantly than you've ever dreamed. God allowed this technology to rescue you, so you have a second chance, one in which you might honor Him."

"Jesus was just a guy in history. I *am* the world's salvation. Stop with the fairy tales," the leader grunted with frustration. "I bring jobs, food, healthcare, necessities, phones, internet, scheduled time away from work...I bring everything people need to live."

Ben continued pacing. "What do I do now?"

"You work for me. We will make a great future for you. One where you have more money and prestige than you could ever imagine." He gestured toward the machine, "This sphere will be an afterthought once you design the next great technological marvel. I know you like to help people, so why don't we work on food replication. No one would be hungry again. With my power and influence, you would have unlimited funds to work with. What do you say?"

Todd jumped in front of Dr. Keith. "Ben, you can't do it. You know he needs you because you are the brilliance behind the technology. Without you, he has nothing. Don't give him what he wants, or your life will be without any hope or real future.

You know you were supposed to have died. If you had, you would have been required to deal with the real Creator; the one who made the heavens and the earth. You *know He exists.* He is the one who designed you and gave you the ability to think and create. If you go with that man," he said pointing across the room, "your future is dark, and there is nothing good in this life or beyond. If you accept the true God, you have an unending future waiting for you with God the Father and Christ Jesus the Son. Come on, doctor."

The man was speechless.

Hudson took the opportunity to look over at Bob, "So, are you proud of your work?"

The military man did not look him in the eyes as he replied defensively, "I did what was best for my country."

"America wasn't perfect, but we were the best nation on the face of the earth," Hudson growled.

"We're better now," he retaliated. "There are more people under our system of government because of my work."

"How could you have been so manipulated by this evil megalomaniac? How could you have lied to me for so long? You *know* I was always honest, fair, and generous with you. I had you over to our home for dinner, yet you were working behind my back?" Hudson stared at Bob with betrayal in his eyes.

"He did what I asked him to do, and he is going to be rewarded very well by his President," the leader patted Bob on the shoulder. "He has no need to justify himself to you.

This is well and good for you all, but it's getting very boring for me," the leader remarked. "Maybe some time to think about my offer is what you need," he said looking at Dr. Keith.

Dr. Keith mumbled as if in a daze, "You've lied to me all along," he looked up at the President.

"I didn't lie to you, Ben. I freed you to create."

"You took me from my work." The confusion cleared and his thoughts crystalized. "You stole my original creation."

"Ben, I've had just about enough of this," shifted the President, ready to silence the words.

Ben was just warming up to his own understanding. "You locked me up under the guise that it was for my protection, then you used me to build a better machine; one you've been employing for your own benefit."

The President's eyes narrowed, but he remained silent.

"You haven't ever done anything for me. I've given my all for you. How is that a god?"

"I am the god of this age. And I am all you need," his voice cracked with the pronouncement.

"No, you are self-serving, proud, egotistical, arrogant..."

"You had better stop, or I will remove the grace I am giving you," spoke the mere man as he neared anger.

"A god should love, and yet you use. A god should be sacrificial, and yet you take. A god should help, and yet you hurt. Through my years of science I've always wanted to have the answers. I rejected Todd's God because I couldn't see him or touch him." He walked the length of the small room before walking back. "And yet everything I do is about using that which I can't see and touch. I work in the theoretical. I design that which no one can see or understand. That's my life, and yet I've rejected the God of the universe because I couldn't see Him or touch Him? How foolish I've been."

Todd and Sara looked at one another and recognized each was praying silently for the scientist.

"God is everywhere. I can see His design in the universe with its precision and movement like a fine Swiss watch. With all of our technology and brilliance, we have no real idea how the universe was created. Lots of theories, but no one really knows.

God is in life. Look at us," he was getting more excited, "We are so perfectly designed. We can't create life. With our best technology we can only produce a few amino acids in precisely timed and gauged conditions with pre-existing ingredients. There is no way that the right gases and some electricity could ever produce life in some primordial ooze." Finally, he looked at the leader and raised his voice, "If you're God, then make something out of nothing."

The President was taken aback and remained silent. Todd laughed.

The designer continued, "Darwin was such a fool. You know I used to think that with enough time, and tries that eventually life might occur randomly. *Then* I accepted that after a million years of *evolution* we could possibly become man – even though that totally goes against the 2nd Law of Thermodynamics. But, I was so blind. I thought I was so intelligent, yet I was the greatest of fools."

"Ben have you had your say?" the President asked, "Because everything you are spitting out now will be held against you at your trial – if I allow one."

"I'm not even close. I always wondered if there was an intelligent designer out there somewhere. The universe is just too well-planned." He shifted into lecture mode. "Do you know that if the constants of the universe were adjusted just one magnitude of measurement either way, everything would cease to exist? Everything is that perfectly calculated.

After spending a short time with these people," he gestured to his friends, "and hearing their prayers and seeing their faith, I know who that Designer is. It is their God, the God of the Bible. And oddly enough, it was your example that brought me to this conclusion.

I put so much faith in mankind, thinking that they would eventually rise to perfection through technology and learning the lessons of the past. Sadly, we just get worse. We must be corrupt from the beginning. We have nothing good in us."

Todd spoke up, "If we are in Christ we are a new creation; that old corruption is gone and the new has come. Doc, we don't have to be corrupt. Christ will pull us out of the mire into a better life."

"I've had enough." The President pulled the gun from his belt and directed it at the doctor. "I don't want to hear any more of this."

"Professor, how do I accept Jesus as my Savior?" the scientist asked genuinely. "This man here is obviously an imposter."

"Just say you choose to follow Jesus and believe that God raised him from the dead. It's about that easy."

"I do," the scientist shouted even as a loud shot rang out in the room.

The President's weapon smoked as the scientist fell to the floor in a pool of blood. Todd immediately dragged him up against a wall as Hudson ran over.

"I told you I didn't want to hear anything else about any other God. I am god." Langley looked at Hudson, "If he dies, I will simply bring him back before all of this Jesus nonsense occurred and still use him for my purposes."

Frantically Todd waved him over, "Hudson, he's bleeding badly. He's shot in his abdomen," Sara sank to her knees and leaned over the man.

Ben whispered through pain, "I still have our plan A," he lifted his arm holding the watch.

Hudson answered, "You're in no situation to leave."

Grimacing, "Hudson, I was on my second life anyway. I really shouldn't be here. I have hope now that I've never had. I'm not afraid of dying like I once was. You three get out of here."

Todd spoke quietly, "Hudson take Sara and correct this."

"I won't leave you!" He whispered.

"If you correct the world, I'll be alright no matter what happens here. If you don't, I'm not going to make it out of this room anyway. I'm trusting God to work in you to fix all of this. You're pretty good at it. Go on, I'll stay with Ben." Looking at his new Christian brother, he spoke quietly, "We have a few more things we can talk about."

A tear came down Hudson's cheek, "I don't want to leave you."

"I expect you back soon," Todd smiled. "Take Sara and go."

"Hudson are you ready?" Ben asked breathing quickly.

Pulling Sara close, the four gripped each other tight.

"What's going on?" the President growled. "He's dying, let it go."

"I'm proud of you, Ben," Hudson whispered, "Now push it."

The designer depressed the liquid crystal screen executing the subroutine that would bring the sphere back. In less than ten seconds there was a pressure in the room that slid the four across the smooth cement floor.

Everyone else within the space was blown across the room, the President included.

After the gust front ceased, Hudson looked up to find the sphere taking the place of several walls. The mission control room was a shambles and all of the people were piled in heaps, many bleeding and several not moving.

"Sara, are you alright?"

"Yes," she replied.

Taking her arm in his he looked toward them, "Well, let's go." He looked at his friends, "Todd, we're going to fix this."

Holding Ben, he smiled, "I know you will. Now go, I've got our friend here."

As Sara and Hudson ran across the room to the sphere that already had its cockpit opening, Hudson was able to hear his friend, partner, and brother in the faith beginning to speak to Ben.

"Ben, let me tell you a little more about how great your Savior is. Have you ever heard the story of the woman at the well?"

The scientist spoke slowly and with a wheeze, "No, I, I haven't." His breath was very shallow, and he winced in pain.

"There was a woman who had done a lot of bad things..."

Hudson and Sara jumped into the steaming vehicle. After touching a few places on the cockpit panel, the top of the sphere began to lower.

People were beginning to move within the space.

Todd continued his story as Ben's breathing became more erratic, "Jesus said to her that if she drank from His well, she would never be thirsty again."

The sphere closed as Todd felt Ben breathe his last. Looking up toward the vehicle, he let a whisper of a prayer escape before adding, "Come on, Buddy, make things right. Dear Lord, please be with them," he prayed as he saw the sphere blink, glow and then disappear amid a torrent of pressure and heat. The room was left with a huge hole where the sphere had landed partially into the floor.

Todd held Ben tight and continued his prayer, "Lord, I don't know why you gave Ben a second chance, but I thank you for accepting him and giving him life. It's going to be a joy to see him again after this life is through."

The professor continued to hold his friend and pray as he saw the President start to rise from the debris caused by the sphere. He was bloodied and dirty but had a look on his face that the professor had not seen up to this point. He rubbed off the dust from his jacket and made his way to the second vehicle.

Bob saw the President and called to him, "Where are you going, sir?"

The President looked at him and responded flatly, "To kill a pair of traitors. Come with me, I'll need your help."

Bob reluctantly walked across the room toward the world leader who was climbing into the sphere.

"Hudson, you don't have much time," Todd whispered into the air. He hoped his friend could hear.

36 — WEDNESDAY, EARLY MORNING

Hudson checked all systems in the vehicle, he hoped for the last time. At this point, drastic measures were their only option. With Sara buckled in tight and holding onto the straps, the agent placed his palm on the clear glass on the panel and considered the situation. Screen after screen appeared and he discarded each choice. Every potential time and place to land only brought more consequences in the timeline and further risk of losing everything that had been good and right with the world.

"I don't know what to do," the man spoke quietly as he lifted his hands from the dash and into the air.

Calmly, Sara touched his arm and moved her face into his line of vision. "What's the problem, Hudson?"

"I don't know where to go to solve this. It's just too big. One mistake and everything could get worse, or I could undo the good things that occurred in the real timeline, before this man took office." The vehicle came to a stop.

"So, where are we?" Sara faced forward, her expression void of fear.

"We're essentially between time and space. Dr. Keith would have called this 'interdimensional space.'"

"So we're nowhere?" Sara asked with her brow furrowed and her face in his space again.

Hudson laughed, "I love that look that you do."

"What look?"

"That eyebrow thing you do. It's cute."

She blushed and then looked forward again. "I don't think it's cute to be nowhere."

"Oh, we're somewhere, just somewhere no one's been."

"That doesn't help."

"I could sure use some help. I don't know what to do," he said sadly.

She smiled and wove her fingers into his, "Hudson, you're missing the obvious. Ask God. He knows all things – even this place of nothingness. He will show us where to go"

"Sara, God knows where we are, and He hasn't told me anything," he muttered, still working to claw past the fear in his mind.

"All the more reason to pray," she said closing her eyes.

Hudson followed suit.

"Dear Lord," she prayed, "Obviously, we need your help. We don't know what to do, or where to go. So, because you are big, we're going to wait here until you tell us where to go. We look forward to your direction. In Jesus' name we pray and praise You. Amen."

"Well, that was an odd prayer," Hudson frowned along with his own set of furrowed eyebrows.

"Not odd for God. He'll tell us what to do." She sat back with a smile.

Suddenly a speaker began to crackle within the sphere.

"What's that?" They exclaimed in unison. Hudson found the source of the sound.

"*Hello, out there*," the words came through with a fake echo sound from the person speaking.

"What is that, Hudson?" Sara's voice was laced with concern.

"Does anyone hear me?" the sound came again.

"There isn't two way communications in these things, not that I know," Hudson was perplexed.

"Stop talking to each other and answer me," the speaker cracked again. "Hudson, give up the sphere. I'm coming after you."

"Can you hear me?" Hudson asked still uncertain.

"Yes, of course. There was always a plan for another sphere and from the beginning, they were to be connected by an inter-dimensional communication connection."

"Langley, is that you?"

"Well, it sounds like we've lost the formality of the employer-employee relationship," the President responded. "I'm 100 feet off your port bow," he laughed.

"What?" Hudson said with shock. "You'll destroy both spheres if they get too close."

"It will destroy only yours, because this one has been shielded from the trans-dimensional weaknesses yours was designed with."

Silence remained in the original sphere.

"I'd say I have your attention. Hudson, you've been a good employee, but I would like to terminate your employment."

"Bob, I know you're with him. And you need to stop him," Hudson spoke clearly as Sara watched him wide-eyed.

"Hudson, this is necessary to protect the nation. I'm sorry, but in war, there are always losers and winners. This time, I'm going to be part of a great future," Bob answered with more confidence.

"Merge the two spheres, Bob. Goodbye, Hudson," the President spoke with finality.

Hudson had been typing on the sphere, but didn't have much time to be specific, leaving much of the necessary data input blank. Here goes," he looked at Sara with a cocky grin as she leaned back and inhaled deeply to calm herself.

The President's sphere appeared in the space of Hudson's a microsecond after they had vacated it.

"Where did they go? Do you have a lock on them?" the leader asked Bob.

"Yes sir, I can follow them all over the universe," he pressed the execute button, and they left.

"Where are we, Hudson?" Sara asked looking at the console.

"It looks like, 1829. Somewhere in France."

The vehicle landed in a field, colliding with some trees and a barn.

"Why there?" she asked nervously.

"I didn't have time to be accurate. I was just scrolling through screens and had to execute before I could be specific."

"Will he find us?" she looked worried.

"I think he can track this sphere. And if he can, he'll eventually get us," the agent remarked taking her hand in his once again.

"Well, looks like I've found you again," the speaker crackled. "Why aren't we coming in on top of them?" he asked Bob.

"It looks like a failsafe designed into the programming. They will never be closer than a distance of 100 feet. It makes sense, why would someone want to destroy a billion dollar sphere?"

Hearing them speak Hudson continued to type on the console. "Langley, you need to stop now. This isn't in your best interest. You know that."

"Having both of you out of the picture is in everyone's best interest. Bob, remove that subroutine."

Bob began going through menus as the other sphere disappeared again. "They're gone."

"Well, track them. It'll be cat and mouse for a while."

"It's the 1940's, somewhere in Canada," Hudson said, continuing to work on the console. "Sara, we only have a few more jumps in this vehicle."

This time, the machine came to rest on a highway, causing a multicar pile up around them. Because of the sphere's trans-dimensional shielding, the point of contact of any vehicle that touched them was erased from reality. Hudson cringed even as he remembered God's sovereignty and will in the lives of everyone.

"Well, it looks like we're going where God wants us to," Sara professed confidently.

"What do you mean? I'm randomly pushing buttons," Hudson nearly shouted in exasperation.

"We asked God to tell us where to go. I think he's using your hands to do it."

"Well, the problem is that we only have a few more jumps before this vehicle is out of gas."

"Move quickly, Lord," she whispered out loud.

"We're here again. Do you have any rhyme or reason to your jumping, Hudson?" came the insidious voice over the intercom.

"I'm just going to continue running from you. You need to back off, or I'll go somewhere you don't want," he spoke while typing.

"We know you only have a few jumps left. Give in now, and I may just put you in jail for the rest of your life. At least you and your wife won't be dead."

Sara looked at Hudson. He patted her taffeta-covered knee.

"Just as a reminder, in this utopia you've built, we aren't married!" He pressed the execute button, and they left again.

Looking at the power readout, he exhaled loudly. "It looks like two more jumps."

Sara smiled calmly, "Well, make them good."

He went through several menus when he heard the sound again.

"Do you have the failsafe off yet?" the President growled.

"Almost, just another few minutes, and the distance should be set to zero," Bob answered still looking at the console.

"Hudson, this is it. By the next jump, we'll have you," the man said without emotion. "We know you're at the end of your power reserves."

There was silence.

"We also very quickly will have the ability to occupy your space. At that point, it's all over."

There was silence.

"By your quietness, I guess you know that what I say is true. So, because you were a good employee, I'm going to give you a few minutes to say goodbye.

Understand, Hudson, that your next jump will initiate an instantaneous jump on our part. You will be sealing your own fate. I'll turn off the intercom for a few minutes."

The speaker went dead.

Hudson looked over at Sara and stopped working the console, "I'm sorry for bringing you into this."

She looked at him with softness.

"To be honest, I never really had a plan." He dropped his head.

Touching his chin and raising his face to hers, she smiled. "Hudson, you're a good man. In these last few days, you've been amazing."

He just looked at her big blue eyes.

"My life is not my own, and if the Lord decides He wants me more in heaven than here, well then that much the better." She smiled.

"Sara, it just seems like such a loss. We couldn't fix it. We couldn't restore the world to what it was."

"Maybe not, but we did what we were asked to do. That's all God expects of us."

"Wait. Huh." Hudson typed on the console and found a date and time that the sphere had been before. "We're going to go out with a bang," he said with a wicked grin.

She beamed, "If we're going to do it, let's do it right." Changing the subject, she looked at him coyly. "You know, I bet the other Sara enjoyed being married to you."

"Why's that?" he asked with a smirk.

"Well, you are pretty good-looking. Seriously, you're pretty great to look at."

He laughed.

"And, your heart. You have such a big heart. I bet you loved her more than she could have dreamed. She probably felt complete every day of her life with you."

Her words made his heart ache. "Ah, I love you, Sara," Hudson whispered. Leaning down he lifted her mouth to his and felt her warmth fuel him once again. She responded to his touch, and he reveled at her welcome. Reluctantly, he pulled away and pressed his forehead to hers.

Sara opened her eyes and caught her lower lip between her teeth for a moment. "O, um. I'm certain she was very happily married."

Hudson touched her face once again, then pulled her to him for a final infusion of confidence before he had to act. "Are you ready?" he asked quietly. She smiled.

He placed his hand over the execute button and she covered it with her own. "If we do this, we do it together."

He inhaled sharply then smiled. "Well, then let's go."

Sara pressed Hudson's hand onto the console, and the vehicle left its present space.

Bob looked up in the other sphere, "They've left. We're making the tandem jump."

"Where are they going?" the President asked Bob.

"April 17th. Washington DC. This year." Looking up at the President, "The White House?"

"What? No, stop the jump!" President Langley yelled.

"Why? I can't."

"What happens when this vehicle encounters two of the original spheres?" the leader asked anxiously.

"Two?"

"What would happen?"

"This machine can take the space of one sphere, but won't be strong enough to occupy the space of two. There would be an overload. We would explode."

"NO!"

The last word spoken echoed through time for a single moment before being erased from eternity as, simultaneously, Hudson Blackwell's sphere landed in the Oval Office of the White House along with the President's. They each occupied the same space as the sphere Hudson had landed when he and Todd had arrived back from Israel the first time, six months earlier.

Thinking ahead, he had encoded the landing time for after he and his partner had left the People's House but knew the President would still be there. As Hudson's sphere encountered its earlier self, an explosion large enough to destroy the White House erupted within Washington D.C. Then, when the second sphere came into the space, the effect compounded to level five city blocks. Enough force was generated to fracture the Washington Monument causing the top third fall to the ground.

In addition to the destruction to the nation's capital, a wave front of a magnitude that could not be calculated encircled the earth. All of the underground lab system was removed including a time correction for every change that had occurred since the President had started his plan.

Essentially, the world returned to its earlier timeline as if nothing had ever happened. Hudson, Sara, Todd, and Dr. Keith sacrificed themselves for the greater good of humanity.

Knowing that Hudson and Sara were on a one-way mission, Todd bowed in prayer without ceasing. And as he saw the wave front coming, he knew that they had been successful in their task, and that – one way or another – the world would be better for their efforts.

John 15 echoed through Todd's mind as he watched the wave front coming toward him deep in the underground cavern that had held the second sphere. He thought it a fairly peculiar verse in that situation. Nothing about comfort, peace, or future hope. Instead, he thought of John 15:13.

When these few words were initially spoken, they were about Christ and the sacrifice He would make for all mankind. Todd knew the Lord had brought these words to his mind for a different purpose. *There is no greater love than when someone lays down his life for his friend.*

As the tumult of time change was about to overtake him, Todd smiled and thanked God for his friends Sara and Hudson and their ultimate sacrifice.

37 — WEDNESDAY MORNING

Todd awakened with a jump. Sitting up as if he were under fire he looked around and found himself in bed. The sun was beginning to make its way through delicate curtains hanging in windows as his eyes acclimated to the space.

"Where am I?" he asked out loud as he patted around on the bed. Feeling a figure next to him he fell to the floor in surprise.

"What happened?" his Jewish wife's concerned face popped over the side of the bed to look at him. "Are you hurt?" she queried in her heavily accented English.

Todd stood up, realized exactly where he was and breathed a sigh of relief. He crawled back in bed and cuddled up next to his very pregnant wife.

"Oh, Aaliyah, I've missed you so much," he hugged her.

"Did you fix world?" she asked nonchalantly leaning over toward him.

"I, uh, don't know. I don't even know how I got here?" he let his hands smooth the gown over her blooming belly. "What's happened the last few days?"

"Things got more and more wrong after you left." She blinked groggily. "But I also remember you not ever going." Struggling to sit up in bed, she inhaled sharply with a realization. "I remember two ways. One where you left to help Hudson and another where you were here the whole time." She sat there confused with her head cocked to the side, "How can I remember two things?"

He sat up next to her, "You went through time like I did, so we know you're rooted to the original time line. But somehow you remember another timeline, one where none of this may have occurred. Do you think everything is returned to normal? I wonder what happened to Hudson?" he thought out loud.

He jumped from the bed, leaving his concerned wife behind him and picked up his phone.

"Todd," she said with a heavy accent, "What are you doing?"

"All I remember is Hudson and Sara leaving. I have to see if they're alive." He dialed the phone.

"Did they die?" she became concerned.

"I hope not," he said as the phone rang. "Come on and pick up," he threatened the phone.

After close to ten rings, the other end of the line came to life.

"Hey, buddy," Hudson answered with a bit of humor.

"Are you alive? I mean, of course you are," he spoke rapidly. "All I know is that you and Sara left. What happened? Did you do it?"

"Todd, I'll bring you up to date on all that later."

"Well, is everything back? Did you give us our lives back?"

"The best I can tell from a quick search of the net is that the President died six months ago in a tragic unexplained explosion at the White House. Because he hasn't been around since then, none of what he did in the other timeline occurred. It's as if nothing has ever happened."

"Praise God," Todd said on the other end of the line at his home in Kentucky. "How did we get back here?"

"It looks like we were restored to the original positions in time and space that we *should* have had if none of this craziness ever occurred. I'll bet you'll have taught a few seminary classes you won't remember."

"Great, it got me out of a little work," he laughed. "How's Sara?"

"I don't know yet," he replied nervously. "When I awakened I spent a minute on my tablet to discover the situation at hand, and then you called. I haven't seen her yet."

"Let me let you go then," the professor interrupted. "I pray everything is back the way it should be. I'll call you in the next day or so, and we'll work through this."

"Thank you, Todd. I want you to know that you are the best friend I could ever have."

"Hudson, it's been an honor saving the world with you. I pray you find everything as it should be."

"Me too, buddy. Bye," Hudson ended the call and looked around the room.

Hudson grabbed his robe and walked down the hall. He entered his son Michael's room and found the little boy all wrapped up in his blankets. "Thank you, God," Hudson whispered. He patted the little snoring boy on his head, rubbed his back, and left the room.

A few feet down the hall, he went into the next room, where he found his daughter reading in bed. "Amy, you're sure up early," he spoke quietly.

"You are too, Daddy. Did you sleep well?"

"Yeah, honey, I guess I did." He kissed her on the cheek, and she went back to her book as he left the room.

Coming to the end of the hall, he walked down the stairs and rounded the corner to the kitchen where he saw Sara. Looking at her demeanor he grew concerned. "Good morning, Sara," he said hesitantly.

He watched the woman going through photo albums they kept on a bookshelf beside the fireplace. Dressed in the pink robe he had given her for Christmas and with her hair tied back she looked up at him. After several silent seconds she finally broke the awkward tension. She looked down at the photo album, "Is this who I am?"

Hudson's heart broke. His wife was not restored in the timeline. "Sara, do you not remember any of this?" he motioned around the room as he sat across from her at the kitchen table.

"No, I don't remember this house, or any of the places or events I seem to have been through. I see myself in picture after picture, but it isn't really me. Is this my life, I mean Sara's life?"

Hudson was quiet as he thought through the situation. "What do you remember?"

"I remember my old life; work, family, friends. I can recall everything we went through the last few days, but I don't know anything about any of this," she responded picking up the books and moving to put them away. "Is my old life still there?"

He stood to join her at the fireplace. Looking her in the eyes, he spoke gently, "Sara, I think all of that is gone. When we crashed at the White House, everything the President had done should have been erased."

"How can that be?" she asked with a tear coming down her face. "If my world never existed, how do I remember it? How did I go through it? Why don't I know about any of this?"

He touched her hand, "I was concerned that this could happen. I'm sorry, I never mentioned it to you, or gave you a choice in the matter."

"What do you mean?"

"Sara, once you went through time, you were locked to the timeline you were in when you jumped." Taking a deep breath, he closed his eyes. "I hoped it wouldn't happen, but it looks like it did.

I'm so sorry. We had to rescue you, and in our haste to get away, I didn't think about how this might affect you until after it was done. Once you jumped with us, there was no way to bring you back to what you know… or should have known. That is unless we totally failed and the President got his way." He lifted his eyes upward. "God, please help us."

"How did I get here?"

"When we corrected the timeline, you were physically restored to where you should have been, but mentally, you remember everything else but this life."

She pulled her arm away. "So what do we, or I do now? I have nowhere to go. Clearly, we're married," her eyes drifted to the sparkling set of rings on her finger. "But, for me, we are not. I only met you a couple days ago. And this isn't my house. Even though most everything here looks like what I would have, the other Sara picked them out." Here she paused and looked into her tea cup, twirling the tea bag string hanging from the side. "I'm even drinking tea out of her cup," she sniffed.

Hudson just sat there and listened, praying God would work through her fear and doubt.

"What do we do now? Will my parents even know me?"

Hudson spoke softly, "You're parents know you, of course. But they know the *you* that is married to me." Taking both of her hands in his he worked to find the right words, "Sara, I know you feel like you've been transported to another planet. But you can be certain, that, no matter what, I will work through this with you."

"Evidently, everything in the world has been set straight but me, is that what you're saying?" Panic and pain flitted through her eyes as she tried valiantly to quell the sobs building up within her.

"I wish it weren't true, and there is a possibility that some of your world might still be out there. But from what I can tell, yes, you are all that remains from the world you knew before." Hudson grieved for the woman who was his wife, and who would never be the same.

She pulled her hands away and stood from the table. As she did she heard someone tromping down the stairs. "Mom, what's for breakfast, I'm hungry!" Michael shouted around the corner, appearing in just his pajama bottoms and scratching his back side.

"Hey little guy, won't you go back to bed for a few more minutes while I talk with your uh,... mommy," Hudson interrupted trying to keep him away and walking him back to the stairs.

"No," she said gesturing him toward her. A tear came down Sara's face when she saw the boy. Seeing her eyes and thin features on the child's sweet face, she knew he was hers. Kneeling beside him she offered him a motherly grin, "How did you sleep, little one?"

"Not good. I dreamed about monsters all night." His little boy words made her smile even more and she pulled him into a big hug.

"Oh, honey, I'm sorry," she said patting him on the back. As he wriggled from her grip, she noticed his crooked britches and twisted them straight again before he could get free.

"Mom, I am reading this great book, let me tell you about it," Amy's voice hit the room before she walked in, fully dressed and with her book in her hand as she entered the kitchen.

Sara looked past the boy to the girl.

"You see, Mom, it's about this princess and a crazy spell is put on her…"

Sara heard nothing she said after that but thought she was looking in a mirror. The blond hair, fair skin and round, blue eyes could have come from nowhere else. She stood up and looked at the young lady continuing to talk non-stop about her book. Her eyes grew soft with motherly affection at what she saw around her.

Hudson just observed. He saw grace under pressure. It was his Sara. Different life experiences, of course. But his Sara.

"Mom, I'm hungry," Michael said.

"Michael, don't interrupt me. I'm telling an important story," Amy chastised.

Sara smiled. "Sweetie, why don't you tell me your story while I make some breakfast?" She looked at Hudson, "Does everyone like pancakes?"

Hudson nodded minimally.

"What about fruit in the pancakes?"

"Yeah, do that, Mommy!" Michael shouted.

"Well, fruit-filled pancakes it is," Sara announced with some energy. "Some people call them crepes, and they are very yummy."

She walked automatically to the pantry, talking to herself, "Now if I was to put a skillet in this kitchen, I would put it right here." She opened the cabinet, found it there and smiled.

"Hudson, we have much more to discuss, but it is important that these little people get some food right now," Sara spoke. All the while pulling items from different parts of the kitchen with ease.

The man smiled and walked into the living room watching the interplay between the three. As he sat in his recliner and heard his daughter talking without a break about a story and his son playing with toys on the table, he watched Sara. His Sara. But a new Sara too.

He was reminded about how much he loved her. He remembered why he married her and felt his heart grow closer to her than it had ever been.

For most people watching, they would have seen a woman cooking breakfast for her family, but Hudson saw much more. He saw a woman who had given up everything because of him. But a woman who was going to make the best of it for two children she did not even know.

The road ahead would try them both, he was certain. Surely her learning curve was about to be crazy steep as she stepped into the role of homemaker, room mother, Sunday School teacher, and all the other things Sara had taken years to grow into. Learning names and histories of so many people they had relationships with would be the most challenging. Somehow, he felt she would embrace the task before her.

On the other hand, the idea of courting her again brought a hint of excitement he had not anticipated. How many guys got to enjoy that first thrilling chase of the woman you love, twice? He looked forward to learning all the experiences she had had through the years without him. Charming her with romance would be especially fun at this point in his life, with so much more confidence than the green kid he had been the first go-round of dating her.

Most appealing of all; the day when he might finally make her his once again – but for her, for the first time. For that – for her – he was willing to do whatever it took to make that happen.

Hudson had literally been through time and space for her. He had taken down the most powerful man in history for the woman working in the kitchen with his two precious children. He knew the greatest mission was still ahead, but he was up for the fight. He would do everything possible to make the woman he loved, love him again.

Sara looked over her shoulder and grinned at him as she mixed ingredients in a bowl with Michael playing and Amy telling stories. Hudson stood and walked into the kitchen. They were the first few steps in what would be a marathon before them, but he had the strength to finish it. And he could tell by the look in her eyes right now that she did too.

He laughed out loud and clapped his hands, whispering behind her as he passed, "Let the chase begin."

EPILOGUE

THREE MONTHS LATER

The hospital room overlooked a large parking lot in Louisville, yet the blanket of snow that had fallen the night before gave it a much more picturesque look. For Dr. Todd Myers, it was the most beautiful place in this world or any previous.

Holding his new baby daughter in a recliner next to the window gave Todd the most joy he had ever felt in life. Aaliyah caressed his arm from her hospital bed and looked over his shoulder at the new little life. Together, they reveled in the wonder and awe of how God brings people together to create life.

It was peaceful and still in the plain yet tasteful room. The night before had been busy with a good amount of activity, but now the hospital staff were giving the new parents time to relax with their small child. Todd picked up a tiny hand to examine again, when there was a knock on the door.

Seeing a friendly face peek through the door he gestured with his free hand. "Hudson, come in!" he welcomed as the baby grumbled at her daddy's loud wake up call.

"Oh, Hudson, it is so good to see you," Aaliyah called out as she gestured for him to come in.

"You mind if I bring someone else in?" Hudson asked still behind the door.

"Sure," Todd responded with a smile.

The door opened, and Hudson walked in with Sara hand in hand.

Aaliyah and Todd both yelled, "Sara!"

Todd stood up with the baby as Sara went over to him.

"Oh, how beautiful," she said. "May I hold her?"

He handed the baby over and allowed Sara to sit in the recliner.

Hudson hugged Aaliyah, "How are you feeling?"

"I am tired," she said thinking through her words, "But am well, and blessed."

"What about you, buddy, are you going to get this fatherhood thing figured out?" Hudson asked jokingly.

"I'm ready to slow down, that's for sure. The old ball and chain is trying to make me pretty domestic. I may have to stop doing things like traveling through time," Todd laughed.

Aaliyah raised her eyebrows, "What is… ball and chain?" she asked looking at Todd, somehow knowing he was taking a cheap shot.

Hudson and Sara laughed.

"I'll, uh, tell you later, honey," Todd smiled, giving her a hug. Content to enjoy the day, Aaliyah just smirked at his escape.

"You two didn't have to come all this way from Washington. We could have sent a few pictures," the professor said.

"Where else would we be when our best friends have just had a baby?" Sara cooed at the baby.

"You are sure kind to come." Todd sat on the edge of the bed, "So what is going on with you two?" Todd subconsciously reached for his wife's hand, thankful for the woman in his life.

Aaliyah inclined the bed so she could be better involved in the conversation.

"I think we're very good," Hudson answered looking at Sara. "It has been slow going at times, but the counseling you've done with us has really kept us focused on what God wants and not what we want."

Todd interrupted with sudden enthusiasm, "You know, I may write a book on this. How to counsel people from different dimensions," he gave a childish smile.

Hudson sat on the windowsill beside the recliner and leaned toward Sara and the baby. "I'm not sure it will be in great demand, Professor, but anyway. We, of course, started over. From the very beginning. There have been many late night conversations after the kids are in bed, many date nights spent learning and re-learning all about one another, and, obviously, much prayer."

Todd assumed his natural role of pastor and counselor easily, "So what does God want for the two of you?"

Sara had been hugging the baby and looking closely at her when she got into the conversation, "God wants us together. He wanted us together in Hudson's timeline and in my own for His purposes." She smiled at the baby happily.

"What do your children know about change?" Aaliyah asked.

Hudson looked to Sara to answer, "They don't know anything is different. For all they know, I've always been their mom. Hudson has spent hours walking me through events, favorite toys, books and music. He's come up with hand signals to help me know when not to pursue an issue and when to bring something up. It's been almost like a game. Granted, a very exhausting game," she shifted positions with the little on in her arms. "But it's been so worthwhile. I love them like a mother from the beginning, and I grow closer to them each day." She looked back at the baby.

"The kids are very happy," Hudson added. "In fact, they think it's cool that their mommy fixes them crepes now instead of plain pancakes, and that she can speak French, and can paint like you wouldn't believe. Honestly, it's been a new adventure every day."

"What about your sleeping arrangements?" Todd looked at Hudson.

"We didn't want the kids to think I was sleeping on the couch because I didn't love their mom. But for goodness sake, Sara had so much thrown her way that first day. So, yeah, I slept on the floor for more than a month. Sara slept in the bed. Believe me, my back is grateful she finally let me up there."

"Your back?" Todd asked with a wicked gleam in his eyes.

"Yes, Todd, my back. Is there any other question you'd like to ask with the ladies present?" he returned with laughter in his voice.

"My question is, are you married again? How does that work?" Aaliyah asked looking over at Sara.

Both Blackwells smiled as Hudson made eye contact with Sara.

"Well, that's part of the reason we're here."

"Tell me," Todd begged, "Sara why else are you here?"

"My world has turned upside down. And, even though in the eyes of God and the law I've been married to Hudson for over ten years, well," she paused, trying to keep her tears at bay and find the right words. "I've never exchanged vows with Hudson officially. Well, we did by ourselves one night," Sara turned three shades of pink. "And, we've decided to honor the original wedding certificate for the kids, so we consider ourselves married but…"

"What is it Sara?" Aaliyah asked.

"Well, we are married, but, for me. Well, I've never been able to say 'I do'. And I would like Hudson to make me a completely respectable woman for our third child – at least in my own mind, since I'm the only one out of place in the timeline here."

"Wait. Third child?" Todd asked.

Standing up, Sara smoothed her hands over her flat belly, "I'm about six weeks pregnant," she beamed.

Hudson hugged Sara out of sheer joy, and Todd went over to hug the two together. "What a blessing," he smiled.

"Can I hug someone?" Aaliyah asked from her bed.

All three surrounded the bed and she embraced them with tears.

After everyone else shed a few tears, Todd regained his energy, "So when are *we* going to do this wedding? And believe me, I can throw you the best wedding you've ever seen. I know a perfect organist; we can do the ring and candle things. How many people are we going to invite? We can call it a renewing of your vows – you know, for the sake of everyone who knows you've been married for ten years."

"We?" Hudson laughed.

"Okay, you."

Sara, sat back in the recliner and shook her head at the ideas. "Todd it's not like that."

Aaliyah knew what Sara was about to say, and she grabbed her husband's hand.

"Of course, every woman dreams of a beautiful white wedding with the bridesmaids and reception. Yet, somehow I've already had that. I have lots of pictures of it. Evidently, half my dishes and cookware were wedding gifts. I don't want to be selfish about this, and I am blessed to be in the life the Lord has given me. So, what I really want is just a Pastor to allow me to say 'I do.'"

"Buddy, can you marry us?" Hudson looked at his friend. "We don't even need a license. We just need to say our vows in the presence of witnesses, really, and you two…well, you two are the best and only choice."

"Hudson, I'll do anything for you and Sara. When do you want to do this?"

Sara stood happily, "What about now?"

"Now, here in this room!"

"Sure, Aaliyah can be my maid of honor," Sara said with a smile.

Aaliyah nodded in agreement. "Yes, Todd, let me see them get married. Sara, let me have my baby."

Sara prepared to hand the child to Aaliyah when the woman reached instead to the nightstand and lifted three pink roses from the vase sitting there.

"Sara, you told me once before you were you," she smiled, "That every bride needs a…what is word…flowers?"

Todd answered, "Bouquet."

"Yes boo-kay." Aaliyah laid the flowers on the bed and lifted her child from Sara's arms. "Please take these for your boo-kay, Sara. I am honored to be your maid of bride." Sara lifted the pink roses from the bed and worked to keep tears at bay. Pink roses. Her mother's bridal bouquet had been of pink roses. She thanked God for His providence yet again.

"Well, I've got my Bible, are you two ready?" Todd asked becoming more formal and straight.

Sara began to breathe a little more quickly and fanned her face to stop the tears.

Moving the recliner to the other side of the room Todd moved the couple to the window, "Here you two stand here."

Sara took Hudson's arm and looked up at him in the eyes. "Hudson, I love you no matter what time we're in."

"Well, I've always loved you, baby," he whispered as he kissed her sweet lips.

"Hey, whoa, you two aren't married yet. Or you are, just, let's do this thing the way you want to do it, okay?" Todd realized he had suddenly lost control.

Aaliyah laughed and cried simultaneously.

Both smiling giddily Sara responded, "Okay, we'll be good, right, my love?" she spoke into the eyes of her husband of the past and future. Todd grunted. They smiled and stood straight.

"That's much better." Pastor Todd stood tall with his Bible in his hands.

"By the way, what's your baby's name?" Sara asked.

Aaliyah replied, "Destiny. I was told it means that things will always happen no matter what comes."

The agent smiled. Unable to stay away from her another moment, Hudson pulled Sara into his arms and looked into her eyes as Todd began, "Dearly beloved…"

Initially the explosion at the White House was thought to have been the work of terrorists. However, those involved with the sphere eventually traced the energy signature to the device itself. Not knowing how it got there, and who piloted it, a second story of a gas leak was used to explain the destruction and thus hide the ultra-secret project from the world.

Conspiracy theorists to this day explain it as an extra-world event. Some say aliens wanted the President removed where others believed people from another dimension were trying to change the future.

Cox Manufacturing was mothballed, with Hudson leading the project. He labored long to ensure it would never be used again, yet with a technology that powerful, the agent always knew there could be potential problems from someone resurrecting it and trying to repeat the actions of the President.

It had been a long year, and Hudson had learned that a true friend is hard to find but worth the search. He realized that his wife was the greatest blessing in his life and far stronger than he ever knew. And finally, he came to know that His God really could supply all his needs and would get him through every difficult time. Not once did God remove trouble from Hudson's path, but He never let go of his hand, and He guaranteed that the agent always made it to the other side.

Hudson would have never asked for the experiences he was given, but crazy enough, he would not give up one of them for everything in the world.

Printed in the United States
By Bookmasters